fool's errand

fool's errand

louis bayard

alyson books
los angeles | new york

MANUFACTURED IN THE UNITED STATES OF AMERICA.

THIS TRADE PAPERBACK ORIGINAL IS PUBLISHED BY ALYSON PUBLICATIONS,
P.O. BOX 4371, LOS ANGELES, CALIFORNIA 90078-4371.
DISTRIBUTION IN THE UNITED KINGDOM BY
TURNAROUND PUBLISHER SERVICES LTD.,
UNIT 3 OLYMPIA TRADING ESTATE, COBURG ROAD, WOOD GREEN,
LONDON N22 6TZ ENGLAND.

FIRST EDITION: JUNE 1999

99 00 01 02 03 **a** 10 9 8 7 6 5 4 3 2 1

ISBN 1-55583-494-9

LIBRARY OF CONGRESS CATALOGING-IN-PUBLICATION DATA
   BAYARD, LOUIS.
     FOOL'S ERRAND / LOUIS BAYARD.—1ST ED.
     ISBN 1-55583-494-9
     I. TITLE.
   PS3552.A85864F66 1999
   813'.54—DC21   98-55139 CIP

COVER ILLUSTRATION BY JULIANNA PARR.

To my parents, my first readers

To Don, my rock

PART ONE

1

Funny that it began with a nap. Naps usually filled him with a nameless dread. Every time he put his head on a pillow, he would remember something he needed to do—something to clean (though he wasn't really that clean) or a book he'd been meaning to read. Or he'd develop a sudden fear of embarrassing himself: mumbling an old boyfriend's name, say, or drooling or some other act still undreamed of, outside civilization's parameters. But nothing, finally, explained how unacceptable it was to be lying there—in daylight—*lying* there while the rest of the world was awake. How did people do it?

On the day in question, though, a Sunday in March, Patrick had been trailing clouds of sleep deprivation. All week long he'd been sleeping poorly, and the night before, three teenage boys had broken into his car, which was parked behind his Victorian row house on Capitol Hill. Patrick might have slept till morning unawares except a neighbor on the other side of the back alley saw the crime in progress and yelled at the boys until they ran away. Then he knocked on Patrick's door to explain what had happened, and just as Patrick was about to thank him and go back to bed, the neighbor mentioned that the police had been called and were on their way. Patrick called twice over the next hour, asking the police not to come. Two hours later a patrolman knocked on the door. He and Patrick waited another half hour for the fingerprint specialist. Still wearing his bathrobe, Patrick led them through the backyard to the car. The first thing he noticed was the Oldsmobile's steering column, which had been peeled open like a can. The second thing was the glass from the rear left passenger window, which had resolved itself into smooth, glittering candy pebbles on the gravel.

He fell asleep around 5. Around 6, his downstairs tenant, Deanna, woke him up to tell him about his car: She'd seen it during her morning jog. This left him only a few minutes of sleep before he had to get up for his violin lesson. His teacher—a radiant freckled woman named Sonya, with a river of auburn hair—lived only three blocks away, but 7:30 on Sunday morning was the only time of the week they could get together. Patrick was not improving. He was mired about two thirds of the way through Suzuki Volume 2; so to distract him, Sonya discussed her latest fertility exercise, a variation on something in the Kama Sutra. She and her husband had been trying to have a baby for four months.

At 8 o'clock Patrick called his insurance company, then called AAA because he couldn't turn his ignition and needed a tow. The tow truck driver came at 9:30 and fiddled with the steering column until Patrick was able to drive it himself, four blocks to the local Exxon, which had a wall covered with photographs of members of Congress but never enough mechanics. The car would be ready by tomorrow, they told him—Friday at the latest.

At 10:30, his boyfriend Alex called to remind him they had brunch with Gary and Robert at Sequoia at 11, followed by a 1 o'clock brunch party at Grant's house. The first brunch actually began at 11:30 because Alex, who lived in Adams Morgan, had to drive all the way down to Capitol Hill to pick up Patrick, then all the way back to Georgetown. Patrick and Alex had a running disagreement about which area had fewer parking opportunities: Alex said Georgetown, and Patrick argued for Adams Morgan. ("That must be why you never come to my apartment," Alex said.) By the time they got to the restaurant, Gary and Robert were freely drinking Bloody Marys. Patrick realized he didn't know which was Gary and which was Robert.

"Guess what?" Alex said, by way of excusing their lateness. "Someone broke into Patrick's car last night."

"Did they take anything?" asked Gary/Robert.

"No," Patrick said. "They looked through my tapes, but they didn't take any."

"I would think not," said Robert/Gary.

"Actually, they were trying to hot-wire it."

"Which gives you a sense of their experience levels," Alex said. "I mean, hot-wiring an '87 Oldsmobile."

"Oh, no, no, no," said Gary/Robert. "That's just the kind of car they want. It goes straight to the chop shop. Especially the GM cars because all the parts are interchangeable."

"Then why—?" Patrick began.

"Why what?"

"Why can't they fix my fucking car before Friday? If there's this whole universe of interchangeable parts."

"Patrick's still a little upset," Alex said.

"I wish they'd *taken* the damn thing. What would it matter? Five hundred–dollar deductible either way. It wouldn't matter."

"Oh, no, no, no," Gary/Robert said. "Then you'd have new car payments. Your insurance rates would go up. You wouldn't want that."

"You wouldn't," Alex said.

They were only 20 minutes late to the second brunch, but it

didn't matter because it was buffet. The house they went to had a Colonial Revival facade but an interior that seemed to belong to an earlier, more cramped era. Half of the vestibule was taken up by an elaborate umbrella stand with ceramic handles, delft blue. The low-ceilinged living room was bisected by a long paisley-upholstered chesterfield running perpendicular to the wall, which made the three men sitting on it look like a gallery of disembodied heads.

Grant, the host, had been restoring the house for the last three years. He was demonstrating his new pocket doors when suddenly he wheeled on Patrick and asked, "Do you know how long it took me? Just to do that stretch of crown molding in the corner?"

"No."

"Three months," he said. "I worked on it every night for three months."

"Well, it—looks nice. I guess it's worth it."

"Oh, I do it because I love it. This is sex for me. If it adds to the house's value, all well and good, but—I do it because it's sex, you know?"

Besides the chesterfield, there were precisely two chairs in the living room, both cabriolets that didn't seem meant for sitting. This meant that guests had either to cluster around the three people on the chesterfield or form alternative knots around the kitchen island or the dining-room table, which Grant had had custom-distressed by a man he knew in McLean. Patrick, momentarily deserted by Alex, wandered ineffectually among the three rooms, feeling more and more the weight of the low ceilings, the weight of people's conversation. He listened to men his own age discussing things he would never have thought to discuss: simplified employee pensions, the storm proofing of summer houses in Delaware, the antiwrinkle properties of Preparation H.

More than anything else, he realized, he wanted to lie down.

"Grant," he said. "I'm going to give myself a tour."

He climbed the stairs, but the groaning of old nails, the dull mottled texture of the handrails, his own weight on each tread— it only made him more tired. So he came back down the stairs and turned the corner, passed down a short hallway, and came to a small empty room. It was a study or library of sorts, outfitted by the Bombay Company. The wallpaper was forest-green, and the Macintosh computer was almond. Patrick dropped, almost faint-ed, onto a chintz-covered claw-foot love seat. He leaned his head against an HP LaserJet printer.

I am not going to sleep. I'm just going to close my eyes. It'll be almost as good as sleep.

He closed his eyes, but the eyes themselves were vibrating with anxiety. *No, no,* they were saying. *You don't want this; you don't want to fall asleep.*

And then a voice which was not the voice of his eyeballs broke in. "Oh, sorry."

Patrick opened his eyes. A cranberry Shetland-wool sweater hovered before him, attached itself to a pair of gray denim pants, then slowly reconfigured itself as a man. A tall man with dirty-blond hair and a powerful neck and a lopsided smile and a chin that quietly asserted itself.

I'm not alone, he suddenly realized. He snapped his head for-ward. "No, it's—"

"You look tired," the man said.

"I'm very—I'd like to sleep."

"Let go, then."

"I'm sorry?" Patrick was struggling now. The man's voice was beginning to recede.

"Cast off," he said.

And Patrick was going to say something, but now his own voice had receded and a gloaming was upon him, and the man in the Shetland sweater was wrapped in a cumulus cloud.

Even now, with his eyes definitively shut, Patrick felt that some etiquette was called for. *Should I ask him to sit down? Does he want to watch me sleep? Is he still there?* There was no way of knowing. Something was slipping out of Patrick's reach…It was Patrick…

He awoke ten minutes later with a great gulp of air. He looked around. No one was there. He hastened back to the living room, wondering if anyone was there, and, of course, everyone was there, except the man he had just talked to. He wandered through the dining room, the kitchen, poked his head into the bathroom, which had two matching white terry-cloth bathrobes hanging from what looked like a meat hook. Before he could head back to the library, he felt Alex's hand in the crook of his arm.

"Grant knows somebody who knows your boss."

"Oh."

They left the house at about 4. It was startling to realize that Alex was the one driving. It must have been startling to Alex too because he talked all the way home.

"It's a *nice* house, and I know he's put a lot of work into it. I mean, the tile alone. It's just not the kind I'd choose for myself. It doesn't have that simplicity that draws you to a house sometimes, do you know what I mean? It's that feeling like 'Yes. OK. This is a *house.*' Except, listen, Grant was telling me the molding was original to the house, but I don't see how it could be. It's Home Depot, don't you think? By way of Sherman Williams. And even if it's original, it doesn't go with the low ceilings. Or the exposed beams."

"Everyone there came in leather jackets," Patrick said.

"Yes?"

"I think it's odd, that's all. Leather jackets over ties. Leather jackets over sweaters, angora sweaters."

"Well, some people look good that way."

"What I mean is: Why? There must have been a meeting where this was decided, everyone instructed to wear leather jackets. Why wasn't I invited to the meeting?"

"You're tired."

"You always say that, and it's—I don't always say things because I'm tired."

"No, it's just that some things you're more *likely* to say when you're tired. Which is why you should learn to take naps like the rest of us."

"Well, you know, now that we're on the subject and everything, I did take a nap. In Grant's library. In fact, somebody walked in on me."

"Who?"

"I don't know; I've never seen him before. He was wearing a Shetland sweater."

"A Shetland sweater?"

"Yeah, he was about your height. Curlyish hair? Blondish, dirty blondish…"

"I never saw him. Did you really take a nap in Grant's house?"

"Well…yeah, I was giving myself a tour of the place, and I just kind of sat down. And started nodding off, and then he walked in behind me."

"Well, didn't he tell you who he was?"

"No, he left."

"Grant must know him, then."

"It's funny; I didn't see him when we came in. He wasn't there when I came back."

"Grant must know him."

Repeating himself was Alex's way of ending a line of inquiry. *That could only work on adults*, Patrick thought. *Children would never buy into it*. It was funny how much he missed driving his own car. He had no sense of time anymore. Before they were halfway across town, they had already reached his house. He blinked a couple of times in disbelief.

"Do you want me to come in?" Alex asked.

He stood at the car door, hesitating. "If you want. I mean, I'll probably go to bed early."

"Whatever."

"No, come in. That's fine."

"No, that's OK."

"Well…whatever, right? I mean, dinner tomorrow night."

"Yeah."

"So…I promise I'll be better company, OK?" He started to close the car door and then stopped it in mid swing. "I'm kind of pissed about my car."

"I know."

"I don't know when they'll be done with it."

"Well…"

"Good night." He leaned into the car, and they kissed.

"Oh! Next weekend," Alex said. "I think we should clean your front windows, OK?"

There was always something a little awkward, a little improvised about the way they parted. Alex never said the same thing twice—although what he said usually had to do with cleaning Patrick's house—and Patrick never said the same thing in response. Maybe it was because they didn't live together—they had passion but no rituals. Even the kissing was expository. Sometimes they didn't even kiss: Their lips just stopped about an inch apart, and then they smiled as though they'd really done it.

He watched Alex's car dawdle to the stoplight at the end of the block, then turn left. He was not at all tired. He was convinced he wouldn't be able to sleep. Why had he taken those ten minutes at Grant's house? He would never make them up. Never, as long as he lived.

Later that night, lying in bed, he thought about the man in the Shetland sweater.

Cast off, he'd said.

Like it was the easiest thing to do in the world. Like it was just a matter of…Patrick envisioned himself floating in a marina, big and cumbersome, displacing all the water that was meant for the yachts, feeling the moon's pull toward sea. The rope that bound his ankles to the pier was fraying, unraveling…and now it had broken off…The current tugged him…The water cradled him…The sky painted his face…

Cast off.

2

The next morning he could barely remember where he'd been. He lay in bed, staring up at the blisters of paint and the hemoglobin stains on his ceiling where rainwater sometimes leaked through. He was 32 years old and three months. His hair had already begun its inexorable crawl up the scalp, and whenever he saw himself in a mirror, he was shocked at how pinched and severe he looked—the high forehead; the high, gaunt cheekbones; the whiskers darkening—like a Spanish ascetic.

He was 32 years old and three months, and the only hope he could muster this morning was that somehow his car would be ready. But it wasn't. The claims adjuster didn't arrive until Thursday, and the new steering column didn't arrive until Friday, and the new steering column turned out to be as dysfunctional as the old one, and the garage mechanic, dangling a dead cigarette from his mouth, told Patrick that the next one wouldn't be in until the following Monday. Or Wednesday.

"I'm going to leave the city," Patrick said.

"No, you're not," Alex said. "You're just upset."

Actually, he had been thinking of leaving the city since last November. That was when someone came in the middle of the night and stole the shrubs from his front garden. Walking out the front door the next morning, he had almost failed to grasp what had happened because the thief had been very fastidious, had cleaned up after himself. Patrick was halfway down his front steps before he realized that the four yew shrubs that once enclosed the flower bed were now gone. He stared at the holes where the shrubs used to be and began laughing. His neighbors walked right by, afraid to ask why.

Just last month someone had taken a pot of black-eyed Susans from his backyard. In retaliation Patrick had nailed a pot of peonies to his front sill. A week later he came home to find the pot still in place but the flowers gone: the thief this time had lifted them bodily from the pot and had used the excess dirt to inscribe the words FUCK U on Patrick's windowsill.

"That was gratuitous," Alex said.

"Why don't we just keep walking?" Patrick said. "Keep walking and never look back. I mean, what keeps us in the city?"

"Because it's worse out there," said Alex. "Think about it, honey: Are you going to feel any safer walking into some general store in West Virginia with a half-starved dog on a chain and Confederate bumper stickers and deer heads on the wall?"

It was impossible to answer because Patrick didn't feel safe anywhere anymore. He didn't even feel safe with Alex, and they had been together a year and a half. There were times, he admitted, when together they achieved something close to relaxation, but something always came along to disturb it. The other night, for instance, hadn't they been conversing amiably about the absence of traffic planning in Northern Virginia and hadn't Alex then said, apropos of nothing, "My friends don't understand why we're together"?

And hadn't he then felt that acidifying sensation deep in his esophagus? "What's the difficulty?" he asked, and even asking the question was hard.

"Oh, I don't know. We're different, I guess. We like different things."

"That's not true. We both like movies."

"That's true," Alex said, "but we like different kinds of movies. You've never seen an Arnold Schwarzenegger movie, for instance."

"Yes."

"And I've seen every one."

"I can't see—is this a ground for divorce? Is this mental cruelty?"

"No, it just shows we're different."

"But we're *supposed* to be, aren't we? What's—I don't see what's wrong with being different from each other."

"Nothing, it's just different."

"But according to your friends, it should be enough to keep us apart."

"Well, it hasn't."

He knew by now that Alex didn't really mean to upset him. It was just a function of their relationship. Sometimes he thought he could actually trace the trajectories of their respective conversations, see exactly where the lines of meaning were diverging. Other times it was more difficult. Once, without realizing it, they spent ten minutes conversing about two entirely separate topics. Alex was talking about S/M lifestyles, and Patrick was talking about living in New York, and they didn't realize their error until Alex said, with an air of finality, "Well, it's a lot to go through just for an orgasm."

Was it any wonder, then, that Patrick could not breathe easy during even the most casual conversations? When he told Alex about the problem with the car, for instance, he felt almost certain that Alex would say something mild and reassuring, but he wasn't quite certain. And then Alex went ahead and *validated* his uncertainty by saying, "Honey, why do you even need a car?"

Patrick closed his eyes. "I need my car, I *use* my car."

"Well, I was just thinking. I mean, you take the Metro to work. And if you wanted to, you could do all your shopping within three blocks of your house."

"Where? Where could I do my shopping?"

"I don't know—Eastern Market?"

"Eastern Market? People get—*things* at Eastern Market. They get—omelets and pig's feet; they don't get *groceries.*"

"Well, there's a Safeway, isn't there?"

"Ten blocks away there's a Safeway. You want me to—to *portage* grocery bags for ten blocks."

"I was just asking a question."

"You have a car too, you know."

"I know I do, and sometimes it's more trouble than it's worth, and I think sometimes if I didn't have one, I wouldn't really miss it."

A Volvo was screaming at them. Alex was a bad driver (in addition to being bad with directions). Every time they drove across town, someone would honk at him for drifting into the lane, and Alex would look puzzled, as though there were some honking conspiracy.

Patrick sat silent for a minute, reformulating his strategy. "All right," he said finally. "Tell me this. How would we ever see each other without cars? How could I ever visit you?"

"You *don't* visit me, Patrick. You never come to my apartment."

At least you could say this about their conversations: They usually circled back to a common motif. It was almost restful, and because they were both nice people, they didn't like to argue, and they searched for ways not to be angry. Usually, five minutes after an argument, one of them would say something banal, and the other would say something banal back. On the occasion of the car argument, they drove in silence to Patrick's house, and as Patrick got out, Alex said, with a determined breeziness, "Don't forget about Saturday."

"What's Saturday?"

"I know I've told you about this; haven't I told you about this? Scott and Jeffrey's commitment ceremony. The University Club."

The invitation to Scott and Jeffrey's commitment ceremony might profitably have been read beforehand, but Alex didn't show it to him until after it was over. It was on creamy mauve paper, and it read: "Please join Scott and Jeffrey as they consecrate their lives together. The only intoxicant will be life. The only animals will be dancing." If Patrick had read this beforehand, he would not have spent so much time looking for beer; nor would he have wondered why the grooms were wearing tuxedos with rope belts and canvas espadrilles. He would still, however, have had trouble making sense of the music, which came at him from all directions. In the anteroom a string quartet played Bach minuets; in the ceremony room an African-American choir sang "Ain' a That Good News?"; a female impersonator roamed the crowd mouthing the words of a Gloria Estefan song. Just before the ceremony, one of the grooms grabbed a microphone and began singing "Volare." Each groom had written personalized wedding vows, and each vow concluded with "My lover, my conscience, the disturber of my peace."

The climax of Scott and Jeffrey's commitment ceremony came when Scott (suffering from an especially virulent flu) collapsed into the wedding cake. He was wearing a white tuxedo, and the lavender frosting clung to it like a lichen. His new husband, assisted by one of the best men, carried him to a nearby sofa and draped a kilim over him. "Please don't let this dampen your spirits," the husband told them. "Scott would want you all to be partying."

About five minutes before the groom fainted, Patrick spotted

Grant at the end of the receiving line, wearing a V-neck tennis sweater and flannel trousers—cocktail napkins were spilling out of his pockets. Patrick walked over, extending his hand.

"Grant! Hey! I wanted to tell you how much we enjoyed seeing your house. It was so…I mean, God is in the details, right?"

"So am I," said Grant.

"Oh, beautiful place. I was talking to one of your guests—I can't remember his name."

"Which one?"

"He was blondish, I think, kind of a big guy, with a thrusting chin. He was wearing a Shetland sweater."

"A Shetland sweater?"

"I feel bad; he was asking me about some environmental issues, and I promised to get back to him, but I forgot his name."

"Did he come with somebody else?"

"I didn't see him come in, but I thought maybe you knew him."

"No." Grant's eyes were starting to wander. "I don't remember him."

"Well, that's funny."

"Yes."

"I thought for sure he knew you. Maybe I just assumed…"

"Yes."

"I mean, who knows? He could have been crashing your party!" Patrick laughed.

"Ha."

They were five feet away now from the grooms. One of the streamers had detached from the ceiling and was sweeping through the room like a jungle vine, and a young girl in a black velvet dress—the only child there—was laughing and chasing after it.

"Anyhow," Patrick said, "we were both raving about your pocket doors."

3

On the way home Alex said, "I'm glad you and Grant are getting to be friends."

"Oh, yeah."

"You know, he gives money to the National Conservation Alliance. Did I tell you that? I think he's in the Millennium Club."

"I think you told me that. Or he did."

"Aren't you supposed to fall on your knees when you meet a major donor?"

"Knees, yes. We're no longer sucking dick."

"I was just thinking, if you want to be director of development, you should get to know your donors."

"You're assuming I want to be director of development."

"Well, until you can come up with a reasonable alternative." Alex glanced at him. "Is there a reasonable alternative?"

Patrick thought, *It is really awful not being able to drive your own car.* "I'm working on it," he said.

"You don't like it when I look out for your career."

"No, I like it very much."

"And you don't like my friends."

Actually, the first time he met Alex's friends, he'd been puzzled because they were so unlike Alex. They were all older for one thing—the youngest of them was 40—and quite large all of them; you would almost call them sizeable, except they had tiny voices. There was at first something staggeringly familiar about them— the way they called each other "girls," the habit they had, whenever one of them said something shocking—one of them was always saying something shocking—of making clutching motions over their clavicles and screaming, "My pearls!" or sometimes just "Pearls!" And yet at the same time, they seemed to have an entirely alien frame of reference, cryptographic. The only allusions he could even recognize were from *The Women*: Alex's friends all identified with the much-divorced Countess. "*L'amour! L'amour,*" they moaned.

Alex's friends were, in fact, the occasion of their first major fight. It was the night of Gustave's birthday. Gustave was a bit of an odd man out in the group because he was half Cherokee and didn't speak much. He was valued because he laughed at everything. His friends threw him a party at the Pop Stop, and they brought whole acres of mocha ice cream cake and drank Diet Cokes. And then the gifts came out, like a cultural catechism: pink flamingoes, scented lubricants, magazines with titles like *Bore* and *Thrust*, frilly underwear, a padded bra, and finally, a gaudy strand of fake pearls, which prompted the entire table to break out with "My pearls!" and make clutching motions around their clavicles. Patrick turned to see if Alex was thinking the same thing he was, but he couldn't tell; Alex simply looked patient.

Afterward, they were walking together down 17th Street, and Patrick, deliberately modulating his tone, asked, "Is it possible that effeminacy is a political act?"

"What do you mean?" Alex said.

"Well, I mean the way that lesbianism can be a political response—oppressive male power structures and stuff. I mean, is effeminacy a statement? Like women sleeping together is a statement."

"What are you talking about?"

"Well, I was just thinking about your friends."

"My friends."

"Yeah."

"My friends are *effeminate*."

"Well…it doesn't matter."

"Effeminate how?"

"You know. Mincy itsy-bitsy."

Alex's jaw went crooked. "Mincy itsy-bitsy."

"It's not a problem or anything."

"Then why would you bring it up? You're clearly *troubled*."

"I'm not."

"You think they're somehow less of a *man* than you are?"

"No, not at all. I mean, we're all men, right? Even if you love men, you're still a man."

Alex's anger was actually charming then. He could remember Alex being as angry as he knew how to be, and all Patrick noticed was how the anger flushed all the green out of his eyes and left the brown flashing and contracting. Alex called him later that night, and before Patrick could say anything, said, "You really don't think you're gay, do you? You don't think you're one of us."

This was not true. Almost always, he felt like he was one of them. How could he not? Wherever he was, *they* were. Pick a street. Pick a restaurant. How could he go to a *gym* and not be one of them, the baseball-capped, action-shorted acolytes of definition. Now and then he would find himself studying one of them dispassionately, or he would catch sight of *himself* in the mirror—struggling through his biceps curls or his lat pull-downs or his triceps push-downs, a single harsh blue vein striping his neck, another bisecting his forearm, his upper lip retracting from his teeth, his entire face dissolving in sweat—and he would think: *Why are we creating these muscles? What are we going to do with them?*

Still, he was regular about his workouts. He was an elder in his gym. He found himself flirting with men he had flirted with seven years ago. He had never once, though, to the best of his recollection, encountered the man in the Shetland sweater. Not anywhere.

Did I dream him? he wondered. And when he dreamed about him that night, he actually asked him that question—extraordinary presence of mind!—but the man began pulling his sweater over his head, and Patrick was grieved by this and hoped he would stop, but the man disappeared into his sweater. And Patrick mourned. He cried like nobody's business.

4

"What I would like to know," said Marianne, "is how you can remember what he looks like if you were fuckin' asleep."

Patrick was still resolving that in his mind. His sense was that for about two seconds he had been completely awake, his retina switching open like a camera shutter, sealing the image onto his cortex.

"Unless you dreamed it," Marianne said.

"I don't think I dreamed it."

"But he was cute."

"I don't know, he wasn't really my type. That's not the point."

In fact, there was no particular point to their talking about it at all, no particular point to his bringing it up. It had just come out unbidden at the end of their evening, as things tended to do on their evenings, their bimonthly salons, as Marianne called them, held almost exclusively in her apartment, Marianne presiding like Madame du Châtelet, Patrick her Voltaire in training, always agreeable to a theme, always recumbent. Tonight, for instance, he was collapsed in her director's chair, his butt almost touching the ground. He was on his third glass of Maker's Mark. Marianne was a full level above him, on the edge of her glass coffee table, wearing plum tights, sequined high heels, and a large roomy T-shirt that read HELLO MY HONEY. She was a big girl who carried her weight well, and she had large cocoa-colored eyes and translucent skin. And a gift for gesture. Now and then she would twirl her wine glass around her head as though she were incanting.

Tonight the name she was incanting was Victor. Victor was the new masculine presence in her life. They had Internetted. In his last communication, he had included a quotation from Robert James Waller and had signed off, "Yours, Victor."

"I think it's the *yours*, really," Marianne said. "In retrospect, I think it's what I've been waiting my whole life for. A man who signs off with *yours*. I am *yours*."

"Is he?"

"Well, I don't know, honey, these things take time. It's only the second E-mail."

"But you're his."

"I suppose I am. I mean, he's just stuck in my brain; I can't think of anything else. Oh, Patrick, he's so sweet and wet—you'd just love him."

"Then bring him around or something."

"No, no, not yet. It's too fragile, it's—I don't even want to breathe on it too hard."

"Well, you'll keep me updated, then."

"Of course. And you'll do the same with Mr. Shetland."

And how he blushed! When was the last time he had *blushed* in Marianne's company? She had even proposed marriage to him once, and he hadn't blushed at all: He had simply deferred the question, knowing that they both understood each other. He knew many of the things that came out of her mouth were proposals—theorems about her future. But they were almost never about *his* future. So his embarrassment embarrassed both of them, and they busied themselves cleaning the place, dumping the wine bottles in Marianne's overflowing recycling bin, pouring the tortilla chip flakes out of the ashtrays that Marianne still kept around to remind her of when she smoked. They were unnaturally quiet with each other, and when she handed Patrick his coat with an unpracticed formality, he almost flung it down and ran. Instead, he dawdled for a minute, and then he shook his head and said, "I'm not sure he even remembers me. I doubt he does."

"But he understands you."

"I don't know. He knew I was sleepy."

"That's more than you did," she said.

His father called him the next morning. For some mystical reason, his father always went through the receptionist; he never called on Patrick's direct line. Patrick had long ago ceased mentioning this.

"Pattie, me boy." The Beatons were Scottish by ancestry, but Mr. Beaton always said Patrick's name as if they were sitting together in an Irish pub, next to a darts board, beerily embracing each other. "Me beamish boy."

"What's up, Da?"

"I've got a prospect," said Mr. Beaton, "but I can't tell you about it."

"This is why you're calling me? To tell me you can't talk about it?"

"Well, I can talk about it, but I can't talk about it now. But I'm calling to say I might be in town sometime soon."

"When?"

"I don't know."

George Beaton's timetable was not available to anyone. As Patrick's mother liked to say: "He wasn't just late to our wedding, he was late to our divorce." The lawyers had almost given up on him when he staggered through the door an hour and a half late. Someone had tried to steal his car, and he wouldn't have minded so much, but his samples were still inside. At the time, Mr. Beaton was selling cutlery from his trunk. Since then his entrepreneurial career had become still more diffuse, to the point where Patrick honestly couldn't say at any given moment what his father did for a living. It depended.

"Whatever," Patrick said. "Just let me know."

"How's Alex?"

"He's fine. He's *driving* me everywhere. My car's been in the shop for three weeks."

"Fuck's sake."

"First it got broken into. And now they've discovered some problem with the engine strut. Do you know what an engine strut is?"

"I know it well."

"Well, they're hard at work on it. I think, before this is through, I'll have the finest engine strut in the postnuclear world."

"You know what I'm going to say, don't you?"

"Yes."

"You should have taken my Infiniti when you had the chance."

Actually, Mr. Beaton's Infiniti was not really his. It had belonged to somebody of indeterminate gender whom Mr. Beaton was convinced would sell it to Patrick for a song. Patrick was sentimental, though, about his Oldsmobile. Every night now, he passed the service station where his car was being held—they kept it parked on the street because there was no room in the garage—and it seemed to be drooping more each time he saw it, its fender curled in despair. "Don't worry," Patrick would say. "I'll be back."

"They're not charging you garage fees, are they?" Mr. Beaton asked him.

"No."

" 'Cause I once lost a Toyota Celica that way. It just got cheaper to leave it there, you know?"

"I remember."

"I miss that car." Mr. Beaton's voice was reedy with longing. "Well, now, tell me, Pattie, whatcha working on?"

And it caught him off guard, just as Marianne's remark had done the previous evening. "Nothing much," he said. "Stuff."

"Well, there's always stuff, isn't there?"

If he had been honest, he would have said, "Da, I'm drawing." It hadn't been his intention. He'd been on the phone with one of the vendors, haggling over production deadlines, and he'd begun doodling—restlessly, edgily—on the back of an annual report envelope, and gradually the scratch marks resolved themselves into the outline of a face. And the face stared back at him—not even a face, a cavity, really, but already acquiring an identity. And the identity didn't change no matter how much he tried to fill in the cavity; no matter how imperfectly he approached it, the identity was still there. So his incompetence didn't frustrate him; it almost touched him. He didn't mind that the hair was a little too tightly curled, that the mouth was too full, the eyes further apart than they needed to be—oh, he would never get the eyes right.

He spent more than half an hour on it, all told, his door closed, his computer aswarm with screen-saving tropical fish, his eraser working as furiously as his pencil. And when he was done, he couldn't look at it for a while. He folded it up and tucked it inside *The Chronicle of Philanthropy*. Then he took it home with him, and that night, just before bed, he pulled it out and looked at it one more time. Then he crumpled it up, and he walked over to the trash can next to his bed—a trash can his mother had given him when he went to college, emblazoned with clematis and fleur-de-lis—and he held the wad of paper over it and watched it drop into the chasm. *Cast off*, he thought, wryly.

The next morning he retrieved it.

To celebrate the return of his Oldsmobile, Patrick decided to treat Alex to a Caribbean restaurant in Adams Morgan, only a couple of blocks from Alex's apartment.

"Are you sure?" Alex asked.

"Of course, I'm sure."

Halfway through the meal the hostess announced that there had been a fire in the kitchen and everyone would have to leave—except for Alex and Patrick, who could stay and finish their meal. As the two of them ate, though, it became clear that the fire was gaining force. Clouds of smoke were surging through the cracks in the closed kitchen doors and engulfing them, searing their nostrils, lashing their faces and hair and hands. Their eyes began to water, and deep inside their chests their lungs were oscillating like accordions.

"Firemen on their way," the hostess said, grinning tensely. "You see."

Globules of sweat began to leach through Patrick's shirt, and he watched with a dire enchantment as the sweat ran off his hands and onto the rim of his plate. He looked up and saw Alex, sunburnt, clasping his trachea.

"What's wrong?"

"I think my throat's closing up."

"Do you want to leave?"

"Um…maybe."

They got as far as ten feet down the street before the hostess caught them. She was breathing almost as heavily as they were and still grinning and waving a bill in front of their faces. "You gotta pay," she said.

"What do you mean?"

"You almost finish your meal. You gotta pay."

They argued with her for about ten minutes. Alex did most of the talking because they both knew that Patrick's anger tended to make him inarticulate. Still, the best Alex could do for all his glibness was to get himself a free meal for some other night, given that most of his red snapper was uneaten. (Not surprising: Alex hardly ate these days.) Patrick, on the other hand, had put a major dent in his blackened chicken, so he was out of luck.

"We need the money," the woman said. "Got inspectors coming next week."

In the end, of course, they paid—or Patrick paid, as he had said he would.

"The snapper wasn't bad," Alex said. "What I tasted."

"Good."

"Maybe I'll go back Tuesday night."

"Fine."

What a fool, he thought. To think going to dinner could spill a little joy into his life. Or getting his car back. Or snuggling with Alex. Sometimes he believed the only uncomplicated joy he experienced on a regular basis came from calling a daily, pre-recorded cafeteria menu service. Not a day went by that he didn't call. He had no idea even where the cafeteria was (the number had been given to him by a friend) but the woman who announced each day's meals had a Southern accent so pure it was almost fictional, and she seemed to ask nothing more of life than the chance to announce the day's specials, the grills, the baked potatoes, the salad bars, the hamburger bars "with all your fixin's." She would linger with special relish over the yogurt options, and now and then a particular item made her fairly detonate. "*Suc*cotash!" she would cry. "Beef with *oh-ster* sauce!" She never finished without offering a song. One day she sang, "I'm the happiest girl in the whole U.S.A." And Patrick didn't for one moment doubt that she was.

I could be that way, he thought. *Couldn't I? Sure I could.*

There were two messages waiting when he got home: one from Marianne, updating him on her progress with Victor, the other from his father, asking for copies of the Washington, D.C., and Northern Virginia phone books.

Joy. Define joy.

Joy came from having more than answering-machine messages and spider plants to come home to. Joy came from other things. From pets, perhaps. Not a dog—too much parenting. Fish? Too little parenting. A cat? Maybe. *Maybe, but do they return your emotional investment?* There was something a little *withheld* about cats—a nagging sense that you were being billed for their time.

It would just be nice, he thought, to have something undemandingly sniffing you or licking your face or waking you up before you were ready.

That night in bed, unable to sleep, he felt his thoughts drifting back toward Scottie. Scottie was the name he had given the man in the Shetland sweater—the name flowed ineluctably from the region, from the Shetland Islands, Britain's northernmost point, swept by gales, lashed by frigid oceans and salt-marsh grasses. Home to small ponies, small sheepdogs, and large silent Scottish fishermen. Big-handed, strong-necked men—men like Scottie.

The name was necessary because Patrick's greatest fear was that Scottie would become an abstraction. Which made the drawing equally useful because, imperfect as it was, it forced him to think of the man in purely physical terms, to think: *No, his eyes were a little smaller, weren't they? But lustrous, a quality of humor in them. The chin wasn't quite so pointed, the whole contour a little softer.*

He forced himself to think about tangible things: where Scottie grew up, where he went to high school, where he got laid, the model of his first car. What was he doing right *now*—at this exact point of consciousness. Sound asleep? Probably. He slept well, probably, snored like a hippo—he knew how to cast off. Night after night, he cast off.

Or maybe he wasn't asleep. Maybe he was sitting up in bed, reading a magazine—*Civilization, The New Republic, Harper's*—behind on his magazines, thinking really he should cancel some of his subscriptions; there wasn't enough time in the day.

Or was he *out* somewhere? *Out* was the one place Patrick couldn't track him. He couldn't get the picture in his head: Scottie on the prowl. Sniffing around the dim, smoky corners, the condom machines, the chiaroscuro dance floors. Whirling though clouds of stimulants. Swinging his shirt over his head like a bolo.

It wasn't possible. *Not Scottie.*

Then where was he?

Patrick closed his eyes. *If I just empty out my head, I might get a clue, a message of sorts.* But all that happened was he went to sleep—which, he realized later, was much as Scottie would have wanted.

5

"Oh, my God, look." Alex was kneading Patrick's shoulder, gesturing with his free elbow toward a triumvirate of men striding down the opposite side of 17th Street. The men were dressed a little warmer than the weather was: cutoff jeans and Bermuda shorts, tank tops in sorbet shades, boat shoes and flip-flops. The man with the bird tattoo on his right calf was the only one Patrick recognized. His name was William, and he was a local television personality—the backup traffic reporter on a Fox-affiliate news show. Once his helicopter had almost crashed into the Potomac.

"I can't believe it," Alex whispered.

"What?"

"Do you know William and Thomas?"

"Which one is Thomas?"

"The shorter one, with the pompadour flippy thing."

"Oh."

"Did I tell you? What happened with them at J.R.'s? Oh, it's wild: A couple of months ago, right, William sees this guy standing by the pinball machine at J.R.'s, and I guess his heart stands still, or *something* stands still, but what can he do? Thomas is there—they've been going out a *year* now, although how they've stayed together that long—so all William does is make goo-goo eyes at Mr. Pinball and go home. But then the very next day, what does he do? Puts an ad in Glances."

"Huh."

"And the *day* the ad appears," Alex said, "William gets a call from Mr. Pinball. Heavy breathing over the phone. They make a date, one thing leads to another, pretty soon lollapalooza. So now William's leading this double life, right? One night Thomas, the next night Mr. Pinball. He's getting it coming and going."

"But then."

"But *then* it turns out that the *Pinball*—is Thomas's personal trainer."

"What are the chances?"

"Of course, William doesn't know this. But one day Thomas and the Pinball are chatting in the gym, and the Pinball's bragging about this new man in his life—what a generous *endowment* he has, what an interesting *birthmark* he has."

"Bingo."

"Shit hits the fan."

"How do you know all this?"

"Thomas told me."

"I didn't you know you were friends."

"We're not," Alex said. "We work out together. But you know what? I *think*—the guy who just went by with Thomas and William? That was *Pinball*. Because Thomas kind of pointed him out once, and I remember he had enormous trapezius muscles."

"So they're out for a threesome."

"God, what kind of—you know, I think sometimes I'm too old-fashioned. I could never go in for that. *Arrangements.*"

"Don't worry."

"I think I would just giggle or something."

Alex giggled as he said it: He was in a giddy mood this evening. They had just left Trumpets, where they had stood in the same place for about an hour. They hadn't needed to move because Alex kept seeing people they knew—people Alex knew—people with exposed undershirts and hair cut down to the follicles, men squeezing limes into the club sodas they nursed through teeny straws, gravitating in Alex's direction like metal filings.

"That was fun," Patrick said, setting his jaw.

"I'm glad you said that," Alex said. "No, I am. I think about this a lot, and I really think getting out more is a good thing. For you. 'Cause it's not healthy to be Ol' *Broody* Butt."

"You're right. No more Broody Butt."

"A little's all right."

Later that night they were sitting in Alex's small apartment. Sitting apart: Alex on the love seat, Patrick on one of the caned dining-room chairs, nothing but a cactus separating them. They were sharing a citrus cooler because it was the only thing Alex had in his refrigerator.

"I wonder," Patrick said. "Do William and Thomas brood?"

"They *should*," Alex said. "I hope William's learned his lesson, anyway."

"Yeah, get that birthmark taken care of."

A small decorous laugh dropped from Alex's mouth, and then he fell silent. The windows were open, but no air was spilling in. Somebody in the next apartment was singing along with Eartha Kitt: "I wanna be evil...I wanna spit tacks..."

"You know," Alex said, "I almost did a Glances ad for you."

"You're kidding."

"Oh, not when we first met. It was for our first-year anniversary. I was going to pretend like we'd just met each other somewhere. Like it was all still fresh. I think that's kind of sexy."

"Why didn't you do it?"

" 'Cause you would have hated it."

"Why do you think that?"

"Because you would've. You would've been embarrassed and—you would've hated it. You wouldn't have spoken to me for a week."

Patrick felt he should protest a little more, but Alex had been too definitive. For the next hour or so, they said barely a word, and Patrick went home alone after promising that he would let Alex clean his shed tomorrow.

On the way out, he slipped into a 7-Eleven and got a copy of the *Blade*. Sitting in his car, he flipped to the "Glances" section:

> 20TH AND P. You: blond, in red Alfa. Me: in light green T-shirt and running shorts. We smiled. You drove on. Let's go through the green light together sometime.

And:

> ROBERTO. We met too briefly on Sat 5/28, near Columbia Rd. & Kalorama. Next time let's get down to briefs.

Did people read "Glances" because they thought their own descriptions would come up? Or was it the randomness that was so thrilling? As if AIDS had never existed. As if everyone were in the first days of liberation, emitting radio waves of libido, brushing against each other and leaving behind broken-off stingers…

Even before he was seriously contemplating it, Patrick was composing in jest.

You: man in Shetland sweater. Me: too tired to speak. Let's meet for coffee when I'm better rested.

Well, it *had* to be in jest; Scottie wasn't the kind of person who would read "Glances." Oh, maybe, with friends, gathered around a big late-night tureen of coffee, some off-brand gourmet blend, or maybe brewed chai. But, no, Scottie was a reader, wasn't he? He would be sitting alone that time of night, reading *The Palm at the End of the Mind* or something, in some bohemian place where people carved Nietzsche into the tables. He'd be drinking his chai. The *Blade* would be on the table next to him. Maybe he'd eye it once or twice, nothing more.

Over the next few days, though, a kind of syllogism gradually impressed itself on Patrick: *(1) If we are to accept that Scottie and I are alike, in some still-unproven way and (2) I read Glances, (3) isn't it at least likely that he reads Glances—at least occasionally?*

And so the jottings that had assembled flippantly in his brain began dribbling out onto paper, and he would labor for periods of five, ten, 15 minutes—whatever he could snatch away during the work day—seeking the proper code.

It was a struggle, of course, because he couldn't give away his identity. There could be no name, for instance, no phone number, no mention of Grant's house. Other people read Glances too.

Me: almost dead to the world. You: telling me to "let go." Thanks for the go-ahead. Would like to let go with you.

No. No. Sounded like an out-of-body experience. Too metaphysical. Had to be lighter-hearted, raffish.

You: wavy dirty-blond hair, lopsided smile, cranberry Shetland sweater. Me: a little weary. Would be happy to "cast off" if you're in the same boat.

This was more to the point. But would Scottie remember the exact phrase he'd used? Would he know what his smile looked like? And what about the Shetland sweater? Maybe that was too explicit. He'd already confided that detail to somebody, hadn't he? Grant, certainly—Alex too, come to think of it.

He ended up taking all his scribblings home with him. That night he crumpled them up—just as he'd done with the drawing. And just as he'd done with the drawing, he dropped the crumpled paper into the trash can by his bed, except this time, instead of having it around to tempt him the next morning, he took the crumpled paper directly to the garbage can outside and buried it underneath two trash bags.

And then, the next evening, the message came to him. It happened as he was riding home on the Metro. He was looking out the window, feeling the comfortable bulk of a large, Bible-reading woman against his flank, looking at a Hispanic woman in a decrepit camel coat, her lips drooping, her head snapping in and out of sleep—and then his own reflection mysteriously appeared in the Metro doors.

Me: in the library. You: in the doorway. Couldn't linger cause I was in the Land of Nod. Join me in the land of the living.

The next day, Patrick faxed it to the paper. And it was only a few days later, when he received his call box number and instructions, that he began to think through the consequences. He was now cultivating an extramarital affair. Wasn't he? Wasn't that precisely where this was heading?

Then again, what exactly did he want Scottie to do? Which of the conceivable scenarios was appropriate? Scottie phones: passionate mutual declaration, immediate assignation. Scottie places a counterad: teasing double entendres, a scattering of clues, the continuation of the game.

Scottie remains silent: an enigma in wool.

It was all a little murky. As hard as Patrick fought to keep visualizing him, Scottie resisted. So Patrick found himself hoping after a while that Scottie *wouldn't* answer his ad because…

Because I don't know how to love him.

That Friday, Alex came over to his house for dinner and brought the *Blade* with him. Neither of them opened it or even mentioned it the entire evening; it sat there half on, half off the corner of the coffee table. Like a prop waiting to be reset by the stagehand.

"Oh!" said Alex. "Did I tell you about Thomas and William?"

"No."

"They're back together again."

"I didn't know they were ever apart."

"Well, they were *less* together, and now they're more together. But in the weirdest way. 'Cause what happened was *Thomas*—who was so pissed off—decides, OK, I'm going to put my *own* ad in the paper. But instead of a 'Glances' ad, he puts in a regular personal ad. You know: 'Hot GWM, 34, seeking multifaceted, hard-bodied stud.' Something like that."

"Uh-huh."

"So he waits a couple of weeks, and then he gets a response. In this plain brown envelope with this *really* familiar handwriting, an even *more* familiar photograph inside. One guess who."

"Pinball."

"William! Answered Thomas's ad, having no idea it was Thomas's ad!"

"Huh."

"So, instead of being upset by it, they both figured it was fate's way of telling them they belonged together. And now, according to Thomas, the sex is amazing."

"Wow."

"I would hate to think there's any kind of moral to this," Alex said, suddenly becalmed. "I mean, it's interesting, but it's not enlightening, is it?"

"I think the moral is to be as little like Thomas and William as possible."

Even as he said this, he felt the shiv of hypocrisy lancing him between his ribs. He almost groaned. The newspaper with his delicately coded advertisement buried inside stared back at him from its perch on the coffee table. He could imagine it falling at any moment, making a great clang.

"You look tired," Alex said.

6

It's warm, Patrick thought. *When did it get this warm?* It was Saturday afternoon, and his eyelids were closed, and Alex must have thought he was falling asleep—napping again!—because he nudged Patrick's cheek with his big toe.

"You awake?" Alex asked.

"I am."

"Everything OK?"

"Oh, yeah."

"I mean, not that anything's wrong."

"No, I'm fine."

They were lying at odd angles on Patrick's bed, still naked. They had been taken by an unexpected wave of passion. It had surprised the both of them. They lay there, a little embarrassed, the perspiration clotting on their skin, the air suddenly languid and fluid. Downstairs, the Saturday mail was being passed through the mail slot.

Alex reached out to grab Patrick's toes. "I wonder why some times are better than others," he said. "I know it's supposed to be that way. It's just…sometimes there doesn't seem to be any reason."

"Does there have to be?"

"No. Maybe it's better if there isn't one."

They lay there for another few minutes, not saying a word, breathing almost synchronously. Then, abruptly, Alex got up and excused himself. Patrick closed his eyes. He could almost fancy himself drifting off to sleep—*sleep!*—here in the middle of the afternoon. Hadn't he learned by now?

But as he closed his eyes, a strange thing happened. Without planning or expecting it, he tumbled backward about 16 months, and he landed on a particular day, which was the very day he met Alex. In an unprepossessing little square on Capitol Hill known to locals as "Dogshit Park." A Saturday afternoon in late January, and it must have been unseasonably warm because Patrick, on his way home from the gym, had decided to sit for a few minutes on a park bench, his gym bag by his side, an empty water bottle in his right hand. There was nothing particularly lovely about the park in January. The tulip beds were muddied over and daubed with fragments of leaves. The homeless people lay still in their Bonus Army tents; only the tent flaps shivered a little.

The only other living things in the square were a young man and his dog. The dog was an Airedale, and the man ran his hands through the dog's dusty, redolent coat and grabbed him around the belly and threw him to the ground and then threw himself on top. For a few minutes, the two of them were a single riotous wheel, rolling, gathering speed as if they were rolling downhill— first the dog on top, then the young man on top—and the dog's yelps of pleasure reached higher and higher frequencies, and the pitch of the young man's laughter ratcheted upward in response. Patrick was entranced. He had never seen such happiness, such high spirits. And without thinking, he picked up a stick that was lying at his feet and hurled it at them. The stick flew just over the young man's head, missed it by two inches, and the young man's head jerked up, his face flushed and vibrant.

"Sorry," Patrick said. "I meant it for the dog."

Slowly, Alex rose from the ground, and the dog, still in a dream of excitement, danced around him in mad circles, not yet recognizing the stick. Alex bent over, picked up the stick, and softly flung it back to Patrick's feet, and now the dog understood; he took off with a purposeful grunt and a scattering rush of claws, and Alex followed deliberately behind him. Patrick almost flinched as the dog, braking too late, skidded into his shins, but he kept his eyes trained on this creature of mud—this creature with the perfectly composed features, hazel eyes, the limpid profile like something out of an old *Photoplay*.

Alex stood there for a moment, smiling, searching for something to say.

"He's not really my dog," he said finally. "I'm just house-sitting. My building doesn't allow pets."

"No?"

"Unless they're human."

"You asleep?"

Patrick looked up. Alex, still naked, was sitting on the edge of the bed next to him. His hand was making slow caressing movements on the section of the down comforter closest to Patrick's head. His eyes were fixed on the newel just over Patrick's head.

"No," Patrick said.

"I know this probably isn't the right time to talk about this," he said. "I mean, there's never a right time, is there?"

Patrick never actually budged while it was happening. He lay there with his head at the very edge of his pillow, waiting for the familiar symptoms: the constricted lungs, the contracted diaphragm, the burning in the esophagus. And as he waited, Alex kept talking, almost free-associatively.

"I just don't feel it getting better, you know? You just get farther and farther away, you *disappear*. It can't just be *my* decision, right? We must have both decided it; I don't know when. Do you want me to go right now? Or I can stay a little. Whichever you want. Do you want me to call tonight? This sucks."

Patrick was so zealously monitoring his own symptoms that he failed at first to notice Alex's. He had never seen Alex cry before.

Alex got up from the bed and began dressing. With his shirt halfway on, he stopped suddenly and said, "I'm sorry, could I— could I just clean your miniblinds before I go?" And then he started sobbing again. "It would make me feel better."

7

Patrick had been 25 the last time he'd broken up with a man. He could remember spending entire days in a state of morbid wakefulness. Driving his car, he would come to a halt at stop signs and remain there for minutes at a time. Street people on Pennsylvania Avenue would approach him for money and then look at him and change their minds. *Grief must repel people*, he'd thought. *It must be a kind of antipheromone.*

Things were different this time. He was surprised at how competent he was. The day after Alex left, he planted a whole row of impatiens in his backyard and then found himself chatting for over half an hour with his downstairs tenant. They had never spoken for more than ten minutes in the two years she had been renting from him. Deanna was at least a decade older than he was. She was unmarried, slightly overweight, with a mop of unruly brown curls just starting to gray, and—this struck him for the first time—a sensual voice: low and beautifully modulated. Why had he never noticed that before?

It suddenly occurred to him that he might learn things if he paid more attention. During his Sunday morning violin lesson, for instance, he found himself listening with great care to his violin teacher, Sonya, who was now using hypnosis therapy to become more fertile.

"I refuse to take fertility drugs," she said. "Because those eggs wouldn't be *mine*, do you see what I'm saying? They'd belong to the drug, and that means the *baby* would belong to the drug. Like one of those crack babies—except you couldn't wean him off it."

"Do you and your husband ever think about adoption?"

"Every *day*, we talk about it, but it's like—we're artists, right? We need to *create*."

And suddenly Patrick was consumed with the desire to comfort her. To tell her that she would have children and they would be beautiful and gifted and unforgettable. Suddenly he was *awash* in empathy—for Sonya, for Deanna, for every living organism—and he couldn't understand it. Was it just a sublimation of his self-pity? Which was not so sublimated that it didn't come out at unexpected moments—like when he discovered he was low on toilet paper. Alex had always reminded him when he was low on things, and since Patrick always promptly forgot, Alex began writing the items down on a special stylus pad he had bought Patrick for his birthday. Over time, the items assumed larger and more urgent letterings. "DENTAL FLOSS!" one message read. "SPRAY STARCH OR DIE!!!"

Alex spent most of his waking moments cleaning. He cleaned things that Patrick would never dream of cleaning—attic shelves, paperback books, the clock timer on the oven. He mopped under the bed twice a month, he polished door knobs, he dusted the individual leaves of the ficus plant. He cleaned the undersides of tables. Last summer he'd taken apart Patrick's gas grill so he could check the venturi tubes for spider nests.

One evening, a little after 11, Patrick had found him voraciously scouring the porcelain in the upstairs bathtub.

"Why do you always work so hard when you come over?" Patrick asked.

"My place is so small," Alex said. "It doesn't give me enough to do."

Would Patrick's house ever be that clean again? Who would pry the dust out of the louvers in the closet doors? Fluff the pillows on the love seat? Scrub salmonella colonies out of the kitchen sink? Refold Patrick's underwear, organize his shoes, polish his reading glasses for him twice a week, though he hardly ever wore them?

All the millions of incremental improvements wrought by those twitching fingers—who would ever do them again?

Whenever Patrick toyed with calling Alex, he compensated by calling other people. His first call was to Marianne. Before he could draw breath, she was off and running about Victor, who persisted in believing she was a vegetarian, and she wasn't sure whether it would be easier to disabuse him of this or simply *become* a vegetarian, and if she *did* become a vegetarian, could she offset it by taking up smoking again—and Patrick finally jumped in and said it: "Alex and I broke up."

"When?"

"Last week."

A brief silence, an outraged silence. "And you waited all this fuckin' time to call me?"

"Yeah, I don't know. I didn't feel like talking about it."

"Well, you shouldn't have let me go on like that."

"No, I enjoy it."

"Oh, honey, I'm sorry." He could see her now, sitting Indian-style on her divan, swathed in a pink silk sweater and tights, stroking the stem of her wine glass. "I know what you're going through," she said. "I mean, I been hit by that bus. I got permanent tire marks."

It was true. Marianne had been deserted by at least two men as well as one woman. The woman's departure was particularly galling because it had come at the end of a brief lesbian experiment that Marianne was just about to call a halt to anyway, and the other woman had beaten her to it. Patrick had never met any of Marianne's intimates: She kept them as sequestered as the Gnostic Gospels.

"Alex *was* kind of a putz," she said.

"No, he wasn't," Patrick said.

"Well, he cleaned too much. And he never liked to eat."

"No, it's not that. He just—he has a complex relationship with food."

Of course, it hadn't always been that way. When they'd first started dating, Alex could break bread with the best of them: He once ate ten biscuits—an entire can of Hungry Jacks—at a single sitting. But something happened, something estranged him from the whole biological imperative of eating. One of Patrick's lasting memories was of the night they celebrated Alex's birthday at the Inn at Little Washington. It took Patrick several weeks to save the money for dinner, and in all that time he never once asked himself if he was contributing to Alex's pleasure. Halfway through the third course, Alex lifted his napkin to his mouth, then let it drop to the floor. His eyes closed, and he began breathing, laboriously, like someone strapped to an oxygen tank.

"Eat," he groaned. "Why do people *eat*?"

Why, indeed? thought Patrick. Why do people do anything? Why does someone roll in the mud with a dog and then never allow himself—or anything else—to get dirty again? Unless it was the duress of being with somebody else throwing you out of whack.

"Alex wasn't the putz," he said. "*I* was. I was the whole problem."

"That right?"

"Not because I did anything *wrong*, exactly. I just never—I never opened up. I wasn't affectionate, I wasn't *present*. When I think back I can't remember a single time when he was really, truly happy around me."

"More fool him," Marianne said loyally.

"No—the first time I ever saw him, I thought he was the happiest thing I'd ever seen on God's earth. I didn't think anyone could be that happy. And I never saw him that happy again, and I think that must be a function of me. I mean, that seems kinda logical."

"Naw, it's more complicated. And maybe less flattering to you. 'Cause Alex's happiness isn't dependent on you. People are happy or they ain't."

"I don't agree. I mean, sure, Alex may not be any happier *without* me, but I think I was—probably—largely responsible for making him unhappy. And it's not a source of pride, it's just the way it was. I wish it weren't."

"Well, you can't change it, you know. Haven't I told you people don't change anymore once they're 30? You're past the magic line."

"I know."

"So you just have to find someone you can make *less* unhappy than you made Alex."

Later, he called his mother, who reminded him that he was still young. He called his sister, who said she had never thought Alex was right for him, although she didn't know exactly who *would* be right for him. His sister was still in the grip of a kind of social Darwinism: She saw homosexuals as evolutionary dead ends and was afraid of what natural selection would do to them if they didn't watch out.

"Especially with all this gene therapy," she said. "I think you're going to be so lonely."

Patrick's father was next on the call list, but Patrick decided not to make any mention of Alex when he called: He had always found it best to let his father do the talking. Mr. Beaton had just returned from the Williamstown, Mass., library—he repeated the word *library* several times, as though it were a code. He told Patrick he was "planting seeds."

"Any hints?" Patrick asked.

But Mr. Beaton was being coy. He would say only that he needed to hook up with some important contacts in Washington, which would take him to Patrick's door sometime within the next three weeks.

"How long are you planning to stay?"

"Well, Pattie, if you could put me up for a week, I'd be most obliged. After that, I can get my own place somewhere, maybe a three-month lease."

"Wait a minute. You're *moving* here?"

"No, no, not exactly. Not really. It's temporary, it's *ad hoc*. Till I get the venture rolling."

"Do you have investors this time?"

"Not worrying about it. If I've learned one thing, Pattie, you get your *idea* first—you refine it, you make it sing. You build a better fuckin' mousetrap, the investors come leapfrogging your way."

After he got off the phone with his father, Patrick called his mother again. "Do you know what Da's up to?"

"How should I know?" she said. "I've had another burglary."

"What do you mean 'another?'"

"They've taken my Rolex watch and my one-carat."

"So you really looked this time?" Burglary was the only form of hysteria to which his mother was prone. "You checked the back of the closet?" he asked. "The attic?"

"I've looked all over. They're gone. Whoever did it was very good because there's no sign of entry."

"Do you know if Da still has health insurance?" he asked.

"Likely not. Oh, honey, as soon as I'm through with the police,

I'm going to send you a motivational video. It's called *How to Carpe Your Diems*. By a very nice man—I can't recall his name—and I don't want you to dismiss it in advance; I want you to really listen to what he has to say. Because you have your whole life ahead of you. How old are you now?"

"Thirty-two."

"Exactly! You're just getting warmed up."

That night, exhausted from watching AMC Classics, he wandered out to Mr. Henry's and sat at one of the outside tables. He ordered a club soda. (Since Alex's departure he hadn't had the slightest inclination to drink.) A knot of off-duty Marines wandered by in a great bullying mass, bare-scalped, thick-necked, their muscles barging out of civilian shirts and corduroy shorts. And then right behind them, like a fun-house reflection, came a crowd of gay men—none of them under 35 and all of them stuffed like penitents into jeans and gaudily filigreed boots—on their way to Remington's, the local country-western gay bar, some of them already practicing their line dance. "*Hoo*, girl!" one of them screamed. "You go, girl!"

The pay phone was right inside the door. As Patrick dialed the number, he realized that it was one of the few phone numbers he had ever committed to memory.

"Hello?" Alex sounded cautious, as though he already knew who it was. For two seconds Patrick thought about hanging up. *It's a pay phone, they can't trace it.*

"Hi," he said finally.

"Hi."

"I don't know why I called."

"Well, it's—"

"I was thinking about getting a dog."

"What?"

"I was just thinking you always wanted me to get a dog, and I don't know why I never did, exactly, except dogs are such a *commitment*. Like kids, really. But I met this woman the other day—people hire her to walk their dogs while they're at work, and I was surprised by how inexpensive she was, and very nice, not that walking is all there is to having a dog. I understand that. And I know a cat would be less commitment, but I don't think of myself as a cat person, I mean, even less than I'm a *dog* person—"

"Patrick."

"What?"

"Can I call you later? I can't really talk now."

"That's fine. I can call you back."

"Actually—I haven't—I'll probably be moving soon."

"Oh."

"I know we need to talk. Can I give you a call sometime next week?"

"Whatever," Patrick said.

"Is everything else OK?"

For a moment, he held the receiver away from him, stared at it with a clinical revulsion, as though it had bubbled out of a bog. An old woman stumbled out of a nearby bathroom, and over his head someone was tuning an acoustic guitar. He was sweating, he realized.

"Patrick?"

He didn't hang up, just left the receiver dangling. He dropped a $5 bill on his table, then walked quickly home.

And he slept badly that night. His sheets were clammy. Waking the next morning, he couldn't believe it was still the weekend. Sunday stretched before him—he wasn't entirely convinced Monday would get there, but it did.

That was the day Scottie answered the ad.

8

Why here? Patrick thought, with a sudden jolt. *Why did I pick this place?*

He scanned the room, trying to see it the way a stranger would see it. It was a place. It was a cheap Italian place in the middle of Arlington. Once it had been a cheap Japanese place, and it still had an uncomfortably low ceiling, with wooden trellis work and an unreconstructed sushi bar. And why hadn't they just kept the original waiters too? The new ones wore tight black polyester pants and creased white shirts, and as soon as he sat down, they jammed a menu into his face, and he said, "Actually, I'm expecting someone," and they just kept the menu where it was, suspended in front of his face, and they wouldn't leave until he took it.

Oh, God, oh, God, God, God. Patrick clutched his unopened menu. *Why did I pick this place?*

Because it was the first one that had come to mind. For some reason. For some fucking reason.

Well, it's full at least. That's a good sign. Half carafes of cheap Chianti. Prosperous suburban couples planting their elbows on the tables, downing chunks of cold bread, gesturing with their ziti, leaning toward each other over flickering candle bowls sweating wax.

"Hi."

Patrick looked up. A man was standing in front of him.

"I'm Rick," the man said.

Rick.

"And I'm hoping you're Patrick. Or I've just made a big fool of myself."

Patrick nodded. "That's me," he said.

"Nice to meet you."

"Nice to meet you, Rick."

Say it. Rick Rick Rick Rick. *Why should it be so jarring?* Rick. Rick Rick Rick Rick Rick Rick. *I mean, what were you thinking? There would be no name? The whole world has names. Given names. They don't need you to invent their names for them.* Why hadn't he just *asked* for the name over the phone? All he'd said was, "Oh— hi. I think you answered my ad," and it sort of went from there, sputtering on for maybe two minutes, and then the relief of quickly setting a time and place, except who would have thought it would be this place? Who would have expected it to be like this? Patrick and Rick, *Patrick and Rick.* Dinner. Together. Here.

"I'm sorry I'm late," Rick said. "I had trouble finding parking."

"Oh, it's—it's hard here. They need more parking."

"Yeah."

A waiter jammed a menu into Rick's face, and Rick began to study it, and Patrick began studying him, and it was funny because Patrick's greatest fear had been that he wouldn't be able to speak for ten or 20 or 30 minutes, but in fact it was only 20 seconds before he actually spoke, and the words just dropped artlessly out of his mouth so that he was as surprised by them as anyone.

"You're not him," Patrick said.

And the man named Rick looked up and smiled a little. "No," he said. And then he bent his head back down to the menu and seemed to recall something and looked up again and said, "You're not him either."

That was the most stunning thing. The notion that there had been a counteryearning, a counterexpectancy that Patrick was not meeting, had never been prepared to meet. He felt his heart wobbling inside his chest, he felt his windpipe squeezing out air. He said, "The gnocchi's not bad here. It's usually one of the specials."

"Oh, wow, I haven't had gnocchi in ages."

"I wouldn't get the house red, though."

"No?"

"Well, I mean, you can get whatever you want. It's just—it made me sick the last time I was here."

"You mean you threw up?"

"No—no, not quite."

"But you felt sick."

"Yes, sick."

"Well, then, we probably shouldn't drink it."

"No." Patrick fell silent, began scratching the closed menu. "But everything else is—you know, it's *fine.*"

"Yeah?"

"I mean, it's a place. I just thought—you know—not pretentious."

"Oh, it's fine."

"So—whatever you get—I'm sure will be fine."

"The bread's good."

Maybe it really *was* good too. It was gone, anyway, after about five minutes. Patrick had eaten a good three quarters of it. Not only had he eaten it, he had *savaged* it. He had torn it apart with his teeth. Swallowed entire chunks in single gulps.

"Big salad," said Rick, through muscular jaws.

Patrick was startled. *When did the salad arrive?*

"I didn't expect this much salad," Rick said.

"I should have gotten some."

"Well, you still can."

Rick was seriously eating too, bless him, eating with gusto. He was *corralling* his food—first the salad, then the gnocchi—rounding up each errant dumpling and tossing it into his mouth as though it were one of Ulysses' men. Patrick hated to interrupt him.

"Rick. Can I ask you something?"

"Hm."

"You don't have to answer if you don't want. I was just wondering who…who it was you were expecting, exactly?"

Rick sat back from the table, still chewing. He locked his hands across his chest, fingered his class ring. "Well, it was kind of a long shot. See, I work in a law library. Big firm on K Street—I won't bore you with the name."

"Good. I hate lawyers."

"Yeah, me too. Anyway, this happened—about three weeks ago," Rick said. "I was checking in some *ABA Journals*, and I looked up, and there was this guy sitting there, going through one of the D.C. Code volumes. And he looked really *tired* but also really—punchy, I guess, like he didn't care anymore. So that made him kind of attractive, I guess. He had kind of—deep-set eyes and a lock of hair that came over one of his eyes. Blond hair. Like he was playing hide-and-seek."

"Did you say anything to him?"

"No. We kind of stared at each other, but…We were both busy, I guess. I did sort of want to stay and talk."

"So then you saw this ad, and the ad mentions a *library.*"

"Yeah, and I thought, *Hey, maybe that's it, that's the guy.* I knew it was a long shot."

"What did you think the Land of Nod meant?"

"Land of what?"

"The ad said I couldn't linger 'cause I was in the land of Nod."

"Oh, I don't know. I thought it was some case he was working on. You know: Nod versus Reno or something."

Rick was wearing knee-length denim shorts and athletic socks and work boots and a short-sleeved rugby shirt and, underneath the shirt, the crispest, whitest undershirt you ever saw. He had compact, muscular arms, coated with black hair—Irish-black hair over pink skin. Straight black eyebrows and small vibrant gray eyes. A face that asserted itself in an easy, masculine way. He was nice-looking.

"What do you do, Patrick?"

"Oh, I work for the National Conservation Alliance."

"That's—"

"An environmental group."

"Like Greenpeace."

"Actually, not at all like Greenpeace. But like every environmental group except Greenpeace."

"Oh, OK."

"I'm surprised we don't all show up at each other's workplaces, we're so easy to confuse. Sometimes I have to look at the stationery to make sure I've gotten the right one."

"Tell me what do you do for them."

"Development," Patrick mumbled. "I shake people down."

"Well, that's cool. You're—fighting the good fight."

"Uh-huh."

For dessert, they ordered cannolis. They ate daintily, with knives and forks, as if they were apologizing for the way they'd been eating before. Now and then, Patrick would look up, and Rick would be looking down at his plate, chewing in slow motion, and then Patrick would feel embarrassed for some reason, and he would look down at *his* plate.

"I hope you're not disappointed," Rick said.

"What do you mean?"

"Well, you know. I'm not the guy you were looking for."

"No! Oh, no, it's fine. I mean, I'm not the guy *you* were looking for, right? So, hey…I'm glad we met. I like meeting people."

"Yeah."

"It's really good. Meeting people."

"I agree."

"I'm—" Patrick stopped, started again. "I should tell you I just broke up with my boyfriend."

"Yeah, I figured."

This caught him up short. He felt bare, suddenly. Easily and ruthlessly exposed. He wanted to be brittle, laugh the whole thing away—*Why, hello! You see right through me!*—but all he could do was mutter: "Really?"

"You just seem a little spooked, that's all."

"Spooked."

They didn't speak again for a few minutes. Patrick was starting to feel desperate. He was hoping that one of the waiters would come over and speak to him, about anything—gnocchi, Middle Eastern politics, Ramadan, anything—but the only waiter he could see was looking the other direction, erasing dinner specials from the blackboard.

"You ready to go?" Rick asked.

"Oh, yeah," he said eagerly. "Let's go."

They split the bill, nodded to the waiter, stepped gingerly down the steep stairs to the street below. A breath of coppery air met them as they opened the door. It was the middle of June.

"Is this your Oldsmobile?" Rick asked.

"Mm-hmm."

"How old is it?"

"Eight years."

"Still run well?"

"Oh, yeah."

Now and then, Patrick did feel the absurdity of having an '87 Oldsmobile, but tonight there was something remarkably comforting in it: the burgundy paint, the ratty trim, the graveyard of bugs on the grille, the whole unrelenting boxy *squareness* of it. It would protect him.

"Well, I'll give you a call," Rick said. "Would that be OK?"

"Oh, yeah, that'd be fine."

"I don't know," Rick said.

"What?"

"Whether to shake hands or—kissing is a little premature, I guess."

They compromised by hugging. Patrick drove home alone. He called Marianne almost as soon as he got through the door.

"I went on a date tonight," he said.

"Well, look at you," she answered. "Alex's body not even cold in the ground."

"Yeah, well."

"Did you like him? Tell me everything. Was he sexy?"

"Actually—I just realized I don't want to talk about it. I'm sorry."

"Oh, come on."

"Well, he was—he was very cute. I don't know. He was nice. He's not…"

"Yeah, I know."

"So I don't know."

"Well, listen, honey, at least this one's *real.*"

Patrick jerked his head back.

"Oh, now wait," he said. His voice was getting away from him. "You're—come on, you honestly think I *imagined* the guy in the library?"

"I'm not saying that. All I'm saying is, this one's breathing and he's here."

And there was something to be said for that. He thought back to the clinch, just 20 minutes ago, how he and Rick had moved toward each other, and his brain had kicked into a higher gear. *Why are you hugging?* it was asking. *Why are you hugging this man named Rick who is not Scottie? What business do you have hugging him?*

But Rick's back shifted and rolled through his rugby shirt. His hand found the small of Patrick's back, his hair was scratchy against Patrick's neck. The *feel* of a man—there was something to be said for it.

And then a surge of inexplicable loyalty went through Patrick. *What about Scottie?* Scottie would have felt like something, too. Many things. The scrape of his day-old beard. The calluses on his big fisherman's hands. The warm, mentholated vapor issuing from his nostrils. His breath: toothpaste or onions or grape Nehi or…

Hugging Scottie would have been real. With all that entailed.

9

That night he dreamed of Alex. In the dream Alex was standing only a few feet away, but it might as well have been a hundred feet because there was no getting to him. Every time Patrick made a move, an enormous structure reared up before him—a carapace, not impervious, exactly, but forbiddingly complex, circular. Patrick spent all his time simply negotiating it, and Alex remained where he was, clearly framed but no more reachable than Scottie. After what seemed like hours of labor, Patrick sat down to catch his breath, and Alex said, "You've been going about this all wrong," and Patrick said, "What do you mean?" and Alex said, "You need a guest pass."

Two days later, Rick phoned. Patrick didn't know who it was at first because he was whispering.

"Who's this?"

"It's Rick."

"Why are you whispering?"

"Oh, I'm still at work."

"Oh."

"I don't really have much of an office."

Of course! He worked in a law library. He lived among texts. Patrick could close his eyes and almost see it: Rick in his gray shirt and cloth tie, crouched between the stacks, his eyes darting about, the overextended phone cord snaking between the shelves.

"Well," Patrick said. "I mean—you're allowed to have personal calls, aren't you?"

"No. Yeah."

"Do you want to call me later?" Patrick asked.

"No, it's OK."

"'Cause you could always pretend I'm a girlfriend, right?"

"It wouldn't matter."

Patrick felt a tingle crawling up his spinal column. *It wouldn't matter!* What was so attractive about that statement? The fatalism of it. The suggestion of corporate oppression. Oh, there was a tingle, a definite tingle.

"All right," Patrick said. "Let me posit some statements, and you can answer true or false. This way you won't incriminate yourself. All right?"

"OK."

"You—you had a nice time at dinner."

"True."

"You're calling because you'd like to go out again."

"True."

"You have a particular day in mind."

"False."

"False."

"Well, it's—"

"OK, well—"

"No, it's—work is kind of rough this week."

"Me too."

"I'll call you next week," Rick said, lowering his voice.

"What?"

"I'll call you next week." Raising his voice now.

"OK."

"OK?"

"OK."

There was a pause on the other end: Rick was talking to somebody. Then suddenly he was back on the line, speaking in a low urgent murmur. "I just wanted to hear your voice," Rick said.

"Oh, that's—"

"I'll call you later." And then he was gone.

That night, seeking guidance, Patrick called Marianne. She had just returned from a Yanni concert.

"Yanni?" Patrick said. "This has gotta stop."

"Victor likes him. What can I say?"

"Yanni."

"I know, I know. Honey, we're working on it. I'm still teaching him how to dress, OK? It's a 12-step deal." She said seeing Yanni was a kind of rite of passage, except she wasn't sure what it was a passage *to*, unless it was a place where critical distinctions ceased to matter.

"Hold on," Patrick said. "Someone's at the door."

The bell rang three times before he got there. Patrick looked through the fish-eye lens and saw someone he had never seen before. For a second or two he hesitated. Then he opened the door to get a better look.

The man was about Patrick's age but at least four inches shorter—maybe 5 foot 6 or 5 foot 7—dark-complexioned, with heavy beard stubble, a well-combed head of black hair, heavy-rimmed glasses, and large blue eyes, startlingly pale, as though some layer of iris had been ripped away. He was small—slightly but economically built, well-distributed—and he was wearing a white Oxford shirt streaked with sweat.

"I'm Seth," he said. His voice had a soft faraway echo of the Bronx.

"Hello."

"Are you Patrick?"

"Yes."

"May need to talk."

"Can you give me a minute? I'm on the phone."

"Kind of important."

"OK, I'll call you later."

"Your boyfriend's living with my boyfriend."

"All right."

Patrick went back to the phone. "Marianne, can I call you right back?"

When he returned, Seth was still standing on the front stoop, looking like a particularly earnest canvasser, and Patrick had a momentary notion that if he subscribed to something, Seth would go away. He didn't show much sign of moving, though, even when Patrick motioned him into the living room. He obeyed only after giving it a few moments' consideration, and they sat catty-corner to each other, Patrick on the love seat and Seth in a decrepit mission-style rocker. Neither spoke for a time.

An animal, Patrick thought. *It would be useful at times like this to have an animal—"She's part Persian, part Abyssinian."*

He found himself staring at the gray blots on the love seat next to his right thigh and wondering if Alex would know how to get them out. Of course Alex would know. Some solution of tonic water or baking soda or crow's-foot oil.

"Do you want a drink?" Patrick remembered to ask.

"Something fizzy."

"Club soda?"

"Be fine."

Actually, it wasn't club soda, it was seltzer water, but Seth didn't notice. He didn't even drink it at first; he rested his drinking hand on the miniature Adirondack chair that sat on Patrick's coffee table.

Patrick sat with his hands clasped between his knees. "To eliminate suspense," he said, "I'm assuming that when you say 'my boyfriend,' you're referring to Alex?"

"Yes."

"And Alex is living with—"

"Ted."

"Who is *your* boyfriend."

"Ex. Yes."

"And they're now living together."

"Yeah, you didn't know. Figured. Sorry." Seth's teeth slid through his lips in a quick, apologetic motion. He moved his eyes around the room. *He's shy,* Patrick thought. *This is hard for him.*

"They moved in together just last week," Seth said.

"Last week?"

"Yes."

"Last week."

"Yes." Seth smiled again or grimaced or both.

"That's pretty quick."

"I know. I was surprised too. In a way."

"Wait a minute, your—boyfriend…"

"Ted."

"Moved out on you last week?"

"Oh, no, six months ago. Well, *I* moved out."

"I see."

"Except, not my idea."

"Mmm."

"Never is." He was drinking his seltzer now, holding the glass to his lips for several seconds at a time, rolling ice cubes around in his mouth.

"You moved out six months ago," Patrick said. "Alex moved in a *week* ago."

"Yeah."

"And you're telling me there's a connection."

"Well…"

"Am I right?"

"Depends on what you mean."

"I don't know what I mean."

"Well…"

"You should maybe tell me why you're here."

"Um…"

"I mean, instead of *calling* me, say, on the phone."

"Yeah. Don't know. Don't really know." Seth looked up suddenly. "Could we go somewhere? Just sit somewhere?"

"We're sitting now."

"Somewhere that's not your place."

After some discussion they settled on a nearby Mexican restaurant, and as they walked deliberately up Pennsylvania Avenue, Patrick asked himself what exotic subset of deportment could possibly apply to this situation. What was the most decorous way of comporting yourself with the ex of your ex's current boyfriend? It was about one permutation too many, and as he glanced to his right, he was wondering if Seth knew the correct form of address, the most appropriate topics. He was even on the verge of asking, but then he noticed the inch-long chevron of red flesh on the side of Seth's neck.

"Oh," said Patrick, politely. "You burned yourself."

"Yeah," Seth muttered. "I was ironing."

"You were—"

"I mean, I *wasn't* ironing. That was the problem. I was going out the door this morning. Realized I hadn't ironed my shirt. So

I, you know, *grabbed* the iron. Did it right there. On the spot."

"You—you ironed your shirt while it was still on?"

"Yeah." Seth frowned. "Thought it would save time. And it *would've*, quite honestly. If I hadn't had to treat the…" He gestured toward his neck.

They were silent the rest of the way.

Composure, Patrick thought. He had come to suspect that composure was the answer to nothing and everything at the same time. An unbreakable code. Lifting you clear.

The restaurant was abandoned when they got there, except for a young man and woman at a corner table: He was chewing on quesadillas, and she was crying. Patrick could make out only shreds of their conversation. "Dumb…help…Ted Koppel…"

"Do you want a drink or anything?" Patrick asked.

"Margarita. Rocks, no salt."

Their drinks came with lime-and-pink–striped straws. Seth hunched his shoulders over the table, sipped noisily through his straw. Patrick was struck by his eyelashes, which were in near-constant motion. Even when the eyes were open, the lashes were on the move, shivering in a kind of autonomic flirtatiousness. In the overhead light they actually seemed to be shimmering.

Patrick asked: "Do we know each other?"

"Um…no. I've seen you. Parties and stuff."

"Oh. I must have seen you too, then."

"Well…" Seth stopped sipping and made some indeterminate motion with his shoulders. "I've heard people talk about you," he said. "Someone once described you, I remember. 'Nice-looking,' they said. 'In a sneaky way.'"

"In a *sneaky* way?"

"Yeah."

"What does that mean?"

"Sneaks up on you, I guess."

"Oh."

"Boo."

"Yes."

"Think they meant it nicely. Can't remember who it was."

Until now, Patrick had attributed Seth's speech rhythms to alcohol—he figured Seth had been drinking earlier in the evening—but he was beginning to see this was the underlying architecture of Seth's speech, the rush of declarative sentences—hardly even sentences, really, the subjects pruned away, the predicates split asunder or just dropped, the direct objects hanging desolate. The pattern was hard to detect at first because the inflections were all over the place, rising when you least expected them to, dropping as suddenly: post-tonal speech never quite finding its center.

"What about Ted?" Patrick asked. "Is he nice-looking in a sneaky way?"

"In an arrogant way."

"Well, you must miss him. I mean, you obviously care about who he's living with."

"I do. Don't know why. 'Poor thing, sir, but mine own.'"

"Oh, that's—Shakespeare."

"Ted subscribed to the Shakespeare Theater. His firm gave him tickets."

"Oh, a lawyer."

"Yeah, I know."

"What?"

"I hate lawyers too."

"I don't hate them. I mean, not really."

"Everyone hates them. Like tax collectors in the Bible. Today, Jesus would have to take lawyers. As disciples. To prove his tolerance." Seth inclined his head a few inches. "Although, I'm Jewish," he said nonsequentially. "So what do I know?"

"Why did you and Ted break up?"

"I don't know. Because I put on weight? I don't know."

"You put on weight?"

"I'm sure you noticed. Just a little shelf. I can't hide it."

"That wouldn't matter, would it?"

"Not sure. It was a symbol, I think."

"Symbol of what?"

"Lack of control. I eat when I'm anxious. Can't help myself."

Again, the grin slipping through the tightly guarded aperture of his lips. There was something a little wet about him, about his eyes, his face—as though he'd been pulled from a womb. Patrick didn't know whether to stare or look away.

"It's funny," he said. "Alex actually *lost* weight when we started dating. We used to joke about it. He used to call me his little tapeworm."

Seth leaned forward. "Anxiety-related?"

"It must have been," Patrick said. The vision of Alex at the Inn at Little Washington, staring at his plate with an existential terror. "You know, I think about it sometimes, and I realize how— *selfish* I was, really. I was always focused on my own symptoms. I would actually measure my heart rate sometimes just to make sure I was *really* feeling anxious and not just faking it. But I never gave a thought to whether *he* was anxious."

"What did you think he was?"

"I don't know. Vaguely—chronically dissatisfied."

"People don't lose weight from that."

"No."

"Although who knows? Who knows why people lose weight? Maybe fat cells get depressed. Take their own life."

"Stupid," the woman at the corner table was saying. "Can't help it…"

Patrick was gazing at the lime-coated ice at the bottom of his glass. He saw his little straw lying unused on the place mat and wondered if he should put it back in the glass. There seemed to be no end of issues to consider. What should he do with the straw? Who should pay for the drinks?

"Excuse me," he said.

He had assumed he was going downstairs to visit the john, but in fact, the phone was there too, in a larger, even emptier room than the one upstairs. The walls were festooned with straw hats and streamers and maps of Oaxaca and photomurals of delighted Mexican people. Patrick winced as he passed them.

He got Alex's new number from the computerized message at his old number, and he dialed slowly, emphatically. As he dialed he felt a wave of blood wash up his throat, through his jaw and his cheeks, and he realized that the spirit of inquiry in which he had believed himself to be calling was now draining away with each ring of the phone.

"Hi!" An unfamiliar voice. A voice he had never heard before. "You've reached Ted and Alex.…" There was a slight pause, and then Patrick recoiled as two rapid dog barks filled the receiver. "And that's Virgil. We're not in now, so please leave a message, and we'll get back to you as soon as we can. Right, Virgil?" Two more dog barks, perfectly timed, then a long preparatory moment as the machine patiently skimmed through the existing messages, then a particularly ear-splitting beep at some unheard-of frequency, some frequency only Virgil could appreciate, and then silence. Patrick stood there a moment, his lips frozen in place.

A dog! Alex found a man with a dog!

Coming upstairs, he was conscious of the need to convince

people that he had in fact gone to the bathroom. *How can I convince everyone that I went to the bathroom?* But as he surveyed the room he realized that no one was looking at him—not Seth, not the waiters, and certainly not the young man and woman in the corner because they had their own distress to think about. She was blotting away tears with her napkin, and he was reaching across the table to clutch her free hand. "I don't care," he was saying. "We can talk about other things. We don't have to talk about GATT…"

Patrick pulled out his chair, sat down in a slow, controlled motion. He jiggled his margarita glass. He listened to the rattling of the ice.

Seth said: "You called them, didn't you?"

"Yeah."

"I would've too."

"Does Ted have a dog?"

"Does now. Got one the day after I left. Always after me to get a dog. I never would."

10

It was Seth who insisted on paying. "I'm a lobbyist," he said. "We do this." And as they walked back down Pennsylvania Avenue, Patrick asked himself what special interest Seth could possibly lobby for. He kept dropping back a little to get a better look, trying to imagine Seth as he would look to a Senate staffer, what sort of wardrobe he might be capable of. Strange icebreakers—they end up feeling sorry for him; he looks so needy. But there must have been something needy about Patrick too because he couldn't think of any better way to kill time on a June evening. The phone call to Alex seemed like many hours ago. Now he was enjoying the feeling of walking. The great glass dome of summer hadn't quite sealed everything in; the air still had currents.

"Almost summer," Seth said.

"Yes."

"Makes me sweat."

"Well, it—makes all of us sweat."

"No one sweats more than I do. Unfortunate."

And it was true. Seth's shirt had great circles of sweat spreading from each armpit. An involuntary look of fear must have crossed Patrick's face because Seth said, "No, it's OK. I always do this. Gets better around mid July."

"Huh."

They stopped in front of Patrick's house. Through the window of the English basement, he could see the silhouette of his tenant, Deanna, bowing her head over some reading.

"You know," Seth said, "it may not be what you think."

"What am I thinking?"

"That Alex—um—cheated, maybe."

"Oh."

"Don't think he did."

"Why?"

"Just knowing Ted, I guess. He doesn't like to share."

"Ah."

A taxi slowed to a halt next to them, and the driver looked at them expectantly. Seth made a dismissing motion with his hand, but the driver stayed there, and because he wouldn't leave, they were both uncomfortable again. Patrick jammed his hands into his pockets. "Would you like a drink or anything?" he asked.

"No. You're awfully polite."

"Well…"

"Hadn't counted on that."

"What did you count on?"

"Don't know, really." Seth was balancing on the sides of his feet, like a child. "Don't know."

"You were expecting a scene, maybe? You thought I'd—what? Scream at you, pull out a *gun*? Set myself on fire?"

"No, no, no," he said. "No, no, no." The cab finally pulled away, and Seth craned his head to follow it. "Still," he said, cocking his head and looking at Patrick from almost a coquettish angle.

"Still what?"

"No, it's personal," Seth said.

"That's OK."

"I was wondering. I mean, if your, um, feelings aren't hurt—why aren't they?"

The question seemed entirely abstract—at least Patrick answered it abstractly. "Maybe they are," he said.

"Of course."

Patrick plucked a stem of clover from between the sidewalk bricks. He shook himself a little, woke himself up, and then he looked back at the house, still struggling for an explanation, and then he began speaking about Scottie.

Afterward this would strike him as a bit miraculous. Although by then he had already told two people—Marianne, who, of course, had every right to know, and Rick, who for a time had *been* Scottie. So why shouldn't he know? No, the secret was already out, and yet who could explain why, looking into Seth's whiskered face, with its unnatural, laserlike eyes, its furtive grin, Patrick should suddenly think, *Oh, tell him, for God's sake. Why shouldn't he know? Why shouldn't everyone know?*

He must have talked for a good five or ten minutes, glancing at the ground, at the sky, at Deanna's illuminated head in the basement window—looking everywhere but at Seth. And even so, there were things he didn't say. He didn't confess, for instance, that he had placed the "Glances" ad *before* Alex had left. And there was a worse omission—much worse. He never really found a way to say how Scottie had become wedged in his consciousness.

What would have been adequate to that?

Understand me, he could have said. *I can attend to things, I can walk and talk, but I can't get rid of him, the* idea *of him. I can't confront him exactly. Or ignore him. He's just there. Apart from everything else. Always there.*

Maybe that would have been enough. Maybe at least if he'd

tried explaining it, Seth would not have said what he said, which was, "So this guy was really hot?"

"I don't know," Patrick said, shrugging impatiently. "He wasn't my type."

"Well, what does he look like?" Seth asked.

"Um—kind of blond, dirty-blond hair. Wavy. It might be curly, actually, if he let it grow longer. And the eyes were bluish-gray, very penetrating color. And a really strong chin and kind of a firm mouth, very masculine, attractive mouth. And he was tall, maybe 6 foot 1 or 6 foot 2. Um…broad shoulders, I think. He was wearing a Shetland sweater but—you know—he filled it out."

"Uh-huh."

"And—I don't know. I can see him, but I can't describe him very well. Oh, wait, I drew a picture of him."

"A picture?"

Shit.

"Do you have it?"

Stall him—stall, stall, stall.

"You know, God, it's funny. I can't remember where I put it," Patrick said, making an embarrassed grimace.

"Just wondering, 'cause—maybe I know him."

"Yeah, no one at the party seemed to. He just kind of disappeared. A friend of mine thinks I dreamed him."

"Did you?"

"It's possible, I guess, but no, he doesn't *fade*, really. The way a dream does. I don't think I'm imaginative enough to have dreamed him."

"Maybe we all dreamed him," Seth said. "Maybe I'll dream him tonight."

"Well…" Patrick laughed for the first time that evening. The margaritas were finally doing their trick. "Just so you know, he's *mine*."

11

When the phone rang later that night, Patrick was sitting half-conscious in bed with a book of poetry in his lap. The book was *The Palm at the Edge of the Mind*, which he had come to believe, mystically, was Scottie's favorite book. *We'll have so much to talk about*, Patrick thought, his eyes filming over. *We can talk about our favorite poems*—and then the phone jarred him awake.

"Pattie!"

He looked at the clock. It was 11:45. Eleven forty-five. In the evening.

"Pattie?"

"What's up, Da?"

"Me beamish boy."

"Where are you?"

"Just off the Garden State Parkway."

"Oh."

"My room's got a fabulous oil painting. A starfish, Pattie. On a rock. You want it for your living room?"

"No."

"You ready to see your lovin' pa?"

"Yeah, can you—can you be a little more specific on the time?"

"Well—I'm thinking *Tuesday* night now. Thinking I'll stop off in Wilmington first, go see your mother's cousin Barbara."

"Cousin Barbara?"

"Yeah, she just married some R&D man at DuPont. Fella's sure to know a lot of people in the industry—"

"Wait a minute, did she invite you?"

"How could she invite me if she doesn't know I'm going to be in town?"

"So you're just going to show up—"

"Well, I'll *call* first. I'm not a savage, Pattie. Now look for me sometime Tuesday night. I'll be driving a yellow Acura. And don't concern yourself entertaining me, either, I've got *work* to do. Quiet as a fuckin' nun, that's me. You and Alex won't even know I'm here."

"Oh, Da, I was going to tell you about Alex—"

"Sorry, Pattie, I'm out of change."

"He's up to something," Patrick said.

Marianne looked up from her Cobb salad. She was now eating salad exclusively because she didn't want her new boyfriend Victor to believe she wasn't a vegetarian. She hated salad. "Of course he's up to something," she said. "He always is."

"Beyond the usual something. I mean, for one thing, he said he was calling from a hotel, but then he had to get off the phone because he was out of change. Which would indicate he's sleeping in his car, which means he's dead broke. Again."

"Hell, at least he's got a car."

"Oh, please, it's never *his* car. God knows how he gets them. They always belong to a friend."

"Did he tell you his new idea?"

"No."

"That's too bad. I'm kinda lookin' forward to hearing it. I

mean, it's gotta be better'n that last piece of shit. What was it? The National Thanatology Center?"

It almost hurt to remember that one. Mr. Beaton had conceived the notion of a hot line—1 (900) R-U-ALIVE—specifically tasked with telling people whether their favorite celebrities were dead or not. As Mr. Beaton had explained it: "How many times do we sit around and talk about some old singer or politician or movie star and then someone says, 'Hey, are they still alive?' And no one fucking *knows*! 'Cause if you're not in the limelight anymore, you might just as well be dead. Like Shirley Booth, Pattie. I thought she'd been dead a good 20 years, and then only a couple of years ago I wake up and find she'd just kicked the day before. I had no idea she was alive! That's why people need this phone line, yes? So they can call from any place in the country any time of the day and have someone tell them, 'No, Shirley Booth just died.' Or 'Yes, Fay Wray is still alive.' And then they can really make the most of the time they have left with their particular celebrity. Or if the celebrity is dead, they can finally come to terms with it. They can grieve, for Christ's sake!"

You couldn't call the idea a failure, exactly, because it had never really left Mr. Beaton's head. Somehow, though, he had managed to acquire some modest funding for it, and somewhere he had invested it. No one was sure where. America was littered with the corpses of his holding companies.

"Maybe he just needs to find someone," Marianne said. She was staring down at a slice of cucumber that she'd inserted between her lips.

"Another wife?"

"Yeah, you know. A good woman."

"She'd need to be independently wealthy, wouldn't she?"

"Or a masochist."

In the course of his next violin lesson, Patrick asked his teacher Sonya if she knew of any good women.

"What do you mean by *good*?" she asked, pumping his bowing elbow up and down as though it were a jack.

"Kind. Indulgent. Wealthy."

"Listen, if I knew anyone wealthy, I'd get 'em to pay for one of those really expensive fertility treatments. Except, who knows? All the egg swapping they do these days, I'd end up with kids in every corner of the world. They'd all sue me for back support."

It was not clear what should be done to a house in preparation for Mr. Beaton's arrival. Patrick wondered if he should do all the things that his father would ask about. Like cleaning the gutters. Except he realized after borrowing a neighbor's ladder and easing himself onto the eaves that he hated climbing back down ladders. So, to borrow time he sat there at the edge of the roof for about 15 minutes, pretending an interest in the street below. After a few minutes he wasn't pretending. A man in a wheelchair scooted by, waving as he went. Down the block, a woman reputed to be insane was dutifully tending her tree box—the same place she spent most of her days and nights, kneeling in a permanent attitude of prayer, shaking her watering can like a censer, naming every root, twig, every atom of soil.

Patrick wondered if she would mind calling the fire department to come get him down.

Then the phone rang, and this was the only impetus he needed. He shinned down the ladder in about 15 seconds and ran to the front door, but it was locked. He ran to the back gate, and that was locked too. So with an alacrity that surprised him, he scaled the fence and found the back door unlocked, and all this time the phone was still ringing, endlessly as in a dream, and it never occurred to him that it couldn't be *his* phone (which would have deferred to the machine after the fourth ring) until he burst through the back door and found it staring back at him from the kitchen counter, mute and undisturbed, and the ringing still echoing, somewhere off in the distance. He stood there, panting, disbelieving.

And then the phone really did ring.

"Hello?"

"Hi, it's Scottie."

The air stopped about halfway up his throat, and the moisture blew from his eyes. The phone connection began to crackle.

"Patrick?" the voice said. "It's me. Rick."

"You—why did you do that?"

"What?"

"Call yourself that."

"I don't know. 'Cause—you thought I was him?"

"Oh, yeah, I just…"

"What?"

"I don't remember telling you his name."

"Well, you didn't, really."

"Oh."

"You whispered it. To yourself, kind of. When we were—when we were hugging the other night."

"I whispered it?"

"Yeah, I just figured Scottie was the guy from the ad."

"God, I'm—" He covered his eyes. "That's embarrassing. I'm sorry."

"No, no, it's cool. I mean, it's not like—you know—I think it's only bad when you do it during sex or something."

"Oh, God, I promise I won't—" And then he stopped himself. And they both laughed. And Patrick said: "I think that was a premature ejaculation."

"Oh, well."

"I won't do that either."

"We could just have dinner instead."

"Dinner?"

"Or *supper*. Do you call it supper?"

"No, I call it dinner."

"Then that's what it'll be."

12

Should he have told Rick he was busy? *Do people still pretend they're busy?* he wondered. *At my age?*

He needed some remedial program, clearly, some interactive multimedia tutorial for reentering the family of man. What, for instance, was he to make of the fact that his second date with Rick took place, like the first one, in a bad Italian restaurant? What did that signify? And what was the meaning of the woman who greeted them at the door in an unruly henna wig, a floral blouse, and a wraparound skirt? Why did she hate them?

"I suppose you'll want to sit in the garden area," she said.

"No," Rick said.

"'Cause we don't have any tables there. There's no room for you there." She grimaced and pulled away.

"I've never been able to sit in the garden area," Rick said.

As they ate, Patrick's eyes were drawn to a blind woman in a mouse-gray smock who was sitting motionless in front of a piano, her hands poised over the keys. As he watched, she stood up and began feeling her way along a long stucco wall—followed by an old man with an accordion. They were probably heading for the garden area.

"How come you call him Scottie?" Rick asked. "Is that his name?"

"No, it's just—he was wearing a Shetland sweater."

Rick's eyes didn't lose a shade of their brightness.

"From the Shetland Islands. Which are—which are Scottish."

"Oh, well, that's cool. I suck at geography."

"I do too," Patrick said. "I guess there's not much demand for atlases in a law library."

"Oh, hey, I forgot to tell you! I saw that guy again. The one I thought was you. I mean, the one whose ad I thought it was."

"The guy in the library?"

"Yeah, he came by again. We actually talked this time. It's funny; I was kind of embarrassed. I wanted to say, 'Hey! Guess what I just put myself through for your sake?'" He stopped chewing for a moment. "That didn't come out right."

"No, I'm an ordeal."

"No, no, you're great. Anyway, I like you better than him, anyway."

"Well, maybe if you asked him out or something, you'd—maybe you'd have things in common."

"Oh, God!" A great snort came from deep in Rick's belly. "What are you thinking? I'm too busy to date anybody else."

When the phone rang later that night, Patrick really was asleep. Later, he couldn't remember if he'd said hello.

"It's Seth. Are you home?"

"Of course I'm home."

"I mean, would you be home if I came by in—half an hour?"

"I'll be asleep."

"Oh! What time is it?"

"It's ten after 11."

"Oh."

"What's it about, Seth?"

"Can't talk about it over the phone. See you at 11:30."

He actually got there closer to midnight, and Patrick didn't feel tired at all. He'd even managed to put on a bathrobe and slippers and to set out a plate of Pepperidge Farm cookies and a pot of Lemon Zinger tea, and he put Seth on the love seat and put himself in the rocker, and it felt for a moment like Seth was a gentleman caller or a cousin just home from college and someone was in the next room waiting to take all the dishes away.

Seth looked more alive than usual. He wasn't sweating, for one thing, and everything about him seemed crisper, including his shirt. He looked like someone who could have once lived with someone named Ted.

Patrick made some polite conversation about the heat, about the cookies, about property tax assessments, and Seth sat there with his hands squeezed between his thighs, now and again resting them on his knees as though he were about to stand up. He seemed to be waiting for an inaudible cue. Patrick went back to the kitchen, boiled some more water, made some more tea, brought out more cookies—and whenever he looked at Seth, Seth was looking back at him. So Patrick kept chattering, which was odd, because he had never been a chatterer. Tonight, it came quite naturally.

"My mother's been having an awful time with gypsy moths," he was saying.

"I want to help you," Seth said. It came out strangely, though, with the word *help* dropping almost out of hearing range.

"Help me what?"

"That's what I want to talk to you. About."

"Why do you want to help me?" Patrick asked.

"Never mind."

"Never mind what?"

"It won't make sense to you."

"Tell me."

"I'm just—I'm an altruist."

"Um…" Patrick set his tea cup down. He cradled a tablet of shortbread in the joint of his index finger. "Seth, no offense, but I'm not sure I should—given that we don't really know each other very well, and I can't possibly guess what your motives are—and maybe more important, I'm not sure what it is I need help with."

"Well, you haven't found him yet. Have you?"

"Haven't found…?"

"Scottie!" Seth's eyes rolled in exasperation.

"That's—" Patrick stopped himself. He had been about to say "That's true," except that underneath it was something he'd never resolved. It was something quite crucial.

Did he *want* to find Scottie?

Was that what he genuinely, verifiably *wanted*? Was he doing anything that would make that happen?

"Find Scottie," Patrick repeated, softly, and even saying it didn't make it any clearer.

Seth's teeth began sliding around behind his lips. "Two heads better than one," he said.

"But this is—this is very odd."

"How so?" Seth cocked his head to one side.

"Because! Because I hardly know you. You hardly know *me*. You don't know Scottie at all."

"Yes?"

"So—please tell me *why*. Why should you want to find someone you've never met?"

"Well, I have thoughts. On the subject. I do." Seth's eyes were half shut, as though he were getting ready to recite a poem. "After talking with you. And getting to know Alex."

"You know Alex?"

"Oh, of course. Of course. Getting to know Alex." Seth's eyes were completely closed now. "Giving the whole matter a lot of thought. Because I don't have a life. What else is there to do but—think about other people's lives? Giving the whole matter a lot of thought. I have to tell you. It was a mistake, Patrick."

"What?"

"The breakup!" Seth's eyes opened now, surged from their sockets. "A *large* mistake. You're meant to be together."

"Me and Alex?"

"Oh, you resist, I know. Perfectly understandable. Wounded feelings, sense of betrayal, wuh-*wa* wuh-*wa*. But you know— you're *going* to figure it out."

"Figure out…?"

"How much you want Alex back. Sooner or later, you'll figure it out. And with my help? It'll be sooner."

"Wow." Patrick had to laugh; he couldn't help it. The more he thought about it, the funnier it got. "You're kind of confident, aren't you, Seth?"

"Oh, nothing to do with *me*. It's *you*. Alex too. Alex wants the same. It's just—you're both too pigheaded. To let it happen."

"Well…" Patrick let his head drop back. It was past midnight now, wasn't it? This was the time of night when other people were sleeping. "You know, since—since Alex is hanging his hat somewhere else, I think the chances of a reconciliation—"

"You don't see. It's the old song. It all depends on you."

"How?"

Seth's lips seemed to disappear inside his mouth. For a moment, he looked almost toothless. "From talking to you," he said. "Talking to him. It's very clear. Alex didn't leave because of *Ted*. You don't understand. No one leaves because of *Ted*. It was because of you."

"So?"

"So he'll come back. If you're ready to be with him. Which you will be."

"When?"

"When you find Scottie. And you realize he's—not Scottie. Just a man in a Shetland sweater."

Patrick started to speak, then stopped himself. He was too mystified. He could feel the creases etching into his forehead, feel his entire face crumpling with the effort to understand.

"So your whole purpose in helping me find Scottie," he said, "is to *disillusion* me?"

"Oh, yes. We're going to kill him off."

"And then—OK, we kill off Scottie, and then—what? I go back to Alex?"

"Yes."

"Get down on my knees."

"Yes."

"*Plead* for him to come back."

"Yes."

"We'll assume he comes back."

"Yes."

"This is absurd."

"Of course."

"And then what?"

"And!" said Seth with breathtaking vehemence.

"What?"

"And!"

Patrick sat back in the rocker and let out a short breath. "Ted," he said wearily, "comes slithering back to you."

"Maybe." Seth's head began to bob a little. "I'll need to lose the weight."

A stillness fell over them. Patrick nibbled around the edge of his shortbread, and even that was too much noise. *If only I had an animal,* he thought. *To help me at times like this. Or a grandfather clock, ticking away, some kind of pulse or backbeat.*

"Listen, Seth," he said finally. "I have to be honest. I find your logic twisted."

"Course it is."

"I mean, do you honestly think we're just a bunch of dominoes, and you give one of us a little nudge, and the rest of us all come toppling down in this nice pattern?"

"No, computer analogy's better. I program you all. Let x = y. From there it's all binary logic. Which is what it's all about, yes? Who to be binary with?"

Patrick stuck out his legs, contemplated his slippered feet. Softly, almost to himself, he said: "Ted is worth all this labor?"

"Oh, it's not just Ted. It's the intellectual challenge, yes? The *cerebration.* An abstract principle becomes concrete."

"Scottie being the abstract principle."

Seth nodded. "Fascinating problem. Right out of a metaphysics textbook."

"You don't think he exists either?"

"On some plane." He spread his hands into a tablet. "Probably a better one."

13

Seth left a little before 1 o'clock, looking no sleepier than when he arrived. Patrick wasn't sleepy either; he lay in bed for another hour, half-clothed. He was waiting for a sign. He was waiting for something that would tell him unequivocally whether to accept Seth's proposal.

But how do you make a sign come to you? he thought. *And how do you recognize it when it comes?*

And in the absence of a sign, how would he know what Scottie wanted him to do? He tried to imagine Scottie as he would look now, in the thick of summer, in the miasmal heat. The kind of clothes he would be wearing: Bermuda shorts, maybe, or freshly pressed linen trousers, baggy, flowered bathing trunks. What would his bare forearms look like? Or his calves—how would his calves swell and taper down to the ankles? Or his hamstrings, those mesmerizing areas behind the knee. What did his hamstrings look like?

It was almost too much. Patrick found himself wanting to unravel the Shetland sweater, all those layers, all the early-spring wrapping, but it wouldn't quite come off.

And then he fell asleep.

Seth called him at work the next morning.

"How did you get my number?" Patrick asked.

"Good detective," he said. "See? I'm good."

"Yes, you're good."

"Are you still thinking about it?" he asked.

"Um...yeah."

"Trail's getting colder, you know. *Brr, brr.* Every day a little colder."

"Well, I'm kind of busy right now. My father's coming in to-morrow night."

"Oh, too bad."

"No, it's just for a visit; it's fine."

"I mean it's hard. Attending to your love life. With a parent around."

"I suppose."

"Last time my dad was in town? He offered to get me a pros-titute. Female. So I'd know what a woman was like."

"What was she like?"

"Don't know. Didn't take him up on it. I regret it sometimes."

Mr. Beaton arrived around 9:30 Tuesday evening in a yellow Acura that was still wheezing five seconds after he turned off the ignition. He was wearing soccer cleats and a royal-green jogging suit with peeling white stripes that ran the length of each leg, and he was carrying exactly two pieces of luggage: a crinkle-nylon gym bag, overstuffed, and a gray hanging case with a mysterious foot-long gash.

"Me beamish boy," he said, hugging Patrick with his free arm.

"I thought you were going to be here two hours ago."

"Ha!" He gestured to the car. "The baby got a little tempera-mental on me, Pattie. Turned a little skittish on the Baltimore-Washington Parkway—I had to talk her through, but we made it, praise God! And who would this be?"

Patrick turned around to find Deanna leaning against the wrought-iron railing that led down to her apartment. Her arms were folded, and she was wearing a cream blouse and a pleated skirt. For the first time in Patrick's memory, she was wearing lipstick.

"Oh! Deanna, this is—my father. George Beaton."

"How are you, Mr. Beaton?" she said.

"Floating with the angels," said Mr. Beaton, "now that I've clapped eyes on you."

"Your brogue sounds a little Scottish," Deanna said.

This was unusual. Mr. Beaton's brogue usually convinced people on first hearing; it was only after he got to know someone that he dropped it, and even then people persisted in believing he was Irish.

He inclined his head a few notches and said in a tone of great magnanimity, "I was born somewhere in the Irish Sea."

"Well, I'm glad you're keeping Patrick company," Deanna said. "I worry about him sometimes."

A little spark of irritation went off in Patrick's head. He hated being talked of in third person. He listened to his father expounding on the trip from Massachusetts, embroidering in the epic style, and he was surprised to hear Deanna responding at a different level—naturalistically, querying him about the traffic density on the Delaware leg, the construction on the inner Beltway stretch—and the only way Patrick could express his annoyance with both of them was by refusing to look at them. He occupied himself outlining the contours of Mr. Beaton's luggage with his foot.

"Well, I suspect you'll want to relax now," Deanna said. "It was very nice meeting you."

"Are you named after Deanna Durbin, by any chance?"

"No," she said simply, and that was the end of it somehow. Deanna nodded to them both and began strolling down the street—who knew where? Her arms moved like little pistons, and her skirt had gathered behind her knee; it seemed to be climbing up her leg.

Patrick turned to ask his father something, but he wasn't there. He wasn't in the car either, and then Patrick noticed the front door still open. He poked his head through the doorway and found his father collapsed on the love seat; one of his legs was hanging off the couch's arm.

"Jesus, what a trip," Mr. Beaton said.

"Oh, I'm sure."

"Pattie, do try to remind me, tomorrow I've got to take the car back. Is there a—Budget whatchama anywhere?"

"Rent-a-Car? I think Union Station, maybe. Hey, have you eaten?"

"Oh, no." He shook his head. "I'm on a new diet, Pattie. Nothing but—uh—bananas and cabbage and fruit shakes."

"A diet?"

"Purging all my toxins, son, all the shit that's been building up inside me—year after year. Year after year, son, so you get to the point, it's either the poison or you, right? Something's got to go."

"But you're so thin."

He was, in fact, even thinner than when Patrick had last seen him, and that had been more than a year ago, during Mr. Beaton's impromptu motor tour of the Eastern Seaboard. The trip was to celebrate Mr. Beaton's emergence from Chapter 7. Anxious to break in his new MasterCard, he had taken Patrick and Alex to dinner at Red Sage, and holding his margarita like a lantern, he offered up a prayer for debtors and scofflaws and took an enormous quaff of his drink, more than his mouth could contain. Little creeks of tequila spilled off his chin.

Now, lying on Patrick's love seat, he seemed hard-pressed even to open his mouth, and the rest of his body had shuddered to a stop. "It's not just food either," Mr. Beaton was murmuring. "I hardly drink a thing now. Except cognac, and that's only when the bowels need coaxing."

No one would have guessed from looking at them that they were related. Patrick was taller by three inches and had his mother's dark Spanish coloring. Mr. Beaton looked exactly like the Irishman he pretended to be. Sparkly red hair that never seemed to grow very long, pale eyes, and fair, hairless skin haunted by the ghosts of freckles. It was a testament to the force of his personality that he still looked so young, perhaps ten years younger than he was.

"Is Alex coming over later?"

"Oh, right." Patrick began refolding the scarves in the downstairs closet. "Da, I didn't get a chance to tell you. Alex and I kind of broke up."

"Fuck's sake."

"Yeah, it's OK; it really is. You know, it's just—it wasn't working."

"Fuckin' hell."

"It's fine, though. It's better, really."

"Well—who knows why?" Mr. Beaton began massaging his scalp, and everything on his face began to vibrate in response. "Your mother and me, for example. Who knows why? We were young."

Patrick made a mental note to call his mother the next morning. She had remarried 17 years ago, but she still liked to be apprised of Mr. Beaton's whereabouts.

"Hope I can see some of your friends, Pattie, while I'm here."

"Sure."

"How's that Marianne? How's my little sweetie?"

"Oh, fine."

"Still plump as a Christmas goose?"

"Well—actually, she's going vegetarian now 'cause—'cause this guy she's dating seems to think she's a vegetarian. Even though she hates vegetables."

"No!" Mr. Beaton almost howled his outrage. His eyelids wobbled down over his eyes. "She must eat fruit, Pattie. *Fruit.* That's how you slough out the bowels."

He had hoisted both his legs now onto the couch. One of the cushions was jammed behind his shoulder blades, the other was supporting his left elbow. His head had dropped against the antimacassar.

"Da, I have the guest room all made up if you want to lie down."

"No, I'm fine. I just need a minute."

Patrick didn't feel able to sit down himself. He leaned against the dining-room table and watched his father's eyes droop shut, watched the hands start their preslumber twitching.

"Don't forget," Patrick said, "you're supposed to tell me your new idea."

"Abso…" His father gulped. His head rocked a little on the arm of the couch. "Absolutely. I will, I will…"

Patrick had cooked frankfurter stew. It was still simmering on the range. He ladled out a bowl for himself and went back to the dining room and ate in silence, watching Mr. Beaton subside into the cushions. Soon his father's breath began resonating like an ocean, and before long it had acquired a hitch, and the hitch at last turned into a snore, a honeyed, sonorous sound.

Patrick had always envied how quickly his father went to sleep. It always left him feeling a little subservient. He could imagine himself spending the rest of his life in just this fashion: not quite sitting, not quite standing, just sketching an anxious periphery around the man on the couch. Afraid to make a noise because it would break the spell. The only sounds—a rhythmical snoring, the gradual winding down of Mr. Beaton's watch, a slow desiccation.

He could spend the rest of his life just like this, and what a comfortable life it would be in many respects. No more worrying about strange men following him into libraries. No more emotional maelstroms, stillborn relationships. He would be an entirely functional object, like a Gore-Tex winter coat, and when his function was finished, he could just wind down—like Mr. Beaton's watch—like Mr. Beaton.

Patrick flinched. His heart squeezed into a tiny ball.

"Huh," said his father. "Huh-huh…"

Patrick ran up the stairs, taking every other step. He paused once on the landing, then sprinted into his bedroom, made straight for the phone at his bedside. He snatched it up, fumbled for the piece of memo-pad paper he had squirreled away in his pocket, read the phone number once, then twice, and dialed with an agitated care, reviewing each numeral as he went.

"Hi," he said without bothering to say who he was.

Seth answered just as quickly. "Hi."

"Listen, I've thought about it, and I would—I would be most grateful for your help. Finding Scottie."

"Happy day," Seth said.

"And I think we should start right away, like you said. I don't think we have a moment to lose."

PART TWO

14

"He's *goyim*, I suppose," Seth said.

They were sitting at the wedge end of Starbuck's, staring out onto Dupont Circle. Seth was cupping a skinny decaf latte in his hands, and the heat from it had raised sweat along his sideburns.

"I don't know," Patrick said. "He might be."

"You don't go for ethnic?"

"No, I—I do. Sure."

"I only date *goys*. If Arthur Miller were gay, he'd be me. Looking for the Shiksa God."

"Well, no, I've dated at least two Jewish men—that I know of." He felt unaccountably silly.

"I've done a cop," Seth said suddenly.

"You mean—"

"A policeman."

"No, I meant—"

"Had sex."

"Yes."

"Actually, he was National *Park* Police. From Queens. Met him through a personal ad."

"Is it—dangerous working for the park police?"

"We never talked about work. We only had two dates."

"Oh."

"Only bring it up 'cause he could be helpful, yes? Looking for our missing person."

Patrick stared down at his cup. He was drinking tea, which he rarely did during the day. He always felt he was offending people when he asked for tea. "Except Scottie's not really missing," he said. "He's only missing to me."

"Sure." Seth yawned, stretched an elbow behind his head. He wiped his glasses against his shirt sleeve. "Wish we had a picture of him," he said.

"Well…actually, I do."

"Oh, yes. Of course. The drawing."

"Now, remember, it's not very good."

Patrick pulled the piece of paper from his shirt pocket. It had been folded over and over again; it was so wrinkled, it looked almost checkered.

Seth pursed his lips, pushed his chin toward the paper.

"Did it go through the dryer?" Seth asked.

"It got mangled."

"*You* drew it?"

"Yeah, the mouth isn't right. And the hair is kind of off."

"It's not bad," Seth said. "Wait." He flipped the paper over, smoothed it a couple of times with his fist. "Got a pencil?"

"Pen."

"Give, please. Tell me where you went wrong."

"Well, it's like I was saying, the hair isn't quite that curly. It's more wavy."

Seth began scribbling on the back of the drawing, using his free hand to block Patrick's view. "Wavy," he murmured.

"It's dirty blond too, which I couldn't figure out how to do. And the mouth isn't really that full. I can't really describe the mouth. I want to say humorous."

"Humorous," Seth echoed dully.

"And I couldn't get the eyes at all."

"What color were they?"

"Gray, I think, but very lit up. Not large. Ovalish but not al-mondish. If that makes any—"

"What about the nose?"

"Well, not aquiline, but—kind of classical-looking. Very straight and, I don't know, unremarkable, really. A nice nose."

"*Goyim* nose," Seth muttered. "Shape of the face? That about right?"

"Yeah. A little more chin, like Dudley Do-Right. And the eyes—were maybe closer together."

"Huh." Seth sketched a little longer, then scratched out, then started over again. After about two minutes he set down the pen and pushed the paper back to Patrick. "What do you think?"

It was only then, for some reason, that Patrick remembered: Scottie had returned to his dreams last night. How could he have forgotten that? Maybe because the dream was so prosaic. All Patrick could remember was sitting in a very high-backed wooden chair, almost like a pew, and Scottie coming from be-hind and bending over and kissing him on the top of his head—very casually, ritualistically, as though they kissed like this every day without thinking about it. *How was traffic? Did you pick up the milk?*

And Patrick woke up thinking that this was where all his other dreams had been tending. That this was their final ex-pression, definitive and eternal.

"Well?" Seth said. He was sitting back on his stool, his hands frozen in a claw shape.

"It's very good," Patrick said absently. "You're very good."

"I wanted to be a police artist once."

"Oh, and now you're a—"

"Lobbyist, right."

Patrick looked down at the picture again. The sun coming through the window seemed to make Scottie's complexion chalky even as it burned away the wrinkles in the paper. "I don't think we'll ever get the nose right," he said.

"What about a profile?"

"I don't think I saw him in profile. I never saw him anything but head-on."

"But it's close?"

"It's very close."

"Well, then."

Seth stood abruptly. For the first time, Patrick noticed that he was wearing long pants. Long twill pants in early July. He looked even hotter than usual: The glass enclosure had the same effect on him that magnifying glasses have on insects. The sweat had turned gluey on his skin, and the black stubble on his jaw looked like a splash of makeup.

"How should we start?" Patrick asked.

"Give me a couple of days. No, a couple of weeks. I want to take the picture around."

"Take it around?"

"Yeah, a few bars. Maybe a couple of gyms. Show it to some people I know." Patrick must have frowned because he said, "Don't worry. I won't mention your name."

"I don't care."

"No, no, no. Don't want people to know you're on the make."

They dumped their cups in the trash and stood deferentially for a moment, waiting to see who would leave first. Patrick led the way. As soon as he stepped outside, a column of hot air rose through his feet. He staggered a little.

"Excuse me," Seth said meekly. "You're—blocking…"

"Oh!" Patrick leaped to one side. Seth got only a foot farther before he too had to stop and gather his breath. They stood there on the pavement of Connecticut Avenue in a mild trance while nearly naked men walked past them.

"There's one thing," Patrick said.

"What?"

"He may not be gay."

"Huh." Seth's head bobbed thoughtfully. "Well, he *was* at the party."

"Yeah."

"Was it the kind of party straight men would go to?"

"Not really. I mean, it wasn't the kind of party *I* would go to."

"Unless he was a realtor. They go anywhere."

"He was too relaxed to be a realtor. He has some secret, I think. Some secret way of living. He knows how to do it."

"Very good," Seth said. "We'll debrief him. When we find him."

At moments like this—with the heat soaking through them, with the whole world baring its skin—the absurdity of their arrangement came home to Patrick with the force of a brick. What was he thinking? What richness of embarrassment was awaiting them: Patrick and his sweaty gumshoe? They walked across Dupont Circle, squinting up at the sun, making a deliberate beeline around a knot of bicycle messengers, and when they reached the other side, they stopped suddenly, as if they didn't know where to go from there.

"Well," Seth said finally, giving a spastic jerk of his head. "I go this way."

"OK."

"Very exciting. Can't wait."

"You'll…" Patrick felt quite helpless for a second, as though he should be dabbing his eyes with a handkerchief. "You'll call me if you find anything?"

"You'll know as soon as I do. Sooner."

"Hello?"

"Hi, Patrick, it's Rick."

"Oh, hi."

"Ha. This time you're the one who's whispering."

"Oh, it's—my father's sleeping on the couch."

"It's 6:30."

"Yeah, he just kind of falls asleep sometimes."

"I wish I could do that. Just nod off whenever I wanted to."

"No, you don't."

15

"I forgot," Seth said.

Patrick was holding the phone receiver in one hand and clutching his pillowcase with the other. When was the last time someone had called him this early in the morning?

"Forgot what?" he asked.

"To ask about his voice. What does Scottie sound like?"

"Um...I don't know—very...um..."

"Are you all right?"

"No, I'm *tired*, that's all. It's..." What time was it? Six o'clock? Five thirty? "He was..."

"Gruff."

"No. No, he was—it was *pleasant*. A pleasant, you know—voice. Not—you know, not effeminate or anything." Even half-conscious he could hear Alex's silent reproach. "Regular—*schmo* voice."

"He sounds a little bland," Seth said.

Patrick blinked. His cheek reddened as though it had been slapped.

Bland?

He sat up in bed, his mouth forming soundless words. What could he possibly say to that? *You're crazy!* That's all he could think to say. *You're crazy if you think Scottie's bland!*

Scottie wasn't bland. To even suggest that he was—was a function of Seth's cultural constructs or—or a function of Scottie's being refracted through *Patrick*. Or *maybe*—Patrick hoisted himself up still higher, leaned back against the headboard—maybe there was a case to be made for *transcendental* blandness, which was to say that Scottie's blandness was not blandness at all but was a hologrammatic patina of blandness *underneath* which—underneath which lay serenity, self-knowledge, fathomless stillness…

"You know," Seth said, "there's something very sexy. About Shetland sweaters, yes? The way they hug the collarbone."

"Yes," Patrick said, feeling mollified all of a sudden. "He has a very nice collarbone."

That afternoon Seth called him at work.

"One other outcome," he said, "we haven't considered."

"What?"

"He may be taken."

It was perhaps the most sensible objection that Seth had raised so far—and it was the one that concerned Patrick the least. Why was that? Because the possibility of actually *finding* him was so remote that every other obstacle shrank in proportion? It seemed to Patrick that if they could find Scottie—or, more accurately, *prove* him—then the existence of a nominal third party would cease to matter. Because if someone who might not exist turned out to exist, then couldn't someone who might exist turn out *not* to exist? Just as easily?

"You're right," Patrick said. "He may be taken."

That night at around 8:30 a policeman pounded on Patrick's back door to tell him someone had broken into his car.

"No," Patrick said.

"You own an Oldsmobile Cutlass Ciera?"

He was about to tell them it was a clerical error. His car had been broken into only two months ago. But the policeman was already leading him out back, through the unlocked gate, and Patrick was following, still in his work clothes. He stopped just outside the back gate and stared at his car.

It was almost a replay of the last scene: the steering wheel ripped open, the screwdriver sticking out of it like a hypodermic. The only thing different was the point of entry: This time it was the right rear window that had been shattered.

"One of your neighbors heard the brick going through the glass. Unfortunately, we were not in time to apprehend anyone."

"Were they the same guys?" he heard himself asking.

"Same?"

"As broke in the last time?"

"Well, maybe," the policeman said. He was a big, bluff fellow with a blond walrus mustache. "Maybe."

"Was it the same neighbor?"

"As...?"

"As last time."

"It could conceivably be," the policeman said.

"Jesus, Pattie!" Mr. Beaton had come up silently behind them. He was standing there in his jogging suit, rubbing his eyes. "They fucked you all over again."

"You may want to think about getting a Club, sir," said the policeman.

"You didn't get a Club, Pattie?"

"No."

"After that last time?"

"I meant to get one."

"Oh, Pattie, I never go anywhere without a Club. I mean, depending on the car."

Maybe the whole world was now lining up to persecute him, was that it? For the crime of not getting a Club. He closed his eyes, opened them again: Nobody had gone away.

"Well," his father said, "thank God they didn't take your tires. They did that to me once."

Patrick turned and walked deliberately back into the house. He fetched a broom and a dustpan from the kitchen closet, and when he returned, his father and the policeman were chatting like summer-camp buddies. Patrick began sweeping the shards of broken glass into the dustpan. He had a momentary sensation that Alex was standing right behind him with an open trash bag, advising him on how to keep the glass from tearing the plastic.

That night he lay in bed wondering what Alex would have said. He would have had something to say about the Club. *I should have reminded you…I can't believe we forgot to get a Club…* His jaw would have been tense from the effort of sharing the blame. Patrick would have been touched.

He closed his eyes and saw Alex's naked belly stretched out on the bed, the almost invisible trail of brown hair leading down from the navel. He remembered how sometimes when they had sex, Alex would arch his back and drop his head so far back that it seemed to disappear.

The next day, Patrick had the car towed to the same service station, where the mechanic estimated the repairs would take two days, perhaps seven, depending on when the claims adjustor arrived.

Walking down Pennsylvania Avenue, Patrick saw two men who were unaccountably grinning at him. He stopped and began inspecting himself, wondering if he'd misbuttoned his shirt. They stopped too.

"Patrick?"

"Yes."

"How have you been?"

"Fine."

"We haven't seen you since—when was it—Sequoia?"

Sequoia.

With Alex. The brunch. The brunch *before* the brunch with Scottie...*of course!* The names came to him in a reflux movement: *Gary and Robert.*

He still had no idea which was which.

"You're looking well," said Gary/Robert.

"Thanks."

"How's your house? Is it still leaking?"

"No—actually, it was never leaking."

"We're having the same problem with our dormer window. The flashing."

"Oh."

"It's been so long," said Robert/Gary. "I don't think we even *told* you about our flashing. It's been a couple of months, hasn't it?"

A blue convertible flew past them; the belt of the driver's raincoat was stuck in the door. "Actually, this is very ironic," Patrick said. "The last time I saw you someone had just broken into my car. And last night it happened again."

"Oh, my God."

"Maybe the same people, who knows?"

"The Oldsmobiles," said Robert/Gary. "Always the Oldsmobiles."

"Did you have a Club?" Gary/Robert asked.

"They sawed right through it," Patrick said.

That night the mechanic working on his car called. "Sir, you have a definite problem with your engine strut."

"That's what I was told the last time."

"Well, sir, whoever handled it last time did not take care of the problem."

"You guys handled it."

There was silence now, except for a squawking sound from deep in the garage, the protestation of a muffler. "Let's look at that baby one more time," the mechanic said.

"You poor motherfucker," said Marianne.

"It's my fault," he said. "I should have gotten a Club."

"Screw the Club—get a gun or something."

"Hey, do you want to go out for dinner tonight? I need to get away from my dad for a bit."

"Oh, honey, I'd love to, but Victor and me got tickets to some dance thing."

"Some dance thing?"

"Yeah, I think it's Senegalese or Cameroonian or something. One of his colleagues gave 'em away, and what can I say? Someone gives me a free ticket, I'll do anything."

"All right. Let me go; I've got a call on the other line."

It was Seth. He was breathing hard.

"I feel like Inspector Javert," he said.

"What's happening?"

"I'm on the hunt." Startlingly, he began declaiming. "Valjean!" A bogus British accent in full plummy-voweled cry. "Valjean! You shall not escape me. I shall never tire."

Listening to Seth ranting, Patrick felt himself growing increasingly abstracted from their situation—as though he were reading about it in an old newspaper.

"Charles Laughton," Seth said. "Gotta love him."

"What's happening?"

"No luck at JR's or Trumpets. I'm heading over to Badlands now."

"What…" He could feel his heart begin to flutter. "What exactly are you doing?"

"Just talking with people. I'm a lobbyist, Patrick. I *talk* with people."

"I feel like I should be helping."

"No, no, you can't be associated with it."

"Remind me why?"

"People would know. You were on the make," Seth said. "It could get back to Alex."

"And Alex has to think I'm lonely and pining away and…"

"Something like that."

"What about Ted, then? He finds out you're running around to all these bars…"

"Oh, he won't care." Seth said it like a kid skipping fifth period. *They won't care.*

Patrick said, "Someone broke into my car last night."

"No way! Did they leave any messages?"

"Messages?"

"Propaganda? Slogans?"

"No."

"Scrawled in blood? On the windows?"

"No, nothing like that."

"Well, that's good," Seth said.

16

Nine days after Patrick took his car to the garage, a mechanic named Luigi called to tell him he had to pick up his car.

"Why?" Patrick asked. "Is it fixed?"

"In the way. Gotta clear it out."

"Is it fixed?"

"We close 7."

Patrick got there by 6:50 and found Luigi gone but the window and the steering column both restored. He couldn't take the car home, though, because his keys were gone.

"I know what you're thinking," said the owner, a gum-chewing woman in fuchsia lipstick.

"What am I thinking?"

"We're making copies of your keys. We're scamming you."

"No."

"I swear on my grandmother's—"

"Look," Patrick said. "Why don't I just run home and get my other set of keys? I'll be five minutes."

"Oh, we're closing," she said. "But listen, we won't charge you for keeping it another night."

As he trudged the four blocks home, Patrick realized how much he missed Alex. Which was perfectly natural, he thought:

You always miss people when you're in extremis. And then a rebellious thought made him stop in his tracks. Was it really *Alex* he missed? Alex would not have been particularly helpful in a situation like this. He was never the best of sounding boards: He instinctively bounced your complaints back to you. "What's the big deal?" Alex would have said. "You don't need your car tonight, anyway."

Still, better than nothing, Patrick thought as he reached for the front door knob—as he tried to estimate the force it would take to rip the door from its frame. *Significantly better than nothing.*

His father was snoring on the love seat. Without stopping, Patrick went to the kitchen and picked up the cordless phone and held it in his right hand and stared at it, thinking: *Who? Who can I bitch to?* And then he started dialing, and he was surprised to learn he had already memorized the phone number.

"*El*-lo." Rick tended to answer this way at home, with the emphasis on the first syllable, and even more puzzling, he always answered by the second ring. Patrick wondered sometimes if the phone was actually attached to him—the way a marching band musician's music is attached to his shoulder.

"I'm leaving the city," Patrick said.

"*Oo ant,*" Rick said.

"What?"

"You can't."

"Are you eating?"

"*Eanut utter.*"

"Right out of the jar?"

"Yeah."

Patrick almost dissolved at the thought. *Out of a jar.* Why was that so enticing?

"*Oo* can't leave," Rick said, "because I haven't seen your place yet."

"Why do you want to see my place?"

"'Cause." He took a long swallow. "'Cause it's yours. How am I supposed to know what you're like if I can't see your place?"

"Well—I'm not sure you'd find me here. I mean, when Alex was around, it was more like *his* place, even though he didn't live here, and now it's just my father's—*crypt.*"

"Oh, come on," Rick said. "It's yours. You just don't know it. I bet you're all over it."

"Well…"

"It's got your smell, right?"

"It has a smell."

Sometimes he thought it was the smell of whoever had last been in it. Seth's smell, for instance, which was not the smell of sweat but of some kind of cologne or aftershave that was either very expensive or very inexpensive. Patrick was always on the verge of identifying it but never quite could.

In fact, he was always encountering Seth at a disadvantage. Seth no longer identified himself when he called. He didn't even say hello; he just plunged in with a random declarative statement that had no obvious rejoinder but gave the impression that they had already been talking for a long time. Seth would call him at work—say, in the middle of the afternoon—and the first thing out of his mouth would be "Go figure." And Patrick had to stop and remind himself that Seth could not be responding to something he had just said—because they hadn't been talking.

"Go figure what?"

"It's just funny," Seth said.

The night Patrick got his car back (the chassis still vibrating despite the new engine strut) Seth called again, a little before midnight. Patrick was still awake. He was awake all the time now.

"I don't care what you say," Seth said. "It's freaking."

"What?"

"I thought Scottie was so *generic*. Thought everyone would kind of know him. Or someone who looked kind of like him."

"What? It hasn't worked out that way?"

"No," he said, his voice faltering a little. "It's destroying my faith. In stereotypes."

Patrick tapped his finger against the alarm clock. "Um…"

"What?"

"I know I'm not supposed to be interfering with this process or anything, but I have to admit, I'm kind of—*curious*, you know about the—about the line you're taking. I mean, what I'm wondering is what you *say*, exactly, when you walk up to someone? In one of these places."

"What do I *say*?"

"Yes."

"When I show them the picture?"

"Yes."

"You mean I didn't tell you? About my little front?"

"No, you—no, you didn't."

"Oh, see, I just tell them I'm a lawyer. Representing the young man's great uncle. Patio-furniture king Herbert Barca de Jongh. Who's just passed on, left his young nephew a considerable sum—"

"Barca de Jongh?"

"And tragically, the young man's family no longer has his current address. Little history of alienation, not worth detailing. Upshot? They're trying desperately to find him now."

"And do they—do people buy this?" Patrick asked.

"Well, they usually ask for a finder's fee."

"Oh."

"Which might be a problem for you. If they actually find him, I mean."

"Mm."

"On the other hand, many hands. Light work."

After a while Patrick could anticipate, could almost *feel* when Seth would next be calling—like a drop in the barometer. Perhaps Seth was beginning to sense this, because the next time he called, he insisted on delivering his report in person.

"Doesn't feel right," he said. "Just doing it over the phone. Clandestine meetings, that's the ticket."

It was August now, and Seth, for the first time in Patrick's memory, was wearing shorts—knee-length madras shorts. It didn't seem to help him. They were sitting in Bread and Chocolate, surrounded by floor-to-ceiling glass, and the sun was smiting Seth with the force of a diamond laser. *He is melting,* Patrick thought. And it was true—his whole body was disintegrating. The whorls of black hair on his legs bled into each other like an intricate tattoo. The only part of him that looked dry were his black-rimmed glasses, which appeared to be floating on his face.

And yet—such was the effect of their growing acquaintance—Patrick no longer found Seth's sweat off-putting. If anything, the perspiration seemed to call the planes of Seth's face into relief, give them a mandarin handsomeness (interrupted only by the startling lavalike quality of the eyes). Alex would look the same way, sometimes, coming back from a run—his face flushed, his cheekbones mysteriously defined.

Seth picked at the mound of cottage cheese on its pale barge of iceberg lettuce.

"You have news?" Patrick said.

"Well—not yet." He readjusted his glasses. "No, there *is* something. I showed the picture. To someone at the Frat House."

"Yes?"

"And he thinks it looks like someone he sees at Remington's. Sometimes on Saturday nights."

"Remington's?" Patrick put down his fork. "That's right across the street."

Seth nodded, dabbed his forehead with a napkin. "Indeed," he said. "That's where you'll find me tonight."

"No, wait! No, it's silly for me not to go. Think about it, Seth. I'd recognize him faster than anyone."

"No," Seth said. "No bars, remember? You're brooding."

"Oh, come on."

"Pining. This is our deal, yes?"

Why? Patrick thought. *Why did I agree to this? What peculiar desperation led me to agree to this?*

Seth said, "You probably are anyway."

"What?"

"Brooding."

"I always brood," Patrick said. "Alex used to—never mind."

"Yes?"

"He used to call me Ol' Broody Butt."

"*Charmant,*" said Seth. His lips opened into that shockingly white, half-apologetic smile. "If I see someone," he said, "anyone even close—I'll let you know. I'll run to the nearest phone. Call you collect." He nodded once, as though to confirm a mutual signal, then pushed his salad plate away. It was half uneaten.

"You don't want anymore?" Patrick asked.

"No, can't afford to. Have to lose 12 by the end of the summer." He brushed a sticky strand of hair away from his forehead. "It can't be water weight," he said.

"My father's on a diet," Patrick said.

"What kind of diet?"

"I don't know, it's—fruits mostly. He's trying to purge all his toxins."

"That's why he's here? To purge his toxins?"

"No, he's working on something."

"Well, that's good. To be working on something."

"Yes."

"As long as it's just *some*thing," Seth said. "As soon as it becomes a *thing*? Watch out."

17

Patrick still didn't know what the something was. His father had promised to brief him and never had. And Patrick hadn't pressed because, quite honestly, it was best sometimes not to know and also because there was a certain decorum that existed between them, a disinclination to push into unwonted intimacy.

On the other hand, they already *were* in unwonted intimacy. It had been a long time since they had lived in such proximity. Mr. Beaton had now been in Patrick's house for three weeks, and he showed no signs of leaving soon. Once, about a week after his arrival, Patrick had asked him if he was having any luck locating a place, and his father said, "Oh, Pattie, these goddamn slumlords! An honest fella can't make his way these days."

So there he remained, sleeping away half the afternoons and most of the evenings on Patrick's love seat—almost always in the same position: one leg tucked in and one arm dangling off. Patrick would leave him there in the morning and find him that evening in almost the same position, still dressed in his 1970s forest-green jogging suit with the peeling white stripes. If he wasn't sleeping, he was almost always watching television—usually Showtime, not because he preferred it but because Patrick didn't have a remote and Mr. Beaton couldn't read the channel buttons on the bottom of the TV set and Showtime was the channel that came on first. Some nights Patrick would come home and find him sitting stiffly in the mission rocker, only a few feet away from the screen, gaping at a direct-to-cable feature.

"What's this?" Patrick would ask.

"Pattie, I have no idea." He would start gesturing at it, a little fearfully, as though it had barged in through the door. "This woman kills men by sucking out their hearts during sex."

"Da..."

"And I think she must be keeping their genitals in a cupboard."

Patrick had expected his father to start stinking. But the jogging suit, though it never came off, always looked clean and pressed, and his hair was always shampooed and freshly combed. By all indicators, Mr. Beaton had just enough energy to struggle upstairs to the shower and back down again—and no more.

Or maybe he was a kind of actuality, siphoning energy from his surroundings. Evenings were quiet. Patrick never turned on the television or the CD player. Even when his father was awake, he found himself tiptoeing through the living room. He made all his phone calls from the upstairs bedroom; sometimes he even ate there. After about two weeks Patrick called his mother.

"I'm worried," he said. "Da's hardly moving."

"I know," she said.

"What do you mean? He's done this before?"

"Of course he has. It's one of his cycles."

"I don't remember it."

"Oh, dear, he wouldn't do it in front of you and your sister. Whenever he felt it coming on, he'd just go away to some motel for a couple of weeks and come back when it was over."

"Wait. You mean that was…"

"His business trips, yes."

Patrick felt a ripple of resentment. Shouldn't he have been briefed on all this by now? Shouldn't there have been full disclosure of all the genetic land mines waiting for him?

"Well, how come Da never went to a doctor? There must be some medication he could take."

"Oh," his mother said, "I don't think they've found the drug that would be a match for your father."

In the absence of psychiatric intervention, Patrick devised a therapy of his own. Every evening he spent about five minutes gently interrogating his father, asking him how his day had gone, what the prospects looked like, whether he'd remembered to bring an umbrella when he went out. His father wasn't hostile to these inquiries; he just seemed helpless to come up with answers. If you asked him how he'd enjoyed the weather, he would look at you with a sort of numb panic, as though you were quizzing him on material he hadn't read yet. He couldn't answer because, in fact, he hadn't left the house. He was living in about eight square feet of space.

Patrick had thought his father's isolation so complete that he was surprised when over lunch one day Marianne said, "Oh, honey, I forgot. Your dad called me the other day."

"You're kidding."

"He's so sweet. He said, 'How's my little Marianne? How's my cutie?'"

"Well, you're—you're always the first person he asks about."

She cupped her chin in her hands. "I think he called 'cause he thinks I can be helpful or something. With his little project. He asked me if Daddy knows anyone in the defense industry."

"Defense?"

"I said, 'Mr. Beaton, Daddy's field is agriculture. He's an ag commissioner. He's into farms and shit. Grain silos.'"

"And what did he say?"

"He said, 'Well, fuck, I thought he did missile silos.'"

Patrick swept his hands across his face. "I'm scared."

"What?"

"My father. Armaments."

"Oh, let him play," she said.

Marianne was wearing a cerulean jumper and matching globe earrings. Lately, she had taken to extending her eyeliner a fraction to give her eyes a Eurasian exoticism. She was glowing with health. Patrick found himself marveling once again at her complexion, which had survived years of smoking and still seemed to have its own current, its own energy supply.

"How's Victor?" he asked. "How's RCA Victor?"

"Oh." She began fanning herself with her napkin. "Patrick."

"I assume that's good."

"Did I tell you about the flower?"

"No."

"Every day he sends me a single goddamn flower. Is that incredible? It gets to my office, rain or shine, by 10:30 every morning."

"Wow."

"And it's never the same flower, 'kay? One day it's a gladiolus, and next day it's a daffodil, and next day it's a tiger lily. It's crazy. I don't think he's repeated himself yet. This morning it was a bird of paradise."

"That's nice. What does it mean?"

"It doesn't have to mean anything."

"No, I mean—what's the point? He sends you a flower every day; it has to have a point, doesn't it?"

"Oh, just shut the fuck up. You clearly don't understand how this works."

"At least you're eating chicken now."

"Oh, Christ, Patrick. This vegetarian stuff, it's—it's messing with my mind. Did I tell you about my dream? I dreamed the other night I was 'bout a hundred thousand pounds heavier than I am *now*, and I was in this store called The Fatted Woman. And all this place did, this little boutique, was, they sold horse-riding equipment to obese women: big ol' boots, jodhpurs as big as circus tents, the whole bit. And there's this skinny woman behind the counter, and she's telling me, 'Oh, someone will be along shortly to *aquarianize* you.'"

"Aquarianize?"

"Yeah, I know, shouldn't it be *equestrianize* or something? Anyway, I'm standing there waiting to be—*aquarianized*. And I turn around, and behind me, Patrick, is this long, long line of enormous women, probably about a mile long. 'Bout two zillion tons of woman, and all of it waiting to be aquarianized."

"Wow."

"And I just—a shudder went through me, Patrick. Cause all I could think was, *Those poor fuckin' horses.*"

It was Sunday night, the night Seth had chosen to patrol Remington's, the country-western bar. He had promised to call with an on-the-spot report, so Patrick stayed up late reading Wallace Stevens poems. He read them like a cryptographer, trying to decipher the enemy's next maneuver. He looked for tropes, linguistic signposts. Eventually he settled for just finding the word *Remington*, but it never appeared.

The phone rang at 1:22. Patrick wondered why it sounded so muffled, then he realized he'd been asleep. He snatched up the receiver. "Seth?" he said.

"Zilch."

"Oh." His head fell back on the pillow. "You're kidding."

"Been here four hours. Can't find him."

"Oh, God."

"I even did a line dance. Terrifying."

"Well." Patrick was exhausted, suddenly; he could have slept through seven moons. "Thank you for trying."

"Oh, my pleasure. Do it again next week."

"No, that's OK."

"Deal's a deal."

The next night, Patrick went to Remington's himself. He got there early; the beginner's dance class was still in progress. Ten pairs of solemn men cantering in a circle like high-bred fillies, their arms linked in *American Gothic* poses, their faces taut with concentration. "Inside turn," cried the teacher, a 50-ish man in pointy-toed boots. "Cape position. And stop looking at your feet! This ain't skydiving."

Watching from the balcony overhead, Patrick wondered, *When Scottie and I dance—who will lead?* Maybe there was an easy way of determining these things. Maybe it depended on who was taller, but which of them was taller? That had never been established.

Maybe Scottie stood here. Right here. Maybe he looked down just as I am doing. Maybe he wondered if he was a leader or a follower. Or else he already knows. *He knows which one he is.*

Was it almost too much to consider? That on at least one evening in the recent past, Scottie had been right here, two blocks away from Patrick, spinning out a few more hours of life, oblivious to their joint destiny?

If Scottie was here, he thought, correcting himself. *If Scottie is.*

18

"So tell me," Seth said. "How was it?"

"How was what?"

"Remington's."

They were having lunch at a restaurant called Ciao Baby, and because it was summer, someone had taken the windows away. The portals opened directly onto the sidewalk, and the diners were a kind of *tableau vivant* for the passers-by, except that none of the passers-by was bothering to look.

"Don't tell me," Patrick said. "One of your moles spotted me."

"No, no, no. Intuition. Blind luck."

"Well—he wasn't there. I knew he wouldn't be."

"Ah. Well." Seth took a forkful of grilled tuna. He was eating more today. Patrick reached for a piece of bread and then remembered they were at the cheap tables: There was no bread.

"I'm going to hit the leather bars tonight," Seth said.

"No!"

"What?"

"No, not leather, that's—"

"What?"

"He won't be there! He's not—he's not leathery."

"Oh, I see," said Seth dryly. "Like my high school calculus teacher. Whom I caught last year. At the East Coast Mr. Leather contest. Wearing buttless chaps."

"That's fine."

"Patrick. We're not saying Scottie's *there*. Just someone there might know him."

"Oh, all right. Fine. Do what you want."

"Highly observant people, the leathers."

Once again Seth promised an on-the-spot report, and once again Patrick stayed up late waiting for his call. When midnight came he was sitting in bed listening to his father's susurrations from the downstairs couch. (Mr. Beaton still refused to use the guest room.) The Wallace Stevens volume lay unopened on his bedside table.

Not leather, he thought. *Scottie doesn't need leather.*

As it turned out, Seth never called. Patrick fell asleep around 2 and woke up about four hours later. He wasn't sure if he had just woken up or just fallen asleep. He looked out his bedroom window. People were already on their way to work. The tires of their cars made whishing sounds, as though the pavement were wet, but there had been no rain for a week. Next door, bumble-bees were swarming in a stand of lavender.

When was the last time he had dreamed about Scottie?

At 8:30, just as he was about to walk out the door, the phone rang.

"Hello?"

"It's Rick."

Instinctively he turned, and his eyes found his father's limp form on the love seat. "Rick. Hi."

"I want to see your house."

"Um…" One of the cushions had squished Mr. Beaton's face into dewlaps. Dry gurgling sounds were coming out of his throat.

"Now?" Patrick asked.

"No, not now. I was just sitting here eating my bran flakes, and I thought, *Wait a minute. I still haven't seen Patrick's house.*"

"Well, you know, my father's still here; it's kind of tricky."

"That's the best way to learn about people, don't you think? Meet their parents."

"I'm not sure that would be helpful. In this case."

"Oh, come on. I'll stop by after work."

Stall! Stall!

"Well…" Patrick closed his eyes, bunched up his cheek muscles. *Think!* "It's funny you say that…" *Think harder!* "'Cause I've never seen *your* place either. That's been troubling me. A little bit."

There was a pause, a long pause. And then Rick said, "How about tonight?"

"Tonight."

"We'll have dinner at my place."

There must be, Patrick decided later, *built-in limitations on my ability to evade, a quota system of evasions per minute.* He had learned nothing from their last date. There was still no emergency kit of excuses, nothing to prepare him for sudden incursions like this.

And yet he didn't *not* want to go. If he were honest with himself, he could see there was something—how to qualify this?—something *not* unappealing, not uninviting about going.

And what else do I have to do? he thought. *Watch Da snore? Tiptoe around my own living room?*

Seth finally called in the afternoon. "I've decided," he said.

"What?"

"Going to get something pierced."

"All right."

"Not sure what it is yet. But it must be visible at all times."

"So…nipples are out."

"And penises. Oh, the whole piercing thing! Know what it is? It's white people, right? Trying to recreate the dignity of African royalty. Form of cultural reparations."

"I'm assuming you didn't find anything."

"No. But Achmed was out last night."

"Achmed."

"The usual bartender. King Daddy they call him."

Patrick wondered if Seth was by now a minor celebrity in bar circles. He could easily imagine the conversations sprouting up:

The same guy approached you?

Something about patio furniture.

He wouldn't stop sweating!

More than once, Patrick had asked himself if Seth's tactics could have the effect of driving Scottie further from sight. And yet, what other options did he have at hand? What ideas had he come up with on his own? He was the most maddeningly passive quest hero one could imagine.

"Going back there tonight," Seth said with a percussive sigh. "Want to come?"

"I thought I'm supposed to stay away from bars."

"Well, you already blew your cover with Remington's." Patrick was surprised by the layer of contempt in his voice. "Never mind," Seth said. "We'll dress you up. No one will recognize you."

"Actually, I'm having dinner with a friend tonight."

"Oh."

"A woman friend," Patrick said hastily.

Afterwards, he wondered why he'd lied. It was alarming to think he needed to play along with Seth to that extent: foreswear all dates, spend each evening in a kind of eternal suspension, waiting for something to resolve—for what? For Alex to come back? What would that mean, anyway? Alex coming back...

Most days, he realized, he still wanted to call Alex. Call him at work, perhaps, and avoid the answering-machine dog. But the plan always foundered on the same obstacle, which was, How do you even begin such a conversation?

Hi, Alex.... Well, hi there, Alex.... Well, hi there, Alex, it's Mr. Guess Who!... Well, hi there, Alex, it's me....

Or just *Alex? You're a dog-owning, lawyer-loving piece of shit!*

There were several options. There was an unlimited number of options.

Rick's building was one of the anonymous stone edifices on the north side of K Street, and as Patrick pulled his car over, he wondered for a second if he'd gotten the *right* anonymous edifice. There were no places to park, and a Federal Express truck was blocking him in front, and behind him a taxicab was kissing his bumper and honking mindlessly. Patrick had a queasy hankering to chuck it all, abandon the car and sprint off into the sunset, and then Rick poked his head through the open passenger window.

"Hi!" he said.

"Oh, hi!" Patrick giggled. "I didn't recognize you in your—suit." It was an expensive-looking suit too: taupe tropical wool, double-breasted. "I thought librarians wore cardigan sweaters and stuff," Patrick said.

Rick wrapped the seat belt around him with a flourish, as though it were one of his accessories. "It's too hot for cardigans," he said.

They had driven for about a minute in silence when Rick said in a taut voice: "Is this car safe and everything?"

Patrick looked over. Rick's entire body was palsying. It was almost liquid.

"Oh, I'm sorry. I should have mentioned it. Something's wrong with my engine strut."

"I thought they fixed that."

"No, they were supposed to. I mean, they *said* they did, but I don't think they did."

"I don't think they did, either."

Patrick didn't know what to say. Every time he looked over, Rick was trying some new technique for stabilizing himself. At first it was bracing himself against the car door. Then it was pulling the restraining belt further into his body until it was almost bisecting him. At one point he even balled up his hands into fists and began pushing up against the roof of the car.

"I'm sorry," Patrick said. "I should have mentioned it."

He watched his own hands vibrating against the steering wheel. The shaking no longer bothered him, for some reason. He had found its still center.

"I think I may have to go to the bathroom," Rick said.

"Well…we're almost to the bridge. How far is it after that?"

"About five minutes."

"Do you think you can hold on that long?"

"I—I don't know," he said. His entire voice was vibrating now. His eyes were dancing in their sockets. "I'll try," he said.

It took them precisely 14 minutes to get to Rick's Rosslyn apartment building. As soon as they stopped, Rick jumped out, slammed the door, and began galloping toward the building. Reaching the front gate, he flung it open, called out "201!" and bolted up the stairs.

Patrick followed at a leisurely pace. He found the apartment door half open, and as he walked in, he deliberately closed his eyes for two seconds before opening them again. And nothing happened, so he closed his eyes again.

What was he expecting, anyway? Did he expect anything? Maybe an intimate, wood-lined affair with clutter and cat hair and African memorabilia. But Apartment 201 was a large, modular two-bedroom unit with limestone carpeting and ladder-back chairs. An empty fish tank sat on a walnut sideboard. Running the length of one wall was a built-in, bleached-oak bookcase with symmetrically arranged cubbyholes full of flower arrangements, framed photographs, china pieces—and a few books. Patrick ran his eye along the titles: Fodor's guides from 1991, a monograph on Georgia O'Keefe, something by Tom Peters, an old paperback copy of *The Road Less Traveled*, at least three workout books dating from the mid 1980s.

A pair of lips connected with the back of his neck. "What do you think?" Rick asked.

"Hi. Yeah. It's very nice, it's—I was just thinking if I were— you know, a librarian, I wouldn't want to even *look* at a book when I came home at night."

"Oh, it's not really a bookcase. It's more like a curio cabinet."

"It's very nice. It's very clean."

"Here," Rick said. He handed Patrick a folded-over piece of paper, stained and discolored.

"What?"

"Order something. It's my treat."

It was a take-out menu from a local Korean restaurant. The restaurant's motto was "Good food and high responsibility."

"I'm a moo shoo man," Rick said.

Patrick ordered garlic chicken, and they ate on Rick's couch, with paper napkins, using the *Post* Metro section as a tablecloth.

Patrick was touched. He had expected a home-cooked meal, and this was somehow homier. And what an appetite Rick had! He ate every one of his pancakes, and when he had finished with those, he brought the little cardboard pail to his lips and drank up the last remnants of sauce. He rubbed his mouth with the back of his hand.

It was 8:30 now. Outside, the gaslights were suddenly visible through the arms of an elm tree. The planes coming into National Airport were making strident lawn-mower noises. Annie Lennox was playing from an audio center somewhere deep inside the front-hall closet.

Rick said: "You know what?"

"What?"

"We still haven't kissed."

And it was true, they hadn't. *Why haven't we?* Patrick wondered. *Is it my fault?*

Rick had changed from his work clothes into a solid-blue polo shirt and gray parachute pants and black high-top sneakers. The skin on his arms was freckled, and his eyes looked even more youthful at night, beneath their full, Irish-black eyebrows. He was awfully good-looking.

"Well," Patrick said. "We'll just—have to."

19

It wasn't a moan, the sound Rick made while he was kissing. It was something shorter and leaner, monosyllabic, something like *grm* or *shm*. Ruminative, as though he were constantly reconsidering the situation. Which he may have been doing because he wouldn't quite open his mouth fully. And he never opened his eyes, which was just as well, Patrick thought: People's eyes always looked strange up close; they looked like they belonged to someone else. But after a while Patrick began to wonder. *Is he imagining someone?*

And then a woeful thought occurred to him: *Is it Scottie? Is it Scottie he's imagining?* He remembered what Seth had said—how maybe they had *all* dreamed Scottie.

"This is great," Rick said, rubbing his hands along Patrick's back. "*Grm. Shm.*"

It was over in about 12 minutes.

Afterward, Patrick excused himself and took a shower. He stood there for a while, not even soaping himself, just letting the water burble through his hair and down his arms and onto his feet. Then behind him the curtain parted, and Rick stepped in.

Patrick's head locked in place. He was transfixed with panic.

OK—OK, it's all right…I'll just—pretend not to see him! No, that's ridiculous. He's right there. He's two feet away, Patrick, you can't—there's no escaping it.

In a matter of seconds they would be washing each other, and for some reason, it was the most intolerable idea Patrick had entertained all evening. *It's too early, it's not right!* This was what you did after several months of acquaintance and then only periodically after that, a kind of ritual lathering, once an equinox.

He turned now, and Rick was advancing, smiling at him through the plane of water that separated them, and Patrick was feeling the cold hard chrome of the faucet in the small of his back—no room for maneuvering.

"All done!" he cried. He wrenched the curtain open. Did his voice really sound that unnatural? He didn't care. He leapt out of the tub, grabbed a towel, sprinted for the bedroom, leaving little lagoons on the floor as he went.

When he was finished dressing, he poked his head out the bedroom door and saw Rick standing in front of the bathroom mirror, still naked and flossing his teeth, working the minty string as furiously as a sander belt. And Patrick's response was the same as it had been in the shower. This was too intimate. This was more than he needed to know.

"I understand," Rick said.

Patrick was on his way out the door, already scanning the parking lot for his car. "You—sorry?"

"It's hard. When you're coming out of a long relationship."

"Oh."

"I mean, I assume that's why you're—"

"Yeah."

"Kind of antsy."

"Well…"

"It was a very nice time."

"Yeah, it was. Really, I'm—it's not that I don't like you, I do. I do, and I don't quite know why you're interested in me—but, you know, I'm *grateful.*"

"Listen," Rick said. "I'll leave it up to you. Think about it, all right? And if you want get together again, call me."

"OK."

"All right?"

"All right."

Arriving home, he found Deanna leaning once again against the wrought-iron railing that led down to her apartment. She was wearing a soft floral dirndl, and her skirt was spread out on either side of her like a canopy: It looked as though she were concealing someone. But her face had that same benign, unexpectant look it always had, and as Patrick approached, she loosened her grip on the railing and gave him an easy smile.

"Lovely evening," she said.

"Yes," he said.

They lingered for a moment in the hazy, fishy air, neither of them saying a thing, and Patrick remembered that it was this very possibility that he had most dreaded when deciding whether to take a tenant.

"Your—your toilet thingy," he said. "Not acting up, is it?"

"No."

"That's good."

"Flushes like a charm," she said.

"Good."

They remained standing there for a few more seconds, and then Patrick slapped his thighs, as though he were just now standing up from an hour-long jaw. "Well," he said. "Gonna tuck in."

"How's your father?"

"Oh, he's fine. Kind of—taking an extended vacation."

"Good for him," Deanna said.

"Yeah."

"Vacations are good," she said.

It was 10:30 when Patrick got through the door. He knew Marianne would be up; she believed that going to bed early was a failure of nerve, and in fact, when Patrick called, she answered the phone instantly, with a quick outrush of air, as though she had been hedging her bets with amphetamines.

"Hi," he said. "You alone?"

"Oh, yeah."

"I went on a date tonight."

"You big tramp. Who?"

"That guy Rick. The one who answered the ad."

"Oh, wow."

"So that's all."

"No, that's not all. Tell me how it went."

"I don't know," he said, truthfully. "I don't know; there's something a little odd about him. I mean, he's a law librarian, right? But he hardly has any books in his apartment. Just curios and CD-ROMs."

"Uh-huh."

"And he wears Italian suits to work."

"Does he have a beeper? Maybe he's got his own drug cartel or something."

"Oh, I don't know, he's very attractive, he's very nice. Very, you know, *relaxed* about things, which is kind of refreshing."

"No sparks?"

"Well—there are *sparks*, but I'm not sure what kind. You know how when you're in high school lab and you sometimes mix the wrong things together and you get that burning kind of smell and everyone turns around and stares at you and the teacher's running for the extinguisher?"

"Which means danger."

"Well, sometimes it's danger, and sometimes—it just means you fucked up. You mixed the wrong things together."

Marianne made a clucking sound. He could actually see her switching the phone to the other ear, settling in. "Patrick," she said, "you're certainly entitled to fuck up. It's not like everyone's gonna hold it against you."

Not everyone, he thought. *Just Scottie. The man I'm supposed to be waiting for.*

Later, Patrick went to check on his father and found him, for the first time since his arrival, sleeping in the upstairs guest room, in the bed that Patrick had first made up a month ago. Maybe it was the different venue: Mr. Beaton's breathing was less labored than usual, and his body seemed to have realigned itself into a posture of submission. His hands were curled up into little balls, the kind that children sometimes make when they rub their eyes.

Watching his father sleep, watching the small pale toes unconsciously flexing and straightening themselves, he found himself visited with an image of Scottie, elusive but palpable. Scottie standing not in front of him but right next to him, almost out of sight, standing there and holding Patrick's hand. And the two of them gazing down, as proud as parents. *Look! Isn't he cute?*

And as if aware of their joint presence, Mr. Beaton rolled his head toward them and from somewhere deep in the Land of Nod said, "Schmuck."

He said it very distinctly, and there was no doubt in Patrick's mind whom he meant. No doubt, either, in Scottie's mind because he pulled his hand away and flung the word back over his shoulder as he left the room.

Schmuck!

20

"What a glorious day, Pattie!"

Patrick pried one of his eyes open. His father—or someone who looked just like him—was standing over the bed wearing a recently pressed seersucker suit, with a yellow-and-teal polka-dotted bow tie. He had showered, shaved, and tucked the *Post* in a neatly folded bundle under his arm.

"Don't tell me you always sleep in this late," Mr. Beaton said.

Patrick opened his other eye and stared at the alarm clock. It was 6:20.

"You know you have rats, don't you?" his father said.

"I have—"

"They went after the sourdough bread. Knocked it off the counter, took a nice big chunk. Greedy!"

"I've never had rats before."

"I should have told you. You know, I heard them all the time when I was downstairs, but I thought I was just dreaming, except no one dreams about rats every night, do they?"

"Probably not." Patrick dragged his fingers down his face.

"Well, I'm off," Mr. Beaton said, executing a quick shuffle step. "Oh, Pattie, you don't mind if I take the paper with me, do you? I didn't have time to read it this morning."

"Go ahead."

"Oh, and you're out of orange juice, but I'll pick some up on my way back. And this weekend, I'm cleaning your oven, Pattie, because it's not safe in there; you're violating some kind of federal law, I know it."

Patrick listened to his father gavotting down the steps and out the door. A few minutes later he heard the moaning of the garbage truck, followed shortly by the rumble of the recyclables truck. He lay there for another half hour, unable to move. Then he got up and went down to the kitchen.

The sourdough bread lay on the counter. The aluminum foil surrounding it had been torn away and a huge divot scooped out. Patrick stared at it, trying to picture what had happened, the whole process, the scaling of the loaf, the puncturing of the foil—but what came to mind instead was not an image but a sound: the tune his father had been whistling as he went out the door. "How Much Is That Doggie in the Window?"

So he wants a dog too.

That afternoon Patrick called Marianne. The first words out of his mouth were: "He lives."

"Who?"

"My father. He woke up early today, he put on a suit, and he went out."

"Well, come on, that's a good sign, isn't it?"

"Yes," he said dubiously. "Except it means he's getting ready to lose all his money again."

"Fish gotta swim, Patrick."

He laughed. It was heartening sometimes that he could laugh about his father, although it usually meant regarding him from a safe distance—the way you'd look at, say, a squirrel rooting up your vegetable garden.

"So how's Victor?" he remembered to ask. "Did he send you a flower today?"

"A dwarf campanula."

"Oh, my."

"Yesterday it was a sour fig, if you can believe it. It came with a little identifying tag. I think he must have stolen it from somebody's garden. I can't imagine a florist having this shit."

"A thief for love."

She whooped. "Or something," she said.

Mr. Beaton was leaving the house every morning now, before Patrick awoke, and every evening he returned looking as clean and dewy as fresh money. Every day, he had his shoes repolished by a very nice man at the Farragut West Metro stop, and you might have thought Mr. Beaton himself was being burnished and buffed daily. Even his bow ties (he had at least five) looked as crisp at the end of the day as they did at the beginning. His movement was more elastic now; his face was pinker; the folds of skin that used to hang off his jaw roused themselves, surged up into his cheeks.

Was it the seersucker suit? Patrick pondered the possibility. Did the suit have some sort of transforming power? Patrick was feeling a little depleted himself lately, and he actually toyed with the idea of going into his father's room one night, trying the damn thing on. He imagined himself stepping into the magic suit, waiting for the flood of life force—but he never got the chance. Mr. Beaton wore the seersucker about as often as he had worn his track suit—except when he went to bed, when he pulled from his garment bag a tartan flannel nightshirt with a mysterious monogram: ZFM.

"Is that yours?" Patrick asked casually.

"Very dear friend of mine, Pattie. Gave it to me when I was staying in Utica. During a blizzard. Along with a stuffed elephant and a flask of peppermint schnapps."

As always, Mr. Beaton's explanations raised more questions than they answered. *Utica? When was he there? Who's ZFM anyway? His girlfriend? His child?* Mr. Beaton was one of those expansive, voluble people who actually told you very little—usually much less than you needed to know. Patrick still had no idea, for instance, what his father did during the day, what business he was pursuing—how he planned to live the remainder of his days. One thing at a time. It was enough to know the nightshirt came with a stuffed elephant.

Mr. Beaton was no closer to finding a place of his own, though he did make a show of running through the ads in the *City Paper* and making some follow-up calls, and twice he drove out to inspect places. Each time he came back disappointed.

"She hates dogs, Pattie."

"You don't have a dog."

"Anyone who hates dogs hates people too. She had mean little eyes, son."

And that's all he would say. The subject rarely came up again, and Mr. Beaton would never say how long he intended to stay in Patrick's house or how long he intended to stay in Washington—or, indeed, anything about *anything*.

And what explanation, finally, did he owe Patrick when Patrick had never told him the most important thing—had never once mentioned Scottie?

There was no one to blame for this but Patrick. His father had given him the openings. There would be moments when Mr. Beaton's motor was temporarily idling, when a mutual quiescence had settled on them and they were in some kind of proximity and Mr. Beaton was inquiring vaguely about Patrick's welfare, and it would have been the simplest thing in the world for Patrick to open his mouth and say, "Da, I met this guy. I met him 137 days ago." Patrick was keeping track. He was ticking off the days one by one in his little appointment calendar, committing each new day's number to memory. "I met him 137 days ago, and he may well be—no, he almost certainly is—the man I will love for the rest of my life, and I let him get away. And I can't seem to find him again."

It would have been difficult, he knew, to explain the exact nature of his feelings because they changed from minute to minute, in a way that kept him from ever defining them. At times it seemed he experienced Scottie as a vacancy—as a chain of anesthetized nerve endings. And at other times he would have been grateful for vacancy because Scottie occupied such a specific location in the chamber of his stomach and it was so palpable a sensation, so bound up with the sensations of hunger and ulcers, that he began to think it must have a physiological root. He wondered if he might even find Scottie briefly indexed in the back pages of a medical journal. He envisioned himself prostrate on a cold metal platform, his abdomen palpated by one of the nation's leading gastrointestinal specialists, imagined gazing up at the X-ray screen and seeing the contents of his own stomach unspool before him and suddenly beholding, like a telltale cluster of nuclei, Scottie's image—the chin thrust forward, the eyes coming together, the lips relaxing into a graceful lopsided smile—seeing *that* image emblazoned in the shadows of organ and bone. And hearing somewhere in the recesses of one ear, the bearded doctor clucking his tongue: "Scottish venereal disease. Worst case I've ever seen."

So Patrick's feelings were intense to the point of physicality, and yet they were never deranging; they never came close to severing him from reality. The very opposite—the more Patrick thought about Scottie, the more anchored he felt to an unprovisional truth. Over and over again in his mind, he returned to the dream he'd had, and the dream seemed more real than anything he experienced on a daily basis. He was sitting once again in a high, pewlike wooden chair, and once again Scottie came up behind him and kissed him on the top of the head, kissed him the way any man arriving home after a long day would kiss his spouse—the same way they'd kissed yesterday and the day before and the day before that, the way they would kiss every day thereafter.

And Scottie said, "Traffic was bad tonight." And Patrick said, "Oh, honey, did you remember to pick up the milk?"

And the two of them were not even mindful of their own banality; they heard nothing but melody. *Our daily litany*, Patrick thought. *Fuck the world.*

He could have told his father all this—all this!—but he never said a word. He never opened his mouth. And as the days passed, the openings grew less and less frequent because Mr. Beaton was now compensating for his weeks of catatonia by talking incessantly—during the evening news, during dinner, after dinner, from behind the bathroom door, from beneath his bed covers. Bosnia, shock treatment, cabala, snow boarding, the professionalization of leisure—everything was meat for his happy jaws. Patrick began genuinely to welcome the interruption of phone calls, even from telemarketers, although being on the phone didn't necessarily discourage the flow of language. One night, for instance, Seth called in the middle of Mr. Beaton's treatise on sweetheart necklines, and the monologue was still going on five or six minutes into the phone conversation.

"Should I call back?" Seth asked.

"No, it's OK."

"Can you hear me?"

"Yeah—actually, you sound kind of hoarse."

"Oh, I just got back. From my men's meeting."

For a moment Patrick wasn't sure whether Seth or his father had said that.

"I know, I know," Seth said. "You thought only straight men did that."

"Um…"

"Think about it, though," Seth said. "Why shouldn't we be part of the men's movement? Are we not men?"

"Yes."

"Are we not just as fucked by the patriarchy? As straight men?"

"In our own way."

"There you are."

"That still doesn't explain why you're hoarse."

"Oh, see, what we're doing. We're getting in touch with our inner warriors. Mine happens to be a screamer."

"Ah…"

"So sometimes I wind up screaming. For about two hours straight."

"And that doesn't bother the other warriors?"

"They have their own baggage."

The more he got to know Seth, the more helpful he found it not to follow Seth's tangents all the way but rather to hold off for a bit and then revisit them with the intention of finding resolution. With the inner-warrior business, for instance, he waited until the next day to call Seth at work. He said, "Tell me. Did you start the men's movement thing *after* you broke up with Ted?"

"Are you kidding?" Seth said. "Ted put me on to it. Said he wanted sex with a warrior."

"And?"

"He found another warrior."

That was the first time Patrick had heard anyone describe Alex as a warrior. He would never have regarded Alex as a warrior of any kind, although maybe *everyone* was a warrior in Seth's world, fighting for Ted's galloping heart.

"Oh, there is something," Seth said. "To tell you. Scottie-related."

"What?"

"Never mind. I'll stop by Saturday."

"Tell me now."

"Can't. I would, but I can't."

"You mean you *can*, but you won't."

"No, I can't. I can't, so I won't."

21

Seth did at least give an estimated time of arrival—10 o'clock Saturday morning—and Patrick, for reasons that he didn't bother to articulate, had decided his father should be out of the house when Seth arrived. So he conceived a fictitious errand to Hechinger's involving lava rocks and lighter fluid, and Mr. Beaton not only agreed to it but did Patrick one better by deciding to throw in a visit to the National Arboretum.

"A fella needs the tonic of wildness, Pattie."

"OK," Patrick had said.

"Thoreau."

"OK, then."

So Patrick was alone when the time approached, which would have been fine except that a few minutes before 10 he was seized by the peculiar notion that he was entertaining. And there was no time to entertain. Quickly, he emptied a box of Wheat Thins into a cut-glass bowl and set the bowl on the coffee table, then threw down a hunk of Havarti dill cheese, and then he filled a carafe with orange juice. Then, as he was surrounding the food with concentric circles of Christmas napkins, he thought: *What am I doing? Wheat Thins and orange juice? Twenty Christmas napkins for a single visitor? It's just Seth, for God's sake.*

Before he could take them away, though, the doorbell rang. And when Patrick opened the door it seemed to him he must have been clairvoyant because Seth *wasn't* alone. He had brought a guest. A well-built man, perhaps 30, with lean wide shoulders and a V shape so exaggerated, it looked almost prosthetic. The man was brown as nutmeg, with close-cropped blond hair and sideburns cut at different lengths and a well-sculpted Aryan face—high cheekbones, Cupid lips, blue eyes, and a heroic forehead—features you could study for a long time because they didn't move.

"This is Adam," Seth said.

Adam extended his hand, and Patrick, effectively silenced, took it and held it for a few seconds…until he heard Seth's discreet cough.

"Oh, I'm sorry. Come in." He beckoned them through the door. "Um…" He looked around absently. "Havarti *cheese*? Or…*Wheat* Thins?"

"Nice hardwood floors," Adam said.

"Thank you." Patrick motioned him toward the love seat, and Seth, without any prompting, quickly followed, wedging himself onto the free cushion.

"Adam is a—a wellness consultant," Seth said.

"Oh."

"Which is very interesting, don't you think?"

"Yes, that is." Patrick began slowly lowering himself into the rocker.

"Particularly as it relates to your business."

Patrick stopped himself in midair, then dropped into the chair with a soft grunt. He slowly crossed his legs.

"My…"

"As I said to Adam. At the Y the other day. I said, 'I know a—

small but progressive employer. Interested in raising the quality of life. Of his workers.'"

"Yes?"

"So I said I'd—take Adam to meet you." Seth had been training his eyes on Adam the entire time. The effect was to leave Patrick feeling almost floodlit. The heat rushed to his face.

"That's...*workers*," he said.

"Now I know you're busy," Seth told him. "So we won't take long. Maybe Adam could just leave you his materials."

"Well." Adam frowned a little. "It would be helpful to know a little more about Patrick's business."

"Uh-huh."

"Only because I like to personalize my wellness strategies wherever possible."

"Of course," Seth said. "Of course. Patrick?"

Patrick uncrossed his legs, then crossed them again, then ostentatiously reached for the cheese knife. "It's a little hard," he said, "to explain." He tried to cut himself a thin swath of Havarti but came away with a large hunk. "To the layperson," he said. He stared at the hunk of cheese. He rubbed it between his fingers. "It's quasi-statistical," he said. "And it's empirical..."

Adam nodded. "Numbers," he said, forebodingly.

"Numbers," Patrick said.

"Numbers," said Seth.

Adam brought his finger to his lips, as though he were shushing them. "I've found," he said, "that people who are very quantitative are often not terribly qualitative."

"Uh-huh."

"And *wellness*, when you come right down to it, is about intangibles. It's about the things that *can't* be quantified, only *sensified*."

"I see," Patrick said.

"Do you see what I'm getting at?"

"I see." He leaned his head against the corner of the rocker, then pulled it back. "Oh! I just remembered. Before we continue, I have a business—thing. Before we continue, I need to talk to Seth about this thing of business. Which will not take more than a minute, if that's OK?"

"I'm in no hurry," Adam said grimly.

"It'll be just a minute. Seth?"

Seth looked up as though he were just learning his name.

"Seth?" Patrick repeated.

Seth got up, began to follow. Patrick caught him gently by the arm, and it was only a few quick locksteps before they were in the kitchen.

"What the fuck are you doing?" Patrick whispered.

Seth said nothing. His lips were puckered. His eyes were quivering like a compass needle.

"You bring this guy to my house," Patrick said. "Without any warning—under blatantly false pretexts—expect me to play along…"

The wet, involuntary smile had crept through Seth's lips. Exasperated, Patrick lowered his voice even further. "What is up with you?" he asked.

Seth made a sucking sound, and his mouth opened into a grin of reptilian brilliance. "Well?" he said at last.

"Well what?"

"*W-e-e-ell…*"

"W-e-e-ell what?"

Seth's eyes darkened. "I guess not," he said.

"What are you *talking* about?"

"It's not him?"

"Who?"

"Scottie."

"Scottie!"

"*Shh...*"

Patrick pressed his hand to his forehead. "He looks nothing like Scottie."

"He does. Look." From his pocket Seth pulled the original drawing—in fact, an intricately folded photocopy of the original drawing—and held it up to the aperture of the kitchen doorway until it came into alignment with Adam's head in the living room.

"Adam!" Seth called.

Adam turned his head. It was like the transverse motion of a coin: the etched profile moving, acquiring dimension, the planes of the face traveling toward the eye. He held his head in place for several seconds, not even questioning their scrutiny.

"See?" Seth said. "The nose, very straight. The eyes, ovalish but not almondish. The strong jaw."

"But no—no, I told you, Scottie has more of a curvy cartoon jaw. Like Dudley Do Right."

"Hm. So that's not just the caricature."

"No. And the hair is *dirty* blond, not blond, and I said *wavy*, remember?"

Seth shrugged. "Thought he might have cut it."

"And he's not nearly as tan as that. And the eyes are a little bigger and grayer, and the nose isn't—it's not *patrician*, it's just straight. And the *humor.* I know I mentioned the humor."

Indeed, it seemed to Patrick he had never seen a face so devoid of humor, of animal enjoyment. *The face of wellness.*

"Can't you get him out of here?" he asked.

"OK," Seth said equably.

"Soon?"

"OK. Do I have permission then?"

"To...?"

"Jump him."

"You're kidding."

"What? He's hot."

"Well, jump him somewhere else. My father'll be back any minute."

"We can't leave *yet*," Seth said. "Be rude."

"All right. OK, you have five minutes to get him out, OK? And I refuse to be of any more assistance. You have to carry this by yourself."

They walked gingerly back into the living room. Patrick repositioned himself in the rocker, and Seth sank slowly into the love seat, coiling his body so that it was facing Adam. He leaned his cheek against one hand and, with the other hand, made little flower patterns on the couch between his thigh and Adam's thigh. His eyes began to press against his glasses, and the long feathery eyelashes actually seemed to dart in and out, like a blind madly scrolling and unscrolling itself. *Fascinating*, Patrick thought.

"So, Adam," Seth cooed. "Wellness consultant. Is that like— teaching aerobics?"

"No," he said tersely. "Everyone asks me that, and it's just— it's such a small way of thinking. I advise businesses on how they can improve the well-being of their workforce."

"Oh."

"And it's not just exercise." He cocked his head in irritation. "I thought you understood that. It's nutrition, it's ergonomics, ventilation, mental health—"

"I can see that."

"—scatology."

There was a pause; Patrick was the first to crack. "Scatology?" he echoed.

"Oh!" Adam said, smiling for the first time in their brief acquaintance. It was like a guilty secret. "Don't get me started."

"On what?"

"Well—you see people have a hard time understanding what it is to be well. So one thing I always like to tell them is to celebrate their bodily functions. Which is very hard to do in our culture because we've been taught that belches are bad, farts are bad, shit is bad. And they're not bad, they just *are*. Your body has to purify itself, right? To keep itself healthy?"

"Yes. Yes," murmured Seth, running his finger now in the divide between the cushions.

Adam was warming to his subject now, he was leaning forward, wrapping his strong brown hands around one knee. "That's why they're called bodily functions—your body is *functioning*. Don't suppress it. Don't be ashamed. Celebrate it. The fart you just cut. The dump you had this morning."

Patrick believed that if he just stared at the ground long enough, the two other people in the living room would be revealed as illusions.

"I was wondering," Seth said in his most insidious tone, "how you feel about urine streams. I mean, *clear* is the way to go, right?"

As he escorted them to the door five minutes later, Patrick noticed that the box of Wheat Thins from which he had been serving had been gnawed open at one corner. *Did that just happen?* he wondered. *Did Adam eat it while I wasn't looking? As a fiber supplement?* Then he remembered: His father had left the box out on the kitchen counter last night.

"Here's my brochure," Adam said, holding out a little paper triptych.

Patrick unfolded it, scanned the various panels on vitamins and antioxidants, correct typing posture, "burning while you're earning." He studied Adam's strangely blurry black-and-white cameo portrait and the inked-in lines of sunlike radiation emanating from it. He carefully refolded the brochure, tapped it against his chest, took a quick backward glance at the box of Wheat Thins.

"Do you know anything about killing rats?" he asked.

22

"Do you know anything about killing rats?" he asked Sonya. He had just finished his 17th performance of the chorus from *Judas Maccabaeus*. His intonation was getting worse the more he played it. Sonya told him he had a fear of success.

She pondered his question now, waggled her bow speculatively. "You mean like *rat* rats, right? Not *men*."

"No, rat rats. Norway rats."

"Wow. You know, before I was married I used to use those, you know, *humane* traps. But I couldn't bring myself to look at the things once they were trapped—the noise they made! I couldn't do what you're supposed to do, which is take them in the woods and set them free. I mean, I just couldn't *touch* 'em. So they died of starvation, which is probably the least humane way to go."

Rodent poison was one of the many things Sonya banished from her house in order to keep her womb pure. The womb was still empty, unfortunately: She and her husband were having no luck conceiving. They had staked everything on alternative fertility treatments because of their ingrained distrust of the Western medical establishment. And here it was, a year later: They had covered the entire Kama Sutra, consumed many gallons of synthesized ginseng soup and Thai horseradish, and were no closer than when they started.

"I really think it's mental," she told Patrick. "I *really* do. I think—no, relax your elbow, that's right—I think, you know, when I'm ready to—no, see, your wrist is tightening up again. Do you feel that? Do you feel how tight that is?—I mean, emotionally, spiritually, biologically *ready*—God, look at your neck; ouch—then, you know, it'll happen, it—Hey, aren't you sick of this piece? Yeah? Let's just go on to the next one."

"I don't get it," Seth said.

"What?"

"Such a small town, D.C."

"True."

"*Gay* D.C.—even smaller. Smaller than Mayberry. Smaller than Dogpatch."

"True."

"And we still haven't found him." Seth creased his mouth into an inverted U shape. He fingered a tiny bead of sweat on his hairline, then casually flung it away. It was the middle of August, and finally, as promised, he was starting to look cooler. "How's your sandwich?" he asked.

Their debriefing lunches had somehow turned into a weekly ritual. The only thing that changed from week to week was the restaurant. Today's was a New Orleans bar that looked like it had once been a fire station: It had high ceilings, tightly spiraled iron staircases, and opening onto M Street, large portals that you could almost see dalmatians skidding through. Patrick had ordered an oyster po'boy, and Seth was staring down at his Cajun Caesar salad, joylessly playing with a crouton.

"I've hit every bar I can think of," he said. "Some bars twice.

Canvassed Dupont Circle. Walked down 17th Street. Stood through all those *Golden Girls* reruns at J.R.'s. Gyms, restaurants, coffee shops. Nothing."

"Well—listen, I know you've made a hell of an effort. I *really* appreciate it. I really—"

"People *recognize* me now. They run up to me. 'You found that guy yet? The patio-furniture guy?' Which is scary but reassuring, yes? We've generated awareness."

Patrick slowly rotated his plate. "You're not…" He rotated again. "You're not going to attract the wrong *kind* of attention, are you? I mean, Scottie's not going to end up in a police lineup, is he? Or in the papers—or on *Hard Copy* or anything."

"Of course not," Seth said. His face looked absurdly serious. "Not even Barbara Walters. We stand firm."

Patrick nodded quickly, blotted his lips. "It's just—I worry, you know? I don't want to turn Scottie into some—*notorious* thing, you know what I mean? Like something they'd do a very special hour of television about. I want it to be more intimate than that."

"It will be," Seth said.

"I know that sounds silly."

"No, no, no."

"I just—" Patrick broke off. There were times—this was one of them—when he wasn't sure whether Seth was soothing him or mocking him. It had become an increasingly nagging question. Was Seth's deadpan concealing an active, living relish of Patrick's discomforts? A contempt for the whole process?

Or maybe Seth really was empathizing. Maybe the two of them had some strange unacknowledged commonality. Could it be that the way Patrick felt about Scottie was akin somehow to the way Seth felt about Ted? That Ted elicited the same quality of abstract, overpowering yearning—and seemed just as far out of sight some days? There was no easy way of knowing. Patrick hated to probe, and Seth, who was so forthcoming about so many things—who would tell you about his first blow job, his recurrent hemorrhoid struggles—was oddly mum about Ted.

About the man who's driving this whole thing, Patrick thought. *The man we're doing all this for.*

Seth had shoved his half-eaten salad away from him. His arms were crossed now. He looked glum. "I'm down six pounds," he said.

"Congratulations," Patrick said.

"Thanks."

"So did you…" How to ask this. "Did you get *healthy* last weekend?"

"What? With Adam?" Seth gave a dry chuckle.

"I guess he didn't play along."

"Well, he started to. I don't know. Sex is not one of the bodily functions he celebrates."

"Oh."

"Something a little unhealthy, I guess. About sex."

"Yes."

"The things it makes you do."

"Oh, yes," Patrick said.

That evening, for the first time in nearly four months, he saw Alex. He was on his way home from work, walking down 18th Street, part of the horde streaming toward the Farragut West Metro station, when he paused at the northwest corner of K Street to wait for the light and spied at the furthest periphery of his vision a man—a man in a starched white shirt and olive trousers carefully entering codes into the NationsBank ATM.

Something about the way he pushed the buttons—the way the fingers paused briefly at contact and then moved deliberately forward, with the whole body following behind—made Patrick turn even before he recognized who it was.

It was Alex, ten feet away, gathering money.

Patrick's mind went almost blank. He forgot for a moment where he was, where he'd been going, what he was looking at— and then an associative memory seeped in. He remembered how Alex had always chided him for forgetting to take his ATM card out of the machine and how Patrick had protested once: "It's no big deal. I've never had any money stolen."

And Alex said, "No one's ever broken into your house either. Does that mean you should leave your keys hanging in the front door?"

And then, after thinking it over a few seconds, Alex added: "Oh, that's right—you do that too."

Patrick almost laughed now, thinking about it. There had been such a comic air of defeat in Alex's voice. *Oh, you do that too.*

And now the machine was making its scraping noise, and the bills were sliding from their orifice, and Alex was plucking them with his right hand, and, yes, with his left hand he was carefully removing the ATM card and returning it to its special fold in his wallet—doing what all correct beings should do—sliding the cash neatly into the bill compartment, closing the wallet, placing it in his back pocket. And any second now, he would turn and find Patrick standing there at the corner, and they would have to greet each other, and some communication, some escalation of meaning would have to occur.

Patrick shook himself. He hurried into the intersection, jogged to the other side.

The wonder, really, was that they hadn't bumped into each

other before—their offices were only four blocks apart. Alex worked for an automobile manufacturers' association. He was a meetings and conference planner—one of those rare cases where a man's personality finds perfect outward expression in his job. It may have been that what saddened Alex the most about his two years with Patrick was the way the relationship refused to be organized, the way it missed deadlines. Surely if you gave something two years to shape up—if you set clearly defined performance goals for it—it would have to respond. It would have to acquire some of the organizational rigor that had been invested in it.

Does Alex still plan meetings? Does he still work in that building? Patrick had no idea. He knew nothing about this man anymore.

Except Alex was skinnier—that much was obvious. The brown woven-leather belt had cinched his waist like a tourniquet. Clearly, six-course meals at the Inn at Little Washington were no longer a part of Alex's universe.

What does this mean? Patrick wondered. *Is he unhappier? Has he just given up on the whole food thing?*

Or was this what accrued from living with Ted? The strict physical culture that Ted imposed on his men—Seth, for instance, who was even now, months after their breakup, frantically shedding weight. And who knew how many others had been discarded—would be discarded—on similar grounds?

For the first time in his memory, Patrick found himself worrying about Alex. A strange sensation. He had become so used to thinking, every time something happened or failed to happen, every time he encountered some problem with his house, with his car, his life, *Alex would take care of this. Alex would know what to do.*

And as the eastbound Orange Line train bore him home,

Patrick reminded himself: Alex had known what to do. Alex had done it.

"*Hel*-lo."

"Rick! It's Patrick."

"Patrick," he said evenly.

"I know it's been—I've been meaning to call—"

"Hey, whatever. I've been busy."

"Yeah, well. Yeah. So, hey," Patrick said, "do you want to get together some time?"

"Um…sure. Actually, I was going to see if you wanted to go to Wolf Trap."

"Oh?"

"Next Sunday night. The National Symphony Orchestra's playing."

"Wow, that'd be great."

"You don't mind Steve and Eydie, do you?"

"Steve and Eydie."

"They're the special guests," Rick said. "It's, like, some salute to their careers."

"The NSO is saluting Steve and Eydie?"

"Yeah, I know it's kind of silly. I just—I sort of grew up on those records. My parents were always playing them. You know, "Blame It on the Bossa Nova," that kind of thing."

"Uh-huh."

"So, is that OK?"

"Yeah, it's—"

"I mean, it's not just Steve and Eydie."

"No, I—I like good marriages."

23

"Steve and Eydie?" Marianne said.

"Shut up—you went to Yanni."

"So I did," she said. "So I did."

"Anyway, you don't go to Wolf Trap for *music*, you know. You—you sit out on the lawn, drink the wine, wiggle the toes, that kind of thing."

"You should take your dad," she said.

"Oh, right."

"What?" she said. "Too early for him to vet the boyfriend?"

"First of all, as you know, Rick is not my boyfriend. Second of all, Da's got *plenty* on his mind as it is."

Of course, he was only speculating here. As far as he could tell, his father's major preoccupation now was ridding the house of rats. Mr. Beaton shared Sonya's abhorrence of rat poison. "That shit never goes away, Pattie," he explained. "It just recycles through your environment. You wake up one morning, your left nut's missing."

So his initial stratagem had been to spray the kitchen counters with a resinous Clorox-and–lime-juice solution—a very good friend of his from Banff (*Banff?*) had told him this was the most repulsive substance you could throw at a rat. It certainly imparted a distinctive scent to the kitchen and did a good job of preserving the occasional rat footprint—like a kind of fossil on the countertops.

"Well," said Mr. Beaton after a few days, "these guys are not as fastidious as Canadian rats."

He decided then that the problem was intrinsic to the house's structure and spent one afternoon crawling about on the kitchen floor, nailing little squares of plywood into the baseboard wherever he saw chinks. The next day, he patrolled the perimeter of the house, cramming in wads of lemon-soaked newspaper wherever he found breaches. At one point during his inspections, he ran into Deanna sitting on the back patio. She was reading a Graham Greene novel but set it down in favor of watching Mr. Beaton squirt lemon juice up one of the gutters.

"Good morning," she said. "A little corrosive, don't you think?"

"Let's hope so," he said.

The rats weren't too disturbed by any of this; they kept on chewing. They chewed whatever they could get their teeth on: bananas, apples, melons, cardboard. In short, they *thrived*—they were quite possibly the most contented rats in Christendom— and it was only a matter of time before Mr. Beaton availed himself of capitalist ingenuity. One evening, Patrick came home to find his father holding, like a chalice, a shopping bag from the Sharper Image—faint credit card fumes issued from it.

"Just the ticket, Pattie!"

"What?"

"It's a—a *sound* thingy. It sends out this high-frequency sound, drives rats crazy. Makes 'em run for the hills."

"Oh, yeah, I've heard about those. You turn it on when you go to bed—"

"And leave it on and leave it on until the rats finally move away. It's like leaving your stereo on too loud. Except only the neighbors can hear."

That night, they unwrapped the device, a small black hermetic box that emitted two frequencies: high and higher. Mr. Beaton wedged it against the refrigerator kick plate, flipped the switch, and tiptoed away like Wile E. Coyote. The next morning they found rat droppings stretching across the kitchen counter in a kind of hieroglyph.

"See, Pattie?" Mr. Beaton said. "We're scaring the *shit* out of 'em."

The machine continued transmitting through the day and the following evening. Later that night, Patrick, fast asleep for once, felt a hand jarring him awake. It was his father.

"Come see, Pattie!"

The two of them crept downstairs, their knees creaking, the steps creaking back. Mr. Beaton put a finger to his lips and motioned for Patrick to go forward. Patrick's heart caromed inside his chest as he moved in agonizing increments toward the kitchen doorway, flattened himself against the wall, and craned his head until he was just able to see into the room.

There were about five of them, making crazy beelike motions on the moonlit kitchen floor. Each time they approached Mr. Beaton's device, they made a high-pitched piercing sound and hastened away—but only a few feet away. Their sport had been slightly complicated, but roughly half the kitchen remained their fairground.

How large they were, Patrick thought. He gazed with rapt horror at their sadistic overbites, their tails trailing behind them like gummed-on string. He remembered Winston, the hero of *1984*, foreswearing love and ideology because a pack of creatures just like these were heading straight for his face. *I wonder if I would have done the same thing,* Patrick thought. *Would I have given up Scottie? Many things, certainly, but Scottie?*

"I think we need an exterminator," Patrick said.

His father, at the bottom of the stairs, closed his eyes and tilted his head, as though he were adjusting a headset. "It's…"

Blinking away sleep, the two of them remained there another minute, mesmerized by the bursts of rat squeal over the high-frequency ostinato of the black box. "It's almost like music, isn't it?" said Mr. Beaton.

For some reason Patrick's sleep cycle was becoming more synchronous with his father's. Saturday morning, for example, they both woke shortly after 8, in virtually the same post-operative stupor, and they wandered about the house like each other's shadows, speaking in vowel combinations. A little past 9, the phone rang.

Patrick grabbed it. "Eyo?"

It was Seth. "Listen," he said. "I've got a new candidate."

"No. No, it's too early…"

"I just met him. Walking his dog."

"No."

"Patrick, listen to me. I'm almost positive. Almost 96% sure. Ninety-seven percent sure. It's the Scotsman."

"No."

"He wants to meet you."

All the questions that should have occurred—that would have occurred with a few more minutes of consciousness—didn't. Everything was just a layer of static behind Patrick's eyes.

"My father's here," he said at last, a little desperately.

"Well, tell you what," Seth said. "We ring the doorbell, yes? If it's *him*, you say 'Come in.' If it's *not*, you say, 'Oh, I'm—I'm doing something. I'm very busy doing something.' And we scram instantly."

For the next few minutes, Patrick went through the rituals of making coffee, separating grapefruit sections, boiling water for his Cream of Wheat—and the more he tried to distract himself, the more the tongues of dread lapped into his stomach. There was something a little terrifying, he thought, about Seth's methodology. *How does he lure all these people over here? Don't they know better? Didn't their mothers ever warn them? About people like him?*

And then the dread subsided for an instant and a new thought broke in: *What if it's really Scottie?*

That, of course, was the seedling of hope that nothing could quite crush—not Seth, not Alex, not his father, not his own ineffectuality, not the months of waiting, of doing nothing as frantically as possible. It was always there, germinating: the inconceivable possibility of Scottie. The possibility that 152 days after the first sighting everything could be transformed in one second.

Oh, shit!

Leaving his coffee half-drunk on the counter, he bolted upstairs, ran into the bathroom, examined himself dolefully in the mirror. A fitful night's sleep haunted by the sound of rats scurrying in the eaves above his bed had transformed his hair into a kind of lopsided cone with a pompadour rising in front. He turned on the faucet and began splashing water on his head. The more he splashed, though, the less his hair wanted to absorb, and when he took a comb to it, the comb lodged halfway toward the scalp and wouldn't disentangle itself.

"Shit!"

He ran to the shower, turned on both knobs with a quick wrench and then sprang back as the water cascaded over him, dislodging the comb and drenching his T-shirt from the chest upward. He gasped, ripped the shirt off, and began wringing it over the toilet with one hand, while with the other he groped blindly for the comb on the bathroom floor.

And then the doorbell rang.

"I'll get it, Pattie."

"No!" He yanked the shirt back over his head and bounded down the steps, running his fingers madly through his hair, watching the drops of water fly off him like a human car wash. He reached the bottom of the stairs and saw his father sitting at the downstairs table, holding the sports section in one hand and looking at him with incipient terror.

"I think it's just a friend of mine," Patrick said, hysterically calm, sweeping a few last strands of wet hair off his forehead. "Or—you know, it might be anyone; we'll just—we'll see, won't we?"

He walked very deliberately to the door, and then another thought burst into his consciousness. *Walking his dog.*

The man that Seth was bringing over—the man now at the door—had been walking a dog. Which made him a dog owner. Or at the very least, a dog lover walking somebody else's dog the way Alex had been walking a dog when Patrick first saw him. A dog lover who would expect the man sharing his life to be a fellow dog lover, to be up to the commitment of keeping, walking, loving a dog.

It was almost too much. He stopped four feet from the door. The breath was leaching from his chest.

The bell rang again. "Pattie?" his father said.

"Yes, all right."

He gripped the doorknob, closed his eyes, and turned.

24

The first thing he saw when he opened his eyes again was Seth, who was wearing nothing except a yellow tank top and a pair of blue nylon running shorts cut high on the leg. He didn't even have shoes on; it was less clothing perhaps than he had ever worn before. Baffled, Patrick let his eyes rest there a moment before shifting them with an almost muscular act of will toward the man on Seth's right, toward the man who was even now peering over Patrick's shoulder.

"Oh."

Either Patrick made the sound or his mouth shaped itself to make it. And for a few seconds nothing else was said.

A pendulum, Patrick thought. That was the only organizing metaphor he could arrive at. *The Scottie Pendulum*. It had swung entirely in the other direction.

In place of last week's Teutonic hard body stood a pleasant-looking, doughy, ginger-haired man wearing a flannel shirt with torn-off sleeves. He had large fleshy arms and hands that seemed even larger—hands for hurling Bavarian villagers out of your path. His eyes were deep-set, with fleshy lids, and his top lip curled upward to expose two prominent, yellowing front teeth. He weighed perhaps 240 pounds.

"This is Torvald," Seth said.

Torvald, still staring over Patrick's left shoulder, gave a curt nod, exposed a few more of his teeth, leaned one of his big hands against the door jamb.

"Nice to meet you," he said.

Seth was grinning so tensely that his two rows of teeth seemed to be merging together. "Well?" he said.

"I have a guest," Patrick said, drawing out each word. "Currently. But you guys could—swing by another time."

Seth let out an exaggerated sigh. "Oh, God," he said. "Oh, I knew it. We should have called." He took Torvald's elbow in a proprietorial grip. "Come on, let's go."

"Pattie!" His father's voice boomed out behind them. "Where are your manners? Have them come in."

Patrick might still have been able to get the door closed if Torvald, craning his head in a politely curious motion, had not already fastened on something inside the house. "Ooh," he said, in a blank, uninflected tone. "Ooh," he said again. "I love it."

And before Patrick could bar the way, Torvald had taken a few long strides into the living room and was laying loving hands on Patrick's secretary desk. Stroking the burnished cherry surface, dabbing at the leaded glass cabinet, caressing the iron cabinet key.

"Did you *buy* this?" he asked no one in particular.

Mr. Beaton, standing a few feet away in his Utica nightshirt, said, "That, I believe, was bequeathed to Patrick by my late mother-in-law. May she—" He stopped himself. "May she reap what she sowed," he said. Grimly now, he extended his hand. "George Beaton."

Patrick, his hand still on the door knob, began to recover himself. "Oh! Da, this is—Torvald? And…" He motioned to the solitary figure on the doorstep. "That's Seth."

"Pleased," Seth said, stepping forward and blinking rapidly in the electric light.

"May the road rise up be-*forrr* ye," said Mr. Beaton.

"You didn't tell me he was Irish," Seth whispered.

"Where are you gentlemen bound this morning?" Mr. Beaton asked.

There was an awkward pause as Patrick and Seth first caught, then avoided each other's glance.

"To the mall," said Patrick.

"To the auto show," said Seth almost simultaneously.

"The auto show at the mall," Patrick said.

"The upper-case Mall," said Seth. "The *Mall* mall."

"Well," said Mr. Beaton, "you'll be wanting a cuppa joe before you go, I think."

"Great. Coffee's great," said Torvald, looking up from the secretary. "Hey, you know what? *Iced* coffee would be even better."

"Iced coffee it is."

Mr. Beaton disappeared into the kitchen, and for the next two minutes they could hear his high tenor voice humming "The Java Jive." The sound of it seemed to transfix them because they didn't move: Torvald remained at the secretary, Seth about two feet inside the house, and Patrick suspended between them.

At last, with a tiny shrug, Seth walked over to the rocker. "Torvald," he said, easing himself into the chair. "Tell Patrick what you do."

"Oh. I teach antiterrorist driving techniques."

"Say again?" Patrick said.

"It's a service for diplomats and State Department employees. Say you're posted to some high-risk country like Colombia or

Iran or Bosnia—some place crawling with terrorists—the theory is that you need to know how to protect yourself. So we teach people how to evade pursuers."

"Where do you do this?"

"Some place out in West Virginia; I can't tell you where."

"He—uh…" Seth scratched the bridge of his nose. "He demonstrated one of the techniques on the way over here. We did a full 180 going down Constitution Avenue."

Torvald shrugged. "Not like the real thing. Normally, you have to do it going 55 on a water-slicked speedway. It's like a dream come true for some people."

"Like one of those 1970s cop shows," Patrick said. "Quinn Martin production."

"He also gets to take people to shopping malls," Seth said. "Follow them around. So they get used to being—*surveilled*, I guess. Is that a word?"

"Surveilled?" said Mr. Beaton, reentering the room. He had gone deep into Patrick's cabinets to produce a mahogany-stained serving tray, on which he had placed four cups of coffee, a glass of ice, and a matching sugar bowl and creamer. "Now, please help yourselves," he said, seating himself at the dining room table. "Surveilled *is* a word but not a nice-sounding word." He planted his elbows on the table and stared into his coffee. Patrick could see he was deliberately calming himself: When he raised his head again, his eyes were bright and watery. "So." He smiled at Torvald. "You're involved in national security."

Torvald nodded curtly. "But my real love is antiques."

"That so?" said Mr. Beaton.

"Right now is a very exciting time. I'm in the process of opening an antique shop in Frederick, Md. I'm going to call it Armoires Are Moi. Of course, it won't be just armoires."

"No."

"And it won't be junk either. Do you know what I mean? None of those Eisenhower-era board games. Junky old almanacs and *Look* magazines. Cheesy neon place settings. None of that."

"Of course."

"Needless to say, I'm always on the lookout for interesting pieces. Frankly, I'm a little compulsive about it. I'd walk ten miles on my hands if I thought something nice would come out of it. That's how much I believe in what I do."

"There you are."

Torvald transferred his gaze to Patrick, slowly unveiled the rest of his teeth. "So how much?" he asked.

"How much?"

He pointed to the secretary. "For taking it out of your life? How much?"

"Um…" Patrick ostentatiously turned his gaze to Seth. Seth was studying his own feet.

"Unless," Torvald said, "you want me just to make an out-and-out offer."

"No…"

"I mean, I probably shouldn't tell you this, but it's the *perfect* complement to this Pembroke desk I found last month in Ellicott City."

Seth was up on his feet now, smiling shyly and sidling over to Torvald, clapping him on the shoulder. "I'm sure I said Patrick was only—*thinking.* Of selling it, you know. Not a done deal or anything."

"That's funny," said Torvald with a quizzical smile. "I think *done deal* were the very words you used."

"Huh." Seth grinned, shook his head. "Wow. Are you sure?

Done deal. *Done* deal."

"As I *understood* it," said Torvald, turning back to Patrick, "you couldn't bear to look at the thing anymore."

"Couldn't *bear*?" Seth said. "Was that the word?"

"I was *told*," Torvald's mouth tightened. "I was told there was some *tragedy* associated with the secretary, some bad association."

"Um..." Patrick felt the familiar passivity steal over him again. He couldn't speak. He couldn't defend himself. He had a dreamlike sense of his legs spinning uselessly beneath him. In short order, Torvald would be absconding with his secretary—and Patrick would not only have to give it up, he would be lucky to save the rest of his furniture.

For a few moments no one spoke or moved. *An animal,* Patrick thought. *It would really be helpful at times like this to have an animal.* Then George Beaton raised himself from his chair, cleared his throat, and gave his nightshirt a judicial tug. "Yes," he said. "Yes, there was a tragedy; I'd be lying if I said otherwise. Last summer—" He paused, took a swallow. "Last summer that heap of wood fell and killed a boy."

Torvald put a hand to his throat.

"And, yes, it was terrible," Mr. Beaton said, rising to a rhetorical pitch. "*Yes*, it was a terrible thing, but as I have told my son, You cannot blame yourself. And you *certainly*—" He flung his arm toward the secretary. "You certainly cannot blame this hunk of carpentry for doing what gravity tells it to do."

"I don't get it," Torvald said. "It's flawless. There's not a scratch on it."

"No," Mr. Beaton said, smiling ruefully. "The scratches are..." He jabbed at his own chest and fell silent.

"Patrick!"

The voice came from behind. Patrick spun around. A man

stood in the open doorway, illuminated and darkened by the sun. He had cautiously extended his head into the house and now withdrew it as the people in the room turned to regard him. Patrick blinked twice, began inching toward the door.

"Is this a bad time?" Rick asked.

25

In that instant, Patrick was aware of two things. First, he had left the door open. This was perhaps the surest sign that Alex was no longer in his life. Alex had been flexible on some matters but never on leaving the door open while the air conditioning was running. "Dollars," he would chant whenever he caught Patrick or somebody else doing it. "Can you see them? Dollars flying out the door."

The second thing Patrick realized was that he was wearing a soggy T-shirt, and the combination of indoor and outdoor climates had left his nipples frigid. That was about the only declarative statement he wanted to make right now. *Please know that my nipples are frigid.*

Rick had brought his whole body inside the doorway now. "I was just—*around*," he said. "But I can see you're busy."

"No, no!" cried Mr. Beaton. "Please. Please come in. I'm George Beaton, Patrick's father."

"I'm Rick."

"Pleased to—no, don't hang back, come *in*. We want a good look at you. Let's see now. You know—you know Patrick, obviously. I don't think you've met Poorwall?"

"Torvald."

"*Torvald*, and then—Christ, tell me your name again?"

"Seth." The shoeless man moved in utter silence toward Rick, extending his hand like a duchess. "It's Biblical."

"Pleased to meet you," said Rick.

"*Enchanté,*" said Seth.

"Excuse me." Torvald had crossed his beefy arms and was leaning against the secretary like a stevedore. "I need some clarity here, if you don't mind, on whether or not this is actually for sale."

Patrick looked down at the ground. "It's just—I'm sorry, we *can't*. You know, it wouldn't be fair. To the memory of..."

"Scooter," his father prompted. "Little Scooter."

"I see." Torvald uncrossed his arms, dusted something invisible off his wrists. "*Well,*" he added, "I can't say I accept your decision, but of course, it's your decision to make, so I must respect that. It was certainly very nice meeting all of you. I hope if you're ever in the Frederick area, you'll stop by and visit." He went to the door, paused briefly at the threshold, removed a business card from his shirt pocket, held it between his two outstretched fingers—then put the card back in his pocket. "Goodbye," he said.

Is he going to do a 180 in front of the house? Patrick wondered. He braced himself for the screaming tires, for the garbage cans flying through the air, the car alarms blaring...

Seth tapped him on the shoulder. "I have to go," he said.

"OK."

"*Go* go," Seth said.

"Oh! The bathroom's right..." He gestured toward the room off the kitchen, but Seth was already marching up the stairs. "Straight ahead," Patrick called up feebly.

"Well," said Mr. Beaton, "you and Rick have a beautiful day waiting for you."

"Actually, Da, it's kind of hot. It's supposed to get up to 98."

"Oh, yes, a *scorrrr*-cher."

"You didn't tell me he was Scottish," Rick whispered.

"But you must have a cuppa joe before you go," said Mr. Beaton.

"I really can't," Rick said. "I have to meet a friend for lunch. But listen, Patrick and I are going to a concert this Friday—if you'd like to come?"

No. No, no, no, no.

"W-e-e-ell…" His father shook his head gravely. "I find lately that music triggers petit mal seizures in me."

"Oh, I'm sorry."

"No, they're very, very petit." He gave Patrick a broad wink. "Nothing to worry about."

"Toilet doesn't flush very well," said Seth. He was laboring down toward them like a chambermaid.

"No," Patrick said. "No, it doesn't."

"Sometimes I think there's a poltergeist in it, you know," said Mr. Beaton.

"That explains the little pinch I felt," Seth said. He stopped at the bottom of the steps, as though he were presenting himself for inspection. Patrick inspected him. His tank top had narrow black-and-white vertical stripes, and his shorts had wide green-and-yellow vertical stripes. What was really surprising about him, though, was the paleness of his shoulders—the way they contrasted with his dark-complexioned face and hairy arms—and the muscular definition in his lean torso. An athlete—who knew?

Seth's long eyelashes were unfurling now. In Rick's direction. "Are you going back to town?" Seth asked.

"Union Station," Rick said.

"Would it be imposing? I mean, could you drop me off? At the Metro?"

"Sure."

"Not out of your way?"

"Of course not—it's right there."

"Very nice of you."

"Not at all."

There was an undeniable note of menace in the air, but Patrick couldn't quite tell from where it was emanating. Mr. Beaton was smiling benignly, bracing his coffee cup against his belly; Seth was moving with deliberation toward the door; Rick was backing onto the doorstep.

"I'll see you Sunday," Rick said.

"Yep."

"It was nice to meet you, Mr. Beaton."

Looking a little like the Ancient Mariner, Mr. Beaton walked over to Rick and gently placed a hand on his left shoulder.

"Rick, is it?"

"Uh-huh."

"Do you know anything about killing rats?"

When Patrick called later that afternoon, Rick answered in the usual breezy fashion, on the usual second ring, and they began chattering as if nothing had happened, as if they hadn't even seen each other that morning, and Patrick began to feel somehow that they had resumed without either of them having to make a point of it.

"I liked your father," Rick said.

"Oh. Yeah, he's…"

"Yeah."

"He really is."

"Now *Seth…*" Rick let the name hang there for a few moments. "Is a little odd."

"Well, yeah."

"What does he do again?"

"He lobbies on behalf of mattress manufacturers."

"Does he always sweat like that?"

"Um—apparently it stops around September. I'm sort of used to it."

"He kept *talking*, you know, the whole way to Union Station. Something about inner warriors. He asked me if I'd found mine yet."

"What did you say?"

"I said, 'No, I don't think I have one.'"

"And what did he say?"

"He told me I haven't met the guy yet who can draw it out of me."

"That's interesting."

"Do you think it's true?" Rick asked.

"Well—I don't think anything Seth says is necessarily *true*."

"But if I had an inner warrior," he said, "then I'd need someone to draw it out of me."

"Yes, you would."

26

"Sorry," Seth said.

It was the first time they had talked since *L'Affaire* Torvald, and they were having lunch not at a restaurant but at a cafeteria, a sweltering place with exposed heating ducts and no air conditioning and a permanent menu display amended in ten places by masking tape. Three Muslim women clothed from head to foot in black were pounding on the lemonade dispenser, and the Pakistani cashier couldn't get his register to work.

"What are you sorry about?" Patrick asked.

"You're—being ironic?"

"I am."

"Then I'm still sorry," Seth said.

"You know, I wouldn't mind so much your bringing people to my house. I mean, it's—it's very nice of you to be so dedicated to your *work*. It's just, it would be nice to know, kind of, what you've told them. In advance."

"I know. I know, and I'm—I'm sorry it wasn't the right guy. I guess I thought maybe Scottie had gained. Some weight. Since you saw him last."

"Some height too."

It was so hot that Patrick was beginning to feel like Seth. The sweat was jumping from his pores. He dabbed his forehead with one of the tiny paper napkins that came out of the dispenser 20 at a time.

"Enjoyed meeting your friend," Seth said. "Rick? Is that his name?"

"Yes."

"Very attractive."

"He's nice-looking."

"Is he single?" Seth asked.

Patrick regarded him for a moment. There had been no change in Seth's tone or attitude: He was still munching tediously on a pita sandwich with bean sprouts and cucumber, still taking tiny periodic sips of lemonade.

"As far as I know," Patrick said.

"What's your father writing?"

"Writing?"

"When I went upstairs. He had this laptop. With all this writing on it."

Patrick set down his iced tea. "My father has a laptop?"

"Didn't read what was on it. Looked like a memo. Or a letter."

"Hmm."

"Wow, you still don't know? What he's working on?"

"We don't—that's not the kind of relationship we have."

Which begged the question of what kind of relationship they did have. A question that might be better considered when it was less hot.

"Well," Seth said, "don't get upset or anything. You may be getting another visit. This weekend."

"Oh, God. No."

"Relax. I'm being much more cautious this time. Really. Going to scrutinize. Screen all the variables. No mistakes."

"I'm—please don't."

"You know what? I won't even come over with him this time. So if it's not the Scotsman—you say, 'Oh, I'm sorry. I'm sorry, you must have the wrong address.'"

"Foolproof."

"Absolutely."

"Please don't do it."

"I must. *We* must."

Scottie Three arrived on Sunday morning. Mr. Beaton had chosen that morning to go to Dunbarton Oaks. A block away, the bells at Christ Church had just tolled the 11 o'clock hour. The compulsive gardener up the street had wrapped her babushka around her head, and an old man was toting groceries down the street in a wheelbarrow.

Patrick had spent a good part of the weekend preparing for just this moment—preparing, that is, by quelling any possibility of hope. So it was that when the doorbell rang and he opened the door and beheld the latest man sent his way by Seth, he could almost bring himself to the point of laughter at how far afield they had come.

Scottie Three. This is Scottie Three.

An extremely tall man—perhaps 6 foot 6—with wildly unkempt dark-brown hair, heavy square-framed glasses, translucent English skin, a slightly pickled look to his mouth, and a slumped, ungainly posture. He was wearing black leather dress shoes, suit pants, and a capacious London Fog rain coat with epaulets that were beginning to pull away from the shoulder.

"Hello," said the man in a dry, languorous voice.

"Hi."

"Mr. Beaton?"

Mr. Beaton. Patrick closed his eyes, but the dismaying scenarios kept scrolling away in the theater of his mind: *He thinks I'm—what? A tarot-card reader? A Motor Vehicles employee? A Cabinet official? What am I supposed to be?*

The disclaimer started to form in his throat: *I'm sorry. I'm sorry, you must have the…* But the words lodged there. He didn't understand what was happening at first. Then he recognized it: that mysterious empathy for total strangers, the empathy that swept over him without warning, when he least expected it— driving by a playground, for instance, and spotting a heavy boy sitting listlessly in a swing or standing aside to let an old woman pass him in the grocery aisle or now, beholding this man on his doorstep, this man in the grip of a fool's errand.

He's probably come here full of hope, Patrick thought. *He thinks I can help him.*

"Yes, I'm Mr. Beaton," he said. And he found himself actually ushering the Scottie impostor in and seating him on the love seat and asking if he wanted coffee or a banana or a defrosted bagel and hovering over him as solicitously as a dean's wife. And why? Why was he bothering?

"Or I have some Wheat Thins," Patrick was saying. "Or some Havarti with dill."

"No, thanks," the man said, waving him off. "Nice day, though, huh?"

"Yeah."

"For summer, I mean."

"Yeah." Patrick stared at the man's coat. "Is it supposed to rain?"

"No."

"I can take your coat if you want."

"Naw, that's OK," the man said, pulling the lapels a little tighter. He sat back on the couch, balanced his right ankle on his left knee, and silently drew a notepad from his coat pocket. He plucked a razor-tip marker from his shirt pocket, uncapped it.

"Where are you from, Mr. Beaton?"

In a way, it was a relief. Patrick had been worried about having to make conversation. Now it seemed he wouldn't have to.

"Pennsylvania," Patrick said. "Near Lancaster."

"Lancaster," the man murmured. "Know it well."

"Are you from there?"

"No, I'm from Wisconsin, believe it or not. I grew up on a dairy farm."

"Oh, yeah?"

"Yeah."

"I'll bet you—see a lot of cows on a dairy farm."

"A lot," the man said.

It would be nice to have a dog or a cat right now, Patrick thought. *It would be nice to know what he does. An economist? With the Agriculture Department?*

"Now—how long have you been living in the area?" the man asked.

"I don't know." *Pollster? Statistician? Print journalist?* "Maybe ten years."

"Do you have any history of law enforcement problems?"

"Um…no," Patrick said. *Criminal law professor? Gun lobbyist?* "I mean—do you mean have I been arrested?"

"Is that what you think I mean?" the man asked.

"I'm not sure." A foolish grin broke across his face. "It's—I mean, no, I haven't been. Arrested. But you know," he said, "you never told me where you know Seth from."

"Seth?" the man asked.

"Yeah, you—Seth?"

"No."

"You know, kind of short and—and whiskery and blue-eyed?"

"No." He shook his head.

And all Patrick thought at first was, *Great. Seth's using make-believe names.* That's when he began sorting through his assumptions, peeling them away like extraneous clothes. One by one, the premises evaporated, and he almost shivered at what he was left with.

"I've…" He stood abruptly. "Can you excuse me? I just have to make a quick call."

"Where's the phone?" the man asked.

"It's—in the kitchen."

"Right in there?" he pointed.

"Yes."

"OK then."

Patrick dialed slowly.

"Hello?"

"*Seth.* Did you send a Scottie over here?"

"No."

"But you said you were going to send one over—"

"No, I told you. I was going to look him over again. Before I did."

"And?"

"It wasn't him," Seth said. "Rejected him out of hand. Didn't bother sending him."

"Then…" Patrick dropped his head until it was resting against the microwave door. "Shit."

"What?"

"Never mind."

The man was drawing helixes on his notepad when Patrick returned to the living room.

"I'm sorry," Patrick said, "I didn't get your name."

"Oh!" The man tapped himself lightly on the forehead. "I always forget that stuff. Hold on." He fumbled through the dozen or so compartments of his raincoat, patting and stabbing until at last he retrieved a wallet, opened it, riffled through the cards, pawed at one until it came out. He talked to himself the entire time: "It's—come on—no—shit—OK, *here!*" He held up a photo identification card. "Bill Lamprecht," he read aloud. "Central Intelligence."

Patrick sat down slowly on the edge of the coffee table. "As in agency?"

"Yeah."

"Wow. I'm sorry. I was thinking you were someone else."

"Who?"

"Well—I don't know exactly, just not—who you are. I mean, I thought you were sent over by a friend of mine."

"That would be Seth?"

"Yes…"

"And who is Seth?"

Good question, Patrick thought. *I'll answer that, and each answer will create another question, and each question will unravel more of the skein—Seth, Ted, Alex, Scottie, love, life, the whole shitty history. Within minutes this stranger will know everything it is humanly possible to know about me and will be none the happier or wiser for it.*

"I'm sorry," Patrick said. "Could you—it would really help if I knew why you were here."

"Oh, I think you know, Mr. Beaton."

"I do?"

"I think you do," the man repeated, with slightly less certainty.

"Can you give me a hint?"

"Let me place this in context for you, Mr. Beaton. When an individual repeatedly pesters CIA officials with phone calls, when that individual files repeated requests for patently classi-

fied material"—he began doodling again in his notepad—
"when, on August 23rd of this year, that individual is detected
by security cameras inspecting the perimeter of the Langley
building"—he made a triumphant stroke with his pen—"given
this concatenation of circumstances, I don't think the individual
in question should be surprised to hear from an agency repre-
sentative. I don't mind telling you we're concerned, Mr. Beaton.
We're very concerned."

Maybe it was the final "Mr. Beaton" that broke through the
fog. Patrick reeled as though he'd been cudgeled and then
found himself suddenly becalmed and lucid.

"I believe," he said, "you need to speak to my father."

"Your—hold on." Once again, the man fumbled through his
coat and, from some improbably large pocket, pulled out a
mud-colored dossier. *How did that fit in there?* Patrick wondered.
The dossier had a large exterior but not much inside, only a few
mimeographed pages with stapled-on routing slips. Agent Lamprecht leafed through them testily, licking his thumb, tugging
each page, and then snapping it back down.

"OK, OK—*shit*—all right, here it is," he said. "*George* Beaton."

"That's my father."

"Your fa—"

"I'm *Patrick* Beaton. Son of George."

"The—the *s-s-s*…"

Almost tenderly, Patrick said, "I think your confusion may
stem from the fact that my father is living here. In my house. I
think that may account for the confusion."

The agent turned over some more pages, then closed the
dossier, set it on his lap, and folded his hands primly across it.
"Huh." He gave a quiet snort. "Hey, I'm *sorry* about that. Geez.
You know, the thing is, it's not my case, really. Agent Lorca's on

maternity leave, and I just grabbed her files and ran out the door, and I've been ten minutes behind all day. It's..." He scratched his head. "Color me *pink*!" he said.

Roughly four hours later, Mr. Beaton was seated in one of the dining-room chairs, with his knees and ankles touching, his hands resting on the edge of the table, his head bowed slightly, his eyes studying the floor. Between him and the door stood Patrick.

"What can I say, Pattie? It's a misunderstanding. I'll just call them tomorrow and explain."

"Da, they had xeroxed *photographs* of you. Snooping around the CIA building."

"Well, how else is a fella going to do research?"

"Research for *what*?" Patrick asked. Even as he asked, he realized he was creating a new level of meaning in their relationship. "Research for what?"

"Well—I hate to jinx these things, Pattie. You *know* that."

"I think it's time you told me. I really do."

"Well—see, it's got a provisional name."

"Which is?"

"You really need to know this?

"I really do."

"It's—I mean, if you must know, it's my—Cold War Personal Security System."

Patrick blinked twice. "I'll need a little more."

27

Afterward, what would stand out in Patrick's mind was not so much Mr. Beaton's idea as the lack of conviction it carried. His father, of course, had had a great many ideas in his lifetime—in the past five years alone: a gourmet bean store, a fondue catalog, a solar-powered lawn mower, a weasel ranch—but the ideas had always, at some level, been irrelevant. It was the passion behind them, that was the only thing that had meaning: the way his whole body could become absorbed in the telling, the way his voice could, like a march tempo, create a galvanic response in your own body, sweep you along for a short distance—a very short distance.

But this time it was different. Maybe it was because his hand had been forced too early—he hadn't composed the spiel, he lacked fluency. He spoke in disconnected fragments, and he seemed to lose energy as he went along, spiraling down to a kind of stage whisper. When the words ran out, his hands dropped into his lap, and his head sank to one side, like a marionette's.

"You OK, Da?"

"I must have…" Mr. Beaton exhaled a little, gave his cheeks an experimental pat. "I must have gotten too much sun today."

"You'll call Agent Lamprecht tomorrow?"

"Of course, of course. Yes, of course."

"So what's he up to, anyway?" Marianne asked.

"It's not even worth telling you."

"Patrick, it's *me*, baby."

"Well, he's—he's trying to broker a *deal*, I guess, with the CIA. To start marketing all their old Cold War paraphernalia."

"Paraphernalia?"

"Yeah, all those secret weapons and surveillance devices and little, I don't know, James Bond killing toys—all that stuff we used against the Russians that we don't really need anymore. Unless someone else becomes the Russians or the *Russians* become the Russians."

"Wait a minute. He wants that shit in the hands of the U.S. consumer?"

"Well, slightly sanitized versions, yeah."

"Jesus."

"I know."

"I mean, get thee to a militia."

"No, no, it's not about insurrection, it's middle-class homeowners. He figures crime's on the upswing, right? Criminals are becoming more and more sophisticated, like—little Blofelds. So American families need the kind of fortress they can depend on."

"What? A spy satellite in every home?"

"I guess."

"Oh, Mr. B."

They fell silent for a few seconds, as though they were watching a body being interred.

"You know," Marianne said, "we need to get him a woman."

"I know."

"At least a good lay. 'Cause he's a very attractive man, he's very charming. It shouldn't be that tough."

"No. We could advertise in *Soldier of Fortune*."

The Wolf Trap concert fell on the hottest day of the year. Sitting on his front doorstep late in the afternoon, waiting for Rick to pick him up, Patrick could feel the heat prickling his scalp and chafing his lips and bleeding into his sinus cavities. August had just passed, and his garden had turned brown and brittle—even the zinnias had a tawdry look, as though they'd been pollinated too much.

Patrick made his silent calculations. It was Day 161 in the Year of Scottie—161 days had passed, and he was no closer, and perhaps much further. And he was beginning to lose faith, not in *Scottie*—never in Scottie—but in himself. He wondered how much longer he could hold out. The call of the actual was very strong. The charms of a living, breathing man, with actual hair and shoulders and thighs and hamstring muscles (oh, hamstring muscles!) and a voice and a scent—it was all very potent. Even the prospect of being near it was potent—enough, he thought, to cloud your mind, to make you forsake the other things, the *unrealized* possibilities that had once seemed just as palpable, just as present.

At five minutes before 6, Rick drove up in a sapphire BMW. Patrick squinted at it for a couple of seconds, then took a few halting steps toward it, trying to make out Rick's features through the tinted glass.

Rick lowered the window. "You're coming, right?" he asked.

"Nice car."

"Oh, yeah, thanks."

"It's yours, I guess."

"Yeah, it's kind of old, though."

"As old as mine?"

"Oh, God, no."

They drove across the 14th Street bridge, up the George Washington Parkway. Patrick cracked open his window and sniffed the Virginia air—such a different smell on this side of the river, swampier, more organic. In the early evening sun the cars inching up the parkway had a futuristic sheen.

"I've been looking forward to this all week," Rick said, reaching for his hand.

"Oh—thanks. Me too."

"Whoops, could you close the window? I've got the AC cranking."

The storm hit just as they turned onto Spout Run Parkway. A few soft rumbles, then streaks of lightning, almost perfectly vertical, heading straight for earth. And suddenly they were somewhere else. The sky had gone black. The wind was blowing down chunks of trees, and the rain, heavy and greasy, raised puffs of steam from the road. Rick gripped the wheel and hunched forward, and Patrick sat back and watched the frantic, regular motion of the windshield wipers. Neither of them spoke.

By the time they reached Wolf Trap a half hour later, the storm had finished; an acrid stench met them as they opened their doors. Walking carefully down the hill that fronted the amphitheater, they staked out a few square feet of wet grass, threw down some unused garbage bags, and then laid two beach towels on top. Rick set out their dinner. He had purchased it from Dean & Deluca: spiced shrimp, curry chicken salad, chive potato salad, and tabbouleh. Patrick had brought the beer—it was Schlitz because that was the only thing in stock at the corner store. It was lukewarm from sitting in the car.

They sat aslant the hill and ate their food in silence. The lawn around them began to fill with people, and neither Patrick nor Rick seemed to notice. They didn't even look at each other. They might have accidentally reserved the same blanket. Now and then one of them would steal a glance at the other and smile tightly and keep eating.

I don't know him, Patrick thought. *I don't know him at all.*

Rick's family, for instance—how little he knew about them. Once or twice he had made some gentle inquiries, but the only anecdote he could remember now had to do with Rick's aunt who had been on *To Tell the Truth* in the early 1970s. She had tried to convince the panel she was a state supreme court justice but was exposed by Kitty Carlisle, who asked her what *quid pro quo* meant. She responded, lamely, that it wasn't in her line of law.

"Two of the panelists voted for her anyway," Rick said.

Rick was wearing Birkenstock sandals tonight and knee-length khaki shorts and a blue tank top with obscure Brazilian lettering—something about a carnival, maybe. His arms, with their scattering of fine black hair, were bracing him from behind, and his legs were extended flat on the ground, and he looked about as relaxed as a person can look.

Maybe it's fine we don't talk, Patrick thought. *It means we're comfortable, doesn't it? It means we don't have to fill up the air.*

He examined his plate of tabbouleh. A squadron of gnats had infiltrated it so thoroughly that it was difficult to tell the bulgur wheat from the insects. He threw the plate into a paper bag, bent his knees into something like Indian style, and surveyed the crowd—or rather, the two crowds—the yeasty mix of demographics: bottles of Merlot alongside bottles of white Zinfandel, overstuffed Bloomingdale's shopping bags alongside public-television tote bags and caned picnic baskets with recyclable utensils, the scalloped lines of hair, the gradations of color in the frames of women's eyeglasses. Patrick and Rick were the youngest people there by at least 15 years.

"I love this place," Rick said.

"It's nice," Patrick murmured. He took a couple of breaths and listened to the rattling of locusts.

The sky was still pale when the house lamps dimmed and the members of the National Symphony Orchestra filed in. In the off light they had a sort of phosphorescence, like exotic crickets, and Patrick half expected them to rub their legs together and launch themselves over the audience's heads. The opening strains of Barber's "Adagio for Strings" carried out to the lawn, and Patrick closed his eyes and imagined that the music was actually bearing him somewhere, unraveling the rope that held him to the pier, blowing on the bark. And it was such a familiar sensation, this feeling. He couldn't quite remember when he'd last had it, but it seemed to him he had picked up directly from that last time.

Cast off, he thought.

He woke up an hour later. *Oh, God!* He gasped, lurched toward the sky. He stared about him wildly.

"Enjoy your nap?" Rick was sitting with his knees touching his chest, smiling at him with an infinite patience.

"Yeah, *shit.*"

"What?"

"I hate napping."

"Why?"

"I just *do,* I just—who's that singing?"

"Eydie."

"Oh."

"Are you OK?"

"No. Yeah. I'm just…"

Irritated, he should have said. Immensely irritated and angry and so incoherent, he couldn't articulate any of it. It wasn't worth telling. *Not to someone who can't divine it on his own,* he thought uncharitably. And his thoughts seemed to feed on themselves, to nudge each other further. *Scottie would have understood. He wouldn't have needed to ask if I was OK. He would have known, wouldn't he?*

Rick probed no further, and Patrick lapsed into a stubborn silence that lasted the rest of the concert and continued during the long walk back to the parking lot.

"I hope you had an OK time," Rick said mildly.

"Oh," Patrick said. "It was fine. It was lovely—I'm sorry."

"You're tired."

"I guess so. I didn't think I was."

"Well, sometimes people have to tell you."

They were walking along a long row of combat-parked cars, listening to the gargling of engines, watching the pinwheeling of insects in the headlights. About 20 feet away, three young men were clambering into a big red minivan, a Plymouth Voyager. Patrick watched the lights wink on, watched the windshield wipers careen across the dry window (the driver must never have turned them off), observed with wry humor the telltale pink lambda sticker on the front bumper.

Gay men and their bumper stickers, he thought. He couldn't imagine ever having one himself. They were so hard to get off, weren't they? Those Dukakis and Gary Hart stickers—you still saw them on the road, as permanent as grave markers.

The three young men rolled down their windows and poked their elbows out, and as the van began inching down the lane and as Patrick began edging to the right to clear a path for it, he asked himself what had drawn his attention there in the first place and why he continued looking.

Because Scottie was in the back seat.

28

For about five seconds Patrick didn't move. He watched the big red Voyager as it crawled down the row of parked cars, turned the corner, and made for the exit, and his heart contracted and then exploded, and he found himself running, sprinting toward the escaping van, bursting through knots of slow-walking pedestrians, swinging his body in every conceivable direction just to keep the van in his vision, just to keep that single head in view, that elusive head, with its tufts of wavy dirty-blond hair poking through the vent of an Orioles cap. God, it was the right head, the *right head*—he almost wept at the thought—the head he had been seeking for 161 days—and now it was getting away. The van was sliding through the parking lot, gliding toward the exit, and cars were mysteriously parting for it, giving it wide berth, and within seconds it would be gone. Gone forever.

Should he yell? He could just open up his lungs, couldn't he? Open his mouth and scream.

Stop! Scottie, come back!

But Scottie wouldn't know his name. Scottie wouldn't even hear. The van driver would have turned the radio on, and Patrick's voice would be like some buzzing in the bass; they would adjust the controls to try to get rid of him. They would never know he was there.

A sob shook his chest. The van darted in front of a dawdling Volvo station wagon, cut expertly across the gravel, groaned onto the macadam, grunted, and then accelerated down the road toward the Dulles access highway.

And then everything else, the rest of the world, returned to Patrick's consciousness. He understood that he was standing alone on the edge of the road, staring after a departing van. He understood that his chest was heaving, and sweat was running down his neck, and people were walking by him, carefully not staring. He understood that he was now about 250 feet from where he had been 30 seconds ago.

Rick.

He began running again, back to where he had started—running even *faster* now because he was conscious of having exposed himself, having something to account for. He pumped his arms and hiked his knees and kicked up clouds of gravel. *Just like a little race*, he thought. *I'll say I was doing a shuttle run.*

But as he came to a halt next to the BMW, he could see that Rick's expression had hardened a little, his eyes had gone cool. Patrick stood a few feet away, dripping in his polo shirt, and the two of them regarded each other.

"You know, it'd be faster to drive," Rick said.

"Oh, I—" It helped that he was panting so hard; it gave him time to think. "I can't believe it—old—old friend of mine—from high school…"

The stirrings of a smile passed over Rick's face. "Must have been a very good friend," he said.

"Yeah, he—" Patrick bent at the waist and rested his hands on his knees. Why did he feel so out of shape? "Scott Sander—Scott—"

"Scott Sanderscott?"

"Yeah, I—I think he was Scandinavian."

"Huh."

Patrick gulped some more air. "You know, we called him Sandy, actually."

"That makes sense."

"We were lab partners. In 10th grade biology."

"Dissecting frogs?"

"Yeah."

"Well, it's too bad you missed him."

"Yeah." Patrick was standing up now. His lungs seemed to have folded in on themselves. He took a few more gulps of air. "Wow," he said. "Ol' Sandy. Sandy Sanderscott."

"All right," said Seth. "All right. Tell me everything you saw."

"OK. Well, first, he was wearing a—an Orioles cap."

"Excellent," Seth said.

"And the van was a Plymouth Voyager. But I don't think it was *his* 'cause he was in the back seat. Behind the driver."

"Doesn't matter," Seth said. "What was the license plate number?"

Patrick shut his eyes. "I knew you were going to ask me that."

"You didn't look at the license?"

"I know, I know, I should have. I mean, I kind of did."

"Kind of."

"I mean, it may have had letters in it."

"Letters."

"And if it had letters—then that means it's either from Maryland or Virginia, doesn't it?"

"The search is over," Seth said dryly.

"Well, what does it matter? It wasn't *his* car."

"Patrick. If you'd seen the plate, we could have found the owner. Could have tracked him down. Staked out his house."

"Oh, right, and then what? We attach radioactive tracers and—"

"Don't need tracers," Seth said. "We've got me."

Was there something in Patrick's silence that expressed skepticism? Was that why Seth felt compelled to add what he did?

"I'm harder to shake than a tick," Seth said.

Patrick had occasion to ponder the tick analogy that evening. It was 10 o'clock, and he was standing on the balcony overlooking his back patio. He had long ago ceded the patio to Deanna, and tonight, he thought, it was just as well—when he looked down, all he could see were insects. They must have been spontaneously created by the heat; they were everywhere. Whole battalions of beetles had clustered around a single particle of food wedged between the patio bricks—probably something from his father's breakfast—and taking possession of the balcony railing was a long, black, ciliated organism about the length of Patrick's index finger and so contemptuous of him, it refused to budge when he waved his hand at it.

Of course he doesn't move, Patrick thought. *He knows what he wants*. And he thought of Seth's tick, which somehow became interchangeable with the image of Seth: Seth hovering in the branches of an oak tree, waiting 20 years if necessary for the right host, for the perfect uncovered head, and then, not wasting a second, dropping in a plumb line, his mandible open wide, sinking into the scalp.

That's how I should have been, Patrick thought. *I should have just attached myself to that van. I should have held on for as long as it took*. And he hadn't. He had let Scottie slip out of his life for the second time in five months. And how many more chances would he have?

But then—he stopped himself—what would he have said if he had caught up to the van?

Excuse me. Excuse me, yes, you're the man I've always dreamed of, and I was wondering if we could discuss it over some coffee.

Scottie wouldn't recognize him. He wouldn't remember their initial meeting. All he would see was a strange, panting young man flailing his arms, babbling endearments, calling him by some name that wasn't his.

And you never—what was it his father used to say?—*you never get a second chance to make a first impression.*

Behind him the screen door slid open.

"Son, you've got a visitor—Jesus, tell me your name again?"

"Seth."

"It's *Seth*, Pattie."

Seth must have dressed in a hurry. He was wearing a candy-striped linen shirt so wrinkled that it looked as though it had been pleated horizontally. His shoes were an old, paint-stained pair of Converse All-Stars. In his right hand was a caramel-colored satchel that he held like a clutch purse.

"We've been going at this all wrong," he said.

Patrick nodded briefly, escorted him into the living room, sat him on the mission rocker. For the next 20 seconds or so, they observed a formal silence, listened to the ticking of Patrick's cherry-wood desk clock. Mr. Beaton, with unusual delicacy, had vanished upstairs.

"We haven't been strategic," Seth said finally, rearranging his glasses. "That's been our problem. We've been very scattered. Very *ad hoc*. That's why we've failed. *But...*" He made a little rallying motion with his fist. "We start over again, yes? We admit our failure and then we—we throw everything out. Start over again."

"OK."

"Now, I've been giving it some thought. Since last we talked. Been asking myself, What's the first thing we need to do? The very first thing?"

"Uh-huh."

"The answer came right away. Absurdly obvious." Seth tapped his temple three times in quick succession. "We create a *profile*, yes?"

"A profile?"

"Like they do for serial killers. Very basic process. First we figure out what we *know*, yes? Then we figure out what we can *infer*. And from there? We start zeroing in."

"Sounds like a plan."

"I've taken the liberty"—Seth reached into his satchel, drew out a yellow legal pad—"of preparing a profile myself." He ripped off the top sheet. "Here," he said. "Read, please."

Patrick took the paper, held it close to his face. The first line read: "Things we know about the Scottish Prince."

"The Scottish Prince," said Patrick, in a small voice. "Is that what we're calling him now?"

"We have to dignify it," Seth said. "We have to do *something* with it."

"The Scottish Prince," Patrick repeated.

> Things we know about the Scottish Prince
> —wanders around houses
> —has friends who drive a Plymouth Voyager
> —Orioles fan
> —could live in Maryland or Virginia (or not)
> —is gay (or at least comfortable with those who are)
> —has questionable musical taste

"I don't know about the last one," Patrick said. "I mean, *I* was at the concert too."

"Your point?"

"Well, I mean he could just have a—highly developed sense of camp. Or maybe he was dragged there like I was."

"Maybe *Rick* invited him."

"Please be quiet."

"What? Am I saying something?"

"No one *saw* us. If that's what you're worried about it. Nothing's going to get back to Alex."

"Me worry?"

Patrick gave a shake, resumed his reading:

> Things we might infer about the Scottish Prince
> —not a reader of "Glances"
> —not a bargoer
> —not part of the mainstream D.C. gay community
> —not a loner

"Well, yeah, but—those are all negative things," Patrick said. "These are all things he's not."

"Fine," Seth said. "Give me some positives."

"OK, he's—I don't know where you'd put this exactly, he's very—he's *masculine*."

"Oh, I see," Seth said, sneering slightly. He pulled a pencil from his shirt pocket and began writing. "*Mas*-cu-line."

"Also sensitive."

"Oh, sensitive *too*? How do we know this exactly?"

"Because..."

Because he let me sleep. When you got right down to it, that was the only indicator Patrick had. Scottie had done the most thoughtful thing a man could do in that situation. *He let me sleep.*

"Anyway, I hate that word," Seth said. "*Sensitive.*"

"Why?"

"It's like a code word. It's what they say about sissy kids. Seth is so sensitive."

"Well, leave it off then."

The two of them stared at the paper for another five minutes, bending over it now and again. Their shoulders grew more and more tense, began to merge with their necks, and their hands ranged uselessly across the tabletop, and finally Seth just grabbed the paper and began folding it up again.

"Actually," Patrick said.

Seth stopped folding. "Yes?"

"There's one more thing."

"Yes?"

"He has a tattoo. Just above his left elbow."

29

"A tattoo?" Seth's eyebrows climbed toward his hairline.

"Yeah."

"Why didn't you say so?"

"I just remembered."

"Tattoo of what?"

Think, Patrick. He closed his eyes. He propelled himself back to the Wolf Trap parking lot. He conjured up Scottie's arm—his bare arm! Hanging out the window of the van. The very thing Patrick had most wanted to see: Scottie's bare arm. And here it was again, blowing past him in memory, and he still couldn't get a fix on it. Something kept diverting his attention—some excrescence, a red smear, just above the elbow. He had thought it was dried blood at the time (why was Scottie bleeding?) but now it reassembled itself—not a drawing, a tattoo, a very small tattoo.

"It was a bird, I think. It was some kind of bird."

"A bird?"

"Yeah. Yeah. Absolutely. There was a beak and—some sort of talon deal."

"Like a hawk?"

"No, smaller and—sweeter, I guess. Like a songbird."

"What kind?"

"I don't know, a wren? A robin? Something like that."

"Well," Seth said, elaborately laying the paper on the table and scribbling on it with his pen, "so much for his being butch."

As soon as Patrick got to work the next morning, he closed his door, pulled out a sheaf of pink phone-message slips, and began sketching. His pencil was dull when he began, and 20 minutes later the point had almost disappeared, and he had amassed a pile of perhaps 30 sketches—the heads of 30 birds. Surveying them now, he realized he was even less gifted at drawing birds than at drawing humans. Most of them were slightly embellished stick figures; some were not quite anything. The only thing he seemed able to create was a kind of Disney caricature—the kind of open-mouthed, chirping bird that, if it were a decal, would keep children from running into sliding glass doors. But the creature on Scottie's arm had been more lifelike, hadn't it? More vibrant, ready almost to leap into a new dimension. And, of course, ineffable—like Scottie, like love.

The phone rang.

"So," Marianne said, "have we found that special someone yet?"

His chest tightened; his throat closed up. "Special—?"

"Your dad, remember? We gotta find him a woman."

"No, I—no."

"Well, listen, I'm thinking of this one gal. I don't know if I mentioned her. She's in my step class, and her name is Sally. She's very nice, and she's about the right age—I mean, she's early 40s, but don't you think your dad would want someone that age? I mean, someone younger? 'Cause he's very young, really. And I do think he'd enjoy Sally; she's cool, but, see, her big cause is Tibet. She pickets, like, every week outside the Chinese Embassy...."

The more she went on, the less Patrick felt himself attending to her words. *This is distraction*, he thought. *Avoid it. Focus. Be ticklike.* He tried to stop his ears and meditate on the bird drawings, but they seemed to mock him now, to declare his ineffectuality. So he began staring at the uneaten bagel in front of him; he tried to empty his mind, see nothing but the bagel—but the bagel wouldn't stay still.

"Oh, God," he said.

"What?"

"I—" He was going to say, *I didn't order a raisin bagel.* And as though to corroborate him, the raisins began moving—scampering in precise circles around the bagel's center, diving onto the paper plate beneath, racing toward Patrick's blotter.

"Yuck!" Patrick swept the plate into the trash can with his free arm.

"What?" Marianne repeated.

"Oh, it's—the woman in the office next to me. She started her own compost pile last week, right next to her desk, and now it's—it's Biosphere 3 around here."

"Yuck."

"I'm a little worried about my sandwich, actually."

"That's what you get, huh? Working with them tree huggers."

"That's what I get."

"Hey, listen. I want you to meet Victor, OK?"

"OK."

"I mean, you know, whenever."

"No, that's fine."

He was keeping his voice as neutral as hers, but they both understood how momentous this was. In 14 years of knowing Marianne, Patrick had almost never been afforded glimpses of her amours. It wasn't clear to him why this was—whether it was because his opinion mattered too much or too little.

"Probably next week," she said. "I'll let you know, OK?"

Patrick gathered the bird drawings into a neat pile and stapled them together. He held the sheaf in his hand for a moment, trying to decide whether or not to throw it away and decided, for no good reason, to keep it.

I have to. I have to keep it.

"We're going driving," Seth said.

"You mean—you're picking me up?"

"Of course not. I don't have a car."

"My car then."

"Yes."

"When?" Patrick asked.

"Saturday'll be fine."

"Where?"

"You'll find out."

This time around, they timed Seth's arrival for precisely 9:30, and as soon as the doorbell rang, Patrick opened the door just wide enough to slip through, yelling good-bye to his father and quickly closing the door after him. He needn't have bothered. Mr. Beaton was immersed in his library book. It was called *Rats: The Next Wave*, and he had been reading it consumingly for the last three days. Now and then he would lift his head for a reflection. "You know," he'd say, "if a Norway rat's mother dies, the other mothers raise the orphan. I think that's neighborly."

Closing the door now, Patrick felt his muscles unclench a little, felt the oxygen begin to percolate in his blood. More and more he was welcoming the chance to get away from his father, and this was as good a time as any—the first cool weekend in many, many weeks. People were actually emerging from their homes. The crazy gardening lady had taken off her babushka. Two young men in fraternity T-shirts were winging a frisbee down the parking alley. At the end of the block, a mother was pelting her young sons with hose water, cocking the nozzle like a gun.

No one had metamorphosed more strikingly than Seth, who was back to wearing chinos and was walking to the car now with a real authority, as though he owned it. His posture was straighter; his hair had been freshly cut, cut so close you could see the anointing of gray hair above his ears. He was even shaving closer. It was the first time in Patrick's experience that he could imagine Seth occupying a position in society.

Seth sat impassively in the front seat, his hands curved around the restraining belt. "Drive," he commanded.

"Where?"

"Fourteenth Street bridge. I'll take it from there."

He's enjoying this, Patrick thought. *It's the most enjoyable thing he's done in years.* The thought was actually comforting. Normally, Patrick alternated between being puzzled and guilt-ridden by Seth's interest in his affairs. It worried him to think that Seth might be devoting what little life he had to a search that would bring him no reward—unless it was the roundabout reward he desired, and who knew if that would ever happen? Who knew what would happen?

"By the way," Seth said.

"Yeah?"

"What's wrong with your car?"

Patrick looked over. Seth was shaking so hard, his glasses were bouncing up and down on the bridge of his nose.

"Oh. There's something wrong with the engine strut. Or maybe the muffler."

"Wow."

"Sorry, I've been trying to get it repaired."

"You know, it—it feels like one of those hotel beds—"

Even as he jiggled and jounced, Seth kept his gaze fixed straight ahead. His eyes seemed even more unnaturally blue than usual—the color of glacier water.

"OK," Patrick said, "we're at the bridge. Where now?"

"Bear left. We're going to get off on Route 1."

It felt a little like getting a driver's license. Patrick was suddenly filled with caution. He turned on the blinker, waited a couple of seconds, checked the rearview mirror, the side-view mirror, turned his head to the left, slowly edged into the lane.

"Here's what I'm thinking," Seth said, still looking straight ahead. "Consider: No one in the city seems to know him."

"No one we know."

"Consider the other things: The license plate you may or may not have seen. The Plymouth Voyager. The tattoo. The nautical metaphor from your first meeting—cast off. Significant, yes? Cast off. And then the general attitude of relaxation. Consider the—the choice of concert music."

"Uh-huh."

"To me…" Seth gave a tug on his restraining belt. "To me, it screams one word. It screams *suburbs*. The Scottish Prince is a suburban gay man."

"You really think so?"

"Oh, yes. Not distant suburbs, of course. Not with the lambda decal on the van. The decal tells me near suburban."

"OK."

"Which narrows it down, yes? Narrows the field. Turn right. Now all we have to do is find the appropriate nexuses. Between suburban and gay."

"Nexuses."

"All the places a suburban gay man would be most likely to frequent."

"Such as?"

"Such as..." Seth turned to look at Patrick now. His mouth was grave, and his brows were moving toward each other, and he gave a tiny, almost invisible nod of his head.

"Behold," he said.

To their right reared an expansive, pale brick warehouse with a teal-colored overhang—a warehouse that was even now emitting boatloads of human beings and dozens of overstuffed orange shopping carts. As Patrick rounded the curve, he fixed his eyes into a squint, trying to make out the blue sans-serif lettering on the front of the building, and Seth, perhaps sensing his difficulty, identified it for him, intoned the name with a liturgical hush: "Bulk Barn."

30

Patrick had never been to Bulk Barn. Not even in his fancy. He dimly knew it as a place of high-volume transactions—he equated it mysteriously with exchange floors—but he had never tried to picture it in his mind and had never imagined it as something that could be pictured. Now, as he and Seth scoured the parking lot for spaces, the sight of the pale, windowless warehouse stretching back beyond vision sent knives of cold air into him.

"I don't know," he murmured. And when at last, after a ten-minute search, they found a space, he said it again, a little louder: "I don't know."

Seth was already vaulting out of the car, slamming the door. His chest was thrust out.

"If Scottie's not here," he declared, "Scottie's not anywhere."

Patrick got out too, but more slowly, and he didn't shut his door. "Why here?"

Seth shrugged. "Just part of our demographic."

"So the urban gays come here too?"

"Urban, suburban, exurban—the whole gang." Seth squared his shoulders, straightened the collar on his shirt. "Let's go," he said.

"But don't you have to be a member or something?"

"*I'm* a member."

"How do you—I mean, how do you get to be a member?"

"It's not Mensa, Patrick. Ted got me in."

Patrick closed the door, but it didn't shut all the way. He unlocked it, reopened it, shut it again. "And it's OK if I go in?"

"Sure. You're my guest."

"OK."

"Why are you so afraid?"

"I don't know."

They jostled their way through the glass doors, and as it turned out, the swell of people was so enormous that no one was checking cards. Patrick had to suppress the urge to reach for Seth's hand. They shouldered through several waves of checkout lines, and they were about 20 feet inside the store when a woman ran over Patrick's foot with a shopping cart. The cart contained two large Michelin tires, and he had the momentary illusion that he'd been run over by an automobile.

"Sorry," said the woman, hurrying onward, flinging the word over her left shoulder.

"All right," Seth said. "We're going to fan out. *I'll* work the west wall. *You* work east and—why are you limping?—east and back around down the middle. Conduct your search and meet me at 10:30. At the hearing center."

Patrick took two deep breaths and began hobbling down the center aisle, along the bare cement floor, past blue jeans and air conditioners, past miter saws and basketballs, crates of soda and 9-roll paper towel sets, past ten-foot-high stacks of tennis shoes, past long tables of remaindered books, past vats of condiments. Five minutes later he still hadn't found the back of the store. The pain in his foot had subsided, but he moved with a wincing tread, and as he moved, he kept his eyes trained on the area directly in front of him. He had a notion that the hordes of people around him could best be addressed as a monolithic force, that the moment he began individuating them, he would be swept away by them.

But when he reached the back of the store—felt the reassuring touch of a large hunk of prosciutto in the deli case—he found he could summon the courage to turn around and fully regard things. It was suddenly quite pleasant to do so, to hear the international broadcast system of dialects and accents, accents he couldn't even recognize. To watch the Metrobus driver hoisting a great jug of orange juice over his shoulder. The pregnant woman journeying from sample stand to sample stand and the Hispanic couple hoisting individual towers of diapers that half-obscured their faces. *Children*—children in all postures of sleep, curled inside carts or underneath carts or buoyed in the space between the carts and their parents' arms—a fidgeting, brawling, grinning *army* of children. (Someday, perhaps, Sonya would be here with her own welter of Kama Sutra–conceived kids, buying 100 violin cases or 200 violin bows or a ream of sheet music.) A person could stand here for ten minutes and find enough human variation to last him for a lifetime.

But not Scottie. Scottie was nowhere to be found.

Will you really come? Patrick wondered. *If I stand here for a while? Will you come carrying a big seedless watermelon, a 24-pack of beer?*

And, as always, the act of imagining Scottie reignited his curiosity. Did Scottie drink? Almost certainly he did, but what? Patrick had no answer. He had no answer to anything—what Scottie read, what he did for a living, how he passed his evenings, his weekends. Even the things Patrick had actually *seen* didn't reveal anything. The two people, for instance, sitting with Scottie in the Plymouth Voyager: Who were they? What did they even look like? How long had they known Scottie? All Patrick could say was, there had been two of them—and maybe the numerology mattered more than anything. *Two* others—a couple, perhaps—and Scottie alone in the back seat. *Alone.* Waiting for the still-to-be-identified person who would sit next to him, share his beer, his seedless watermelon, his—his bag of sunflower seeds.

"No luck?" Seth had materialized at his side like a store detective, gripping Patrick's left elbow.

"No."

"Well, it's early," Seth said. He stood a few moments, surveying the long rows of French cheeses. "Do you want to stay here a while?" he asked.

"Sure."

"Good vantage point, yes?"

"Very good."

Twenty minutes later they were back in Patrick's car. Seth had decided, upon further reflection, that the best place to catch people going in or out of the store would be in the relative isolation of the parking lot. "Less conspicuous," he said. "Less distraction."

So here they were, camped between a cherry Saab and a shopping cart hangar, their windows open to the cool air, their elbows hanging out—and they were *staring*. That was all they were doing. Staring at the people spilling in and out of the Bulk Barn doors, staring *hard* and fixedly, and now and again, by a joint impulse, locking on to someone—someone who *might* do, someone who might in certain lights be thought to resemble the man they were looking for—and then their breath would hang suspended, and they would lean forward for a better look, position the man in their gun sights. And then, always, they would shake their heads and lean back and almost simultaneously rub their eyes. That was the strangest part, this final ritual—erasing from their consciousness anything that wasn't Scottie.

From time to time a car would pause in front of them expectantly, and they would have to interrupt their work to wave at the driver. *No*, they semaphored. *We're not leaving. Go away.*

By noontime the Oldsmobile had grown warmer in the unrefracted sun. Films of sweat were forming under Patrick's thigh and in the small of his back, and he realized he was tired. Maybe it was the effort of staring for so long at one place. Maybe there was an actual medical syndrome associated with Bulk Barn: *people* blindness. From looking too closely at people, for too long.

"Do you have fantasies?" Seth asked suddenly.

"Oh." Patrick slumped down in his seat. "Maybe. Sure."

"Would it be weird if I told you mine?"

"Yes, it would."

Seth's face was glowing now, with some hidden wellspring of feeling. He removed his glasses, dabbed at the skin below his eyelids. "I know you'll laugh."

"I won't."

"It's just—you know how it is in there?" He gestured toward the pale brick warehouse, still pregnant with shoppers. "All those gay couples? I mean, just normal boy-boy couples pushing carts. Two boys to a cart. And every couple is recognizing some other couple. And they're waiting in line and—complaining about how long the line is. And loading their stuff in the car. Some ridiculous large quantity of something. And driving off. And there's a dog waiting for them when they get home. Barking before they get through the door."

A dog, Patrick thought. *He's introducing a dog.*

"And we put away the stuff from Bulk Barn, and we feed the dog. And we vacuum. We sweep the back patio. We clean the bathroom. Iron the cloth napkins. Just normal weekend stuff, yes? And the whole time we're saying—I don't know, really stupid, banal things: 'Oh, we forgot the light bulbs.' 'Oh, never mind, I'll stop at CVS tomorrow.' Stuff like that. And if you were listening to us, you'd think, *How boring*. And it wouldn't be. It would just be us." Seth's lips had parted. His tongue was wedged between his incisors, and his eyes were almost opaque. He turned suddenly to Patrick. "Does that make sense?" he asked.

"Sure."

In fact, it made a great deal of sense. It made more sense than anything Patrick had heard in a long time, and its very sensibleness made it—suddenly—profoundly moving. Patrick was afraid he would start crying.

Seth nodded, pushed his glasses back up his nose. "Listen to me," he said, chuckling. "Classic postmodern gay. I fantasize about domesticity. Instead of sex."

The afternoon sidled on. At about 12:50 the sun slipped behind a cloud, came out again at 12:58. The cherry Saab next to them was replaced first by a gray Mercedes, then a dark-blue Volvo station wagon, then a bone-colored Nissan Sentra with a bumper sticker that read: JESUS IS COMING. LOOK BUSY. There was not a single Plymouth Voyager in sight.

At one point—sometime after 1:30—Seth asked, "What are you going to do when we find him?"

And this, unaccountably, made Patrick smile. *When* we find him. What was it about the choice of words that so tickled him? Not just the certainty of success; Seth had always believed he would succeed. Maybe just the tacit acknowledgment that Scot-

tie was *real*. This was new. Scottie wasn't a metaphysical problem anymore. He was empirical, something you might reasonably capture and record—a lost species.

"I'm not sure what I'll do," Patrick said. "I think I'd like to
look at him for a few minutes. Just stand off to the side somewhere and look."

"Make sure he's the one?"

"Well—I've never had more than a few seconds with him. So
I guess I'd just like to be able to *look* at him and know he's not
going away again."

"And then what?"

Patrick peered at Seth over his sunglasses. "I don't know," he
said, speaking more slowly. "Isn't this when I get disillusioned?
Go running back to Alex?"

"Oh, that's right."

"Is that still the plan?"

"Yes."

"And then—help me out here—does Ted go running back to
you, or is it the other way around?"

"Ted does the running. He just won't know it."

"And you'll do the—"

"Waiting."

"You've been doing that a while," Patrick said softly.

Seth shrugged. "That's what I do. I'm good."

The tick. Seth the tick.

"Well, you're better at it than me," Patrick said. "I mean, how
long have I been waiting for Scottie? God."

Except he knew exactly how long. One hundred and seventy-
two days. An almost Biblical amount of time—and no revelation
to show for it, no sign. Just devotions. Just half a Saturday spent
staring at Bulk Barn. And this was only the beginning, surely.

Surely Seth would want to come back tomorrow or the next weekend, or he would devise new surveillance details, new adventures, each one taking them further and further away from the city, from anything that was familiar.

"What time is it?" Seth asked.

"Um…1:40."

"Wow. Gosh." He wiped his hands up and down his face, pinched his cheeks. "Sorry. Didn't think we'd have to wait this long."

"Well," Patrick said, "at least we're doing this in a parking lot. And not in a bar."

"Huh." Seth wiped his glasses with his shirt sleeve. "You don't like bars very much, do you?"

Patrick didn't answer right away. He felt his eyelids drooping; he watched his hands tumble out of his lap.

"The first time I ever went to a bar," he said, "I was by myself, and I walked in, and they slapped a number on my chest—like I was about to run a marathon. And it turned out everyone else was wearing a number, and if you saw someone you liked, you were supposed to scribble his number on a piece of paper along with some sexual innuendo, and it would all go up on this video screen over the dance floor. And you were supposed to keep your eyes peeled in case your number came up. People wore their numbers on their crotches, on their asses. Some people wrote their *measurements* just above their numbers. In my most jaded moments, I couldn't have imagined a more degrading human lottery."

"And no one picked your number," Seth said.

"And no one picked my number."

Patrick began to laugh—first a little burp of surprise and then a running stream. It lasted about a minute. It was very pleasant.

"Maybe we should go home," Seth said.

Patrick looked at his watch: 2:30. Ten minutes ago a heavy-bearded man in a Honda pickup had threatened to hurt them if they didn't give up their parking space. He was only dissuaded from it when a space opened up a few cars down, and he was still sufficiently aggrieved to give their front fender a hard kick on his way into the store. Patrick wondered if the imprint of his tread was still there, pressed into the metal.

"Maybe we *should*," Patrick said.

"We'll try again.

"Hey, listen, I want you to know, I *appreciate* your taking all this—all this time and everything."

"No, no, my pleasure."

"I mean, you don't have to do this. You know that, right? The deal doesn't—you know, five *hours* is above and beyond."

"No, I prefer it like this."

"Like what?"

"Like now."

"As opposed to what?"

"As opposed to…" Seth began to yawn, he stretched his arms to the ceiling. "Well, it's better than being in your car when it's *moving.*"

"Oh."

"In fact, I might take the Metro home. If you don't mind. Still a little nauseous."

31

It was 3 o'clock in the afternoon when Patrick got back home, and Deanna was on her knees in the front garden, planting a bush of rust-colored chrysanthemums. This was another of their unspoken compacts: Deanna did most of the gardening. Not only she was better at it, she enjoyed it more, and the plants seemed to enjoy her more. In exchange, Patrick lowered her rent by $50 a month, but this never felt like enough to him, and now and again he found himself chafing at the sense of obligation he felt toward her—not just for the work she did but for the interest she took. He worried that her interest might some day break free of the garden, rampage through the rest of his house like a fungus.

Maybe that was why he was moving with particular stealth toward his front door. He might have made it too—Deanna's large sun hat was obscuring her vision—but when he was halfway up the steps, she suddenly raised her head, and their eyes met with a kind of static shock.

"Hello," she said simply.

"Hi."

They stared at each other for a few more seconds. Patrick's mind began whirring through a menu of excuses, important errands, reasons he couldn't stay and chat—and then he remembered.

"Hey!" he said with a jollity that he knew didn't suit him. "I've been meaning to ask you something."

"Yes?"

"I was wondering if you've been seeing any—*things* in your apartment."

"Things?" Slowly, she hoisted herself from the ground.

"Yeah," he said. "*Living*—kinds of things."

"Living," she murmured. She gazed at the basement apartment for a few seconds. She thrust a hand into her mess of curls. "Oh, you mean the rats?" she asked.

"Um, sure. That would qualify."

"Well, only…" Her eyes rolled upward as she made a mental tally. "Only the last month or so, I think."

"The last month?"

"Month, five weeks, something like that."

"Oh." He took a step toward her. "Wow, you should have told me."

"Well, I just figured you probably had them too, what difference would a few more make?"

"Yeah—huh."

"Anyway," she said, "I think I've got them under control."

"Oh, yes?"

"Well, you see, what I did was I tried thinking about it from *their* perspective. I thought, OK, if I were a rat, what would keep me from going into somebody else's kitchen? And the only thing I could think of was a *cat*."

"Oh, you got a—"

"Actually, I'm *allergic* to cats. But I went and visited a friend of mine who has a big hairy Persian cat. And she gave me a bag full of cat hair and dander and—cat stuff."

"Uh-huh."

"So I spread it around the kitchen floor, and, I don't know, it seems to do the trick. I haven't seen any sign of them for about two weeks."

"Wow."

"Of course, I'm still allergic," she said, smiling. "So breathing's an issue sometimes."

"Sure."

"But as long as I stay out of the kitchen, it's not too bad. And I don't cook much anyway."

It was perhaps twice as many words as he had ever exchanged with Deanna. And the only reason he didn't continue talking was that he was lost in admiration. He had tragically undervalued her. Her resourcefulness, her forbearance—how had he failed to see it?

She didn't want to bother me. She had rats crawling all over her kitchen, and she just—she took care of it.

"You know," Deanna was saying, "if you want, I can get my friend to fix an extra bag of cat stuff. It's no problem, she just pulls it out of her vacuum cleaner."

"Well, thanks. I'm probably going to get a professional exterminator."

"Oh." Her face clouded over. "Are you sure about that? You know, those poisons get in the ground water."

"No, it's OK," he said. "I think they use those nonchemical trappy things."

"Oh, OK."

"But thanks for the tip."

She nodded, gave him a tentative smile. She was clamping down now on the top of her sun hat, as though they were standing in a strong wind, and Patrick somehow took this as a signal that their conversation was over. But when he turned around, he heard her calling his name softly.

"Yes?" he said.

She had leaned her head to one side, and her large brown eyes had narrowed. "Is that why your father was spraying lemon juice up the gutters?" she asked.

"Um—yeah. Actually, yeah. I don't know why. I guess some friend told him about it."

She nodded. "Interesting," she said, and he assumed she was being satirical, but in fact she looked receptive, reflective. She seemed to be giving the idea consideration. *Just what Da needs*, he thought. *Someone to take him seriously.* And as he began making his way up the steps, his thoughts formed a channel, flowed back to another conversation, to something Marianne had said several months ago.

A good woman.

Wasn't that the phrase? *A good woman. That's what he needs.*

Deanna had turned away from him now. She was bending over the chrysanthemums, pawing at the dirt, pressing the roots, idly fingering the branches of a nearby azalea bush.

"Oh—hey." Patrick said.

"Yes?"

"I was wondering, actually, if you would be—*free*? Tomorrow night? For dinner."

She raised herself again, turned around, brushed something off her forehead, rubbed something between her fingers—and gave him that look of hers, that look of almost mysterious simplicity.

"Tomorrow night?" she repeated.

"Yeah." He pointed his finger toward the sky. "Upstairs."

Of course, getting Deanna to come was the easy part; preparing his father was a little more delicate. From the start, Patrick was working at cross-purposes. He wanted Deanna's visit to look casual, spontaneous, and he wanted to be sure that his father made some kind of formal and indelible impression. So he worked obliquely at first. An hour or so after mentioning the invitation to his father, he said, "Hey, Da, I'm thinking of—I don't know—making something *fancy* when Deanna comes over. What do you think? Only 'cause I haven't really cooked in so long."

"Well, that's fine, Pattie," his father said, raising his eyes briefly and then returning them to his book.

And then the following morning, Patrick said, "You know, Da, I think I may dress *up* tonight for dinner. Nothing special, I'm thinking coat and tie." And his father shrugged because he would undoubtedly be wearing what he always wore—the fucking seersucker suit—which was the one thing Patrick didn't want him to wear. For all its magical properties, he thought, the suit had too much summer in it; it seemed to define his father as a thing of autumn. Patrick's secret hope was that Mr. Beaton would pull his one good blazer out of his still-packed garment bag, and in fact, ten minutes before Deanna arrived, his father—miraculously—went upstairs and returned with the blazer on.

"Well, don't you look nice," Patrick said.

"Oh, you know." Mr. Beaton tugged at the fabric sheepishly. "Just trying to get the mothballs out."

Deanna, for her part, arrived at the door in a china-pattern print dress and an unobtrusive necklace, and she had applied a little eyeliner and a whiff of some retiring perfume. She had also brought a bunch of chrysanthemums, which she spilled into Patrick's outstretched arms.

"A couple of them are from the garden," she whispered.

"Oh, great, great. Da, do you want to put these in a vase?"

Patrick would have done more to facilitate this first encounter, but he was feeling a little distracted at this point. He was not really a cook, so the task of preparing dinner had consumed all of Sunday and most of his good humor. He wasn't sure why he had been so ambitious: grilled salmon with dill, green beans with béarnaise sauce, a sweet potato pie, an onion terrine, and for dessert, an almond-raspberry tart. He wasn't sure, either, why he had followed a magazine's suggestion for warming the bread—but he had. He had kept the store-bought sourdough loaf in its original brown paper wrapping; he had run it under water; he had put the whole thing in the oven—and halfway through the first course, wreaths of smoke began rolling in from the kitchen.

"Shit!"

Patrick grabbed an asbestos mitt, ran to the oven, yanked out the smoking loaf, ran it over to the sink—carrying it at arm's length, like an incendiary device. The smell of tar permeated the air. A blackened heel of crust poked through the wrapping.

"Shit," he said again. He turned the water on and watched a brownish vapor rise up from the loaf. He carried the damp black bread to the other side of the kitchen, held it over the trash can, and—and let go. It made a thick muffled sound and wedged itself at a diagonal, like a broken finger.

Patrick began apologizing as soon as he got back to the table.

"It's some technique," he said. "I read about it in a magazine. It's—supposed to make the crust crunchier and—I don't know what it's supposed to do to the inside—make it softer? I don't know—I'm sure it works, you just have to—you know, keep an eye on it—that's really important, keeping an *eye* on things."

He had hoped the bread might at least stimulate some conversation, but it was now a half hour into the meal, and no one had roused himself to say much of anything. Patrick's excuse was that he was preoccupied with the food. He had decided that the sweet potato pie was overbaked, and this depressed him more than he expected. It struck him as one more indicator of Alex's absence.

Alex would never have overcooked the sweet potato pie. He would never have put a bread bag into an oven. He would have stopped me.

Patrick had more or less expected Deanna to sit there in her cocoon of easy silence, her arms folded in her lap. What he hadn't expected was this muteness from his father, who was compensating for his silence by being unusually fidgety, eating slowly but keeping his hands in constant motion—grabbing the cutlery, reaching for the water glass, decanting the wine, smoothing out his napkin, scratching his sideburns. Patrick had never seen him use so much energy to such canceling effect.

"Hey, Da," he said, and as he spoke he heard the trace of desperation in his own voice. "Da, I was going to ask you, How come they call them *Norway* rats?"

"Well." His father dabbed his lips with his napkin, put the napkin down, picked it up again. "'Cause they're from—from Norway, I think. Originally."

"Oh, they're *from* Norway?"

"Yes." Mr. Beaton's napkin fell to the ground, and he leaned over in his chair and began fumbling for it, and from somewhere underneath the table, his voice came back to them. "Norway. Yes."

The silence must have been oppressive for a naturally garrulous man because after a while he started throwing a few sentence constructions Deanna's way, and over time he even developed a conversational gambit, which was to quiz her about all of

Patrick's friends, none of whom she knew.

"Do you know Poorwall? No? Let's see. Well, there's that fella—I can never remember his name—and you probably met Jack. He comes here from time to time. Old college friend of Pattie's. You haven't met Jack?" This went on for some minutes. Patrick was a little surprised at how many of his old friends and acquaintances Mr. Beaton remembered.

"Oh, well," said his father, "you must know Pattie's friend Marianne."

"No."

"Now that's a shame. It really—Pattie, do you remember at your graduation—?"

"Yes, Da."

"That was *so* goddamn funny."

"I don't think Deanna—"

"Mind you, we hadn't even met Marianne yet. I mean, *I* hadn't. Had your mother met Marianne?"

"It's really—"

"You have to picture it. There we were, standing next to the chancel gate. It was—it was me and Pattie and my ex-wife—and my ex-wife's *mother*, who was not—not a woman of great *humor*, if you understand me."

"Mm-hmm," said Deanna.

"And Marianne—I think she must have been about 100 feet away from us—she started screaming at us. She…" Mr. Beaton put a fist to his chest, as though he were suppressing a gas bubble. "I'll never forget it," he said. "She yelled"—Mr. Beaton cupped a hand to his mouth and began bellowing—"Patrick! Our babies need *milk*!"

Mr. Beaton's face, neck, and shoulders shook like pudding. He wheezed and coughed laughs, and every time he seemed to settle down, another fit of giggling took him, carried him off for another few seconds. After about a minute he was still gasping, still wiping his eyes, taking deep drafts of air.

"Oh my," he said. "My, if you'd seen the look on the mater-in-law." One last chuckle broke from his throat. He began re-filling his glass from the water carafe. "Well, now, tell me, Deanna." He angled the carafe a little closer to the glass. "What is it you do with your life?"

"I'm a social worker," Deanna said.

The cascade of water stopped dead. Mr. Beaton tipped the carafe back, stared at it as though he'd gotten it confused with a creamer. Slowly, he returned it to its original place on the table.

"Oh, well, that must be very interesting, mustn't it? Working with all those…" A trickle of sweat appeared at the corner of his forehead. "Those delinquent children and—and poor families."

"Unwed mothers," Deanna said.

"Certainly, certainly, that's—you're doing God's work, young lady."

The evening never quite recovered. Mr. Beaton subsided into a grave courtesy. Deanna returned to her watchful silence. Patrick looked hard at his plate and, when that palled, began staring at the other two plates.

An animal, he thought. *At times like this it would be nice to have an animal.*

When they had finished the main course, Patrick quietly gath-ered the plates and retreated into the kitchen. He stacked the plates in the sink, began to walk away, then decided he would stay and rinse them and put them in the dishwasher. He would take his time doing it too because he had no intention of returning to the silence, and when he was done five minutes later, something in him still refused to go back. *I can't,* he thought. *I can't go in there.*

He couldn't stay in the kitchen either; one of them might conceivably notice. So, to defer the question he bounded up the stairs.

"I've got to check the iron!" he called. "I think I might have left it on this morning."

He went to his bedside table, opened the drawer, began riffling through the sheaf of bird drawings, the ones he'd made the other day. And as he riffled he imagined the images coming together in a short animated film—a narrative—with clues, buried meanings, inspirational messages. Except none of the images would come together.

Distractions, he thought. He was being smothered with distractions. The thing he *needed* to do, the thing he needed to spend every waking *second* doing was finding Scottie—and what was he doing instead? Hunting rats. Burning sourdough loaves. Playing matchmaker for his feckless, CIA-baiting father. Doing everything except the one thing he had to do.

Scottie, help me. It's the minutiae, Scottie.

Five minutes later, coming back down the stairs, he was already composing excuses for his absence, but a surprising thing had happened while he was away. His father and Deanna had begun talking. Deanna was leaning forward with her arms folded on the table, and Mr. Beaton was doing some fancy prestidigitation with his right hand. He was telling some joke about the Irishman's curse, and as Deanna laughed Mr. Beaton's shoulders began to relax a little. He wiggled his hips and sat back in his chair and grinned like a bandit.

"Oh, Pattie!" he cried. "Did you know Deanna has family in Utica?"

A half hour later Patrick walked Deanna back down to her apartment.

"Your father's very sweet," she said.

"Well, that's nice of you to say. He was a little—*off* at first, but you know, I can tell he's—I can tell he's very fond of you."

"Oh, he's *charming*, Patrick. I'd love to meet his fiancée sometime."

"His…?"

"She must be very refreshing."

32

"His *what*?" Marianne asked.

"Fiancée."

"Oh, my God, you're joking."

"I'm not. I'm really not."

"Oh, my *God*," she repeated. "Did you ask him about it?"

"He just laughed it off. He said Deanna must have misheard him."

"OK, fine. If she misheard him, what did he *really* say?"

"Well, I asked him that. He said he was talking about his *financier.*"

"Oh, that's convincing."

"I know. Like, that's the *last* thing he'd ever have."

"Jesus," she said. "I can't believe it. Mr. B's got some chippy on the side, and no one knew. How did this get by us?"

"The same way everything does."

"Well, then, I'm gonna hold off on fixing him up with Sally. I think we need to get clear on his status first."

"You're probably right."

"I'm not sure it would've been a good fit anyway. She doesn't have the right kind of *humor*, you know? Lots of tolerance but no humor."

"I'd settle for tolerance right now."

For their lunch that week, Patrick and Seth chose an obscure Chinese cafeteria. Patrick piled his plate high with chewy sesame beef, and Seth opted for a pungent form of orange chicken, which he complained kept "talking back to him." It may have been the sheer arduousness of eating that kept them silent for the first 20 minutes.

At last Seth pushed his plate away. "Eight pounds," he said.

"Meaning…"

"I've lost eight pounds."

"Well. Congratulations."

"Thanks. Feels great."

"Good."

"Yep, I'm gonna be…" He rubbed his hands together. "Gonna be ready for lovin'." Patrick looked down quickly, but Seth was already segueing. "I thought tomorrow we'd hit Pentagon City," he said. "Take in Macy's. Take in Bloomingdale's. And then where we really need to spend time is Eddie Bauer. You know, he probably even *works* there."

"Eddie Bauer."

"And then Sunday, thought we'd hit a nursery. Maybe Behnke's—we haven't done much Maryland yet. Then maybe the Arlington Farmer's Market, if we have time. Sunday night, I really think Home Depot or the Pottery Barn."

"Well, first of all," Patrick said, "I can't go tomorrow *morning* because I'm waiting for the exterminator to come."

"OK."

"And I'd suggest *tonight*—but I'm going to a party."

"A party?"

"Yeah."

"Whose party?"

"Oh, you…" Patrick was about to say, *You wouldn't know them.*

Then he remembered who he was talking to.

"Carl and John?" Seth said. "I know them! I'm going there too." He paused. "No, I'm not."

"You're not?"

"I was. But my men's group. Special bowling night."

"Oh," Patrick said. "Warrior bowling."

"Yeah."

"Well, have a good time."

"That's funny. Carl and John. I can't believe you're going."

"Why?"

"I don't know. Seems out of character."

"Why?"

"Don't know," Seth said. "Just does."

"You mean because I'm so antisocial? I'm such an outcast, I wouldn't even go to a *party* if someone invited me?"

"Um…I think you would *go*. Don't think you'd necessarily have a good time."

Patrick had no answer for this. He couldn't honestly guarantee he would have a good time. He couldn't even say why he'd been invited in the first place. He barely knew John. He only knew Carl because they had been volunteer phlebotomists at the Whitman-Walker Clinic—but that had been three years ago, and since then, they had seen each other perhaps five times in passing. So why were Carl and John bothering with him now? Did they pity him? Was that it? Were they reaching out to him? Was he just lodged somewhere in their mental Rolodexes?

And another question: Why was he so painfully, childishly *eager* to go? Maybe it was just the joy of being invited somewhere. Periodically, events conspired to remind Patrick of how few friends he really had. He could count his close friends, really, on two hands, and he barely needed the second. There was

Marianne, of course. A couple of people from work. Some buddies from college and high school—he had to really think hard to come up with anyone else. Sonya? The crazy gardening lady down the street? There were so many relationships he didn't quite know how to classify.

But these enumerations always lent a special urgency to the idea of rejoining humanity—and then too, he was horny, outrageously horny. In the last five months, he had logged exactly one sexual encounter—with Rick—and it was all beginning to show. He was feeling musty, bedraggled. His libido would fire off at all hours of the day—inexplicably, without warning. The other day at the gym, he'd been staring at a tiny man in a skintight wrestling tog with a Li'l Abner pompadour and sideburns that reached down to his mouth and a habit of screaming during his bench presses—and hadn't he needed to run downstairs to the bathroom, sit on the toilet, and wait until the attack passed? It was embarrassing. It got so he couldn't walk by a ginkgo tree—couldn't inhale its salty odor—without doubling over, the urge was so strong.

Scottie was for life. He knew that. But what about the interregnum? What about this long, long period of waiting? There had to be a special dispensation.

"*Hel*-lo."

"Hello, Rick? It's Patrick."

"Patrick."

"Yeah, hey, I'm sorry I was so weird at the concert the other night. I mean, I can't really explain it or anything. I guess I was just—you know, *tired*."

"Oh, no, it was a good time. Really."

"Well, that's nice of you to—listen, I don't know if you have any plans tonight. I was going to this party, and I thought if you weren't—"

"Oh, shoot," Rick said.

"You're busy."

"Yeah, it's—sorry—"

"No, that's—"

"It's someone I used to work with. He's only in town for a couple of nights, so—"

"Oh, that's fine. I waited too late."

"Sorry."

"No, it's fine."

"But, listen," Rick said. "We'll do something again soon."

"OK."

"OK?"

"Yeah."

"Hey, thanks for calling, though."

Shortly after he climbed the high-pitched flagstone steps to Carl's Arlington home, and just before he rang the doorbell, Patrick had a flashing intuition that he wasn't supposed to be there—that Carl and John hadn't meant to invite him, had confused him with somebody else, were in no mood to open their door and find him waiting on their stoop. Patrick *Beaton*? No, no, we wanted Patrick *Seaton*. Or *Bleaton* or—God, how did this happen?

The door opened before Patrick even had a chance to ring the bell. The man opening it looked like Carl with his head shaved.

"Carl?"

"Patrick!"

They embraced, and Patrick lingered there for a few moments. It felt surprisingly good, and he didn't let go until he felt Carl's admonitory pat on his shoulder blade. Patrick pulled back, smiled shyly, made a helpless gesture with his hands.

"It's been a while," he said. "Wow. How've you been? How's—John?"

"Oh, fine. He's closing a deal in the living room."

"A deal?"

"He's a realtor, did you know that? The people wanted to close tonight, and he said just come on over and have a beer and we'll do it in my living room."

"Oh."

Patrick remembered his own closing: a contentious affair in a windowless office on Pennsylvania Avenue; the title attorney's schnauzer had punctuated the proceedings by sinking his teeth into Patrick's ankle. Now Patrick had a strange desire to wander into the living room, to see if beer really facilitated real-estate transactions. But he had no say in the matter. Carl was already ushering him down a shotgun hallway that emptied onto the back patio. Before them reared a great terraced hill, landscaped with boxwood and yew, climbing away into a grove of sycamores. Patrick could have stood there a while, arching his neck, staring up into the trees, but Carl was gripping him by the wrist, guiding him toward a group of people around an unlit gas grill.

"Excuse me," Carl said. "Everybody, this is Patrick. He's an environmentalist."

Patrick winced. He hated the way professions were tacked onto names: *Greta the Gynecologist…Hrothgar the Swineherd…*

"And this is Scott," Carl was saying. "He's a contemplative psychologist. And—I'm sorry…"

"Roger."

"*Roger*, who's a meteorologist with the National Weather Service. And Maggie is a labor statistician. And I don't know if you've met Adam. He's a—"

"Wellness consultant," Patrick said robotically.

"Oh!" Carl said. "You two—"

"Yes," Adam said. "Hello."

"How are you?" Patrick asked. "How's business?"

"Business is good," Adam said, nodding in a slow ruminative arc. He had grown a goatee since their last encounter; it looked almost white against the burnt brown of his skin. He was wearing a tank-top undershirt with a scoop neck that swung down just below his right nipple. It seemed to be *supporting* the nipple, keeping it erect.

"How is *your* business?" Adam asked pointedly.

"Fine," Patrick said. "*Busy,* my God. I just—I haven't had time to do anything. Like your—I'm still reviewing your materials."

"We may need to readjust."

"Readjust—"

"Your spine. I think one of your legs must be several inches longer than the other."

"Oh!" Patrick straightened himself, brushed his knees. "I think I was just slouching or something."

"Perhaps," Adam said.

"Anyway, I think I'm heading for the…" He was going to say beer, but he let the sentence die out and meekly pushed away.

The beer bottles were in a big bucket of ice, and blocking the way was a freckled, red-headed woman in a blue denim jumper. She grinned at him, as though he were an ice-cream man.

"I'm Joanne," she said.

"Hi. I'm Patrick." He paused a moment. "I'm an—an environmentalist."

"I'm a games consultant."

Should I just go for the beer? He knew he would be able to handle this discussion much more effectively if he could just get a beer, hold it in his hand, start peeling the label away.

"You mean like playgrounds and stuff?" he asked, buying time, craning his head around her.

"No, no, I work with law firms, corporations. Mostly in a retreat setting. I lead the employees in various games, stimulate their creativity, their team instincts."

"Oh."

There was no clear route. The only clear route was through her.

"We've found that games really help people decompress."

"I bet."

"Oh, wow!" she cried. "Let me show you this one." Still guarding the beer bucket, she reached suddenly to Patrick's right, toward a tray of canapés. "I did it for the first time at the Xerox Center last weekend." She pressed down carefully on two finger sandwiches, extracted their toothpicks, then passed one of the toothpicks to Patrick. "Here," she said.

"Oh, no, I've—I've eaten—"

"No, you put it in your mouth," she said, demonstrating. "See?"

"You…"

She fished through the pockets of her jumper and came out with a half-used roll of Life Savers. "This is fun," she said. "I was saving this for later, but what the hey? Now, see, I'm going to slide this Life Saver onto my toothpick, right? OK, now what I'm going do is—I'm going to pass the Life Saver to *you*. Right onto your toothpick."

"I think—you know, I think I've done this—"

"And we can't use our hands or anything. Just toothpick to toothpick, OK?"

"I'm sure I've—"

"Here I come!"

"—done this—"

"Pucker up!"

All right, he thought. *All right.*

He clenched the toothpick between his teeth so fiercely that he almost broke it in two. He pondered the horrible thing that was his passivity. Here he was, with a toothpick wedged in his jaw, arching his neck, moving his mouth toward the mouth of a strange woman—this was how he behaved in the company of enthusiasts, as though he had no will of his own, and clearly he had no will because instead of asking the woman to get out of his way, instead of demanding that she let him have a beer, he was doing *this*, knowing how it looked, knowing their awkward, intimate motions were meant to simulate a kiss, understanding the *exact fashion* in which he was humiliating himself—and powerless to stop it.

"*Mm-mmgawa*," said the woman through her clenched teeth.

"Patrick?"

Patrick's head snapped back. His throat tightened, and he whirled around, and as he was doing it, he knew it was the wrong impulse. Because he already recognized the voice.

It was Alex.

33

The amazing part was that as he turned, the Life Saver went with him. He didn't realize he even *had* the Life Saver. He'd assumed there'd been no time to make the relay, that the Life Saver was still making its way toward him—but then it wobbled into view at the end of his toothpick, revolving like a loose tire, and it seemed now to have acquired consciousness, to be weighing its options, deciding whether or not it should drop off—and finally it did. It landed on the brick patio with a quiet clatter.

"Well, this is funny," Alex said.

Which struck Patrick as a restrained judgment. A restrained judgment from the man who had left him five months ago, the man who had not called or written since—and who had now apprehended Patrick not in an attitude of mourning (sorry, Seth) but in involuntary erotic interplay with a woman who was only now—*only now*—relinquishing her sentry duty over the beer supply, sidling away, leaving clear access to the tub. And there was still no good way of getting there, no good way of doing anything because here was Alex. Here was Alex, smiling tentatively, typically unimpeachable in a wrinkle-free cotton work shirt over a crisp white Gap T-shirt, loose-cut jeans, and black hiking boots.

Patrick couldn't move. He couldn't speak.

"I didn't expect to see you here," Alex said. "I forgot."

The toothpick was still in Patrick's mouth. He didn't know what to do with it. Spit it out? Swallow it?

"How are you?" Alex asked.

"Oh." The toothpick dropped now, bounced off his knee, landed about two inches from the Life Saver. "I'm fine, thanks." He ground the toothpick beneath the heel of his tennis shoe. "How are you?"

"Oh, fine. Fine. Wow," Alex said. "It's been a long time."

"Right, yeah. Several months."

"Yeah."

For the next several minutes, the five feet of space between them remained unbreached, even by the other party guests. Patrick could see them all dimly: a young black man in a DKNY T-shirt and purple pantaloons; an older woman with corncob earrings; a bespectacled bald man with a Florida tan; Carl himself, the host, deploying his guests in complex patterns, matching professions. They all seemed to be creating an unspoken perimeter around Patrick and Alex, leaving them to their destiny.

"So you're doing well?" Alex asked.

"Yeah."

"Well, that's good. That's good. You know, I—" He bent his head down, as though he were looking for his own Life Saver. "It's weird," he said. "Practically every day I think I'm going to—you know, pick up the phone and give you a call."

"Yeah."

"And I don't. I don't know why. It's not like…" He looked up again, squinting.

"Well," Patrick said, "I mean, *I* could've called too. I guess. It's hard, I guess."

"Yeah." Alex shifted his weight, took a speculative step forward, then reconsidered. "So you're doing well?" he asked, again.

"Oh, fine, yeah."

"You look good."

"Thanks, so do—I think you've lost weight, haven't you?"

Alex grinned sheepishly. "Probably," he said. "Nothing major." *I don't eat anymore*, he might have said. *Because of you. You completely put me off eating. Forever.* But Alex was already scrolling for a new topic. "I hear—I understand you and Seth are good friends now," he said.

"Seth?"

"Yeah. I think it's really funny how you guys ran into each other. Some sort of—police investigation, wasn't it?"

"Oh, yeah—Seth's very nice. Very interesting."

"Yes, he is that."

"Yep," Patrick said.

"We see him at least once a week, you know."

"I didn't know."

"He comes over for dinner every Monday night. He's very funny."

"You mean funny *strange?*"

"Um…I guess so. In a nice way. He's very fond of Ted."

The name hung there for a few seconds in the space between them. It had the effect of something visible.

"I don't think I've met Ted," Patrick said carefully.

"No. You haven't," Alex said. "We should have you over to dinner sometime."

"On *Seth's* night?"

Alex laughed. Patrick couldn't remember the last time he'd heard him laugh. "Any night you like," Alex said.

"Well—fine. No, that's fine."

"OK. Good."

Something must have loosened between them—that was the only conclusion Patrick could make. Alex was looking at him in a less embarrassed fashion, a more openly curious fashion, and Patrick wasn't looking away.

"You're not angry," Alex said after a while. "You don't seem angry."

"No," he said.

And it was true. He wasn't. It was surprising, maybe, but he wasn't. It's just easier not to be, he thought. He had to husband his resources, after all. For other things. For Scottie. Scottie above all.

"You're looking very well," Patrick said.

"You—" Alex stopped speaking, and his right hand began to flutter uncontrollably. For a few seconds Patrick stared at the hand, tried to decipher its intention, but he got nowhere, and at last, Alex found the words.

"You've got a pine needle," he said. "On your left shoulder."

When Patrick got home that night, his father was asleep in the upstairs room, so Patrick crept into the living room and turned on the television set and turned the volume all the way down. He sat in the rocker, and the silent images flickered over his face. What was he watching? He had no idea.

The phone rang. Patrick sprinted into the kitchen, grabbed the phone off its hook. "Hello?" he whispered.

"Why are you whispering?" Seth asked.

"Because my father's asleep. Because it's past midnight."

"I just wanted to hear."

"Hear what?"

"How Alex is doing."

Patrick closed his eyes. He counted out three breaths. "You must have spies in just about every corner of the world."

"Don't need spies," Seth said. "I engineer things."

"Like…"

"Like who do you think got Alex invited?"

Patrick paused.

"No, you didn't," he said.

"*Mais oui*," Seth answered. "I thought to myself: 'Self, Ted's out of town. Alex isn't doing anything. Why don't I call Carl? Ask him to take pity?'"

A cataract of heat rushed through Patrick's chest, inflamed his neck and ears. He was surprised at how powerful it was.

"Aren't you clever?" he said quietly.

"Listen," Seth said. "If you guys are going to reconcile, someone's gotta get the ball rolling."

"Well, I hate to disappoint you, but I think the reconciliation is a long way off yet."

"Oh, what? Things were strained? A little awkward? That's to be expected."

"Alex is happy," Patrick said. "He's happy the way he is."

"Naw."

"Fine. Believe what you want."

"I will."

"And mind your own business," he said.

"I can't start *now*," Seth said.

Mr. Beaton had viewed the summoning of outside help as an admission of defeat, so on the morning that the rat exterminator was due to arrive, he decamped to the zoo.

"Got a hankering to see the panda, Pattie. Nothing scratches itself quite like a panda."

As a result, Mr. Beaton was not present at 10:35 when the purple-uniformed man from Vermin Vendetta arrived. It was Patrick who opened the door; it was Patrick who welcomed the man with orange hair and pale, drawn face, the man so tall he had to duck through the front doorway, the man who gave off a scent that seemed almost exotic until Patrick identified it as tobacco.

"You got some rats, I hear."

Meekly, Patrick led him into the kitchen, showed him the pack of coffee filters that last night's party had gnawed through, pointed out the necklace of droppings in front of the dishwasher, recounted every incident he could remember, every depredation from the past two months, every lost article of food, every organic and man-made material sacrificed to the vermin overlords.

The man listened with his head slightly averted. His mouth worked in a perpetual chewing motion.

"Yes, sir," he said. "Yes, sir, you got rats."

For the next half hour, Patrick followed him around as he lowered his large frame to the floor, poked his face into crevices, peered behind appliances, felt inside cupboards. He went everywhere—into the living room, out onto the patio, even poked his head into Deanna's kitchen. He moved as deliberately as an equerry, and just as Patrick was beginning to grow impatient—it had been more than a half hour—the man went back to his truck and returned with an armful of what looked to be small cable boxes, which he proceeded to lay out with scientific precision—next to the refrigerator, the washing machine, at regular intervals across Deanna's floor. Patrick heard his small grunt of approval as he wedged the last one into place alongside to the backyard shed.

"I'll come by next week, see how many we got." The man took off his purple cap, pressed it to his chest. "Don't you worry," he said. "They gotta deal with *me* now."

Patrick was going to say something definite in response— something like "I'm happy to know it"—but his mind was occupied with something else, so he said nothing. He led the man back through the kitchen, watched him wind his body around the dining table and the coffee table, watched him duck his head through the front doorway, and it was only when the man was halfway down the front steps that he thought to say anything.

"Excuse me!"

The man coiled himself back around like a centaur. "Yes, sir."

"Can I ask you something?"

"Yes, sir."

"Where did you get that tattoo? The one on your left arm."

34

"Are you sure?" Seth asked.

"Almost positive," Patrick said. "Almost 100% positive."

"The exact same tattoo?"

"In the same position. Just above the left elbow."

"Fascinating," Seth said. "Fascinating."

"And guess what the bird is."

"Tell."

"A *roadrunner.*"

"You're kidding. Like—beep beep? Like Acme Anvils?"

"No, no, not that cartoony. It was more—it was more like the real thing."

"So wait. Let's think now. This must mean something, this must—roadrunner, roadrunner—it must mean he's a—a runner! A jogger of some kind."

"Yeah, I was thinking the same thing, actually—but this exterminator guy said he got *his* tattoo when he was 16. In New Mexico. He said all his pals were getting the same tattoo; it's what you did apparently when you grew up in New Mexico."

"I didn't know people grew up in New Mexico."

"And then I told him I saw someone with the very same tattoo, and he said, well, *that's* where the guy's probably from."

"New Mexico. Interesting."

"It *is* interesting."

"But not—I mean, it's not like they have their own embassy."

"But *still*. It goes into the profile, right?" Patrick said. "It's one more piece of data. We know he probably lives in the near suburbs. We know he probably has a New Mexico—*orientation*. So maybe we should—I don't know, try some—*Tex-Mex* restaurant. In Falls Church."

"I draw the line there."

"Or call the—the New Mexico congressional delegation. Or start a bogus support group. Gay New Mexico Alumni or Refugees. We could advertise in the *Blade*. We could send out flyers."

He knew he was getting silly. He knew it. He could feel the reticence slipping away from him, the edge of hysteria creeping into his voice, and he could feel—how was this happening?—a curious inverse proportion setting in: *Seth* acquiring dignity and restraint. *Seth* saying, "Let's not get crazy here."

And Patrick saying, "Or maybe it's a secret society, you know, maybe we could just *infiltrate* their ranks. Pretend we're tourists or—or drug couriers. From Albuquerque."

"Patrick, we'll explore it."

Explore it! Never mind, Patrick thought. Never *mind* that it was Day 179 in Our Year of Scottie. Never mind that nearly *half a year* had gone by, and they were no closer to finding him, and every clue seemed only to take them further away. Never mind all that—they were going to exercise *caution*. They were going to *explore* it.

"I'll be an old man," Patrick said. "I'll be 95 by the time we find him."

"That's OK," Seth said. "So will he."

Seth had wanted to spend most of Sunday at Tysons Corner Mall, but Patrick, on the brink of committing, remembered he had another engagement.

"What's the deal?" Seth complained. "This is your second previous engagement. You never used to have previous engagements."

"I know, it's—it won't happen again."

It was just that in a weak moment Patrick had agreed to host a group recital for Sonya's violin students, and he remembered now, with a sudden lurch, that it was scheduled for Sunday afternoon. Of course, in agreeing to sign over his house, he had assumed that most of the students were fellow adults, so he was not prepared for the rafts of 9-, 10-, and 12-year-olds that came sailing through his front door a few minutes after 1. They took to his house as though it were a jungle gym—jumping up and down on the love seat, poking their heads up the flue, scaling the banister—and they particularly took to his father, who beguiled them for several minutes with a trick involving a handkerchief and an apple.

They were happy, careless, nerveless children. They held their violins under their chins without a quiver of tension, and their wrists instinctively found the equipoise that Patrick had spent two years trying to locate. When they played their individual selections, their minds seemed to switch off, and as soon as they were done they resumed the conversations they'd been having just before they started—resumed them sometimes in mid sentence. It might have been easier for Patrick if there had more people of his age group, but Sonya's only other adult student was an intense young man named Javier. Javier had invited his mother and two sisters, both of whom arrived half an hour late, after he had already played his Bach minuet. "I hate you,"

Javier told them. "I hate you for doing this to me." But he agreed to play for them one more time, and as he played, they snapped flash pictures.

They even took pictures of Patrick as he did his Schumann scherzo. Normally this would have enhanced Patrick's humiliation, but he found himself so detached from his failure now that he could watch the bow slither across the strings, hear the strangled sound coming back, and find it all oddly comforting. It was as though he were burying the piece for good.

"Yea, Patrick!" Sonya cried, and three of the children applauded by tapping their bow sticks against their wrists.

At the end of the recital, everyone adjourned to Patrick's backyard for a group rendition of "Ode to Joy." Patrick had a niggling worry about his neighbors and an outright fear that Deanna would be listening, but he found his self-consciousness mysteriously fading after a few bars, and he finished the piece with a great flourish of flatness. And then he noticed Sonya. She was leaning against the backyard shed, chewing quietly on one of the tea sandwiches that a student's mother had prepared. The children were filing back into the house, but Sonya wasn't moving, and it wasn't until Patrick touched her on the shoulder that she seemed to register where she was.

"Oh, that's right," she said. "I have brownies in your oven."

"Are you all right?"

"I'm fine," she answered. "I'm just *thinking*, you know? About stuff."

"Is it the baby thing?"

"Yeah."

"It's not happening?"

She shook her head. She gave a quick, hysterical grin. "We, uh, OK, we went to the doctor finally because—because noth-

ing we were doing was *working*, right? And the woman basically laid it out for us; she told us how Roger's sperm count is down
so far, he's basically—shooting blanks."

"Oh, Sonya, I'm sorry."

"I think it's because his mother ate *fish*, you know? She ate
lots of fish when she was pregnant. They lived in a fishing
town."

"Uh-huh."

"So what can you do? I mean, all that stuff happened 30 years
ago, right? All that fish. There's nothing you can do."

They were both staring now at Patrick's kitchen window,
where one of Sonya's young girls—it was hard to tell which
one—was mugging for them. The girl had mashed her face
against the glass until it resembled a kind of face soup, and she
made a fishlike motion with her mouth and cocked her head and
attached two hands to either side of her head and began wag-
gling them.

Sonya smiled impulsively, then bit her lip. Her violin dangled
by her knee. "Damn fish," she said.

Patrick never spent a lot of time second-guessing his
wardrobe, but the historicity of his meeting with Victor was too
great. It took him half an hour to settle on a sports jacket, black
T-shirt, freshly pressed jeans, and kick-ass Italian boots—which
meant he got to the restaurant ten minutes late. He found Marianne sitting alone at a table for three, staring up at the mount-
ed animal heads that ranged across the wall like a taxidermist's
display. *An Italian restaurant*, Patrick reminded himself. Why
was he spending so much time in Italian restaurants? Italian
restaurants that wanted to cross the Mediterranean, plunge a
dagger into the heart of Africa?

"I'm sorry," he said, "I got stuck coming up Wisconsin."

"Jesus, I expect Victor to be late. But *you*..."

"I know. I'm a loser."

Marianne was grinning; she couldn't help herself. She was dressed for work in her navy-blue linen dress with nautical white piping and white faux pearl earrings. Her hair was cut in a new sporty bob and smoothed back in a white headband, and her skin gave off its usual glow of contentment. And something else too, he thought. Had she lost weight? Almost certainly she had. Maybe 15, God, maybe 20 pounds. When did *that* happen?

And why should he be surprised? *Everyone* was losing weight. Seth and Alex and Marianne, *all* of them—losing for love. And his father too, maybe for the same reason, and who knew, Patrick himself might be losing some flesh too on account of love. If he ever weighed himself, he might be astonished at how much of him was gone.

"I can't believe you didn't bring a date," Marianne said. "It's fucking criminal how much *loser* time you pack into a day."

"Well, you know," Patrick muttered. "I've got things to do; I've got Da to worry about."

"Oh, yeah, listen." Marianne made revolvers out of her hands. "I got two more candidates lined up. Now, I know, I know, we still don't know what the deal is with the fiancée, but I figure as long as we don't have a wedding announcement, we gotta just—*plow* ahead as planned. Now, both these chicks I have in mind—they've got potential, but I need to run their specs by you before we do anything else."

"OK."

"And then listen up, OK? As soon as we got Mr. B squared away, we're gonna start on *you*, all right? 'Cause, Patrick?" She leaned across the table, pressed her hand down on his. "There's someone for everyone; I really believe that."

She meant to be comforting, he knew that, but the words just rattled around inside him. Not because he was alone in the world, but because he was conscious of a hollowness, a fundamental regret. He had never told Marianne about his search for Scottie. And he didn't know why. He'd told her about their first meeting in the library, and she'd probed a couple of times after that, and he put her off, and now five months had passed since their last discussion of the subject, and so much had happened— or *not* happened. And whatever had happened Marianne had not been a part of. Which was some form of betrayal, wasn't it?

"Oh!" Marianne gasped, put a hand to her neck. "Oh, my God, I forgot to tell you!"

"What?"

"Oh, you're not gonna believe this. It's too fucking crazy."

"What?"

"Well, how about this, Mr. Wolf Trap? It seems you and Victor went to the *same fuckin' concert*."

"What do you mean?"

"That damn Steve and Eydie thing!"

"The…"

"I couldn't believe it when he told me. I said, 'Victor, what were you thinking?' He said, 'Oh, some buddies from work dragged me there. I didn't really want to go.' He was so sheepish, and I gave him such a hard time about it, you know, that after a while I couldn't admit I knew someone *else* who went. I figured I'd be damned by association or something."

Patrick's mind began to whir.

"Is—" He stopped himself, took a long breath. "Do Victor's friends drive a Plymouth Voyager?"

Marianne frowned. "I don't know."

"Well…" He smiled edgily. "I mean, are they from the suburbs?"

"Maybe. I mean, *Victor* is."

"He's suburban?"

"Yeah, he lives in Arlington."

Oh, God.

Patrick tried to squeeze the irritant from his brain—it wouldn't budge. He made himself laugh. He practically guffawed.

"I was just wondering," he said. "'Cause I think maybe I saw them, I think. Would Victor's friends be gay by any chance?"

Marianne thought a second, gave a laconic shrug. "I don't know; they could be. I mean, he is real comfortable with…" She giggled, lowered her voice into a mock-conspiratorial whisper. "With you people. Hell, he goes to more gay parties than I do."

Patrick nodded.

Gay parties, he thought. Gay parties attended by a young man named Victor. A young, liberal-minded man named Victor who gets dragged by his campy buddies to a concert. One of them drives a Plymouth Voyager, and as they leave the grounds, the man named Victor climbs into the back seat behind the driver, casually hangs his arm out the window.

"Does…" Patrick stopped again.

"Does what?"

Does he have a tattoo? he wanted to ask. And suddenly he couldn't. He couldn't anymore because—because it was *absurd*, wasn't it? It was pathologically ridiculous. It would be the joke to end all jokes. It would be the final declaration of war on reason.

And then he remembered what Seth had said.

It's a small town, D.C. Smaller than Mayberry.

And things like this happened in a small town, didn't they? Things like this happened all the time.

"Well, here he is!" Marianne cried.

A layer of moisture evaporated from Patrick's eyes. Marianne was looking over his shoulder, her face was expanding, brightening. She was curling her fingers, gently waving Victor over to the table, and Patrick was thinking—what else?—thinking of *escape*. How could he get away? How could he get away from here and, by leaving, prevent Victor from being whoever he was, prevent *whatever* it was from happening a little while longer.

"Don't tell me," Marianne was calling out in her mocking tone. "The traffic on Wisconsin. Patrick's already used that one."

There was nowhere to run. He knew that. His back was to the door, and the only other way led to the kitchen, and from the corner of his eye, the lion and leopard and antelope heads on the wall seemed to be hanging in judgment, readying themselves for a nice big laugh at his expense.

There's nowhere to go.

And that, for some reason, made it bearable. It was a bit of a jolt to realize it: He was glad he couldn't escape. He was horribly fascinated. He had to know. He had to. He couldn't wait any longer.

No, he *could*.

No. He couldn't.

And so he turned. He turned to his left, and the only thing postponing the reckoning was that Victor was circling to the right of the table so that the precise moment of their meeting was delayed by perhaps two seconds. And in those two seconds Patrick had come to believe that what he most feared would be the thing most likely to happen. He had almost resigned himself to it, and so he was surprised by the rush of emotion that greeted him when he and Victor finally locked eyes. It left him holding his breath.

There was a silence of perhaps five more seconds before Marianne did the honors. "This is Patrick," she said. "And Patrick, this is Victor."

"We've met," Patrick said.

PART THREE

35

Patrick was standing in the kitchen when the phone rang. He'd been home for almost an hour, and for half that time he'd been leaning against the refrigerator, listening to the ancestral sound of his father snoring in the upstairs bedroom. The sound had so lulled him that the phone seemed to come charging at him from another dimension, smacking him between the eyes. Patrick groped for it, as though it were an alarm clock.

"Hello?"

"Patrick," the voice said.

His head almost jerked away.

"Patrick, I know you're upset."

"No," he said. "I'm not."

"I would say I'm sorry, except I don't—I mean, tell me what I'm supposed to be sorry about."

"Well, wow, where do I start? Let's see. For starters, you never told me your name was Victor."

"No one calls me that. Marianne is the only one in the world who calls me that."

"So Rick is—what? A nickname?"

"No, it's my *name*. It's what my family's called me ever since I was a kid. My father's name is Victor too, so they always called me Rick to distinguish us."

"Well…" He was losing his edge already; he could feel it. "Well, why didn't they call you Vic?"

"Patrick, you don't know my family. They would never call me *Vic*. They would shoot me if I called myself Vic."

Patrick shut his eyes. He could feel it—the anger slipping away. He didn't want it to go. He wanted to nurse it.

"OK," he said. "We'll move on to lie number 2. You told me you were a law *librarian*."

"I know."

"Which must be some kind of grounds for disbarment. Or something."

"Patrick, be honest with me. Would you have gone out with me if I'd said I was a lawyer?"

"Sure."

"You *hate* lawyers."

"I don't."

"You *told* me you hate lawyers. On our very first date."

"I did?"

"Why would I want someone to hate me—I mean, right off the bat? I just want people to—see *me*, not some *lawyer* thing. And I would've gotten around to telling you."

"When?"

"I would've told you."

Maybe, Patrick thought. *If I'd pushed it.* And, of course, he hadn't. He hadn't pushed anything.

"All right," he said. "OK, let's move on to the big one, lie number 3: You somehow failed to tell me you were dating my best friend."

"How was I to know she was—"

"Which would be bad enough, but we happen to be different genders."

"Patrick, what Marianne and I do is not—we're not *dating*."

"That's not what she thinks."

"I'm sure if you asked her directly, she would *not* say we were dating."

"No, she thinks you're getting married."

"Marianne says lots of things. You know that."

Do I know that?

It was a real question. Patrick found himself trying to address it, surround it. Trying to condense his accumulated memory and pack it all into a single frame.

What did he know about Marianne? What sorts of things had she told him in her short lifetime?

Well—she had once pretended to be a descendant of the Medicis. She had once asked Patrick to marry her. Come to think of it, she had once pretended to be the mother of Patrick's child—Mr. Beaton would never forget it. But these were—these were little role plays, weren't they? Enactments of theorems, they had no attachment to reality. No attachment to anything.

And then he realized something.

He had never met any of Marianne's boyfriends. Not a one of them.

Not since college. Eleven years ago. And she'd had at least three or four boyfriends in the past few years alone. At least three or four, and somehow the men always withered on the vine before Patrick ever got around to meeting them. He always took Marianne's word for them. He always commiserated with her, waited patiently for another candidate to come along. He always assumed one would.

But what if they'd never existed?

"All right." Patrick began speaking more slowly. "Tell me this: Does Marianne know you're gay?"

"Sure, she does."

"You mean you've told her?"

"Well—if you mean did I ever come out and say 'Marianne, I'm gay'—I mean, come on, you know how these things work. You don't come out and *say* it; you just—you let people know."

"That's how it works?

"Yeah, you say, 'Oh, wow, that's a good-looking guy,' or something. You let them know right off the bat."

"So she knows you date men?"

"Sure. Probably, sure. I don't describe every *date* for her, if that's what you mean. I mean, that's my own business, that's private."

"So, for instance, you go to Wolf Trap with *me*, and you tell *her* you went with some buddies from work."

Rick hadn't expected that one. He was silent a few moments. "Marianne doesn't—" He stopped again. "I don't think she likes hearing I have dates."

"Because she thinks you're dating her."

"No, she's just very—she's a little possessive."

"Uh-huh."

"Patrick, listen to me, all right? Marianne and I are not dating. If she has some—*fantasies* in that direction, then that's her deal, OK? Not mine. I've never misrepresented myself."

Misrepresented. The lawyer killing off the last trace of the librarian.

"What about the flowers?" Patrick asked.

"What flowers?"

"You send her flowers every day. A single flower. A different flower every day."

"Patrick, I've *never* sent her flowers."

He put a hand to his forehead. He was feeling warm now, uncomfortably warm.

Jesus. I've never seen the flowers either. Not even when I visited her apartment. I took her word for that too.

Something was slipping over his head. He could barely see through.

"OK," he said. "You really have to swear to me now. You have to swear that you've *never* sent Marianne a flower."

"Why would I send her flowers? She's just a friend."

No flowers. And no men, no visible signs of men—except Victor, who was Rick.

"And..." Patrick had to unclench his teeth to talk. "And she never mentioned me? She never mentioned she had a friend named Patrick?"

"Well, yeah, I guess," Rick said. "I never thought about it. It's not that uncommon a name so—I mean, what were the chances you'd turn out to be the same guy?"

What were the chances?

"I'm a little confused," Patrick said.

"I know."

"So—I'll need some time, I guess."

"That's *fine*, that's fine. Just—I mean, I like you, all right? And I'm—I think we have a pretty good time together, and I know the circumstances are a little awkward right now, but—we're adults, right? We can figure something out."

"Yeah. OK, yeah, I've—I've gotta go; I've got a call coming in. I'll—"

"Call me when you're ready, OK?"

"OK." Patrick exhaled. "OK, bye." He clicked to the other line. "Hello?"

"I can't believe it," Marianne said.

"What?"

"I can't believe you and Victor know each other."

"Yeah, it's—"

"You didn't tell me his firm represented your office."

"Oh, well, that's 'cause I didn't know what firm he worked for. You never told me."

"Hey, he's dreamy, isn't he?"

"He's very nice-looking."

"I know what you're thinking."

"What?"

"He's too good for me. He's too handsome and—"

"Are you kidding? He's, like, the luckiest guy in the world."

"Aw, shucks. Gee."

"So…" The blood was massing in his face. "So you guys—I mean, kind of—how far *along* are you?"

"How far along?"

"I mean datingwise. Do you…?"

"Do we…?"

"You know."

"Patrick, what can I tell you? It's just not your garden-variety relationship. I mean, everything is…"

"Yeah."

"It's so *unspoken*, you know? I mean, Jesus, we talk practically every day, and we know so much about each other, it's just so *intimate*. And the other stuff—I don't know, it just seems kinda redundant, you know?"

"Huh."

"I mean, we ain't gettin' *married*, if that's what you're worried about. Not yet."

"Oh, no, I wasn't. I mean, whatever. It doesn't—you know—"

"But I'm really glad you guys met."

"Oh, yeah. Me too."

"I can tell he liked you. He was very comfortable with you."

"Yeah, well, he's nice."

"Ha!" Marianne said. "My two men. Together at last."

He lay in bed that night, fighting off sleep, thinking about fate's whims—thinking that if he had not fallen asleep that fateful Sunday afternoon in the library, then he could have followed Scottie out the door, followed him and never looked back and never met Rick. He would only have met Victor and never met Seth—at least he would not be following Seth to every crevice of presumed homosexual life in the metropolitan D.C. area, and he would be, at this precise moment, happy. And for the rest of his life, happy. If he hadn't fallen asleep.

But Scottie was the one who wanted him to fall asleep. Scottie had told him to. *The Scottish Prince*, he thought, *commanded it.*

He would never fall asleep again. Never again.

36

So he was a little surprised to wake up the next morning. *Wait a minute*, he thought. *I've just woken up, and I could only have woken up if I'd fallen asleep. I must have...*

Fuck! He pounded his pillow. *Fuck!*

He squinted at the clock. It was almost 10. Ten o'clock on Saturday morning. Why hadn't his father roused him? Patrick rolled out of bed, poked his head into the guest room; Mr. Beaton wasn't there. He trudged downstairs; Mr. Beaton was nowhere to be seen. The only evidence of his existence was a half-empty, lukewarm pot of coffee on the kitchen counter. Patrick stared down into the inky liquid.

Candy, he thought suddenly. His father had probably gone to get candy.

For the past week Mr. Beaton had been consuming entire landfills of candy. Patrick would come home every night and find his father sitting on the couch, eating chocolate-covered peanuts directly from the bag—or candy corn or Pez or Smarties or peppermint patties or bite-size Tootsie Rolls—eating them as you breathe air. Patrick had said nothing. This was another of his father's chemical processes, wasn't it? No point in examining it.

But as he stared into the coffee, Patrick began to wonder if maybe this was candy too. Candy coffee. He was about to taste it when the doorbell rang. And for a brief interval, he was resolved not to open the door. There were so many people it could be, and he didn't want to face any of them.

But the person on the doorstep was none of those people. It was Deanna. Wearing her jogging clothes and looking mournful.

"Patrick."

"What?"

She beckoned to him with her index finger, and he followed, followed her as she sketched a deliberate circle around the front of the house, down the side alley, to the back lot. Watched her approach his car, his boxy, rust-colored '87 Oldsmobile, watched her approach, then stop abruptly and bow her head.

Patrick was still not awake—that must have been why his mind worked so slowly, so transitively. His first thought was that he was taller. No, he wasn't taller—his car was smaller. His car was smaller, and it was smaller because it was resting on cinder blocks. It was resting on cinder blocks because—because all four wheels had been removed.

Not just the tires, he realized. The wheels themselves, in their entirety. Tires, rims, discs, hub caps—the whole package. Gone.

The car sat on its dais of cinder blocks like a conceptual artwork or like those cars he had seen in people's front yards in West Virginia—paralytic, permanently grounded. Stripped of its essential *car*ness. Because what was a car without its wheels? Nothing. Nothing at all.

"Oh, my God," Patrick said.

"Patrick, I'm so sorry."

"Oh, wow."

He remembered suddenly what Alex had said when the vandal had stolen the plant from Patrick's front window and scrawled "Fuck you" on the windowsill. *That was gratuitous*, Alex said. And this was the very quality that Patrick felt most keenly now—the superfluity, the hostile excess.

He went back inside and called the police. They told him there was a shortage of available cruisers. He called his insurance company. The woman asked him if it was the same car as all the other times. "Yes," he said. "The same one." He called the service station, and a man with an extravagant Italian accent said, "Bring car in. We look."

"I can't bring it in. It's got no wheels."

There was a pause. "You got flatbed truck?"

"No," Patrick said. "No flatbed truck."

"OK," the man said, breathing deeply. "We send someone over. Maybe an hour, OK?"

Patrick was sitting on his front doorstep, waiting for the mechanic, when two men bicycled past. They stared at him as they passed, then made an arc at the end of the block and pedaled back.

"Patrick!" they called. Almost synchronously, they removed their helmets, unpeeled their biking gloves. "How *are* you?"

It was Gary/Robert. Patrick still didn't know which was which. He would need, in the future, to categorize them as a single biological unit. *A Hydra*, he thought. *A centipede*.

"I'm fine, thank you," Patrick said.

"Alex told us he ran into you."

"Yeah, it was…" He tried to complete his thought, but he wasn't in fact thinking anything. "It was good."

"I love your new shutters," Robert/Gary said.

"Oh. Thank you, they're not—"

"Did your tax assessment go down?" asked Gary/Robert.

"My tax—"

"Ours went down by a third."

Patrick devoted about five seconds to thinking about his tax assessment, then gave it up. Thinking about it made him scrunch up his forehead too much.

"Actually," he said, "my car got attacked again last night."

"Oh, my God," said Robert/Gary. "Did you have a Club?"

"Yes," Patrick said. "Yes, I had a Club. They took my wheels."

"Locking lug nuts," said Gary/Robert.

"I beg your pardon?"

"You should get locking lug nuts. Our Saturn dealer warned us when we got our car. He said Saturn wheels are particularly coveted."

"Did he mention Oldsmobiles?" Robert/Gary wondered.

"I don't remember," said Gary/Robert.

Patrick regarded them for a few moments. He leaned forward, pressing his chest against his knees. "It makes me wonder," he said, smiling thinly. "Every time something happens to my car, I run into you guys."

"Ha! We're car vultures."

"Yes, it could be that," Patrick allowed. "Or it could just be you're the people behind it all. The masterminds. The kingpins."

"Um…"

"Now, it's possible," Patrick said, "it's *possible* you're doing it yourselves. But I'm inclined to think you hire a gang of mercenaries to do it for you. To give you plausible deniability."

There was a pause. Then Robert/Gary began slowly putting on their helmets, refastening their gloves, kicking their legs over the crossbars of their bikes. "Well, hey," they said. "Sorry about your car. Good luck getting it fixed."

"I don't have a motive yet," Patrick conceded. "All I can think is that you're perpetrating a reign of terror. I suppose that's possible."

"It was—it was good running into you. We'll have to tell Alex we saw you."

"But reigns of terror should have more than one victim, shouldn't they? Normally, they involve whole *communities*."

"Bye now."

Patrick stared after their retreating backs. "Whole nations!" he called.

The man from the service station—the same Italian that Patrick had spoken to on the phone—arrived two hours after Patrick placed his call. He drove up in a green pickup truck, and as he got out he was balancing a tire on his head.

"Christ shit," he said, staring at Patrick's car.

"Do you have locking lug nuts?" Patrick asked.

"Naw."

"I was told I should get locking lug nuts."

"Oh, don' worry 'bout that."

"My engine strut still doesn't work," Patrick said.

"You should bring in. We take look."

"I've brought it in. I've brought it in several times. You've taken several looks."

"Jesus, Pattie!"

Patrick dropped his head. He had completely forgotten about his father: Mr. Beaton had chosen this afternoon to stroll in through the back alley. He was wearing poplin trousers and a pinstripe cotton dress shirt and carrying a bag of Russell Stover candy. He was chewing a handful of Gummi Bears.

"Hi, Da."

"Did you call the police?"

"Yeah, they're all over it."

Patrick and Mr. Beaton stood silent for the next few minutes,

watching the mechanic ratchet up the jack, position a wheel, rotate it, sound it, ratchet the jack back down, reposition the jack,
ratchet it up again. Patrick felt himself growing still and rever-
ential, as though he were witnessing a burial at sea.

"You should get locking lug nuts," Mr. Beaton said.

"Naw, don' worry 'bout that," the mechanic said.

"I think God's trying to tell you something," Marianne said.

"What?"

"Fuck if I know, but *something*."

"You mean besides sell my car, move out of the city? Off the
Earth?"

"Oh, no, that's too obvious. That's too—hey, why don't you get
yourself out of the house tonight? Get your mind off that shit?"

"I don't know."

"Oh, come on. Victor and me are goin' to Tracks tonight.
We'd love it if you came."

"That's OK."

"You won't be in the way or anything."

"That's OK."

"I think it's the CIA," Seth said.

"Why do you think that?"

"Reprisal. 'Cause of your dad. He pushed the wrong buttons."

"I'm pretty sure he hasn't been messing with the CIA lately."

"They hold grudges."

"I don't know," Patrick said. "It seems awfully petty."

"The CIA is *King* Petty," Seth said. "Grudge *Emperor*."

This is when you need somebody, Patrick thought.

When it was midnight and you weren't able to sleep and you

were wondering how you could afford to keep your car and you had an insurance deductible that was basically the same as being uninsured and you had a father heading toward diabetic shock and a best friend who was possibly dating the man you'd been dating, except he possibly or maybe even probably wasn't the man you wanted, and you had an ex-boyfriend whose new boyfriend's ex-boyfriend believed everything should be *status quo ante* and maybe he was right, maybe it was foolish to expect better than that, maybe nothing was better.

It was at times like this that you needed someone. Someone to sidle up to you in bed and chew on your ear and take the sting out and walk you into dreamland.

Someone like Scottie, huh? Someone like that.

It wasn't so much to ask. People had asked for much more than that.

37

That night he dreamed he was a member of the Manhattan Transfer. Steffi Graf was standing to his left, twirling a Dunlop racket and singing along, and Patrick was excited but inappropriately dressed. Instead of a tuxedo, he was wearing an Aqua-Lung. He was about to explain it when he woke up.

As soon as he got to work, he closed his door and put his head down on his desk. He was so tired. If he'd been capable of napping—more than once or twice a year—he would have done it then, done it without a second thought. He would have slept through the rest of the day.

The phone rang. Without raising his head he reached for the receiver, dragged it along the desk toward his ear.

"Patrick?" said the voice.

"Hi." He had no idea who it was.

"It's Alex."

"Hi," he said again.

"Are you all right?"

"Yeah!" He jerked his head off the desk. Instinctively he smoothed his hair back. "No, it's just—my *car*. My stupid car." It was Alex. "Nothing worth going into."

Patrick waited. He was curious. Was Alex going to say what

he had always said whenever Patrick complained about the car? How silly it was to own a car in the city? How car owners were just asking for trouble? That's what Alex always said, and Patrick was almost hoping he'd say it now, but Alex didn't say anything. Or rather, he said, "What are you doing for lunch today?"

"For lunch?"

"Yeah."

"Um…nothing really."

"Would you want to get together?"

"Sure. OK."

"Say 1 o'clock?"

"Um…yeah, OK. Where?"

"Well, it's such a nice day, I thought we could just grab a sandwich. Maybe sit out in Farragut Square?"

"That'd be—that'd be good."

And it *was* a nice day. The air was dry, except in the shadows of buildings, where it felt like a splash of cool soda. At the corner of Connecticut Avenue, a Peruvian band was throwing up walls of sound—reed sound and percussive guitar sound. It was fast music, but the people coming out of their offices had slowed a step or two. Women were wearing their good flats, lazily swinging their handbags, sipping from plastic cups of Diet Pepsi. Well-groomed young men in white shirts, with just a trace of a forelock hanging down over their foreheads, had taken off their suit jackets, had draped their ties over their shoulders as they ate salads from polystyrene containers. Everyone looked confident and fully realized, Patrick decided, like commercials for themselves. Even Admiral Farragut, rising up in the center of the square, suggestively clutching a telescope— even *he* seemed absolutely certain of what he was doing.

The benches were all occupied, so Patrick and Alex decided

to sit under an elm tree. Patrick was about to lower himself to the ground when Alex grabbed his elbow. It was a startling act. Patrick almost pulled his arm away.

"Ground's a little damp," Alex said quietly. He pulled a wad of paper napkins from his pocket and began making a little carpet on the grass. It took him almost a minute. Patrick was enchanted. He had forgotten what it was like, having someone make a fuss.

"OK," Alex said.

They sat down. Patrick pulled out his chicken salad sandwich and, mindful of who he was eating with, tossed his tie over his shoulder, tucked a napkin inside his collar, gently placed another napkin on his lap. A pigeon strutted over to his knee and glared up at him.

"How's your sandwich?" Alex asked.

"Fine."

Alex was eating something—eating something!—with apple slices and bean sprouts and honey mustard. He chewed a few times, contentedly, before speaking again.

"I was so surprised," he said. "Seeing you at Carl and John's."

"Why?"

"Well, I guess—I don't know. I guess Seth makes it sound like you sit around the house all day long."

"Moping?"

"Well..." Alex laughed. "Yeah. Something like that, yeah."

"Yeah, well. Seth."

"I mean, don't get me wrong, I was really glad to see you 'cause—the thing is, I've been *meaning* to call you and explain stuff. I know I have to explain stuff."

Patrick stared at the ground. A ladybug was climbing the tassel of one of his loafers.

"The thing is," Alex said, realigning himself on the ground, sitting cross-legged. "I know you're *aware* of my relationship with Ted, and—I was really concerned that you would think that what happened with us was—because of Ted. 'Cause it wasn't. I mean, the Ted thing just kind of—it just *happened*, I guess. Right after—I mean, just like that." He snapped his fingers, a little tentatively, and his mouth made a mocking half grin. "We call ourselves the Rebound Boys," he said.

A mayonnaised cube of chicken fell from Patrick's sandwich, landed in the little trampoline of a napkin he had stretched across his lap. Patrick stared at it in a kind of wonder. He had won; he had protected his pants. *Did Alex notice that?* he wondered. *Does he know I only put the napkin there because of him?*

"You never told me how you guys met," Patrick said.

"Um, it was a while ago actually. He had a friend—do you remember Holly? From my office? He'd come over to visit Holly sometimes, and the three of us would have lunch, and—I guess we had a couple of lunches, just the two of us, but it was never…"

He stopped again. *This is hard for him*, Patrick thought. *Good.*

"I mean, I was with you, and he was with Seth," Alex said. "So…"

"Seth, yes."

Alex smiled. He must have considered Seth safe ground; he relaxed his shoulders. "It's funny," he said. "One of the things I like about Ted is how he's still on such good terms with his exes. I know other people would be threatened by that, but it really just makes me think better of Ted. 'Cause that's the way he is; he's the kind of guy—there's some French expression for it, someone who's comfortable in his own skin, and that's sort of— God, I just can't finish a sentence today. What I meant was, I hoped we could be like that too. Someday. Good friends."

"Uh-huh."

"And I know this stuff takes *time* and all, so I don't want to—I mean, this is kind of my overture, I guess. I guess what I really wanted to say is, I never stopped *caring* for you and all, and I still—*do*, I guess. I wanted you to—" He wound a blade of grass around his finger. "To know that, I guess."

"Well," Patrick said evenly, "I feel the same about you too."

"Well, good." Alex gave his shoulders a shake. "I don't know why I couldn't just call you up four months ago and say that."

"It's hard."

"Yeah."

Patrick was staring at Alex's lowered head so intensely that when Alex raised his head, their eyes met briefly. And that second's worth of contact was so charged with something it seemed to last longer than a second.

Alex was handsome—the remembrance came to Patrick with a little pang as he contemplated the mass of medium-brown hair not yet sacrificed to fashionable salon cuts, the bright hazel eyes, the intense *regularity* of the features—that clean, wholesome profile and the perfectly straight nose, the kind of nose a plastic surgeon would build templates from. Suddenly it seemed perfectly sensible to Patrick that someone who looked so—so *ordered* would need to impose a little order on his surroundings, would feel obliged to be the world's organizing intelligence.

Why had Patrick never allowed himself to be organized?

And why had he never really *looked* at Alex before? While they were still together? It seemed, in retrospect, they had always been avoiding each other's glance. Why was that?

Somewhere, he thought, *somewhere Seth is lurking*. Patrick could almost conjure him up: hiding behind a bench or a bush or training a pair of binoculars on them from an office window. Because this was what Seth wanted, wasn't it? This moment of reconciliation, this feeling of the future—*some* kind of future—opening up.

And yet Patrick didn't feel manipulated. The moment felt earned. He felt like they were capable of many more like it.

Alex was arching his back now, reaching one arm behind his head, stretching his fingers down his spine.

"Do you have an itch?" Patrick asked.

"Yeah."

"You want me to scratch?"

"OK."

When Patrick got home that night, his father was on the couch, eating from a box of donut holes.

"Oh, Pattie," he said, his mouth half full. "That fella called."

"Which one?"

"That one I can never remember his name."

Seth wasn't home, though, when Patrick called back. It was the first time he had ever heard Seth's answering machine. It was a strange, diffident message: "Oh, this is Seth. Um...I'm not here now. Leave a message. If you want."

Patrick didn't leave one, but Seth called back anyway, an hour later.

"You're supposed to tell me who I had lunch with today," Patrick said.

"Who?"

"No, you have to tell me."

"Alex."

Patrick frowned. "I knew it," he said. "You were in the bushes."

"Who else could it be?"

"*I* don't know. It could have been the Scottish Prince..."

"You wouldn't be so coy. You wouldn't even have called. In the first place."

"I would have."

"No, you'd already be running off to Belize. Or Morocco. I wouldn't hear from you ever again."

"And that would bother you?"

"Well, sure. What would I do nights? Oh, I almost forgot, I've got a new place. To look for Scottie."

"Where?"

"You'll find out."

38

"Do you need any harvest pilaf?" Seth asked.

"Why would I?"

"Need harvest pilaf?"

"Yes."

"Because," Seth said. "They have it in bulk. Good price."

They were standing at the southeast corner of the Leafy Glen grocery store in Arlington. A minute earlier Patrick had rounded this corner for perhaps the 32nd time that day and found Seth standing there, staring at the bulk bins, his face strangely contemplative, his mouth twitching, his hand inserted like a surgeon's into the cavity of the plastic bag—and for some reason, seeing Seth like this was jarring.

Why? It made no sense. Hadn't the two of them arrived here in tandem two hours ago? And hadn't Seth been talking all the way here—like an ineradicable radio frequency? Saying how certain he was, how absolutely, mystically *certain* he was that their search would end here?

"If we can't find him in Leafy Glen," he'd said, "he'll never be found."

And when they parked the car and discovered, three spaces down, a Plymouth Voyager—blue, not red—hadn't Seth all but declared victory? All but planted the American flag right there in the parking lot?

"I can smell him," Seth had said. "Oh, I've got him in my nose."

So, for that first hour they'd wandered the aisles together—like one of those couples that Seth fantasized about in the Bulk Barn parking lot—Patrick walking and talking like a replicant and Seth in the grip of a mad gaiety, compulsively grabbing jars and cans and packages off the shelves, twirling them, swinging them in wild arcs around his head. He shouted random greetings to passersby, and now and then he'd stop to call out the information that was printed on overhanging wooden slates. "Sixty-five percent of the human body is water," he would repeat in a tone of awe. "Ribbon pasta is best with creamy sauces."

Once Patrick even caught him kicking his heels together, like a leprechaun. "Whole peppercorns!" Seth cried. "Will last indefinitely if kept in an airtight container!"

By contrast, Patrick found himself growing more and more dispirited as the afternoon wore on. He wasn't sure what about this place so depressed him. Was it the homeopathic remedies aisle? Was it the fact that employees were called "team members"? Was it the framed photographs of organic farmers, smiling pluckily like those starving villagers from CARE brochures? One woman had even posed with her goats. According to the caption, she treated them tenderly, and the goats really seemed to appreciate it. They seemed, actually, to be *in* on the whole deal—coentrepreneurs. Patrick could visualize them all sitting around the counting table at the end of the day, totting up the day's yield, tallying each bill with a little lick and a bleat.

"No, not harvest pilaf," Seth was saying. "Maybe pine nuts. Or orzo. What do you think? Pine nuts or orzo?"

The question puzzled Patrick perhaps more than it should

have. It had never occurred to him to actually shop here. To *counterfeit* shop, yes. He had a great deal of experience with that. He and Seth had been doing little else for the past two weeks. They had spent an entire day, for example, wandering through the men's departments of three separate Macy's and two separate Bloomingdale's. Another day had been given over to sampling dining-room tables at Pottery Barn and pretending to inspect the bridal register at three Crate & Barrels. They'd lost a whole afternoon at Home Depot, just running their hands along plywood.

Once, in the course of their peregrinations, Patrick had stopped in his tracks and said, without thinking: "Maybe Scottie doesn't shop much."

It was amazing how weary his own voice sounded.

"Of course he does," Seth had said. "He can't help it."

Seth couldn't seem to help it either. He was inexhaustible. A kind of suburban camel, able to cross vast tracts of highway and parking lot on very little food or water. He took Patrick everywhere. To antique stores, farmer's markets, Old Town Alexandria eateries. To Hechinger's, Britches of Georgetowne, Nordstrom's. To Borders, the Gap, Quartermaine Coffee. To a pet supply store, a CD trading post, a Shopper's Food Warehouse.

And he never got lost. His sense of direction was remarkable. He could have found his way to the gates of Cerberus and back, and in fact, he only lost Patrick once—at Ikea—and that was because Patrick had agreed to meet him at the Kavaljer wall system and had mistakenly gone to the Björkvalla bed frame instead. For about two minutes Patrick didn't know what to do. How would he ever find his way home?

The more they affected to shop, the more Patrick began to feel they were perpetrating a version of fraud—patronizing establishments with no intention of buying anything. So to relieve his guilt, he had begun making small purchases, anything that would run him less than ten bucks. At Merrifield Garden Center, for example, the scrutiny of a clerk had moved him to buy a slightly scratched watering can and a packet of turnip seeds. In the Pentagon City food court, he'd bought a falafel sandwich and a chicken souvlakia—though he wasn't at all hungry. The guilt came on especially hard at Circuit City—so did the salesman. If Seth hadn't been on hand, Patrick might have gone home with a ten-inch subwoofer.

"They have some beautiful basil," he heard Seth saying now. "Maybe I could make pesto."

Patrick watched Seth sift through a barrel of sunflower seeds, and he wondered if it wasn't the whole spirit of retail that was weighing him down. The ceaseless interchange with mammon. Or maybe it was all the standing.

Now and again he would find himself questioning Seth's tactics. He'd once suggested—he couldn't remember where they'd been at the time—he'd suggested they would be more likely to find Scottie if, instead of scattering in all directions, they remained in *one* place for a long period of time.

Seth, to his credit, gave the idea some thought. "I'd agree with you," he said. "If we knew for sure he would come here."

"I thought you said *all* gay men come here."

"Sure. If they're modern, if they're *enlightened.* Scottie might be—you know, a little medieval."

A medieval prince, Patrick thought. Why were they seeking a medieval prince in a late–20th-century climate-controlled shopping complex with glass elevators?

He hadn't the heart to really question Seth's assumptions, but he couldn't help thinking that the only times he himself had ever been successful in finding Scottie were the times he *hadn't* been seeking him. Clearly some principle of accidental fortune was at work here, and there had to be a better way of engaging it. Couldn't Patrick just go on living his life in normal fashion— as long as he agreed to do it in a state of constant expectancy? So as never to be caught off guard again? So as never to miss another chance?

"Swedish juniper cheese," Seth was saying. "What would that taste like?"

"I don't know," Patrick said. "Maybe gin."

"Gin cheese," Seth said. "Sounds like a greeting. In Taiwan." He bowed to Patrick. "Gin cheese," he said, extending his hand.

Patrick said nothing. Seth studied him for a few moments, then carefully set the cheese down and picked up his bag of pine nuts.

"Some refreshment," he suggested. "A shot of wheatgrass from the juice bar. Just the ticket."

He grabbed Patrick's arm with a jailer's grip, clamped onto the wrist and dragged Patrick for a few feet. Then he pulled his hand away.

"Oh, wow," he whispered.

Approaching them was a tall blond man, perhaps 35, with long arms and deep-sunk eyes. He was wearing desert boots and gray twill trousers and a green chamois shirt—surely, it wasn't that cool outside—and one hand was holding a cup of fresh-squeezed orange juice and the other was holding a huge bunch of Italian parsley, which he had fanned out like a floral bouquet.

"Who is it?" Patrick asked.

Seth didn't say anything. He pressed his bag of pine nuts against his belly and waited.

The man came to an appraising halt, about four feet in front of them. "Hi, Seth," he said in a low and attenuated voice, just this side of drawl.

"Hi," Seth murmured.

The man gave Patrick a pleasant cursory glance before shifting his attention back to Seth. "Aren't you going to introduce us?" he asked quietly.

"Oh!" Seth's bag of pine nuts fell to the ground. He bent down quickly to retrieve it, and as he came back up, his arm made an awkward sweeping gesture in Patrick's direction. "This is Patrick," he said.

"Very nice to meet you," the man said, slowly shaking Patrick's hand.

"And Patrick, this is Ted."

39

The thing was, Patrick had always *expected* to meet Ted. At some point. Somewhere. But he had always assumed it would be from a distance—through a telephoto lens, maybe—from a great enough distance, at least, to formulate an impression, to understand exactly what Alex had accomplished. And to give himself enough time to compose his appearance, draft an opening statement. And now the moment had come, and he was completely *un*composed, completely *un*prepared, shaking hands with the man in question and much too *close*. He couldn't observe anything. All he could do was scrounge for conversation.

"I've heard," Patrick said. "About you. From—"

"I've heard about *you*," Ted said. One of his eyebrows arched slightly as he spoke, and Patrick couldn't be sure whether the eyebrow was insulting him. He found his own brows involuntarily rising in response.

From the corner of one eye, he could see Seth furiously plucking his whiskers—practically depilating himself—and staring at Ted's feet.

"Didn't know you shopped here," Seth muttered.

"Well, I don't usually," Ted agreed. "But now and again I get a hankering to cross the river. I think I'd really have to call it a hankering. I mean, the Leafy Glen on Wisconsin has its moments, but ever since Larrimer's went away, there's no place that really...I mean, even Dean & Deluca gets kind of *impossible* sometimes."

How carefully modulated his voice was, Patrick thought. Even his dislikes had a lulling, honeyed quality—you could warm your hands on the things he didn't like.

"And then the other night, Jonathan and Charles served these, wow, pork medallions in a balsamic herb vinaigrette. And I said, 'Where in God's name did you get this meat?' And they said 'Leafy Glen.' So..." He flashed two rows of perfectly behaved teeth. "Here I am," he said.

"The meats are spectacular," Patrick said, nodding. He said that because that's what the sign over the meat counter had said: SPECTACULAR.

"Actually, this is the second time I've been here," Ted confessed. "Last weekend I got a pound of lamb sausage, and it was..." He folded the tips of his fingers together and gave them a wet kiss. "*Mwah.*"

"I was thinking of getting gin cheese," Seth said.

He might as well have been writing it to the local paper. Ted never shifted his attention from Patrick.

"Where do *you* buy your meat, Patrick?"

"Um...Safeway."

"Oh, in town?"

"Yeah...usually."

Ted's eyebrow dropped now, returned to its point of origin. Patrick was conscious of a difference in their relations.

They stood in silence for a few more seconds, and the only person who was registering physical discomfort was Patrick, who kept twisting his head around to stare down the aisle. As though someone were about to join them.

Oh, Scottie! There you are! I want you to meet a dear friend of mine.

"Well, hey!" Ted's voice came suddenly bursting into his ears—a little eruption of cheer. "Alex and I have been saying for the longest time, we have to have you over for dinner."

"Oh! Well, yeah, that'd be fine..."

"Are you doing anything this Saturday?"

"*This* Saturday?"

"Yes."

"*This* Saturday. I don't—no, I don't think so." He glanced over at Seth, but Seth was still staring at Ted's feet—like one of those Indian servants in the old movies, waiting for the Bengal Lancer to make his wishes known. Patrick gave a quiet cough, but it was useless: Seth was in a trance of humility.

"Saturday sounds fine," Patrick said. "I guess."

"OK, then," said Ted. "We'll say 7:30."

"OK, fine."

Where was Seth? Why wasn't he breaking in? Posing objections? *Oh, no, Patrick, you can't, remember? You're doing that* other *thing—that* thing.

But Seth never looked up.

"Do you need me to bring anything?" Patrick asked.

"Oh," Ted said, "you can bring *that,* I suppose."

He nodded briefly in Seth's direction, and Seth responded by snapping his head up and giving one of his quick, slippery smiles. Ted took a gulp of orange juice and smiled back. It was a slow and wide smile this time, without teeth.

"Isn't he dreamy?" Seth said.

For their weekly lunch they had chosen a canopied burger-and-sandwich joint along 17th Street. The waiter sat them outside at a family-style table, which they shared with two gay pensioners—60ish men who were reading great quantities of newspapers, most of them Thai. Patrick had ordered a club sandwich, and Seth had gone for the chicken pot pie, which, like most of the things on the menu, arrived on a bed of brown rice.

"Who are we talking about?" Patrick asked. "Ted?"

"Of course," Seth said. "Of course Ted."

"Well, you know. He's handsome. He's…"

"Bit of a snob, isn't he?" Patrick started to protest, but Seth cut him off. "No, I'm used to it. It's fine. I don't respect it, that's all."

"I was going to say he's very *cultured* and—well-mannered."

"Oh, it's all part and…" Seth was staring over Patrick's head now, staring at the waiter, who had large, gym-fed shoulders and tiny, tiny legs sticking out of black denim shorts. "Part and parcel," Seth said, finally.

"You're not being very respectful," Patrick said.

"Love forgives," Seth said, shrugging. "Oh, excuse me, Mr. Waiter? I'm sorry, could I get more iced tea? When you get a chance? Thanks very much." He waited a couple of seconds, then gave Patrick an ostentatious wink. "He's cute, isn't he?"

"Your type."

"Yeah," Seth said. "Like who isn't?"

Patrick balanced his thumb on the rim of a potato chip. "Before you give him your phone number," he said, "you need to tell me something: Should I be dreading this dinner thing? With Ted and Alex?"

"Oh, no, no, no. Just the ticket. You and Alex. Together again. The angels singing."

"And Ted making it happen."

"Even better," Seth said.

The iced tea came to them on a big white-lacquered tray, and as Seth took the glass his eyelashes began fluttering like wind-socks. He smiled up at the waiter and asked, "Where did you get that T-shirt? I really like it."

The waiter grunted something about Urban Outfitters and slouched off to the next table. Seth stared after him. "Urban Outfitters," he whispered.

"Something else I need to know," Patrick said. "Why the hell did Ted invite me? In the first place?"

"I'm sure he's curious," Seth said. "And besides, it's *his* place. He controls the environment, yes? Not like—Carl and John's backyard."

Carl and John's backyard. Patrick almost giggled. That was *years* ago, wasn't it? In Seth's mythology it had become a kind of touchstone of illicit passion. Which was pretty funny, really, when you considered how awkwardly Patrick and Alex had re-connected. Patrick with that ridiculous thing sticking out of his mouth—he still couldn't get it out of his mind. He stared down at his club sandwich, with its four toothpicks stripping for the sky, and all he could remember was that strange woman reach-ing across him for the hors d'oeuvre tray, delicately tamping down on one of the canapés—just as he was doing now with his sandwich—pressing down, curling one finger around the tooth-pick, coaxing, tugging…

"Don't do that!" Seth screeched.

Patrick looked up. Seth had buried his face in his hands.

"Don't do what?"

"The toothpick."

"What about it?"

"I can't stand it."

"*What?*"

A shudder ran the whole length of Seth's body, made him

writhe. "Pulling toothpicks," he groaned. "From food."

"You're kidding."

"No!" Seth began waving his hands frantically. "Just—can't you just put it back?"

"How am I supposed to eat my sandwich?"

"I don't know—eat *around* it. Can't you?"

"What if I take out the toothpicks under the table?"

"OK, but—don't make any noise."

"I won't. I'll hum."

Patrick began humming something. He didn't know what it was at first, but then he recognized it: "How Much Is That Doggie in the Window?" He got almost to the end of the song, and then he realized that the toothpicks were all out, so he quit humming in mid phrase. He gently returned the plate to the table.

"OK," he said. "All done."

"Where are the toothpicks?"

"In my pocket."

"OK." A shine of sweat had risen up on Seth's cheeks and forehead.

"You know," Patrick said, "you could've *told* me. I wouldn't have gotten the club sandwich."

"I *did* tell you."

"No, you said the club sandwich is bad here. You didn't say you have a toothpick *issue*."

"Well—I don't like to talk about it. I only tell my closest friends."

Patrick smiled. "I'm honored," he said.

The phone rang while he was throwing out the latest of Mr. Beaton's Whitman's Samplers. It was a small source of comfort that his father was now getting through less and less of each box. Surely it would only be a matter of time before his body began sending nausea signals with each new chocolate nougat. Soon, perhaps, Mr. Beaton would return to the banana-apricot shakes and carrot pulp and seaweed salads of earlier days and then, perhaps, to the paralyzing depression and then, surely, to another doomed venture—who could say what exactly? An international terrorism bazaar? Just recreating the whole cycle made Patrick cross. He snatched the phone from its handset, practically cold-cocked himself with it.

"Hello?"

"Patrick. It's Rick."

His eyes banged shut. "Rick. Hi."

"I'm beginning to wonder," Rick said.

"What are you wondering?"

"I'm beginning to think you're avoiding me."

"No! What are you—no, I've had this work project—*thing*, and it's been eating into my weekends; it's crazy. I haven't had a moment."

"You're avoiding me."

"No! I'm not. I was going to call you, and I just got busy."

"Listen, if it makes you feel any better, Marianne and I had a really good talk the other night. About the future and everything."

"Oh, yeah?"

"And we're—I mean, I didn't tell her about *us*, but I made sure she knew all about *me* and how I'm set up, and—it's all out in the open, and she's fine! Everything's cool."

"Really?"

"Yeah, really. So stop sweating stuff."

"I can't help it," Patrick said. "It's what I do."

"What are you doing Tuesday night?"

"Tuesday night."

"Want to come over for dinner?"

"*Tuesday* night."

He still didn't have it. The Excuse Database. He'd been meaning to get one for months. Something to sift through the parameters, generate the immediately plausible conflict, the commitment you wished you hadn't committed to, but you had.

"Sure," he said. "Tuesday would be fine."

"OK, I'll see you at 7 then."

Two dinner invitations. Two dinner invitations in the space of one week. When was the last time *that* had happened? Someday, perhaps, he would have dinner invitations that filled him with pleasure. Surely few could arouse less pleasure than the prospect of breaking bread with his ex and his ex's lover and his ex's lover's ex: It would be hard to top that. The closer it loomed, the more it seemed to pose a new high-water mark of dread.

Ted and Alex lived in a red-brick, turreted castle off of Florida Avenue. It was originally Ted's apartment: a two-story luxury condominium with access to a rooftop that offered, according to Seth, one of the best views of Embassy Row. Patrick wound up having to park five blocks away. It was a cool night, early October, and when Patrick got out of the car, an errant breeze almost ran off with the red bow he had slapped onto his wine bottle.

Why the bow? It was impossible to say. He had been searching for some gesture, and the wine didn't seem enough of one, but the bow—the bow was too much of one. It was almost childish, wasn't it? He was bad at gestures.

It was a beautiful evening though. There was a field of salmon overhead, with jet trails scratched into it by a giant finger. He could make out the smell of rotting persimmons, and as he passed a brownstone apartment building, a gust of chlorinated air met him. It made him want to drop the wine bottle, tear off his clothes, go for a swim.

Would they notice? he wondered. *If I didn't show up?*

But when he reached Ted's building, Seth was waiting for him outside. They exchanged brief, absurdly formal nods, and Seth leaned into the vestibule door, nudged it open with his elbow. Once they were in the lobby, Patrick looked around for stairs, but Seth went straight to an eccentric-looking, old-fashioned elevator with an open grillwork front. Patrick gaped at it. He didn't know anything like it existed in Washington. He followed Seth into the cage, watched Seth close the grate and poke his fist at a big plunger button. The car rattled and muttered, then, with a grunt of exertion, began crawling up the shaft.

It was a very slow elevator, so they had plenty of time to read the handwritten signs that had been posted at vertical intervals along the wall of the shaft. The signs read: GO BACK! IT'S NOT TOO LATE. YOU'VE BEEN WARNED!

"I helped put those up," Seth said in a tart voice.

After about 40 seconds the elevator shivered to a stop before a heavy wooden door with a brass plate bearing the number 2A. Seth slid the grill back and knocked twice on the door. For a moment nothing happened, and Patrick began to wonder if they had stumbled into a trap—maybe water would start trickling in from the ceiling or the floor would give way or the walls would move in—and then the door slowly opened before them. An unseen hand was pulling it from behind, pulling it by small degrees so that Patrick received an uninterrupted and gradually expanding view of the spacious foyer and the gleaming, wood-lined front room, in the middle of which Alex was standing, his hands folded in front of his belt in a gesture of qualified welcome. He was wearing a formfitting black cotton jersey and floppy jeans, and all Patrick could think was how thin he was. The thought actually energized him. As soon as Seth pulled the grate open, Patrick took a single long step in Alex's direction. He was thinking perhaps something might be wrong, something wasn't happening as planned.

But the only unexpected thing was the beagle that came sprinting from the kitchen, racing for the door and flying straight for Patrick, *lunging* at him with such momentum that Patrick fell back, almost collapsed into the elevator.

"Easy, boy," said Ted from behind the door.

The dog wasn't angry at all. He was overwhelmed, incredulous with joy. He couldn't think of anything better than what had just happened.

And Patrick couldn't remember the last time a living thing had been this glad to see him. As he struggled to regain his balance, he found himself wanting to memorize everything—the damp, yearning eyes, the cocked ears, the strange stripes of black and white around the snout, the autonomically wagging tail, the white collar encrusted with what looked like sea shells.

"Virgil, get down," said Ted.

Virgil. That was his name. *Virgil*.

Patrick had already heard that name, hadn't he? That long-ago summer night, calling for Alex from the bowels of a Mexican restaurant. Virgil was the yelp—the ear-splitting bark on the answering machine.

So you're the one, Patrick thought, staring down. *You're the one Alex left me for.*

"Watch out," Seth said. "He'll pee on you."

40

"No, he won't," said Ted from behind the door.

Alex was moving toward them now. "Look at that!" he cried. "Virgil likes Patrick!"

"Is that unusual?" Ted asked. He was in plain sight now. His arms were folded like a harem guard's. "Don't dogs take to Patrick?"

"More like the reverse," Alex said, smiling. "Patrick doesn't take to dogs."

"No, I..." Patrick began to say. The dog was clawing at his crotch now. "I like dogs. A lot. I do."

"Seth doesn't like dogs either," Ted said.

"No, no, no," Seth said. "I like dogs. Really. Here, Virgil! Here, boy!"

But the dog ignored Seth as unequivocally as Ted had done at Leafy Glen. Virgil had eyes only for Patrick, and he was quivering almost to the point of bursting. Maybe someone really *had* forgotten to walk him.

"Nice boy," Patrick said, bending over and tentatively tapping the dog's head. "Good boy."

It really is useful to have an animal, he thought. *At times like this.* He thought he might be able to spend the rest of the evening doing just this, sliding his hand along Virgil's spotted white-and-brown coat, staring into Virgil's beseeching face—anything to spare himself the awkwardness of being here. But out of the corner of his eye, he saw Ted's hands coming together in a large, stylized motion—like someone clapping cymbals together, except there was no sound.

"Welcome," Ted said. "I don't think you've seen the place."

"No."

"Everyone has to do the tour," said Alex in a singsong voice.

"I'm happy to do the…" Patrick stood up now, looked around in a slight daze. "Is that a Steinway?"

"Oh!" Ted was already halfway there. He moved with great elegance—Patrick couldn't help noticing that—his back straight, his head erect, his arms traveling in short, expressive arcs. Not a single wasted gesture. He swept his hand across the music stand, as though he were dusting it. "You're looking," he said, "at the thing that will keep me here for the rest of my life."

"Oh?"

"Only because it was such hell getting it in here. I don't ever want to face taking it out again."

"Do you play?"

"A little. Not as much as I used to."

"Ted could have gone to Juilliard," Seth announced. "His parents didn't want him to go."

Ted shrugged listlessly, headed for the next room. The tour had begun, Patrick realized. He followed a few feet behind, feeling a little like an out-of-towner trailing after the museum docent. He never quite caught up. For the next few minutes Ted kept advancing in fluid, circling trajectories and carrying on an almost uninterrupted stream of interpretation.

"Well, you can probably guess: The place was built in the

1920s. Thank God none of that art deco business across the street, you know, on that rent-control building? But still very '20s, with the high ceilings, confined space. Now, I'm experimenting with something in the living room; you'll tell me if it works. I've decided to hang all the stuff at waist level. I have a theory about this: I don't think people are used to *seeing* things anymore, so you have to really—*jar* their senses with different perspectives, like that guy, what was his name? In Philadelphia? *Barnes.* Now we're going upstairs. Watch that last step; it's exactly two inches higher than the others, I don't know why. And this is the guest bathroom. Claw-foot tub. That's an antique shaving mirror—I *love* that piece. And this is *our* bedroom. The four-poster lost its original finials, so I bought those carved wooden hands when I was in Bali, and I just kind of stuck them on top. I really like how they look. It's almost like they're *praying*, isn't it? Now, the chest of drawers is *not* a chest of drawers; it's part of a hotel front desk. From an old mining community in Wyoming. The hotel burned down around 1910 or 1920, but this piece survived, if you can believe it. See, it has 96 numbered compartments. Some mornings I just stand there, and I go, OK, are the argyle socks in Number 12 or Number 37?"

Mine eyes dazzle, Patrick thought. Always there had been some part of him that rejoiced at the accomplishment, the sheer competence of gay men. And always another part of him shrank before it. It seemed to him he was shrinking very rapidly now. Each decorative flourish—the cornflower-blue candle floating in a bowl of clear water; the vases of wheat and eucalyptus; the collection of antique chocolate molds; the kitchen with its floor-to-ceiling refrigerator, its chest-high dishwasher, its corrugated tin ceiling, its Smallbone cabinets—each new accoutrement left him a little smaller.

Alex has done well, he thought. *He probably can't believe his luck.*

"Oh, I almost forgot," Ted said. They had come back downstairs. They were standing in the living room now, alongside rows and rows of built-in oaken book shelves. "Seth! Should I show him your thing?"

Seth, crouched by the entertainment center, said something unintelligible.

"What? I didn't hear you." Ted gave Patrick a significant look, lowered his voice to a stage whisper. "He bought this for me at the Kennedy Center gift shop. I think it was for my birthday. See? Little tiny volumes of Shakespeare. In a lucite holder. I said, '*Lucite?*'" Ted grinned, bent his head toward Patrick's, lowered his voice still further: "I shouldn't have said that; he was very upset with me."

"Was not," Seth said. He was peering carefully into a CD tower. "We used to subscribe to the Shakespeare Theater. That's why I got it."

"And it was very sweet," Ted said. "That's why I still keep it in a place of honor. See?"

Seth said nothing.

Ted took Patrick by the arm now, a soft, almost sensual squeeze. "I think we'll sit you over here," he said. "By the ficus. And Seth, why don't you sit on Patrick's left? Honey," he said, casually fingering Alex's earlobe, "do you want to—no, before you do that, I need your help with something." The two of them disappeared inside the kitchen.

Seth and Patrick sat with their hands in their laps: two children at academy.

"I like your lucite thing," Patrick said.

Seth shrugged. "Impulse buy."

They fell silent. It had been a long time since they were this quiet with each other. Even when they were investigating retail outlets, Seth's chatter was a kind of trolley, carrying them along. But tonight he had nothing to say. So it was a relief, after another minute, to hear Ted's voice calling from the kitchen.

"Seth! Guess what we have for appetizers?"

"What?"

Ted lurched suddenly into the room, pointing a long, lethal-looking toothpick in the direction of Seth's heart. A piece of grilled pork had been impaled on it.

"Satay!" cried Ted.

"G-a-a-a…" Seth pulled the cloth napkin up into his face.

"Coming for you," wheedled Ted, taking slow long steps. "Coming for you!"

"Go away!"

Ted crouched further and further to the ground as he advanced—until his head was level with Seth's. He brought the satay stick to within six inches of Seth's ear, then abruptly reared up, pulled the stick away, frowned a little. "Never mind," he said in a soft voice. "Never mind. We'll serve it without the toothpicks, how about that?"

Alex wheeled the dinner out on a blond wooden cart, and for the next minute he and Ted whirled around the table, depositing chopsticks and rice bowls, red linen napkins and a pot of strong, resinous tea. Then came the meal itself, each new item placed ritualistically in the center of the table. Satay sans toothpicks. Steamed pork-and-rice balls. Grilled chicken with garlic eggplant. Chinese broccoli. Stir-fried tofu with bamboo shoots.

"Eat up, everybody," said Alex.

Hungry as he was, Patrick felt unnaturally constrained. Even the idea of picking up a fork struck him as rash and foolhardy. A static formality had shrouded everything—the linen, the bowls of food, the ticking of the grandfather clock, Ted and Alex themselves, sitting fully erect in their rosewood chairs. Even Virgil had subsided into a compliant heap on the hearth rug. Patrick felt mysteriously compelled to be as still as he could possibly be—and he wasn't sure how to reconcile that with eating.

Seth had no such constraints. Three minutes into the meal he had already abandoned his place to gallop over to the CD player, and for the next half hour he engaged in an endless double-guessing of the music. Beethoven's *Eroica*. No, Tony Bennett. No, k.d. lang. Donna Summer. Beethoven again. About halfway through the meal he put on Ella Fitzgerald and Louis Armstrong, and this seemed to satisfy him; he let it play unimpeded. But at intervals he still left the table and wandered around the apartment. At one point Patrick saw him staring out the window, like someone waiting for a taxi.

Neither Ted nor Alex seemed surprised by any of it. They had long ago acquired the habit of referring to Seth in the third person: "Seth's lost weight, hasn't he?" "Oh, Seth would know all about that." "Didn't Seth run into him the other day?"

Patrick was beginning to think of *himself* in third person. He couldn't understand why he felt so detached from his own situation, why he couldn't make himself eat larger forkfuls of food. He was falling behind, he could see that. Even Seth had put more of his meal away, and he was hardly present.

To compensate, Patrick periodically offered compliments about the food he wasn't eating. "The rice balls are excellent," he would say.

"Isn't he amazing?" Alex said, pawing at Ted's biceps. "I don't have to do anything except clean up after him, and then he's so *clean*, there's nothing to do."

That was the key, wasn't it? *He's so clean.* Alex had probably never dreamed—certainly never when he was dating Patrick—that he would find anyone to match him for cleanliness. Ted was not only clean in practice, he was clean in theory. He seemed, if anything, abnormally preoccupied with dirt; it kept coming up somehow. At one point in the evening, Seth lamented the absence of grunge music in Ted's collection, and Ted's first observation was, "Oh, they're so dirty. I just want to give them a bath, don't you?" And when Patrick mentioned a favorite coffee bar of his on 17th Street, Ted said, "God, it's so *dirty* inside. I wouldn't want anything from that kitchen. Oh, and you know they closed down that Ethiopian place because of the rats!"

They should probably close down my house then, Patrick thought. In roughly three hours, he realized, he would be lying in bed, listening to the scuttling sounds of rats in the eaves overhead. The best efforts of Vermin Vendetta had not succeeded in eliminating them, and Patrick had a vague sense that he was the subject of jokes in the rat kingdom.

"Do you cook?" Ted asked him. They were eating coconut sorbet now, and Ted's dessert spoon was politely paused about two inches from his bowl.

"Something like that," Patrick said.

"I figured since I saw you at Leafy Glen…"

"Oh." Patrick had forgotten how he was going to account for that. He struggled for a few seconds, and then Seth broke in: "Patrick was helping me. Find stuff for pesto."

Ted nodded slowly. "You live on the Hill, don't you, Patrick?"

"Mm-hmm."

"I lived there about ten years ago, I think. It was nice but a little sleepy."

"I like to sleep."

"But he doesn't like to nap," Alex interjected. "He hates to nap."

"That's true," Patrick said.

Ted said, "I would *love* to nap, but I can never find the time, do you know what I mean? Today, for instance, would have been a great day to nap, but what could we do? We had to go to the Orioles game."

"He gets box seats from one of the firm's partners," Alex explained.

"I only get it for six games."

"But it's so worth it. My God, these seats have *waiters*," said Alex, "*serving* you. At a baseball game!"

"And then tomorrow's already ruined for napping: We've got that stupid Chamber Society series. I mean, I could nap *there*, but it would be a little rude."

Ted's great achievement, Patrick decided, was his ability to take the sting out of his own superiority. His tacit assumption was that you were equally accomplished, equally prosperous, capable of providing your own litany of achievement if you so desired.

"Marcie Marquand," he said to Patrick. "Do you know her?"

"No."

"She does telecommunications at my firm, and she was asking me about the health insurance ramifications of hiring a lactation consultant—she just had a baby a few months ago—and I had *no* idea, but Tim *Reynolds*—do you know him?"

"No."

"I ran into him at the P Street pool. God, what a scene! I mean, don't you feel you can't walk anywhere without a thousand pairs of eyes following you?" He turned to Seth now. "Don't you just feel so self-conscious?"

"No," Seth said. "Doesn't happen to me."

He was actually seated at the table now, and Patrick stared at him and thought, *How could anyone* not *stare at you?* The blue eyes, igneous and unearthly; the mouth sliding over white, wet teeth; the permanently avid expression, which actually seemed to complete Seth's features, make them more attractive.

But Seth was so muted tonight. And so restless. And no matter how far he ranged, he always seemed to be revolving around Ted, like a meteor. The whole evening, in fact, reinforced Patrick's own gradually developed sense that Ted was their magnetic north. It was even more striking here because of the geometric composition: Ted with his back to the kitchen, staring out, and Seth circling around him, and Alex and Patrick poised on either side, leaning in sometimes when Ted lowered his voice.

"What should we do now?" Ted asked once all the dishes had been packed away, the table wiped down. "A game?"

But they couldn't agree on a game. Seth hated Pictionary. Alex was dubious about charades, and Patrick was equally dubious about Taboo—the last time he'd played it, a fight had broken out.

"I know," Ted said. "We can all pick a color for the upstairs bathroom." He bounded up the steps and returned with two armfuls of paint chips. "We've been meaning to paint in there for months, and we can't decide on the color, so no one goes home until we decide on a color."

For the next half hour they sat in a ragged circle on Ted's expensive Persian rug and perused every wavelength of the spectrum. It was beguiling in a way, and the names were really fascinating: lightning bolt, Spanish omelette, orange sherbet, embarrassed fawn, mad iguana, and Patrick's personal favorite, faux pas.

"Boysenberry!" Alex cried, raising the chip in the air like a bingo card. "That's what it was." He turned to Ted. "That's the color Grant used for his powder room."

Grant? The name left an instant residue in Patrick's brain.

Grant... For the next minute he sifted through dozens of colors and shades, held them up to his eye, stared at them—and attended to none of them. He was wrestling with the name. *Grant.*

And then it came to him.

"Oh!" he said. He hadn't intended to say it out loud, but he had. "That's..." He squinted at Alex. "Didn't we go to Grant's house for brunch?"

"That's right," Alex said. "We did."

And Patrick met a man in a Shetland sweater.

Did Alex remember that? Did he remember anything about his days with Patrick?

"Grant's had a tough time lately," Alex was saying. "I don't think I told you. He got burglarized only a month or so after we went there."

"You're kidding."

"It was the strangest thing. No forced entry. No signs of searching. Whoever it was had access to the keys and knew *exactly* where to go. Didn't need much more than a minute. Grant was wondering if it was some kind of inside job."

Patrick stared at the paint chip in his hand. Somewhere in his head a cannon fired off.

Inside job.

"God," Alex said. "We were there a while ago, weren't we?"

41

"It can't be," Seth said. "I don't believe it."

He sounded distraught. They were walking up Florida Avenue, and Patrick was trying to remember where his car was parked, and Seth was shaking his head in a jittery, seismic pattern.

"You're crazy," he said.

"All I'm saying," Patrick said, "is think about it. *Think* about it: No one at the party remembered seeing him. *Alex* didn't. And Grant didn't, and Grant was the *host.*"

"He could've come with somebody else."

"But it doesn't make sense. Even *I* didn't see him for more than a few seconds. And that was in the library. Not downstairs, not around other people." Patrick closed his eyes, projected himself back one more time, back to Grant's library. "Maybe he just didn't expect to find anyone. You know, if he was *casing* the joint. He wouldn't want to be seen."

"I don't believe it," Seth said. He had stopped now, and his head was lifted at an angle of defiance. "Not the Prince," he said.

Patrick almost laughed. *What a strange journey*, he thought, *for Seth the Tick.* From skeptic to advocate.

That's what comes from hunting someone: You get a little attached.

The two of them stood there, on the west side of Florida Avenue, staring up at an African violet silhouetted in someone's Palladian window. An old man in a tweed jacket walked past them—long tufts of his hair had blown upward like feathers.

"Call Grant," Seth said quietly. "That's the only way we'll know. I mean, maybe they found the guy. Maybe they've already arrested somebody."

Patrick shrugged. "I don't even *know* Grant. I couldn't even tell you his last name."

"Ask Alex for the name."

"Oh, come on, I can't do that. How would I explain it?"

"Well—don't you remember where he lives?"

"The *neighborhood*, yeah. Not the exact house."

"Well, maybe we could drive around. See if any of the houses jars your memory."

"And then what? Knock on the door? 'Grant! You nut! Any luck with the burglar thing?'"

Seth didn't speak. One of the corners of his mouth began to sag.

"Didn't you once date a policeman?" Patrick asked.

Seth rolled his eyes. "Patrick, he was *park* police. He rode a horse."

"I was just thinking, you know, we have a—a mug shot. The drawing. We could show it to the police, see if it turns up anything."

They were walking again, by unspoken agreement, strolling very slowly in the direction they had just come from. Seth had plunged his hands in his pockets and was walking a little bent over, as though he were searching for change.

"You really believe this?" Seth asked. "You really believe Scottie's a criminal?"

Patrick looked straight ahead. He had a notion that he was being tested. "I don't know," he said. "No. I mean, *no*, I don't think that. I don't know."

They found the car about ten minutes later. It was parked on N Street. They had been walking in entirely the wrong direction. Finding it should have been a relief, but it wasn't. They both stopped about ten feet away and refused to go any further. Another minute passed. A tall, pipe-smoking man came by, walking a Dalmatian on a very short leash; every time the dog deviated from the path, the man gave the leash a sharp yank. It made Patrick wince—it made him think of Virgil, who had made a point of sniffing Patrick's crotch as he stepped into the elevator. One last sense experience. Maybe right now Virgil was gazing out the window, the smell still quivering in his nostrils, dreaming about Patrick, wondering where he was.

"So you didn't give me your opinion," Seth said. "Your updated opinion."

"Of what?"

"Ted."

"Oh." Patrick shrugged. "He's—I don't know, he's very good at what he is."

"Hmm." Seth nodded a little. "He's not really. It's all an act."

"Well, then, it's a good one."

"All the same. Alex must know it. By now."

Patrick hesitated. He started to speak, then glanced away, and when he looked back he found he still couldn't meet Seth's eyes. He had to stare at his collarbone.

"They seem very happy with each other," Patrick said.

His tone was mournful as he spoke, and he wasn't sure if that was for Seth's sake or his own.

"Says you," Seth answered. He wrapped his arms around himself, gave his sides a quick rub, then turned his body northward.

"Think I'll walk home," he said. "Beautiful night, yes?"

"You sure?"

"Oh, yes." He made a little darting wave with one of his hands, then shoved both hands back in his pockets and began ambling down the street, moving in crooked lines.

"By the way," Patrick called after him. "Why did you kick me?"

"I didn't," Seth said, still walking.

"Yes, you did. Under the table, in the middle of dinner."

"Haven't kicked anyone since second grade." He kept walking.

"Pattie?"

"Yes, Da."

"If rats were going to eat you…would they go for your eyes first? Or your testicles?"

Patrick was lying in bed. It was midnight. Both of them should have been asleep.

"I don't know, Da."

He wanted his father out. The realization swept over him like a hangover. He was tired of sharing his house. He was tired of being accountable to a 56-year-old man. He was tired of worrying about his father's eating habits, business plans, love life. He was tired of chocolates, rats, seersucker suits, downstairs tenants, violin teachers.

He was tired of everything. He was tired of lying in bed, thinking about Scottie. That may have been the thing he was *most* tired of, and yet here he was, doing it again. Day 201. Day 201 in Our Year of Scottie, and suddenly Scottie could be a second-story man. He could be *anything*. There were so few facts to go on, and almost any theory could be made to fit them. The Shetland sweater? Bulky enough to hide valuables. The tattoo? Initiation to a league of burglars. The two people with him at the concert? Confederates. Working the Steve and Eydie crowd for watches, jewelry, wallets, leaving before anyone could trace them.

So maybe, after all, there was a reason they hadn't found Scottie. Maybe he just didn't want to be found.

Or maybe—and here Patrick's mind took a lurid turn—maybe Scottie was searching for *him*. Because he was the only witness. The only one who could place him at Grant's house.

Yes, officer, that's your man. He thought I was asleep, but in reality I was absorbing every detail of his soul and physical being. That'll teach him!

Oh, it was stupid. It was endlessly, fruitlessly hypothetical—and unreal, like everything else. Like Seth, like Marianne, like Ted and Alex, like his own father.

Like everyone but Rick, he thought, with a sudden wrench of his heart. Rick was actual. Verifiable. And what a charm that had all of a sudden.

Marianne called him Tuesday morning.

"Whatcha doing tonight?" she asked.

"Tonight? Wow, tonight. Having dinner, actually."

"Shit, so is Victor."

"Oh."

"I was calling to see if you wanted to get tanked or anything."

"Oh, wow, that's—hey, we could do it tomorrow night."

"OK."

"Is everything all right?"

"Yeah, it's—I don't know. Victor and me had this talk the other night, and now I'm not sure what the hell's going on with anything."

"What did he say?"

"Oh…well, if you must know, *nothing*, really. Anyway, I'll bore you with it tomorrow night; I gotta go now. I promised Victor I'd get his watch battery replaced."

"OK, call me tomorrow."

Until Marianne called, he could have honestly said he was looking forward to dinner with Rick. The thought of it had lightened his morning a little—but no longer. Driving to Rick's apartment complex, he felt Marianne's presence like a shroud, cloaking his head, oppressing his thoughts. He couldn't shake the idea that he was betraying her.

Because he *was*, wasn't he? And he could no longer argue that it was unwitting—he was walking right into it, eyes open.

So he had half a mind to turn back as soon as he got there, but as he maneuvered the Oldsmobile into a parking spot, he found, to his own alarm, that he was laughing. He was remembering the last time he'd come here. Remembering how Rick, desperate for a toilet, had leapt out of the car, charged up the steps, called out his apartment number as he ran. He would probably never ride in Patrick's car again.

So I'll have to get a new one, Patrick thought. *If we get serious.* And that made him sad a little. He thought sometimes the car was the only thing that understood him.

Rick let him get about five feet into the apartment before bestowing a kiss. It was a businesslike sort of buss, a quick brushing of the lips, with no sound effects. *What was that noise he made before?* Patrick couldn't remember now. Something like *hmm* or *grm*.

"Japanese OK?" Rick asked.

"Yeah, great."

"I was going to order, but I thought I'd better wait for you."

"Oh, you know. Tuna roll, whatever."

He watched Rick disappear into the kitchen. He looked around, made a few halting steps in various directions. He was still not comfortable here. He couldn't find a center of gravity. *Maybe if there were more books*, he thought. Books gave you something to look at, something to run your fingers along.

"Well, sit down," Rick said, reentering from the kitchen. "You're making me nervous."

Patrick looked down. A cream-colored leather sofa had materialized directly beneath him. He fell onto it. It made a strange grouching sound, like the muttering of a bear.

Rick came around from behind, dropped into the space next to him, carefully draped an arm around his shoulders. It surprised Patrick. He didn't know what to do exactly. Bring his knees together? Interlace his fingers?

Rick leaned over, whispered into his ear: "Whatcha thinking?"

"I don't know."

I shouldn't be here—that's what he was thinking.

And yet, if he were to be rational about it, there was nothing clearly offensive about it, nothing clearly culpable about Rick. He had always been very kind, hadn't he? Very patient, easygoing. Straightforward, almost simple. He had never been a second-story man. He had never placed carved wooden hands from Bali on his bedposts, and, most likely, he did not walk dogs on a short leash.

And he was *here*. He was here right now, breathing, his pretty gray eyes lambent, his well-knit frame moving around inside a flannel-textured cotton shirt, his hand softly, almost subliminally stroking Patrick's shoulder.

"It's good to see you," Patrick said, and it was. He shut his eyes, and his lips opened a little, and without willing it he felt his face moving toward the neighborhood of Rick, toward the whole satisfying vicinity of Rick, moving by invisible degrees.

A buzzer sounded.

"Shit," Rick said. "The food."

He rocked himself off the couch, ran toward the door,

pressed the intercom button just to the door's left. "Yeah?"

"Hey, stud!" answered the voice.

Rick turned around. His mouth was open about an inch.

Marianne was downstairs.

42

"Hide."

That was the first word out of Patrick's mouth, and the strange part was, he was expecting *Rick* to hide. It took him several seconds to understand his fallacy, to understand that it was *Rick's* apartment, and Rick had just answered the buzzer, and Marianne would be knocking on the door any second now, expecting to see Rick.

Which Rick, of course, already understood. He was circling in place now, putting up a periscope, scanning the environs for somewhere that Patrick could hide. That was their joint instinct, after all—to conceal. No question of bluffing their way through, improvising a story. *Yeah, I was just kinda in the neighborhood—though of course I didn't know it was Victor's neighborhood, having no idea where Victor lived or anything.*

Concealment, that was the ticket.

"The bedroom," Rick was saying. "No, she puts her coat in there. Um—the kitchen—shit."

They heard the knock on the door.

"Just a minute!" Rick called.

A few seconds of fierce pantomiming ensued—Patrick throwing up his arms in a gesture of helplessness and Rick making jabbing thrusts with *his* arms, which Patrick took for an expression of rage before he recognized it as a directing motion. He turned and discovered the hallway closet, slightly ajar.

The closet?

He squinted at Rick, gave an interrogative backward jerk of his thumb. Rick nodded, advanced toward him with large shoveling motions, and in the face of all this violence, Patrick retreated slowly, fell back until the small of his back felt the cool brass knob of the door. He gave one more questioning glance, then, with a shiver of disgust, turned and crept into the darkness. The door closed quickly and quietly behind him.

So here was Patrick Beaton. In a closet. Sitting on his haunches, his head wrapped in woolen coats and scarves, a Hoover vacuum cleaner stabbing him in the spine, the crook of an umbrella lancing his ankle.

It didn't get much lower than this.

He heard Rick open the door. He heard Marianne's bright greeting: "Hey ya, good buddy!" He heard her distinctive tread on the floorboards and the strange sound of rustling plastic— only a few feet from his head. He was doomed. He knew this, knew it with utter certainty. Within the next few seconds she would be opening the closet door, and that would be it. The end. The absolute end.

"Well, wow," he heard Rick say. "This is a surprise."

"Yeah, hey," Marianne said. "I know you're having dinner and all; I just thought I'd drop off your dry cleaning."

Dry cleaning?

"Oh, and your watch," she said. "I got your batteries."

"Hey, thanks," Rick said. "How much was it?"

"Don't worry about it, honey. Hey, listen, I'm gonna head out; I know your friend's coming."

"No, that's OK," Rick said. "I don't have to pick him up for another couple of minutes."

Great, Patrick thought. *Let's just hang for a bit. Let's shoot some shit here.*

Through the closet door he heard the now-familiar grouching of the leather sofa. The sound of Marianne planting herself, getting ready to stay a while.

"Can I take your coat?" Rick asked.

"Naw, that's OK," she said. "I won't be long."

"You sure?"

"Yeah. Hey, you know what? That piece-of-shit car out there looks just like Patrick's."

The car. Patrick smothered his face with his hands.

"Oh!" he heard Rick say. "I was going to tell Patrick about that. When we saw him the other night. It's so funny, this neighbor of mine has a car just like his. It's probably the same year even."

"With D.C. plates?" Marianne asked.

Oh, the pause was chilling.

"Yeah," Rick said. His voice was starting to fade now, like a radio signal. "I think…just moved from…a couple of months ago…still doesn't have new plates." Then, a little louder: "He works for the Capitol Police!"

Oh, good one, Patrick thought. *He works for the Capitol Police.* There was no question: Marianne was going to rip open that door any second, tip her head back, waggle her tongue, let out a body-snatcher scream.

Patrick held his breath—five seconds…ten seconds—then slowly released it. He closed his eyes, opened them again.

Nothing had happened.

He couldn't believe it. Nothing had changed—nothing except the permeability of the door. Because now he could hear

Rick's voice only in fragments—but Marianne's came through as distinctly as a stage actress's.

Patrick tried to lower his butt to the ground, but a flashlight was waiting for him. It gouged his tail bone. He stifled a cry, rolled the flashlight away, then settled back down. From nowhere a brown suede glove landed on his head. It covered his head like a beret, and a single suede finger crept over his hairline, pointed menacingly toward his left eye. Patrick didn't even bother removing it.

"OK," Marianne was saying, "so I've got this varicose vein, OK? On the back of my knee? Now, the doctor says they can gradually kill it with—with saline solution. Just keep injecting the stuff until the vein collapses. *But*—you have to wear this big ol' ugly brace over it, and even then sometimes the vein turns *brown*. Which is not an improvement, if you ask me."

"*Ruh-wuh-wuh*," said Rick.

"So I said, 'Well, how did I get varicose veins, anyway? I never cross my legs.' And the doctor guy says, 'Crossing your legs? Where the hell did you get that idea?' And I couldn't tell him. I just always thought you got 'em from crossing your legs. And he told me I was as bad as this woman who came by the other day. She said, 'Doctor, my son can't be gay. He's right-handed!'"

Marianne laughed—her most musical laugh. "So I started thinking," she said. "Do I know any left-handed gay people? Maybe they're *all* left-handed, I don't know."

Suddenly, Rick's voice became distinct again—as though someone had turned a knob on him.

"Is *Patrick* left-handed?" he asked.

Deep inside the closet, Patrick jerked his head up.

"Patrick," she said. She gave it a few seconds' thought. "No. No, he isn't."

No, Patrick isn't, Patrick thought.

Slowly he peeled the glove off his head. He shifted his body around, leaned his bulk against a heavy, gray, goose-down parka, reached for the something that was digging into his left thigh, held it close to his face, realized it was a pole socket. He stared at it.

No, Patrick *wasn't* left-handed. And Rick wasn't either—except Rick hadn't volunteered that. That little piece of news. He hadn't said, "Well, look at me, for gosh sakes; I'm right-handed."

And Marianne hadn't said anything either. She'd talked about "they." Maybe *they're* all left-handed, she'd said.

She didn't know. She still didn't know.

"Well, the fuckin' upshot," said Marianne, "is that varicose veins are basically hereditary. So what do you know? One more reason for me to be pissed off at my parents."

Why hadn't Rick made it clear to her? When the opportunity presented itself?

The suede glove sat in Patrick's lap, one crooked finger pointing toward his face.

Because Marianne picks up his dry cleaning.

And then Patrick's mind really got working. It began replaying, like an endless reel, all the conversations he'd ever had with Marianne—all the times she'd ever discussed Victor—and it seemed to him now, as he reviewed the transcripts, that they added up to a single text.

A recitation of sacrifice.

How had he never remarked on this before? She did *everything* for Victor. Whatever a girlfriend did, Marianne had done: Bought him gifts to give his own friends. Cooked dinner for him. Cooked dinner for his family when they were in town. Sewed buttons on his shirts. Took his car to get it inspected. Balanced his checkbook. Picked out furniture for his apartment.

Organized his photographs. Picked up his newspapers when he was away on vacation. Brought him soup and oranges when he was sick. Helped with his laundry. Picked out his clothes.

She had dedicated her life to Victor's service.

Patrick could remember calling her one evening to see if she wanted to go out and Marianne saying, "Oh, I can't. I gotta stay by the phone." And it turned out she was waiting by the phone because Victor might need her to be a fourth at bridge—but only if one of the invited group couldn't make it.

"You know," Marianne had said, "I'm kinda hoping he doesn't call. I don't even know how to play fuckin' bridge."

He never did call.

She brings him his dry cleaning, Patrick thought. *Drives a half hour out of her way to bring him his goddamn shirts. And his watch.*

And as an added value, she adored him—openly and unquestioningly.

Not a bad bargain for ol' Victorrick. And all he had to do was provide enough ambiguity to stoke her romantic interest—without ever satisfying it.

How could he have ever believed Rick was simple?

"Oh, I gotta tell you this story." Marianne's voice was still unbelievably clear, wired directly into the closet. "There's this woman in my office—we call her Teresa 'cause she takes so much interest in homeless people? Anyway, she befriended this guy who sits out on the corner right in front of our office, and this guy is—not *well*, OK? Not *well*, but he tells Teresa his birthday is coming up, so she says, OK, I'll make him a *cake*."

"*Roo-hum-buh*," said Rick.

"So she makes this cake, and the next morning she takes it to him, and he's sitting there with his little bag of belongings, and she says, 'Happy birthday!' And he takes one look at this cake that she's got all frosted and wrapped in aluminum foil, and his face just fuckin' lights up, and he says, 'Oh, thank you! Thank you s'much!' And he grabs it, and he turns it over, and the cake goes splat all over the ground."

Patrick was barely listening now.

"And he takes the *foil*, and he wraps it all around his head and says, 'Thank you, how thoughtful!' 'Cause he's hiding from the Martians, right? That's his whole deal. And here his little friend has just given him the perfect little Martian radar blocker, right? He couldn't get over it. He kept saying, 'Thank you, thank you s'much!' "

Marianne's laugh ran up the scale again, but Patrick's mind wasn't following it.

Oh, he could get a handle on Rick—or at least begin to. But he couldn't understand Marianne anymore.

A woman so pathologically in love that she invented daily flower deliveries, created whole-cloth fantasies, dreamed away every obstacle to their happiness. Why this language? Varicose veins? Aliens from Mars? This wasn't how an obsessed lover talked. This wasn't what a woman would tell the man of her dreams. It didn't make sense.

Oh, Scottie, he thought. *Help me understand. Please help me understand.*

Then the doorbell rang—so loudly that Patrick winced.

He heard Rick gliding toward the intercom. "Yes?" Rick said.

"Got yaw food," came the voice.

The food. Patrick roused himself, inclined his ear to the door. He waited.

"You already ordered?" Marianne asked.

And then Rick's voice fuzzed out again. "Was going to…waiting here…Jim got back…" Patrick could barely make out the words, but he could sense, all of a sudden, Rick's movement. Maybe it was the sound of the floorboards coming from different quadrants, but Patrick had a vision of him needing to move, inventing as he moved.

"Well," said Marianne in a softer voice, no longer plugged in. "I gotta go anyway."

"Oh!" Rick said. "I'll go down with you."

"Yeah."

The door clicked behind them.

Patrick was free now. He was free, but he didn't even think to let himself out of the closet. Another two minutes passed before the door opened, and it was Rick holding it open, and with his other arm he was holding a bag of Japanese food, and the light from the living room was barreling in, making Patrick blink.

Rick held out his free hand, and Patrick took it and hoisted himself to his feet and then took his hand away. They looked at each other for perhaps ten seconds.

Afterward, this interval would assume a larger complexity in Patrick's mind. But at the time all he was conscious of was the need to leave. He would agree to anything if he could just be permitted to leave.

"So...food's here," Rick said, his face twitching into a smile.

"Um..." Patrick made a polite wince. "I'm not very hungry."

"Oh, come on."

"No, I'm—really. I've got to go." He took a large step toward the door, waited to see if Rick would make a counterstep, and when Rick didn't he kept walking. He didn't turn around until he was standing directly on the threshold.

Rick was still standing there, holding his bag of Japanese food. He hadn't moved. "Do we need to talk about anything?" he asked.

"No."

"Are you mad at me for something?"

Patrick thought about it for a moment, gave it serious consideration. "No," he said. And then the unquiet spirit of Alex must have possessed him because he pointed to the closet and said, "You may want to dust in there."

43

"You win," Seth said.

It was a little after 8 in the morning. Patrick and Mr. Beaton had just sat down to breakfast, and Patrick wasn't thinking clearly because when he went to answer the phone, he took his cereal bowl with him—as though he were expecting the corn flakes to speak for him.

"What are you talking about?" Patrick asked.

"I called the police," Seth said.

"Say again?"

"I called the police."

"Um..." Instinctively, Patrick's eyes searched for his father, but Mr. Beaton was still slumped at the far end of the table. "Why did you call the police?"

"To give them Scottie's description."

"Oh."

"Like we discussed. *Your* idea, remember?"

"Wow, OK, you—what did you tell them exactly?"

"Said I was mugged."

"By Scottie?"

"Who else?"

"Yeah, but that—didn't happen."

"Course it didn't."

Patrick stared down at his cereal bowl. The few remaining flakes were wheeling about in endless spirals. He couldn't figure out what was making them move.

"What if they pick Scottie up?" he asked. "What if they arrest him?"

"Patrick." Seth was assuming his parental tone now. "If he doesn't have a record, they won't find him. If he *does* have a record…"

"Yes?"

"He's not the Prince."

"Well…"

There had to be a flaw somewhere. Patrick knew it; he just didn't have the energy to find it.

"OK," he said, "so what did they tell you? The police?"

"The one guy said it was awfully warm. To be wearing a Shetland sweater."

"Uh-huh."

"And his partner said, 'Are you sure he had a *humorous* look?'"

"Uh-huh."

"And they wondered how I could have seen the tattoo. If he was wearing a sweater. But still they were impressed. At how well I could identify him. And my drawing ability."

"Sure."

"I did have to give myself a little bruise. To be convincing."

"A bruise?"

"Yeah, on my—my right shoulder. I just gave myself a few punches. Before they got there. About 12 punches, I think. All told."

Who is this person? That was the question that now and again would come vaulting to the front of Patrick's mind when in Seth's presence. *Who is this person?*

"I told them he pushed me to the ground," Seth said.

"Uh-huh."

"My only fear," he added, "is that they'll classify it as a hate crime. You know, skew the statistics."

"Well, they'd have to know you were gay, wouldn't they?"

"Oh, I *told* them. More convincing that way, yes? Said I was coming out of Badlands. Singing a Diana Ross song."

"Yes?"

"And then Scottie came at me with a knife."

"Wow." Patrick leaned his head against the kitchen wall. Maybe he needed more sleep, maybe that was it. "Yeah, well, listen," he said. "Thanks for calling and—the thing is, I'm kind of late for work, so—so maybe you could—keep me updated?"

"I could," Seth said. "I will."

Patrick carried his corn flakes back to the dining room, set them on the table, then lowered himself into his seat. Mr. Beaton lifted his head a few inches.

"Was that your friend, Pattie?"

"One of them."

"That one—shit—" Mr. Beaton moved his hand slowly across his forehead, as though he were wiping away perspiration. "Begins with an S," he muttered. "Or a T…"

"Seth."

"*Seth*. Why can I never—Seth. Seth." He shook his head a few times in slow motion, then lowered it back toward the table. He might almost have been meditating, but it seemed more likely he was trying to figure out how to eat his cereal, how to *solve* the flakes, which had aggregated into a hard, brown moonscape.

"What are you going to do today, Da?"

"Well…" His father wedged a finger into the corner of his right eye. "There's a—Joel McCrea movie on at—at 3. And before that there's something about—spiders. Large ones. Large spiders."

"No rats?" Patrick asked helpfully.

"No," his father said. He dipped a finger into the milk of his cereal bowl. "No rats," he said.

Patrick must have caught some of Mr. Beaton's torpor because when Marianne called him that afternoon, his first thought was: *Will she mind if I don't talk? Maybe I could FAX my responses.*

"So!" Marianne said. "We're still on for tonight, right?"

Oh, God.

He'd forgotten all about it. They were supposed to have drinks after work; it was all set up, and now—he couldn't do it. He couldn't. He couldn't face her. He wanted to say: *Marianne, there's no point, I already know. The varicose veins. The Martian birthday cake. I know all about it.* And he wanted to say—what? That he would never again make her unhappy. That other people might, but he wouldn't. Except she would have no idea what he was talking about.

"Would you mind if I took a rain check?" he asked.

"Well, fine! You big whiner. Oh, but, hey, listen, I was over at Victor's last night."

"Yeah?"

"And I saw this car that looked *just* like yours."

"Oh, yeah?"

"Victor said it belonged to some neighbor of his, and I thought how weird 'cause it had D.C. plates. But then I thought, Well, Patrick can't be the only one in the world with a piece-of-shit car."

"Thanks."

"Oh, by the way, you know that woman I was going to set your dad up with? Sally the Buddhist?"

"Yeah."

"Well, it turns out she's taken a vow of celibacy."

"Oh."

"I mean, who *knows* if it's permanent? But it'd be a hell of a shock on a first date."

"I guess so."

"So the upshot is, I'm still lookin'. I have to tell you, I thought this was gonna be easier."

"Well, my father's a distinctive type."

"No shit. Is he still mainlining candy?"

"Um…no, he seems to be heading for the catatonia thing again."

"Oh, boy," she said. "Oh, Christ, I better hurry."

Patrick had come to believe he would be playing Beethoven's Minuet in G for the rest of his natural days—and always inadequately. Sometimes he would try closing his eyes as he played— the better to dissociate himself from the sound—but it seemed to be hard-wired into his muscles and neurons. He couldn't escape it. He almost wished someone would intervene, impose a court order, anything to stop him from playing, and in fact, that Sunday, after he'd slogged through one more stillborn rendition, Sonya suddenly took the violin from him, set it down on the tiled coffee table, and said, "All right, here's the deal."

Oh, wow, Patrick thought. *She's going to fire me.*

Or whatever teachers did to unload their students: *You know, Patrick, it's been great working with you, but you're still in Suzuki Volume 2, and you won't relax your wrist, and if I hear you do that to Schumann again, I'm going to kill you.*

And what would he be able to say to her? That he would practice more? That practice didn't help? Nothing helped?

So even before Sonya had said anything, Patrick was ready to pack the violin away, walk out the door. But Sonya said, "We've decided to get a surrogate father."

And it took Patrick a few moments to realign his train of thought. He'd been so closely monitoring his own symptoms.

Surrogate father, he thought.

"Oh," he said quietly.

Sonya was already talking again by this point, and as she talked she made a square around the den of her house, and her eyes were fixed on the small box of space directly in front of her head. "Now it won't involve intercourse," she said. "We're looking more at noninvasive techniques—sperm donation, most likely. On the other hand I do think whoever it is should have a real connection to the child's life. I mean, it takes a village, right?"

"Uh-huh."

"Now, Kevin and I are both very clear on what we're looking for in a potential father."

"You have criteria."

"Oh, yes! Oh, yes, it needs to be someone, first of all, who appreciates *art* without necessarily being artistic himself. Someone with a resilient sense of humor. Politically liberal. Sensitive, egalitarian, energetic, literate. Interested in dietary experiment."

Dietary exp— Patrick felt his eyes enlarging. A trickle like adrenaline circled around his throat.

"Are you…?" He paused, gave his chin a quick rub. He was nervous all of a sudden. "Are you looking for any particular age range?"

Sonya shrugged. "Sperm is sperm," she said. "I mean, I don't think it gets *old*, does it?"

"And would—would the donor be expected to *live* near you?"

"Well, that would be ideal, yeah."

"And—OK, you were saying you wanted him to be really involved with the upbringing. Does that mean, maybe, baby-sitting regularly? Spending a lot of time with the kid?"

"Of course."

"Or possibly—I mean, I'm thinking out loud now—maybe you'd consider *hiring* him as a live-in nanny, kind of?"

Sonya stopped pacing, pursed her lips. "You know," she said, "I hadn't thought about it, but if the guy was suitable and willing and everything, that might work out really well."

Patrick began sketching his own path now, around the coffee table. He didn't even notice his violin lying there or the bow still dangling between his thumb and index finger. His mouth began moving without his knowledge, forming inaudible words.

"OK," he said finally, "how are you planning on choosing the donor?"

"Well—I'll be conducting the prescreening interviews. Then we'll have a questionnaire followed by joint interview sessions with me and Roger. And then, you know, if we have to narrow it down any further, maybe an essay contest."

"Huh." Patrick regarded his bow now. His lips stopped moving, solidified into a smile.

"I may have your man," he said.

44

"Da?"

From the love seat Mr. Beaton made a slow windshield-wiping motion with his hand, as though he were unfogging his brain. For the past hour he'd been watching an old Roger Corman movie, and his body now made an almost perfect hypotenuse with the right angle of the couch. You had the sense, watching him, that if a hole opened up in the floor, he would simply slide on through, disappear forever.

"Da, did I mention Sonya's coming over?"

Mr. Beaton's eyes narrowed a little. "Today? It's not—it's not Sunday morning, is it?"

"Well, no, it's Saturday. See, her schedule's been crazy this week. She's rehearsing with—Slatkin or somebody? I don't know, somebody famous like that."

"Oh." He turned back to the television set. Someone in the movie was screaming.

"And the reason she's coming over *here*," Patrick said, "is that her house is being fumigated. She has lots of different insects, but mostly she has ants. Flying ants." He knew he was explaining too much. "Maybe termites," he added. "They're just not sure. They have to check."

Mr. Beaton said nothing. His head sketched a circle in the air.

Sonya arrived promptly at 3 o'clock, and as Patrick went to open the door he made a point of turning down the volume on the television set. His father didn't seem to notice, and, indeed, it cost him a visible effort just to turn his head in Sonya's direction when she entered the room.

"Well, hello!" Sonya exclaimed, extending her hand. "It's George, isn't it?"

Mr. Beaton took her hand with an air of bafflement—as though it might come off if he pulled too hard. "Yes," he said, softly. "George Beaton."

"Well, it's nice to see you again. I don't know if you remember, we met here a month or so ago. At the violin recital. You played duck-duck-goose with some of my students."

"Oh." His eyebrows did a faint twitch, and the embers of a smile began to stir. "Yes, I remember."

"They certainly had a very nice time with you," Sonya said, nodding fiercely. "You clearly have a way with children."

"Oh, yes. Very nice. Nice time."

Sonya's smile was still in place, but the edges of her mouth were turning up in panic, and Patrick began to feel his own smile freezing into something false and hysterical.

"Well, listen, Da," he said, clasping his hands together, "I know you're in the middle of something, so we'll just get out of your way, OK? I'll just get the—" And then he gasped. The first gasp was nowhere near loud enough—it died somewhere near his epiglottis—so he gasped again, a little louder, and then clapped a hand over his mouth. "Oh, my God," he said.

"What?"

"My violin! I think I left it somewhere. Oh, God, let me think." He gave his cheek a vigorous scratch. "Oh, you know what? I think I left it at the drug store!"

"The drug store?" asked Mr. Beaton.

"Yeah, I was buying some—*tung* oil, I think, and I—set it down to get my wallet out, and I must have forgotten all about it. Oh, wow, I hope it's still there."

"Oh, wow," Sonya said, "you better go over there right away."

"Yeah, you're right. God, how embarrassing. I'm just—wow. Let's see—hmm—hey, Da? Da, I hate to ask, but—would you mind keeping Sonya company? Till I get back?"

His father looked up. "Certainly," he said faintly. "Certainly."

"I'll be right back; it won't be ten minutes." Patrick was bobbing his head like a finch. "Fifteen, tops." He took a few long steps toward the door. "No more than 20 minutes," he said, turning around again. But neither Sonya nor his father was looking at him now. Patrick opened the door, gave them a last backward glance, then walked out.

His feet lingered on the sidewalk bricks as he made the slow journey up the street to Marion Park. It was a beautiful November day—masses of yellow serrated-edge leaves were piled around the bases of lampposts. The park was almost empty, except for a man in a streaked nylon raincoat lying sprawled on one of the benches. Patrick stopped for a moment, surveyed the scene, then, to his surprise, found himself heading straight for the sleeping man—veering off only at the last second to sit on the next bench over.

Now why had he done that?

Because this could be Scottie.

It wasn't so irrational. If Scottie could be a criminal, he could be almost anything, couldn't he? No scenario was too remote. He could be homeless. He could be illiterate and drug-addicted and leprous, the father of four illegitimate children in three different states.

Except he couldn't be. Could he? The man in Grant's library wasn't on the lam. He wasn't in a hurry to go anywhere.

Scottie, he thought. *If you're running—run to me. You can hole up here. We can wait it out. Everything will blow over.*

The man sleeping on the bench next to him had one arm stretched out under his head, and the hand of that arm was curled softly in a gesture of farewell. As Patrick watched, one of his parched, veined eyes opened and fixed him with an inquisitional glare, then wheeled about in its socket and closed again.

Patrick looked at his watch. Somehow 30 minutes had gone by. He made his way home, feeling surprisingly light—light in his feet, his legs, his head. Even the door to his house felt light as he pushed against it.

Mr. Beaton was still on the couch, but he was sitting up now, reanimated, his hands squarely on his knees and his head tilted upward in an attitude of absorption. Sonya was standing directly across from him, leaning against the fireplace, her arms folded and her head drifting toward one of her shoulders. Seeing Patrick, she turned and with a strained cheer asked, "No violin?"

"No, and you know what? I could *kick* myself. I just remembered—on the way back—I think I left it up in the attic!"

"Oh," said Sonya. "You're kidding."

"Can you believe it? All this trouble and—there it is, up in the attic, probably. So I'll just go get it."

"Oh, but you know what?" Sonya said. "I've just called the fumigators, and they need me to come back. Come back home."

"Oh, you're kidding."

"To the ants," Sonya said.

"Wow, that's too bad. Wow. Well, you know, maybe we could pick up again next week. The usual Sunday morning time."

"Yeah."

Her voice went hard all of a sudden. She seemed to have lost all will to dissemble. Patrick peered at her, but her face was closed off now; he couldn't read it. He watched her gather her things and watched his father's face grow at once more vibrant and more abstract, his eyes shining, his lips moistening.

"All set," Sonya said.

Patrick followed her onto the front step, carefully closed the door behind them. They stood there for a few seconds, their bodies pointed in different directions. It felt like the end of a bad date.

"Well?" he said. "How did it go?"

"Um…" She was grimacing now, as though it were an effort to remember, as though everything had happened a long time ago. "I have to tell you, it was hard going at first. You didn't tell me about the depression thing, Patrick."

"Well—I'm sure it's treatable."

"All I can say is, Thank God he started *speaking* after a while, I was about ready to give up. But it did get better; we started chatting, and it was fine, and of course the subject of kids came up. And I asked him, you know, if he ever thought about having more children. You know, never too late and all that."

"Right."

Sonya started to speak, then turned her face to the street.

"What?" Patrick asked.

She was almost smiling when she looked back. He had never seen her look this sardonic—he hadn't thought her capable.

"He said he and his *fiancée* would be having a child very soon."

"His fi…" The word wouldn't come out of Patrick's mouth. He tried to cough it out, but it wouldn't budge.

"I mean, gee, Patrick!" Sonya was grinning now. She couldn't help it. "You might have told me your dad was inseminating someone else."

Once he was back inside, Patrick closed the door behind him and leaned against it. He felt solid and unbreachable now, as adamant as a prison warden. *Seal off the perimeter!*

"Da," he said. "We need to talk."

His father was off the couch now, had taken a few halting steps toward the kitchen but with no clear intention. His only intention seemed to be to *move* again, but Patrick's voice interfered with that, confused the synapses so that even as his head turned, his body kept going a few steps.

"What is it, Pattie?"

"We have a problem here."

"Yes?"

"You haven't been truthful with me." Patrick was surprised at how steady his voice sounded. *I sound like a dad*, he thought. *I could be a dad.*

"I haven't?" said Mr. Beaton.

"No."

"Well, I don't—I'm not sure I take your meaning."

Patrick folded his hands behind his back, took a couple of declarative steps forward. "Well, Da, to begin with—I've now heard from two separate people that you have a fiancée. And neither of those people was you."

"Oh, no," Mr. Beaton said. "No, they misheard me. It was my *financier.*"

"Da, you don't have a *child* with a financier." Patrick's voice was low and firm, but something must have shaken his poise because after a moment's reflection he asked, "*Do* you?"

His father said nothing, just pulled out one of the dining room chairs and sat in it sidesaddle, so his body was facing toward the door.

"So this woman," Patrick said. "Have I met her?"

"Well—not…"

"And she's—I mean, you're really going to have a child with her?"

"Yes."

"And you never told me."

"Well—no…"

Patrick took a breath. "You know," he said, "I guess I should be angry, except—no offense, Da—I'm not sure I *believe* it. Come to think of it, I'm not sure I believe about 90% of the things you've told me since you came here."

He was amazed by his own directness. This wasn't how his family communicated. He must have been channeling some other, more functional clan.

His father wasn't quelled though. He just beat out a little military tattoo on the table. His spirits seemed perversely to be surging. He looked like he could hardly wait for the next sentence.

"Is there anything you want to say, Da?"

"Well—I think I've been honest with you mostly. It's true, I haven't *told* you things, but…" He smiled bashfully. "You *know* I don't like to announce things before they happen, Pattie."

"Da, if you're *engaged*, then it's already happened. If you've fathered a *child*, it's already happened."

He shrugged. "It's not that easy," he said.

Patrick came forward now. He stopped about five feet from his father, but he had to fight the urge to simply keep walking. He felt carried away by his own momentum; he wanted to follow it all the way.

"Da, if you can't be honest with me, then I think—I think it might be better if you lived somewhere else." The momentum was gone now. Patrick lowered his head, slid his hands in his pockets—tried to efface himself. "I want my house back," he said almost inaudibly.

The smile slipped off his father's face. For the next few seconds Mr. Beaton looked uncommonly grave. Then, without warning, he slapped the table and jumped out of his chair, propelled himself forward with such force that he almost collided with his son.

Patrick was genuinely startled. Mr. Beaton's face was only about a foot away now, and it was coursing with blood and oxygen—like he had just sprinted 100 meters.

"You know what?" his father cried. "You're right!"

Mr. Beaton had his two pieces of luggage packed in half an hour. Patrick was stunned to see them coming back down the stairs: the crinkle-nylon gym bag, the gray, rumpled hanging case with the gash running down the side. He'd forgotten how few things his father owned. It made his heart fold in on itself. He was sending his father away. Sending him away before he'd had a chance to acquire a better wardrobe.

Mr. Beaton was wearing the same royal-green jogging suit and soccer cleats that he'd arrived in four months earlier. Except the clothes weren't hanging on him this time; they seemed to complete him. Like regalia.

"Da. You don't have to leave *now*, for God's sake."

"Pish," his father said, smiling genially. "It's best this way, I think."

"Well—where are you going?"

"Oh, there's a B and B a couple of blocks away. I thought I'd go there tonight and maybe tomorrow night hit the Hilton or some place. You know, I won't be in D.C. that much longer."

Patrick could barely look at his father now. He thought at first it must be the guilt—the guilt that was even now clawing at his throat—but, no, it was Mr. Beaton's *happiness*. It was too radiant—like a naked lightbulb.

"I can drive you," Patrick said lamely.

"Oh, no, Pattie, it's such a beautiful day. I need the walk."

"Well—you'll call me, right? As soon as you get settled?"

"Of course! Of course!"

"You're not pissed, are you?"

"Not a bit of it. I just got a little *mired* here, Pattie, and I'm..." He paused, and when he started speaking again, his voice was hoarser. "I'm so grateful to you 'cause this way is *much* better. In fact," he said, shaking his head wonderingly, "I can't tell you how grateful I am."

Patrick didn't know what to say. He was standing in the kitchen, leaning against the counter, feeling completely enervated—where had all his energy gone? All the *air* had gone out of him, and it hadn't returned to the atmosphere—it had somehow been shunted into his father's quivering frame. Mr. Beaton could hardly wait to leave.

"Well," Patrick said, "I'll miss you and all."

"I'll miss you too, Pattie. And this lovely house of yours. I wish I could've killed all your rats for you."

"Oh, well."

"Maybe what's-his-gibbet could do it for you."

"Seth?"

"That's the one," his father said, looking solemn. He nodded twice, affirmatively. "That boy's got the hands of a rat killer!" he said.

45

Normally, Sunday morning was the time for Patrick's violin lesson, but he and Sonya had already postponed it to next week, which left him with a slight but unmistakable hole in his Sunday, one that he tried to elide by sleeping in late. His body, though, roused him at the habitual 6:30. He lay in bed for about half an hour, his hands by his side, staring up at the ceiling, which a year's worth of water seepage had painted a deep sienna. His front window was open, and gradually his ear picked out a sound—a short, repetitive rasping sound—that at first seemed far away—down the street and around the corner, maybe—and then gradually reconfigured itself until he came to believe it was burrowing into the foundation of his house.

He rolled out of bed, ran to the window, peered through the screen. The breath slowly returned to his body.

It was Deanna. On her knees in the garden, digging.

Well, thank God, he said to himself. And then an errant thought struck him. *In November?* he wondered. *Do people garden in November?*

When he went downstairs and opened the door, all he could see at first were Deanna's cotton work shirt and khaki trousers and her enormous straw sun hat, which seemed to conceal her entire head except for the thatches of curly brown hair that slipped out the sides.

The hat rose now toward the sun, and Deanna's unperturbed face met his.

"Hello," she said.

"Hi."

"I know, I know," she said, smiling. "It's too late to plant bulbs. I just let October get away from me somehow. I don't know how, but I did."

"Oh, well, you know, it's—October does that."

"You're right," Deanna said. "It does." She looked down at the freshly dug hole next to her left knee. "I'm not sure *what* will come up next spring. I guess we'll just wait and see, right?"

"Right," Patrick said. "Right."

She picked up her trowel, made a few feeble pokes at the hole, then set the trowel down again and stood up. Carefully, she peeled off her striped green gardening gloves. "Patrick," she said, "I need to let you know something."

"Yes?"

"I'll be leaving next month."

He looked at her blankly. She wasn't making sense. Leaving? Did she mean going on vacation?

"I mean moving out of town," she said, answering his very thought.

His silence must have unsettled her because she added, a little hastily, "I assume there's no problem with the lease. Since it's a month-to-month."

"Oh, yeah! I mean, *no*, it's no problem. I was just—I mean, is everything OK?"

"It's fine. I'm getting married."

"Married," Patrick said.

"I know it's a bit of a surprise."

"Well, *no*, it's just…" *What?* He scratched his head. *It's just what?* "Have I met your—fiancé?" he asked.

"Oh, no, he doesn't live here. He's from New Jersey. We actually grew up together back in Toms River, and we've just—you know, kept in touch over the years, and now it's just—the right time, I guess."

Patrick began to nod. "Oh, OK, that's—congratulations, that's great."

"Thanks."

"Well, we'll miss you."

His eyes settled on the little gopher burrows Deanna had been making. Bulbs. She was planting bulbs: Tulips and crocuses and irises that would emerge several months after she had gone.

"The garden will miss you," he said.

"I'll miss it too," she said. "I would take it with me, but I think it would be happier with you and your dad."

"Oh. Well, actually, my father moved out yesterday."

"Oh."

"Yeah, it's not—he's probably going to be leaving town soon, so…"

"Well, I hope I see him before I go."

"I'm sure you will."

She had turned away now. She was staring at the ground, surveying the holes that had multiplied around her feet, and Patrick thought, *How strange.* How strange that only a few weeks ago he had been planning to marry her off to his father—and the whole time she'd been planning to marry someone else. And the possibility had never even occurred to him. The possibility of Deanna having alternatives.

"Well," he said, "it's been—*nice*, you know, having you here and stuff."

She clamped her sun hat down on her head and looked at him now with a directness that surprised him. "You won't let my flowers die, will you?" she asked.

"No," he said. "Not—not intentionally."

Later that morning he drove the two blocks to the bed-and-breakfast where his father was staying. It was a lovely row house with mock-Tudor flourishes, and as Patrick paused the car a baleful Great Dane got up from the stoop and began trotting toward the car, bearing something in his mouth. Patrick couldn't quite see what it was—a sock? a dish towel?—and he couldn't be sure whether the dog meant it as an offering or as something else. He decided it was something else. He lifted his foot from the brake and drove on.

He was on an errand that morning anyway. He was going to find Grant's house.

He *had* to find it. He didn't necessarily know what he was going to do when he found it. He wasn't even sure there was an actual *point* to finding it. Would it honestly tell him if Scottie was a criminal? And failing that, what else could it do? Provide physical proof of Scottie's existence? The woolen fibers, the bodily residues fossilized on the library floor?

All he knew for sure was, if he could find Grant's house, he would be closer to Scottie. He would be closer to their first point of contact. And that was better than nothing.

But finding the house was no easy matter. His difficulty, he now realized, was that he had not been the one driving to Grant's. *Alex* had driven that day, and so Patrick had only a general sense that Grant lived somewhere in Adams Morgan. He realized too he had only the vaguest sense of what Grant's house looked like from the outside; all his memory was bound up in the inner rooms.

So Patrick began by driving up 18th Street, and for the next hour he steered his Oldsmobile down every street that presented itself. Down California, up Calvert, Columbia, Kalorama, up Champlain, down Euclid, Harvard. Not even noticing the names after a while because they were too confusing. Noticing nothing but the houses, slowing his car to a crawl and swiveling his head from left to right, scanning every building front, taking in every salient architectural detail, every cornice, porch, pilaster, lintel—waiting for the jar of recognition.

And in fact he recognized many things in the course of his driving. He recognized Alex's old apartment building. He saw the Caribbean restaurant that had caught fire while he and Alex were eating. He saw the rooftop where they'd sometimes gone for drinks. He saw the 7-Eleven where he'd been parked when he first decided to advertise for Scottie.

But nothing of Grant. Nothing that would lead him back to the Prince.

After an hour his eyes were spent. He pulled the car over to the side of the road, lowered his lids, and rested his chin on the steering wheel.

Maybe all this labor was pointless. Maybe he could just screw up his courage and ask Alex for Grant's number. He could do that, couldn't he? He could come up with some reasonable pretext.

And even if I can't think of a pretext, Patrick thought, *what does it matter? Who cares?*

Tired as he was of looking, he didn't want to stop driving. He wanted to keep going, and it didn't matter where. So without any clear mission in his mind, he drove back to the center of town, and after a couple of right turns, he realized he was heading for Georgetown. And then the image of the C&O Canal presented itself, triggered a rush of longing that propelled him through the next few blocks, made him park his car near the Four Seasons Hotel and walk quickly down 28th Street, down the stone steps to the canal tow path, which was still muddy from the most recent flood.

People were actually wading in the canal today—wading in November! Patrick didn't dare do it any time of the year. A young boy in nubby long underwear had immersed himself to the knees, and he was holding a long hornet-patterned fishing rod and staring at the point where his line entered the water. Further down, a golden retriever was paddling toward a mossy tennis ball, pointing his snout to the sky and swallowing tiny drafts of air as he went.

And about 20 yards down the path, another dog was coming. A small beagle, not swimming but looking as if it might, wiggling down the path toward Patrick—entirely alone, by all appearances, until the distant figure of an owner materialized some 20 feet behind. The closer the dog came to Patrick, the more it began wiggling, until with just a few yards separating them, the dog was leaping in the air, straining at its leash and making an unearthly whine. Patrick stopped, tensed himself in anticipation.

"He recognizes you!" called the dog's owner.

And it was only a few seconds before the recognition was mutual. *Virgil!*

How had he failed to make the connection? His little friend, Virgil. The only creature in the world that would asphyxiate itself at the sight of Patrick.

Touched, moved beyond belief, Patrick bent over to greet the dog, stroked its vibrating head, accepted the warm benison of its tongue.

"I think I'm going to let you adopt him," Ted said.

Patrick's head whipped up.

Why was he so startled? Because he'd thought only of Virgil? Given no consideration to who was actually *walking* Virgil?

Ted was wearing immaculately faded blue jeans, a cardigan sweater over a white T-shirt, and a corduroy cap that exerted minimal pressure on his head. He held Virgil's leash with a casual grace, as though he were training a filly.

"I thought you didn't like dogs," he said.

"No, I do." Patrick stood up now, cast his eyes about the path. "It's just—you know, the commitment."

"Oh, commitment, yes." Ted's eyebrow did its slow ascension up his face, toward his hairline. "Well," he said, "we certainly enjoyed having you to dinner."

"Oh! Yeah, that was nice. Great food."

"Are you doing anything tomorrow night?"

"Tomorrow night." *Kick in, database. Excuse parameter has been established. Kick in!* "Tomorrow night."

"I was just wondering if you wanted to join Alex and me for drinks after work."

"Oh, OK." *I can't! I'd love to, but I can't.* "That would be fine."

"Say Fox & Hounds at 6 o'clock?"

There's some objection, some impropriety I can't quite discern yet.

"OK," he said faintly.

"Well, that's fine then," said Ted.

"Should I bring Seth?"

Ted's eyes grew a little larger, pulsed outward. For a moment Patrick thought he was doing a Seth impression. Any moment now, he might start sweating, licking his teeth.

"Now, why?" Ted asked. "Why would you want to do that?"

When Patrick got home he found two phone messages waiting for him. One was from Seth, the usual noncommittal stammer: "Um...yeah, it's me, so...whenever..."

The other was from Marianne. And it sounded like the end of the world.

"Patrick! Call me. For God's sake, call me."

He drew a draft of oxygen. Then another. He picked up the phone. He began dialing, holding down each key for a full second, two seconds, three seconds—delaying as much as he could the inevitable connection because all he could imagine was disaster.

Rick had confessed.

That was the only explanation: Rick had confessed. Told her the whole sorry business. The eating of bad Italian meals. The enjoying of bad concerts. The ad in "Glances" and the glove in the closet and the bag of Japanese food and the Oldsmobile and everything, *everything*.

And when Marianne answered the phone, her voice was unusually tight and constrained, as though someone were in the next room. Patrick's heart began to hammer. He wanted it over with. If she was going to accuse him, she should do it now. Tear out his heart and be done.

But Marianne only lowered her voice further and said, "Well, guess who slept on my couch last night?"

Rick, he thought immediately. It had to be. Rick slept on the couch and—what? He—*did* something on the couch—something *to* the couch?

"I give up," Patrick said.

"George Beaton."

"George..."

Patrick wheeled around. His eyes ran to every visible corner of his kitchen and living room. Any second now his father would come stepping out from behind a wall, laughing, and Marianne would start in laughing too, and what a laugh they would both have—the two of them chuckling away!

"George Beaton, father?" he asked.

"The very one."

"Is he—is he there now?"

"Next room," she said, dropping her voice still lower. "Hey, you guys must have had one hell of a fight."

"No! It wasn't a fight at all, it was—*no*."

"Whatever it was, he looked awful. I mean, I couldn't turn him away, Patrick; it woulda been like kickin' a puppy."

"But—no, he told me he was going to stay at a B and B."

"Yeah, he was *planning* to, but then he lost heart or something. I don't know, he swears he only needs a place for a couple of days, and then he's on the road again. But, you know, come to think of it, isn't that the same thing he told you? A couple of days?"

"Something like that."

"The only upside I can see is, it'll be easier to fix him up with someone."

"Um…I think we're beyond that."

"Oh, no, you're kidding. Not the fiancée thing."

"The *pregnant* fiancée thing."

She sucked in her breath. "Oh, boy," she whispered. "Oh, wow." The air came out again, in a wheeze. "Well, shit," she said, "who knew the guy had it in him?"

"Oh, we're congratulating him?"

"Hey, Patrick, come on, at his age? You gotta be happy it remembers where to go."

46

The next morning, Patrick was sitting alone at the dining room table, stirring a bowl of oatmeal, half-consciously perusing the Style section, when he suddenly realized, *I have no distractions.*

By which he meant no half-eaten boxes of chocolates, no plates in the sink, no expectorant rumbles from the other side of the table, no noise at all—just the distant whisper of car tires on the street.

I have my house back. At last.

And it should have been a moment for quiet, extravagant celebration, but something in him was hedging, refusing to party.

Was it the thought of seeing Alex and Ted again? No, he'd confronted that; that was bearable.

Was it the image of his father lying on Marianne's couch? Oh, for all Patrick knew—for all anyone knew—Mr. Beaton was perfectly happy there. Perfectly happy anywhere.

No, Patrick would just have to make himself understand and fully appreciate his blessings. He had his house back. That was all that mattered. He had his house back.

The phone rang, and suddenly Patrick felt almost too giddy to answer. He was enjoying—he was very very close to enjoying his first long stretch of private time in five months.

He answered anyway.

"You didn't return my call," Seth said.

"I know."

"We missed a mission furniture sale yesterday. In Herndon. Perfect for Scottie sighting."

Oh, sure, Patrick thought, suppressing a laugh. *Perfect. Dead cinch.* "Yeah, well," he said, "I got tied up with stuff. My father moved out Saturday, and he's—"

"I have to tell you."

"What?"

"I'm starting to doubt your commitment."

"Commitment," Patrick repeated. He realized he was still holding onto his spoon. He was holding it in a death grip. "You know," he said, "I don't think there's any *question* about my commitment, all right? I have a *life* to live."

"Oh, yes?"

"And when you have a *life* to live, things happen, and you have to—take care of them, and that sometimes takes *time* and—energy."

"If you say so."

"Yeah. I do."

It was a rare gift: Seth could actually grow more infuriating with time. *The tick*, Patrick thought. *Burrowing deeper.*

"Anything else?" Patrick asked tersely.

"There is."

"What?"

"The police thing."

"All right, tell me about the police thing."

"Well…OK, the *good* news is, they haven't turned up Scottie in their files. Which means he's not a known felon."

"OK, what's the bad news?"

"Um...do you know the Pink Posse?"

"Yeah, they're some kind of—oh, wait, they're that gay militant group, right? They fight gay bashers."

"Right, they're the ones who sponsor Eye for an Eye Night. You remember. Anyway—kind of *funny*, really. Seems they found out I was—they heard I was *mugged*. Don't know how."

"Uh-huh."

"So they called. They said whenever I was ready. To speak out. I should call them."

"Oh, great."

"They're also—they're circulating the picture."

Patrick felt his jaw tighten. "What picture?"

"The drawing. Of Scottie."

"Oh, my God!"

"Well, see, I gave a copy to the police. And I guess they showed it to the Posse. So now the Posse wants to—all they want to do is show it around. To some other people."

"Oh, my God!"

"But this could be useful, yes? If they track him down. Saves us a lot of legwork."

"Oh, yeah, if they track him down and—and then *disembowel* him in Lafayette Park. What are you thinking? This is an innocent man, Seth!"

Seth was quiet a few seconds. "There is that," he conceded. "OK, I'll call them back. Tell them they have the wrong drawing."

"Please do."

"I'll do it now."

"That would be best."

Among the people sitting at the outdoor tables of the Fox &

Hounds, Ted stood out like a funnel of light, with his blond hair, his sculpted cheekbones, his eyes receding almost into blackness—he looked like he was being burned down to some irreducible essence. He was sitting at one of the white plastic tables next to the iron street railing, and when he saw Patrick he raised his hand, gave a slight, almost imperceptible twist of his wrist.

"Greetings," he said.

"Hi."

Patrick stumbled slightly as he maneuvered between the tables. He reached out with one arm and slipped his gym bag under the table, then fell back into one of the chairs—and as soon as he did it he realized his error. He had positioned himself against the railing, with his back to the street. This wouldn't do. The only reason to come here was to watch the street life.

"I've never seen you in a suit," Ted said contemplatively.

"Oh, this." Patrick glanced down quickly at his wool pants, gave them a soft involuntary brush. He was all prepared to explain his suit, but then he looked up again and noticed Ted *wasn't* wearing a suit. Ted was wearing black jeans and a teal-colored mock turtleneck.

"So," Patrick said, "is this how lawyers dress these days?"

"I had to leave town this morning. It's such a pain; I'm closing on a beach house in Rehoboth."

"Really?"

"And then I had to stop in Annapolis to see the parents."

"Oh, your…" Why was it so surprising? To learn that Ted had parents?

"Next month they're moving to Myrtle Beach," Ted said, "and I'm supposed to visit them in the spring, but they don't want me to drive. And I don't know a nice way to tell them this, but if I have to spend time in Myrtle Beach, I'm going to need my own car. Otherwise I'll just go mad."

An unshaven man in a grubby flowered shirt approached them from the street side of the railing. He stood over them, glowering.

"I'm sorry," Patrick said, "I don't have any change."

"I'm the waiter."

"Oh. Actually, we're expecting someone."

"Actually, we're not," Ted said. "Alex can't make it."

"Oh."

Patrick was going to make an inquiry, but then he realized it might be impolite, so he said nothing, and neither did Ted, and the silence might have continued if the waiter hadn't cleared his throat twice.

"I'll have a gin and tonic," Patrick said automatically.

"I'll have a Campari and soda," Ted said.

They were quiet until their drinks came. *An hour*, Patrick thought. *An hour. That's the minimum amount of time we'll need to spend here. An hour's worth of conversation.*

He still hadn't figured out a graceful way to change seats. It frustrated him. The only way to glimpse the local fauna was to twist his head to the left as far as it could possibly go. There was no way to accomplish this casually, but he did it anyway and saw at various intervals a cab blocking a Coca-Cola truck, a woman with a wallpaper sample book in one hand and a car muffler in the other, and a young man dressed for summer in a low-scoop tank top—his car keys were dangling from his nipple ring.

Looking at the street was easier than looking at Ted because looking at Ted would mean talking, and he couldn't think of anything they could talk about. It was remarkably awkward. And yet running into Alex had been awkward too, hadn't it? And they'd still found things to talk about, but what *were* they? What were the safe topics?

He could think of only one.

"I talked to Seth yesterday," he said.

"Oh, yes?"

"Yeah, he's—I don't know—what a character, huh?"

"Yes, he is," Ted said.

"So…" He really wanted to change chairs. He couldn't stand having his back to the street; it felt unsafe. "So how long were you guys together, anyway?" he asked.

"Two years."

"Oh, two years."

"It's amazing, really, that it lasted that long. My friends were amazed, anyway. They said we were the oddest couple they'd ever seen."

"Odd how?"

"Oh." Ted shrugged. "Physically, I suppose. Very different types. But you know, I was always attracted to him. He's really kind of nice-looking, I think—almost *Sephardic* at times."

"Sure."

"And, of course, he's voracious," Ted said, never changing his tone. "Sexually."

"Oh."

"You wouldn't think it to look at him, would you?"

"Well…maybe."

"I think it's all tied in to his body chemistry," Ted said. "It's in his pores. Do you know what scent he uses?"

"Um…no, I know it's—it's very distinctive."

"It's Old Spice."

"Oh."

"Do you know why he uses Old Spice? Because nothing else works. I know because we tried everything else." Ted was warming to the subject now; he was leaning forward in his chair.

"When we first started dating, he had this natural—*scent* about him, and I quite liked it because it wasn't a bad scent, it was just *distinct*, you know? But then I started thinking about the career ramifications—because let's face it, he's a lobbyist! He has to sway *Senators*. And I think, when you have this distinct scent, it's very distracting. In fact it's probably almost as bad as having a *bad* scent. Say you're a Senator, right, and Seth is sitting two feet away from you, jabbering away, and you can't hear what he's saying, you can't think of anything else, all you can think is, Here's this *scent* I've never smelled before, and you become obsessed with it, you'd do *anything* if he'd just stop smelling that way."

"Maybe that's his leverage," Patrick said.

"Have you sold your secretary yet?" The voice came from somewhere behind him, rattled in his left ear. Patrick twisted around in his chair and beheld a large, ginger-haired man with big hands and two big yellow front teeth.

Torvald.

Patrick was amazed at how quickly he made the identification. *Torvald. Scottie Number 2. Antiterrorist driving specialist. Antiques enthusiast.*

"No," Patrick said. "No, I still have the secretary."

"I thought I'd check," Torvald said.

They nodded at each other for a few seconds. Then Torvald said, "I don't think you should let the child's death affect you. People die all the time."

Child's death. Patrick's eyes began to flutter. The memory came rushing back.

Of course! The secretary. The secretary couldn't be sold because—because it had killed a child.

"Thank you," Patrick said. "I just—I need some *time*, that's all."

"Well, if you ever change your mind," Torvald said, "you know where to find me."

"I do."

"And I want to tell you something." He was sucking on one of his fingers. "Furniture is for the living," he said. He nodded once and walked slowly southward.

Patrick watched him go—partly from fascination, partly because he didn't want to turn around. He didn't want to see Ted's climbing eyebrow. He couldn't cope with that.

But when he turned around the face was still in place. All Ted was doing was taking a sip of his Campari and inquiring politely: "Someone died?"

"No. It's a long story. We made up this death to—"

"You look nice in work clothes," Ted said.

"Oh. Thank you." His mind shut down for a second. "I'm sure you do too," he said.

The conversation never quite got back on track after that. For the next half hour they indulged in little spasms of small talk—about mutual acquaintances (they had none), about the Orioles, car upholstery, the real-estate market, Teva sandals, domestic help, veterinary hospitals—talk that never led anywhere, talk that trailed off into long, puzzled intervals of quiet. They sipped compulsively at their drinks, let their eyes roam with no clear purpose, assumed exaggerated postures of nonchalance, regularly flung their arms back as though they were about to embrace someone.

Patrick never did find a way to change seats.

They were on their third round of drinks when Ted, smiling now with a mellow fire, leaned back in his chair, joined his hands in a pyramid, and said, "You're not dating anyone currently."

"Um…no."

"That's what Seth said. He said you sit around the house all day."

"Well, that's an exaggeration really—"

"I don't doubt it," Ted said quickly. "Are you still attracted to Alex?"

Oh, wow. Here it was. Half an hour of idle chat, half an hour of filler, and it all came down to this, the whole reason for his being here. The whole reason for Alex not being here.

Back off, Patrick. He's mine.

And knowing what was to come, how could he possibly answer the question? What could he possibly say? That wouldn't be incriminating?

"Well, I don't know," he began, inching his way. "I guess. Sure," he said. "I don't know. I mean, that kind of thing doesn't—go away, does it?"

"Of course it doesn't. That's exactly my point. The human race—and men in particular—are biologically programmed, correct? Programmed to scatter our seed as far and wide as we can. Ensure our genetic survival. It's biology."

"Sure."

Where is he going? He wasn't going where Patrick thought he was going.

"And monogamy, on the other hand, is entirely a social construct. I read it started with the Hebrews. To ensure the orderly disposition of land."

"Oh."

"Many thousands of years ago. So you have to wonder, Why are we still stuck in these archaic constructs? When our genetic makeup—the one immutable thing about us—is telling us something entirely different?"

"I don't know," Patrick said. "Maybe genes get it wrong."

"Genes never get it wrong," Ted said. "The concept of wrong

means nothing to genes. Things *are*. Things are, and you act on them. Like attraction, for example."

"Uh-huh."

"Why should you stop being attracted to Alex just because you're no longer together?"

"Well—no reason, I guess."

"Or why should someone not be attracted to you even if they're with someone else?"

Patrick would have answered, but the kick stopped him. He hadn't expected it. A blunt collision of someone's instep with the tibia of his left leg. Not a hard bruising kick. No real pain to it. Just a form of announcement, a declaration.

Again he started to say something, and again he stopped. Because he remembered that kick. He'd felt it before. Eating dinner at Ted's.

It had come from under the table just like this one. From out of nowhere. And he'd wondered what he could have said to provoke it. He'd thought it must have come from Seth. Or maybe Alex, working off some hidden fund of anger. He had assumed that kicks were expressions of anger. He had never considered their caressing properties.

And now Ted's eyes were doing that thing they'd done on the canal tow path two days ago: engorging, enlarging, moving toward Patrick like the lens of a microscope. And the eyebrows weren't climbing now; they were contracting themselves, focusing the lens, and all of Ted's features seemed to be configuring themselves toward a common end.

"Doesn't that seem sensible?" he asked.

"Oh! Well, you know, it's all natural."

"Precisely."

"I'm not sure I—"

And then he heard another voice clanging in his left ear.
"Patrick?"

Once again Patrick arduously twisted his body around until
he was facing the street—but he already knew who was there.

It was Rick. Wearing a navy-blue pinstripe suit, with a big red
gym bag slung over his shoulder, standing about five feet away
from Patrick and showing no inclination to come any closer.

"Oh, hi!" Patrick said. "Hi. How are you?"

"Fine, I'm just—I'm meeting Marianne for dinner, so…"

"Oh, OK." He felt utterly exposed now, as though he were
being uplinked to the world. He wanted to cut the conversation
short, speed Rick on his way—but Ted couldn't be ignored. He
wouldn't allow it.

"I'm sorry," Patrick said. "I don't think you've—Ted, this is
Rick. Rick, this is—"

"We've met," Rick said.

47

Patrick got home at 8:30, and at 8:31 he called Rick's number. There was no answer. He called again at 9 o'clock, then at successive half-hour intervals after that. He never bothered to leave a message. He didn't want to. He was seeking confrontation, unnatural as that was. He was relishing the prospect.

He called at 10:30, then 10:35, then 10:40. At 10:50 he finally got through.

Rick sounded tired when he picked up. It must have been close to his bedtime. "Patrick," he said. "How are you?"

"Time to come clean, Victor." Patrick waited…one second, two seconds.

"You know," Rick said, "it's kind of late; you're going to have to be a little clearer. Come clean about what?"

"You and Ted."

Two seconds, three seconds…then a brief exhalation from Rick, a sound of concentrated weariness. "What about it?" he asked.

"Tell me how you know each other."

"Patrick, we already explained. We work in the same firm."

"The same firm."

"Right."

"And you can barely say two words to each other? Barely *look* at each other? I can't believe that's how you greet your average colleague."

"Patrick, I hardly know the guy."

"You do," he said calmly.

His viewfinder ran through the few charged seconds at the Fox & Hound. He remembered turning to Ted and—with a sense almost that he was witnessing pornography—seeing the infinitesimal, instinctual narrowing of Ted's eyes, an unmistakably defensive reflex. And he remembered turning back to Rick and being suddenly aware of *distance*, the five feet of space that Rick had put between him and them, space that wasn't going away.

"You know him," Patrick repeated. "I just can't figure out how yet."

He was ready for anything, for Rick to scream, hang up, anything—but nothing happened at first. All Patrick could hear were muted background noises, noises he couldn't identify— maybe Rick was putting his dishes away.

And then Rick's voice was back, sounding wearier than ever.

"All right," he said. "All right, it goes back a little."

"Uh-huh."

"OK, you remember how *we* met, right? How I answered your ad?"

"Of course."

"And I answered your ad because I thought maybe it came from this *other* guy."

"Yeah, I remember. Some guy you saw in the library or something. Some lawyer guy."

"Exactly," Rick said. "Some lawyer guy."

That's all he said, and in the ensuing silence all the inflections of "lawyer guy" reverberated in Patrick's brain and then coalesced into a single theme, a name.

Oh, Christ, this was getting ghoulish.

"*Ted?*" he cried. "*Ted* was the guy?"

"Yep."

"I can't believe it."

"It's a small town," Rick said softly.

A spasm seized one of Patrick's eyes. "So—OK, wait a minute," he said. "If that was *Ted*—I mean, that would have been months ago."

"It was."

"And if that was months ago, then you must have run into him since then."

"Sure."

"And nothing happens? You stare at each other in the library, nothing happens?"

"*No*, I mean—no. I mean, we may have kissed. Once."

"You may have kissed?"

"Yeah."

"Where?"

"In the—the supply closet."

Patrick stopped, made a grimace. "You mean, with all the pushpins and—*staples*?"

"We happened to be getting something at the same time. I don't know, *maybe* it was staples, and he just kind of—closed the door behind us. And he gave me a kiss."

"Kiss like a *peck*? Or a serious kiss?"

"I don't know. God, it was—it was a peck, I guess."

"And when did this happen?"

"A month or so ago. Maybe."

A month ago.

"And then what?" Patrick persisted.

"You know, for someone who doesn't like lawyers—"

"Just tell me what happened. I won't bother you anymore."

The words startled even him. *I won't bother you anymore.* He hadn't meant it to come out that way. He hadn't meant it to *mean* that.

Rick seemed to be considering the meaning too. It was several seconds before he spoke again, and when he did speak he sounded almost resigned.

"*Nothing* happened," he said.

"Nothing?"

"Well, of course not. The guy's *involved* with someone, isn't he? I don't want any part of that."

Very moral.

Patrick had wanted so much to have this conversation, and now he wanted even more to end it. He couldn't figure out a way to do it though.

"How's Marianne?" he asked suddenly. His tone was jarringly polite. "Did you have a good dinner?"

"Yeah. She's—actually, she couldn't stay long, she's got some—houseguest, she said? Someone staying with her?"

"Oh, God!" Patrick threw his head back, gaped at the ceiling. "Oh, wow, I have to call her," he said.

"I know." The life was seeping out of Rick's voice; he was almost whispering now. "So, OK."

"Yeah, OK," Patrick said.

"All right. All right, good night."

"Good night."

Patrick pressed down on the reset button, held it in place for a few seconds—a memorial moment.

Good-bye, Rick.

Then he dialed Marianne's number. He dialed quickly, with a mounting sense of urgency, and Marianne must have felt urgent too because she picked up on the first ring.

"Yello!" she cried.

Patrick pulled the receiver away from his ear. "Marianne?" he said.

"Well, hey! How's it hangin'?"

"Oh, I was just calling—I saw Victor. Earlier. He said you guys were having dinner."

"That's funny. He didn't—he didn't mention seeing you. You know, I gotta tell you, Victor's turned into a real stiff these days."

"Yeah?"

"Oh, I'll tell you all about it some time. Hey! You want to talk to your dad?"

"Um…he's not asleep?"

"Are you kidding? We're finishing off some—oh, fuck— George!"

George?

"George, tell me the name of this shit again…"

From somewhere—perhaps a few feet away—Mr. Beaton cackled back at her, a high-pitched response, foreign and intricate.

"Oh, yeah!" Marianne said. She was back on the phone now, laboriously reciting. "Rou-yer Gui—*Gui*-llet."

"That would be…"

"That would be cognac," she answered grimly. "That would be pretty decent cognac."

"Oh, I can't believe he's keeping you up on a school night."

"It's fine."

"No, listen, *any* time you want to give him his walking papers, you just go ahead, all right? Don't feel any guilt about it."

"Oh, shut up, will you. It's—hey, you never told me about your French teacher."

"My French teacher."

"Yeah—oh, come on, how you threw up on your French teacher? In the A&P?"

"Wait. My father told you that?"

"Oh, the whole sorry mess. He said you were out drinking one night, and Madame Whozit came up to you in the A&P and said, '*Bonsoir*, Patrick,' and tapped you on the shoulder, and you just turned around and—*ROWLLLFFF*—all over Madame Whozit and—wait, George! What did he say after that?"

"*Excusez-moi!*" his father yelled.

"*Excusez-moi*," Marianne said in a quiet, wondering tone. "Patrick, I got so much more respect for you now."

"Thank you."

"I mean, so much more respect."

"Well, OK, I'm going to be hanging up now."

"OK," she said agreeably. "Any message for your dad?"

"No. Just tell him I've got plenty of shit on him too."

"I will, sweetie. I'll tell him. Good night to us all."

A few minutes later he was lying on top of his blankets, still in his shoes, still fully clothed, his hands propping his head up at a slight angle. He was lying so still he could have been a piece of furniture.

Which might make life easier, he thought. People might like him better. How lovingly Torvald would treat him, for instance, if he were constructed of burnished cherry wood and leaded glass panes.

But now his life had become unbecomingly messy. Every time he thought he was getting a handle on things, they would rearrange themselves like an offensive formation.

He'd thought, for instance, that he'd dislodged his father from his life—had actually grieved about it—and his father had just turned up somewhere else, lodged in another host organism. He'd thought his relationship with Alex was resolved, sealed off, neatly consigned to history, but now it had broken free, started calling his name again.

There was a fundamental problem, he realized. It was a problem that colored everything else: Letting go of Alex had depended on his knowing that Alex would be happier without him. But now he couldn't be sure. Was Alex happier? Truly happier?

And in going back over the evening's revelations, he couldn't decide which was more meaningful, his own encounter with Ted or Rick's encounter with Ted. Rick's, after all, was still a little blurry, and Rick himself was an unreliable narrator, and for all Patrick knew, it could have been *Rick* lying in wait next to the staples, and it could have been *Ted* pulling back. But that still didn't explain—it didn't explain Ted's behavior with Patrick, which was maybe just something too sophisticated for Patrick to grasp—a quick mind fuck, a bit of mischief to perpetrate on your lover's ex. An episode of serial flirtation.

Or maybe Patrick had just *imagined* he was being seduced. Maybe he'd misinterpreted.

They only think they're happy. That was Seth's dismissive verdict of Ted and Alex, and maybe Patrick had wanted to think so too. Because no matter what anyone else said, Patrick still believed he was fundamentally responsible for Alex's leaving—which made him likewise responsible for Alex's being where he was now.

Which left Patrick perhaps with only one responsible thing to do.

From the eaves above his head came the familiar scurrying sounds, the ongoing critique of the Beaton rats. Listening to them now made him think of his father. He remembered the night Mr. Beaton had seen the rats skating across the moonlit kitchen floor, had cocked his head and said, "It's kind of like music, isn't it?"

That was some achievement, Patrick thought, *finding the music in rat squealing*. Maybe you could find it anywhere if you knew how to listen.

Day 232, he thought, making a note in his mental ledger. Day 232 and the Scottish Prince further away than ever. Everything else too close.

48

"All right," Patrick said. "Tell me what happened with the Pink Posse."

He and Seth had departed this week from their normal lunch ritual and had met instead for breakfast. Seth chose a place near Patrick's house: a diner/bakery that served cloglike doughnuts and fragrant, greasy omelets and looked, for all intents and purposes, like a hologram. The uniformed women behind the counter carried great synthetic piles of white hair on their heads, and the waitresses stuck pencils behind their ears, chewed gum, and called you "honey." It gave Patrick a bittersweet tang in his mouth: He'd forgotten how much he liked being called "honey."

Seth had already gnawed out the centers of four buttered pieces of toast, and he was staring now at the blackened, uneaten crusts. "The Posse," he said carefully. "All right, OK. It's a little—unsettled."

"Wait," Patrick said. "You *called* them, right? As we discussed?"

"I did."

"And you told them not to circulate the picture. You said it was the wrong picture."

"Correct."

"So what's not settled?"

Seth's lips slid open a little, then closed again. "They didn't believe me."

"They didn't *believe* you?"

"Well, you know, they—they think I'm only waving them off 'cause I'm *afraid*. Of reprisals. I said no, no, no. It was an art-class project. Human portrait exercise. Police picked it up along with some other papers."

"And they still don't believe you?"

"I don't know. I can't tell. Maybe they were pacifying me; I don't know."

"Oh, God." Patrick's head dropped. "Scottie's dead. They're going to kill him."

"No, no, no. Think about it, Patrick. All the months we've spent looking. *We* haven't found him. How are *they* supposed to?"

Seth meant that to be cheering, but it had the opposite effect. It made Patrick's head droop even closer to the formica table-top, made him instinctively curl one hand around his coffee cup. He couldn't get warm this morning. Last night a thin sheeting of ice had materialized inside his bedroom window, and he felt as though he'd absorbed it directly into his skin.

"Are we going to find him?" he asked suddenly. He'd intended to sound casual, but it hadn't come out that way; his voice was toneless, defeated. "I mean, *really*," he said, "are we going to find him?"

Seth looked away, as though the question embarrassed him. He was wearing one of the blackened toast rims around his finger.

"Course we are," Seth said, quietly. Then, dropping his voice still further, he said, "If you would just focus a little."

Patrick felt the old hackles rising up along the back of his neck—the Seth hackles. "Focus," he said calmly.

"You can't concentrate," Seth said. "Last night on the phone. I said, 'Let's hit the pet supply stores. Oh, and let's pose as home buyers. Check out local realty offices.' Didn't even register."

"I've had a lot on my mind," Patrick said.

"Tell me something." Seth's eyes were starting to darken in the fluorescent light. "Tell me something," he said. "Do you still *want* to find him?"

Oh, this old game, thought Patrick. Seth accusing him of insufficient commitment, and Patrick feeling persecuted and wanting to say *something* in his defense—something—except what could he possibly say?

Of course I want to find him! It's the only thing that gets me out of the fucking bed some days. It's just…

It's just, he couldn't be like Seth about it. He couldn't be tick-like. He was a compound-eyed insect—he saw everything through lenses and prisms—or maybe he was like one of those barn owls, swiveling its head in every conceivable direction. Too many things to look at, too many distractions: his father, Marianne, Rick, Alex, Ted—*Seth*—all separate roads. And maybe he could *follow* them all if they led to a common destination, but they seemed to wind along different mountains.

"I still want to find him," Patrick said.

"Good," Seth answered, his voice suddenly breezy. "Then we will. By the way, you haven't said anything."

"About what?"

"The weight!" His eyes lit up again, swelled out. "More than four pounds in the last two weeks."

"Oh. Well, yeah…" Patrick shrugged, spread his hands noncommittally. "Yeah, you look good."

"Even *Ted* mentioned it. Ted said he's never seen me this thin."

Patrick pulled himself up in his seat now, brought his palms together. "Can I ask you something?" he said. "Kind of personal?"

"*Bien sûr*," Seth said.

"I mean, it's not a big deal. I was just wondering—and it's not like you have to tell me or anything—I'm just—I mean, I was just wondering if Ted was—I don't know, *faithful*? When you were together? I mean, as far as you know."

Seth took it as an academic inquiry. He brought a finger to his chin, pursed his mouth. "I think so," he said. "Sure." He thought a bit. "You mean, like sleeping around?"

"Yeah."

"No, he was fine. That way." He dangled his head to one side. "Now *flirting*, of course. He did a lot of that."

"He did? Really?" Patrick felt his voice rising without his consent. "And, OK, that didn't bother you?"

Seth shrugged. "It's what he did. What he does. Doesn't mean anything."

"It doesn't?"

Seth's long, long eyelashes wobbled and fluttered. His mouth opened to admit first a brief flash of tongue, then that double row of startlingly white teeth, glowing like radium.

"You should learn how to flirt, Patrick," he said. "Very good for you. Opens your pores."

Patrick got to work that morning with a raked, steaming throat, and by the end of the day he had a fully realized cold. The next morning he called in sick, and as he sat alone on the love seat watching a television program he never knew existed, wrapped in a terry cloth bathrobe he almost never wore, he realized this was the first workday he had missed in almost 11 months. Eleven months! And he had not taken so much as a long weekend's vacation. It depressed him more than he would have suspected. *I need a life*, he thought. *Anybody's life.*

A few hours later he had swaddled himself in a brown suede jacket and sweatpants and was on his way to Provisions to get a tomato, basil, and mozzarella sandwich when something at the eastern boundary of his vision made him stop about six feet from the corner drug store, pull his hands from his pockets, unclench his body, and stare.

About 50 yards away was a Metrobus stop—a kiosk with clear plastic walls and wooden plank benches. And sitting on one of the benches was a dog.

A dog waiting for a bus.

That was the only interpretation Patrick could make. Of course, he worked for an environmental group—he knew better than to apply anthropomorphic norms to animals' behavior— but it seemed to him that the dog sitting on the bench, the— collie, was it? Not a collie, some kind of mongrel with ratty, uncombed caramel fur and a necklace of white fur where the collar would normally be—it seemed to him that this dog, by all objective indicators, was waiting for a bus. That is, it was sitting on the bench—resting on its hind legs, gathering the forepaws in front—and it was staring straight ahead, as calmly and unthinkingly as any dog would if it were—if it were waiting for a bus.

Patrick began walking toward the kiosk. He stopped about 20 feet away. He might have gone even farther, but from behind him came the sudden whooshing sound of a Metrobus. It froze him in place. He waited, waited until the bus was alongside him and then past him, listened to its gears sneezing, watched it pull up to the kiosk, puff open its doors, disgorge two humans, swallow three more, then groan and heave and grind on down the avenue.

And the dog didn't move the whole time. It kept on waiting.

Maybe it's a mirage, Patrick thought. He covered his eyes with his hand, then took the hand away—and the dog was still there, fully material.

Maybe I'm the mirage, he thought. He gave his cheek a couple of quick taps, then a harder tap, something like a slap. Then, impulsively, he turned around and began walking away, gathering speed as he went. He would go fetch his sandwich. He would go fetch his sandwich, and by the time he returned to this corner, the dog would be gone. It would have become sufficiently bored and would have gone back to its owner, who was even now depositing a check in NationsBank or picking up medication at CVS or—or returning library books.

But when he came back ten minutes later, the dog was still there. Sitting all alone now, but with the same air of infinitely trusting patience. Willing to wait as long as necessary.

How will he pay his fare? Patrick asked himself. *How will he get the coins in that little box?*

Once again Patrick found himself walking toward the kiosk, not even conscious of how he was getting there. The dog still hadn't turned its head, but Patrick could see it more clearly now, could see how it had arranged itself on the bench, how its stillness was, in fact, a bit of an illusion because one of the forepaws was beginning to slide off the edge, so gradually that you might think the dog was just lowering its shoulder, but then the paw actually dropped off, and the dog's whole body arrested itself— and then hurriedly realigned itself. The shoulder reared up again, the forepaws returned to their original perch—began slowly sliding forward again—and the hind legs gathered together underneath, anchoring the animal's bulk.

No, he didn't look comfortable, this dog. And it *was* a he; Patrick had seen that during the brief flurry of realignment. But he did look resigned. Resigned to waiting for his bus—whichever bus it was.

Surely, Patrick thought, surely the owner will come back, come rushing back mumbling apologies, her hands full of shopping bags or library books or vodka bottles. But this dog had no collar, no tags, no leash. And no other humans presented themselves. The population inside the kiosk had disappeared, and the surrounding plaza had been abandoned even by the pigeons.

Patrick moved even closer now, moving on the balls of his feet, holding tightly to the wrapped sandwich in his coat pocket, advancing a yard, another yard, until the dog had no choice now; he would have to acknowledge his caller. And in fact the dog did—with a slight incline of his head, an old-world bow.

Such dignity, Patrick thought. So far removed from his friend Virgil, that desperate creature, whimpering and quivering and wagging his tail, all for love. No, this was a cooler customer—didn't open his mouth, didn't even pant.

But the tail—the tail was stirring just a little bit. And the dog was moving his head now. Wasn't he? Moving it in some undefinable way, perhaps just a motion of the neck. And now—Patrick caught his breath—the dog was lifting one of its ears, like an antenna, and the other ear was quietly rising, and now the dog's mouth was opening, for just a fraction of a second, just long enough to let his tongue make a 180-degree fan, left to right, then dart back inside.

It was encouraging though, that little peep of tongue. Patrick thought it was the most encouraging thing he had seen in months. He was so moved that, against his better judgment, he began speaking. He said, "Come on, boy."

But the words had no effect at all—or, rather, a reverse effect because the dog recoiled a little. He seemed genuinely offended by the request. He seemed to be reevaluating his options.

Lost now—entirely lost—Patrick turned halfway around. Only halfway because a last-minute surge of hope made him sneak a look over his shoulder. But the dog still hadn't budged. So Patrick turned completely away; he started walking. And he had walked perhaps five feet when he heard a sound behind him, a soft sliding sound, a whispering, followed by an even gentler sound, a meeting of paw and ground, a soft dismount.

Patrick couldn't believe it. Had the dog really left his bench? After all this time? After all this waiting he was going to give up on his bus?

Patrick was almost afraid to turn around this time, but he did—he did, and there he was, the caramel-colored mongrel, standing! Wobbling a little, it was true (his feet may have fallen asleep), but standing, and his huge chocolate eyes were trained not on Patrick's face but on Patrick's shoes. He was waiting to see what the shoes would do.

So Patrick began moving. He moved a few more paces, then turned around again. The dog had followed him. Patrick moved another increment, and the same thing happened. The dog followed but from a decent distance, with no inclination to do anything more—no inclination to walk ahead or even alongside. He would wait to see what Patrick's feet did. He would move when Patrick moved, and he would stop when Patrick stopped.

Patrick should have been able to accept this, but he couldn't quite. He found himself needing to know if the dog was still following, and so he stopped at irregular intervals and tossed surreptitious glances over his shoulder, and the dog was there each time—each time just a few paces behind. And as soon as Patrick started walking again, the dog started walking.

It was like that the whole way home.

49

"Hello?"

"Hi...hi, Alex? It's Patrick."

"Patrick."

"Yeah, is this—I'm sorry, is it a bad time?"

"No, no, Ted's making dinner, and I'm just cleaning up a little. How are you?"

"Oh, I'm fine. I was just—I was calling to tell you I have a dog."

There was a pause. Patrick knew there would be a pause.

"A dog?" Alex asked.

"Yeah. I mean, I have him temporarily. He may have an owner somewhere, so—so I'm putting up notices and stuff, but I think he's probably a stray, so I may probably keep him, I don't know."

"A dog," Alex repeated dully.

Which was the very thing echoing through Patrick's head even now, two days after the animal had come home with him. *A dog.* He had a dog. It was almost too strange to contemplate, and yet he felt compelled to tell Alex about it the moment the dog had passed through Patrick's door. And how little coaxing it had taken in the end, the dog simply following Patrick through the doorway, as though a house were just a variant on a bus, still keeping that respectful distance as he quietly inspected the new terrain, reviewed the upstairs bedrooms, making soft slaps with his paws on the hardwood floors. As soon as the dog was through the door, Patrick had thought: *Alex. I've got to tell Alex. I've got to tell him I have a dog.*

Because the dog was, in some mystical way, the key to everything. He knew that. He knew his breakup with Alex was directly linked to his failure to have dogs, and this failure was somehow emblematic of a larger systemic failure on his part. But having a dog changed all that. It meant that Patrick himself had changed, had become the kind of person that a person like Alex could live with.

Because when you took away Ted's good looks, impeccable breeding, exquisite taste, his polish, acquisitions, talents—what was left? *A dog!* That was the critical variable.

"What's the dog's name?" Alex asked.

"Um…I don't know yet. I haven't—I don't have the right one yet."

"Well, where did you find him?"

"He was—actually, he was waiting for a bus."

"Waiting for a bus?"

"Yeah, he was—hold on, I've got a call on the other line… Hello?"

"Turn on the TV," Seth commanded.

"Seth, I've got a call on the other—"

"Turn on the TV. Channel 7."

"OK," Patrick said. "Just a second."

He set the phone down on the counter, strode over to the television set, searched for the remote control in the cavity of the VCR shelf, realized he didn't have a remote, pressed the television's "on" button, pressed 0 and then 7, waited for the slow fade from blackness.

And found himself looking not at a piece of film or a still photograph—but at a drawing, a crude ink sketch of a face. A sketch Patrick immediately recognized—he'd been there, after all, when it was first created several months ago on a table in Starbuck's. Even more than the sketch, it was the *face* he knew, a face now so familiar to him, so present in his waking and his dreaming that having it beamed back to him now was like seeing his thoughts writ in the heavens. He stifled a sob of joy, and it was only after two or three seconds that the context in which he was seeing the face penetrated his thinking—about the same time that the news anchor's voice broke through.

"Police say if you've seen a man resembling this sketch, you should call the Crimestoppers Hotline at 202…"

And in the gibberish of numerals that followed, Patrick's mind switched off almost completely—as though someone had thrown a mantle over his brain. The only thing he could still make out was the announcer's contralto:

> "The suspect was last seen brandishing a butcher's knife and is considered armed and dangerous. Do not attempt to confront him. Repeat: Do not attempt to confront him. Report any sightings to the police."

Scottie's face remained on the screen for perhaps another 15 seconds, but Patrick's sense of time was seriously impaired now: It may well have been an hour. Without turning off the set or even adjusting the volume, he slowly backed away from the television, moving in reverse lockstep, keeping his eyes fixed on the screen until a slight pressure against his right heel alerted him that he was inside the kitchen entranceway. He wheeled around and found the phone receiver still lying on the counter.

"Oh, my God," he muttered. He picked up the phone. "Oh, my God," he said again, more loudly.

"It's not ideal," Seth said.

"Not ideal? Seth, we're into major fraud territory now. You're, like, the Tawana Brawley of gay people."

"Oh, fine, blame me," Seth said. "I didn't do a thing. It was all the Pink Posse. They called the news station, news station called the police. Police gave them the sketch. No one even consulted me."

"Well, you're going to have to phone the station, then. Phone them and tell them to run a retraction or a correction or—whatever TV people do."

"Phone them? Are you on crack?"

"What else do you suggest?"

"Go with the flow! Listen to me. What's the worst that can happen? They find Scottie. They haul him in. Perhaps in handcuffs. A little verbal abuse, nothing serious. They call me up. I come in, say, 'Oh, my God, officer, the wrong man.' Very sad. Tragic miscarriage. Personally apologize. I say, 'Can I buy you dinner tonight? Least I can do. Oh, and I want you to meet a very good friend of mine. He's writing a book on falsely ac-cused—accusees.'" Seth paused a few seconds. "Come to think of it," he said, "that's the *best*-case scenario."

"Oh, yes. Dinner. He can bring his handcuffs. And his lawyer too, with all the litigation papers."

"Well, now you're getting silly," Seth said.

"Oh, I'm getting *silly*? Oh, I'm sorry, I didn't mean to—"

"And anyway, this is basically your fault. Essentially."

"That's interesting," Patrick said. "That's very interesting."

"I mean, if you'd called Alex. When I suggested it. You could've gotten Grant's number. Found out if they had someone in custody. I wouldn't have had to bring in the police."

"Oh, I see, so none of this would have happened if I'd called Alex."

Patrick's stomach did a half revolution. *Alex.*

"Shit," he said. "I've got to go."

"Go?"

"I've got a call on the other—I'll call you later, all right? We'll figure something out."

"Nothing to figure out," Seth said. "It's perfect."

"Fine. Whatever you say." He clicked over without another word. "Alex?"

"Uh-huh?"

Patrick was all set to apologize for the delay, but the voice on the other end wasn't peeved, just faint and a little distracted. *He's probably still cleaning,* Patrick thought. Dangling the portable phone off his shoulder, feather-dusting the CD tower, the Steinway, currycombing the sofa.

"I'm so sorry," Patrick said. "It was Seth—something on TV."

"Oh, yeah!" Alex said. "Did you hear about that? I couldn't believe it. He almost didn't tell us; we practically had to pull it out of him. He was so shaken up."

"I think he'll be OK."

"It's funny you should call though. Your name came up today."

"Oh?"

"Ted was saying we should all go away for a weekend, maybe in December. There's this great B and B we heard about in the Pennsylvania Dutch country."

"We *all*?"

"Yeah, just the four of us. Ted and me. You. Seth."

"Oh."

"Ted says he wants to get to know you better. Oh, and you could bring your dog."

When Patrick got off the phone, the dog was in the same place he'd been a half hour ago: lying on the unmade master bed, his tail mashed against the footboard, his paws supporting his head in an attitude of thoughtfulness—or what would have passed for thoughtfulness if his eyes had been open. Patrick eased himself onto the adjoining square foot of bed. The dog's nose twitched a little, sussed out the new scent, then fell still. A little grunt broke free. Maybe he was dreaming.

Seth's right, Patrick thought suddenly. *It is my fault.*

There was simply no reason he couldn't have called Alex and asked for Grant's number. Even if he couldn't have found a convincing excuse—so what? So what if Alex knew about Scottie? What did it matter?

Unless—and here a clipped, staccato voice resembling Seth's briefly took over the synapses of his brain—unless there were. Uniquely personal reasons. For not advertising Scottie's existence.

Perhaps, after all, there was some part of him, some very small part of him that wanted to be back with Alex.

Who knew if it was true? But Patrick could see that, as a hypothesis, it explained certain sets of facts: his concerns for Alex's future happiness, his secrecy about the Prince, his reluctance to follow Seth to any more suburban outposts. If he really wanted to find Scottie, after all, wouldn't he be willing to do *anything*? Go *anywhere*? Gladly risk televised fraud?

Did he really want to find Scottie? Was he really through with Alex?

Oh, it was absurd—it was beyond absurd. Even if the idea of a reconciliation could be entertained—and even stipulating that entertaining it was more than it deserved—was it really possible? And regardless of what Seth thought, was it desirable? Was it something either Patrick or Alex truly desired?

No, it was ridiculous; it would never happen, not in a million geological aeons. And even—even if it could happen, Patrick wasn't necessarily *keeping* it from happening by looking for Scottie in the meantime. Alex couldn't object to that: He had his *own* Scottie, for Christ's sake. And hadn't Alex always wished the best for Patrick? Looked out for his interests, tried whenever possible to advance his career? Come to think of it, the only reason Patrick ever met the infamous Grant in the first place was because Grant—Grant was...

Patrick stood up.

Because Grant was a supporter of the National Conservation Alliance.

Which meant Grant's name, Christian name and surname, had been at Patrick's fingertips for the last five months. In the cubbyhole of his office, in the goddamn NCA annual report. The annual report, with its comprehensive roster of major donors, the swelling ranks of the Millennium Club.

Grant's name! Waiting for him the whole time.

The next morning, he got to work an hour and ten minutes early. The offices were dark except for the spectral glow of copy machines and computer screens. Patrick opened his door softly, turned on the light, quickly closed the door behind him, threw his blazer over his chair, lunged for the bookcase, for the middle shelf, for its cache of one hundred annual reports, all bound in unmistakable kelly green. Almost panting now, he pulled out the first one on the left and began flipping to the back, his fingers moving automatically toward that familiar end section, that well-thumbed page—the members of the Millennium Club.

Feverishly he ran his fingers down the left edge of the first column, tunneling off his vision, eliminating everything from his field of sight but that first name, that initial letter *G*.

First column—no Grant.

Second column—no Grant. *No Grant.* Was it a middle name? Was that the problem?

Third column. *Come on! Come on, Grant!*

But Grant wasn't there. He wasn't there, and Patrick had only one column left. One column, and if he wasn't there, then everything was fucked. They were back to zilch, back to nothing.

Come on, Patrick thought, exhaling little bursts of steam. *Come on. Give me a G! Give me an R! Give me an A!*

And then—*oh, God! Oh, thank you, God!*—the page echoed the name back to him.

Grant.

Halfway down the final column: Grant Wallberger, Washington, D.C.

Patrick almost burst out laughing. Oh, it was too much. He couldn't bear it. Deliberately calming himself now, he knelt down, pulled the D.C. white pages from the bottom shelf, flipped it open from the back, began riffling, riffling, riffling.

G. L. Wallberger.

There he was. The little bastard, there he was.

And the address? California Avenue. Adams Morgan. Adams Morgan!

Grant, you asshole! I've found you!

He'd found Grant. He'd found Grant. Now what was he going to do with Grant?

Well—he could call him at home—except it was 8 o'clock in the morning. You weren't supposed to call people this time of day. They might still be sleeping. They might get cross with you. They might not tell you what he needed to know.

So Patrick waited. It was hard—it was very hard—but he

waited a half hour, unable to do anything else but wait—unable to read the paper, check his E-mail, get a cup of coffee. He couldn't even open the blinds on his window. All he was capable of was waiting.

And then at precisely 8:30, the very second at which the minute hand of his watch bisected the 6, he called.

He got Grant's machine.

"Hi," said the voice, not quite the voice Patrick remembered. "I'm not home right now, but your call is very important to me, so please leave your name and number, and you may be certain I will call you back. Have a nice day."

The beep sounded in Patrick's ear, and for a few seconds he was struck dumb. He couldn't conjure up a single word. He couldn't begin to explain the reason for his call. And then, just as he was about to hang up, the words came gushing from him in a half-mad torrent.

"Oh, hi! Hi, Grant? This is Patrick Beaton. I don't know if you remember me. I used to go out with—with Alex? Anyway, the reason I'm calling—it's funny because I was talking to Alex the other day, and he mentioned you had—very unfortunately been burglarized, which I was disturbed to hear about. And the reason I'm calling is—is really funny—or *odd*—because a *friend* of mine had the very same thing happen to his house. I mean, very similar to the kind of break-in that Alex said *you* had. And they don't have any leads yet—for my friend's house, for *that* break-in, and I was just wondering if the police had found—you know, anyone, any suspects or anything like that, and—actually, I wanted to call you too about whether you were happy with the work that the National Conservation Alliance has been *doing*, you know, in—in saving the planet. We're always very eager to hear from people—from supporters such as yourself. So, anyway, let me give you my work number…" He spelled out the numbers with agonizing slowness, as though he were speaking to a 4-year-old. "And you can call me anytime, and here's my home number…" Even slower this time, like someone speaking in a time warp. "So anyway, I look forward to chatting with you, and once again, I'm very sorry to hear about your—*losses*, so— OK, thanks, you have a good day, OK?"

He had expected to feel an overwhelming relief when he finally hung up, but what came rushing in were the doubts; they crowded out everything else.

He still didn't *know* anything. He didn't know if it was the right Grant. And if it was the right Grant, would Grant know who burglarized his apartment? Would Grant even bother to return Patrick's call?

Too many uncertainties. He couldn't process them all, and he wasn't used to being this wired so early in the morning. It scrambled his constitution. So he put his head down on his desk—the way his third-grade teacher used to instruct him. *I'm going to put my head down for at least ten minutes, and then I'm going to hoist myself up and crawl the 20 feet or so to the coffee pot (if someone's made coffee), and very gradually I will rejoin the land of living.*

But it didn't work that way. About a minute after he put his head down, he heard a gentle tapping on his door.

His initial instinct was not to answer. He didn't want any visitors. He wanted whoever it was to assume the office was empty and move along. But the caller must have taken his silence for a tacit acknowledgment because the door was opening now, slowly, and Patrick was almost afraid to raise his head, and in fact, he probably wouldn't have if the caller hadn't said his name.

"Pattie?"

And now Patrick's head snapped up. He saw his father standing in the doorway, dressed in clothes that Patrick had never seen on him before: a rust-colored turtleneck under a hounds-tooth sports jacket, baggy light-gray corduroys, calfskin desert boots.

"Da?"

"Can I come in?"

"Oh, yeah. Of course." Patrick stood up hastily, pulled an armchair around to the other side of his desk, motioned for his father to sit down.

But Mr. Beaton didn't want to sit at first. He made a couple of revolutions around the chair, and then he abruptly perched himself at the very edge of it, as though he could barely tolerate sitting, as though any second now he might have to spring up, hurl himself spread-eagled at the window. His hands were folded awkwardly in front of him, and his knees were humming like a turbine.

"Honestly," he said, "I won't keep you long. I've just come so you can congratulate me."

"Congratulate you?" Patrick asked.

"Twice over."

"Um…congratulations. Twice."

Mr. Beaton leaned back a little. His face sketched out the beginnings of a smile. "You're not going to ask me what for?" he said.

"OK, what for?"

And now Mr. Beaton was really smiling—but toothlessly, like an infant.

"I'm engaged," he said.

Patrick blinked once, twice. "Engaged," he said.

"Yes."

"To be married."

"Yes."

It wasn't a surprise, was it? It felt like a surprise, but it wasn't.

Patrick had known all along. Or at least he'd had time to consider the possibility, to use the word *engaged* alongside the word *father*—it wasn't a surprise at all.

"All right," Patrick said, sounding relaxed. "You're engaged. Maybe this time you can tell me who you're engaged *to*?"

His father's face clouded over. For about five seconds Mr. Beaton looked about as confused as Patrick had ever seen him, as though the question hadn't even made sense, except it *had* made some kind of sense because before long he answered it— but in a half-exasperated tone, as though the answer were self-evident.

"Marianne," he said. "Marianne, of course."

50

It was Mr. Beaton's idea to go for the walk. Otherwise Patrick might have stayed for hours in the same position: his arms flopped over the arms of his ergonomic chair, his chin awry, his ankles parted, and his knees clumsily joined together. All things considered, the walk was a good idea, except Patrick realized on the way down that he'd forgotten to bring his jacket with him. He watched his father shoulder through the building's double-glazed front door, and he followed half willingly, already gritting his teeth against the cold.

So the warm spicy summer air that actually met him was more shocking than the cold would have been. He stopped in his tracks, tried to reorient himself. It hadn't been this warm an hour ago, had it? It was late November, almost December, and somehow everything was as balmy as Memorial Day. *Indian summer*, he thought automatically, but that didn't clear things up; it just made them stranger. Why did they call it Indian summer, anyway?

He and his father walked for about two blocks without speaking. Mr. Beaton walked a little bent over, with his thumbs hitched inside his pants pockets—a cerebral cowpoke walk. Patrick's was a more open, straightforward gait: his head erect, his arms deliberately swinging. But this was an affectation. He didn't normally walk that way.

"I don't believe it."

That's what he said, finally, when they rounded the corner onto Connecticut Avenue. They were walking more slowly now, with no clear destination, and Patrick said it again, for emphasis: "I don't believe it."

His father stopped now, gave a couple of short nods. "We sort of figured you'd say that," he said. "Here."

Mr. Beaton reached into the pocket of his gray corduroys and extracted a folded sheet of scented mauve stationery, and even before Patrick took it, the scent had already reached his nostrils, triggered such an instant recognition that seeing the handwriting was just a needless confirmation. He read in a kind of stupor: "Dear Patrick: It's true, goddamnit!"

"So she does know," Patrick said dully.

"Of course she does! You don't think a fella gets unilaterally engaged, do you?"

They were walking again, walking toward Farragut Square, and Patrick remembered suddenly that he'd come here for lunch with Alex just a couple of months ago. And it was warmer *today* than it was then. The sun was washing through the trees like weak warm tea, and the workday was just beginning—people were clipping along in raincoats they hadn't bothered to button—and the only persons occupying the square were a raucous group of helmeted bike messengers waving their walkie-talkies like wands, and a young man in a black suit, sitting alone on a bench with a long green tie dangling between his outstretched legs.

Patrick and his father sat three feet apart on the bench nearest Admiral Farragut. A seagull was camped on the admiral's head, and a couple of yards away, a white squirrel scrutinized them from the parapet of a water fountain.

"So I guess I should ask you some questions," Patrick said. He felt unaccountably apologetic, as though he were back in geometry class asking to go through the Law of Contrapositives again. "I mean—when did all this happen?"

"Well, it depends on what you mean," his father said. "The *engagement* part happened last night but, of course, the whole *enchilada's* been in the works for—two years?"

"Two years."

Mr. Beaton had crossed his legs now. His hand was cupping the left side of his face. "Yes, I think it was two years ago—practically to the day. I can tell you exactly where I was, Pattie, I was staying with a friend of mine in Utica—doing some contract work with a venture capital firm there. It must have been the fifth town I'd stayed in that year. The fifth one, Pattie! I remember it being very late at night, and I was sitting up on this little makeshift cot, with my garment bag to my left and my traveling bag to my right, and I couldn't even remember where I'd packed my toothbrush—and I suddenly thought, 'No. This isn't it. This is not the life for a man my age.' It was then I realized, Pattie. I couldn't live like that anymore. I wanted a *home*. Very specifically, I wanted a nice little bungalow. With a garage and walk-in closets and wooden hangers.

"Well, that got me thinking," Mr. Beaton said. "I spent pretty much the next year, in fact, just kind of *thinking* it through. 'Cause I figured there was no point to having a bungalow if I didn't have someone to share it with. Do you take my point, Pattie? A bungalow *needs* a woman. So I just—I let my mind wander on the subject. I kept asking myself the same question, over and over again. 'Who do I want to share my little bungalow with?'"

"Uh-huh."

"And for some reason—every time I let my mind wander—it kept wandering back to Marianne. Terribly odd! It was honestly the strangest thing in the world because I hardly knew her, you see! The first time I ever met her was at your graduation, when she was pretending to be the mother of your love child." He chuckled to himself gravely. "And then after that I don't think I ever spent more than ten seconds alone with her in my whole life. But I couldn't shake the feeling, Pattie. Over and over again, I kept saying to myself, 'She's the one. She's the one.' My bungalow woman. And after a while I stopped fighting it. I thought, 'Well, here's this delightful girl, pretty and plump as a partridge, with a crackling sense of humor—and come to think of it, I think I love her.' Even if it did happen in a few seconds."

A few seconds, Patrick thought, remembering the cranberry sweater, the lopsided smile, remembering them as vividly as if he'd seen them a minute ago. *That's all it takes sometimes.*

"Well, by that time I had some savings, and I had a—a new project—so I thought, 'OK, George, you get your ass down to Washington. And you see if you can't work out some kind of joint merger with this gal.'"

Patrick squinted at him. "So—Marianne was your whole reason for coming here?"

"Well, not the *only* reason, Pattie. I mean, I wanted to see my goddamn *son*."

"Oh, yeah, I know."

"But yes, she was the motor, the—*engine*, yes. And I tell you, Pattie, the very *instant* I got here I thought I'd made the biggest mistake of my life. 'Cause I knew I didn't stand a chance with her; I'd never stood a chance. I couldn't understand what I was *thinking*. Disrupting my life that way and disrupting *yours*—and all on account of some idle fancy. So it was hairy for a bit, but then after a while I just decided I'd have to gut up! Give it my best fucking shot. So the first thing I did was try to come up with some way of—announcing my intentions, I guess. Letting her know what I was about."

Patrick stared at the thinning circle of shrubs around Admiral Farragut, ran his eyes along the shreds of dead brown leaves flecking the grass.

"The flowers," he said automatically.

His father didn't turn his head, just nodded. "That's where I went most mornings, you see. A different florist every day and a different flower. It was my little daily quest."

"But…" Patrick spread his arms helplessly. "She thought they were coming from someone else."

"Her little friend, you mean. Well, that was a bit of a misunderstanding. You see, I signed all the cards 'G.B.' And she thought that meant 'Good Buddy'—which apparently is the name she uses for that Victor fella."

Good buddy. Patrick's mind began scrolling. Back to Rick's closet. Back to Marianne's hearty greeting as she blew through the front door: *Hey ya, good buddy!*

Good buddy.

"Well, you can imagine how I felt, Pattie. Here I'd been sending her flowers for weeks, and she never said word one, not so much as a thank-you note, and I already knew—from you, I think it was—all about this Victor fella and how she'd made herself a goddamn vegetarian for his sake! And it got to the point I didn't know *what* to do. I just thought, 'You old fool! She's gone and found some nice young beet-eating man, which is what young women do.' And suddenly—it was like my whole world was falling apart."

Oh, it was all coming together now. Those fierce mood swings—the periods of manic energy punctuated by long stretches of paralysis. Nothing but the cycles of love. How had Patrick failed to see them? He'd navigated them himself.

"I don't know why, though," his father said. "I never gave up. It's funny, isn't it? I never gave up hoping. And then when—when we decided I should leave the house—it was suddenly a golden opportunity! Because now I could go and stay at Marianne's, really spend some *time* with her—the first real quality time I'd ever had. And it was just wonderful, Pattie! I mean, she's..." He stopped, shook his head. "She's everything I imagined."

"A few nights?" Patrick asked, squinting. "That's all you needed?"

"What can I say, son?" Mr. Beaton gave a light shrug. "We were staying up late—must have been the third night—and I don't know what gave me the gumption, but I just up and kissed her. And she waited a second or two, and then she kissed me right back. And that was that." He snorted softly to himself, then teased out a grin. "Oh, she's a grand girl, Pattie," he said. "So full of *moxie*, isn't she? And you know the best thing about her? She doesn't mind having an old fart like me around. Says she doesn't like men her own age, anyway."

Patrick was finding it hard to concentrate now. The bike messengers were beginning to shout at each other; he couldn't be sure whether they were fighting or not. And a tiny, white-haired Asian woman in a green raincoat came scurrying past them, and she was carrying two identical black handbags. Why two?

"The thing is," Patrick said and then stopped. He was having difficulty remembering all the wrong assumptions he'd made, all the missteps. "I mean—I thought you already *had* a fiancée. You told Deanna."

"Well, that was Marianne, of course."

"No, wait a minute—I *talked* to Marianne. She didn't know anything about it."

"Of course not, I hadn't quite popped it yet, Pattie. The question, I mean," he added. "I was just getting a little ahead of myself, that's all."

"But—you told Sonya your fiancée was *pregnant*."

"No, I didn't say she was pregnant; I said we were *planning* to have children. Which was very presumptuous of me—considering Marianne wasn't my fiancée yet and considering I'd never really brought up the subject with her—but, you know, your friend was so damn fired up on the subject. I almost think she wanted *me* to impregnate her."

Farragut Square was a strange place, Patrick decided. Very strange. The paths didn't seem to meet anywhere. Nothing felt still. Even the leaves—even *they* weren't still. They shimmered like electron clouds.

"Da," he said, slumping now against the bench. "Did it ever occur to you how much time and—*effort* you could have saved us if you'd come clean? From the very start? If you'd just told me what you wanted to do. I could have—I don't know, *helped* you, probably."

"But none of it was ready, Pattie. The time wasn't ripe. I honestly wasn't sure I could pull it off." Mr. Beaton looked at the ground, smiling. "I still can't believe I have," he said.

"Well—are you going to tell Mom?"

"Oh, in time, yes. I think she'll be a little relieved, don't you?"

"Hmm." Patrick jerked his head to the side. "I don't know."

Mr. Beaton was looking at him sideways now, puckering his lips. "What about you, son?" he asked gently. "How do you feel about it?"

"Um…" Patrick creased his brow. "I don't know," he said. "I guess I'm feeling a little selfish right now. I don't—I mean, I'm losing both of you."

"Oh, well, that's silly, Pattie. Who knows where we'll end up when it's all done? That little bungalow might turn up right next door to you." He said it very matter-of-factly, as though it were an actuarial possibility, and then his voice grew suddenly tight and husky. "I've got so much love left, Patrick," he said.

And Patrick felt his own throat tightening. He couldn't be sure what was causing it—maybe it was the sound of his actual *given* name coming out of his father's mouth.

"I think sometimes love's been my only capital," Mr. Beaton said. "It's about the only venture I've got left." And then, straightening his spine and adjusting the lapels of his jacket, he corrected himself: "Well, no, there's one other."

Patrick's eyebrows started to climb—he felt suddenly like Ted, scaling the rungs of irony. He watched his father fishing once again through the pockets of his corduroy trousers, watched him pull out a piece of business stationery that had been folded over so many times it was almost the size of a paper football. Carefully, Mr. Beaton unfolded the paper, gave it a few strokes with his hand to smooth out the wrinkles, then silently handed it over.

"What's this?" Patrick asked.

"The *other* reason I came here."

The first thing that caught Patrick's eye was the letterhead: the engraving of one of the world's largest publishers. He stared at the name, wondering if it could be an illusion. He ran his finger along the lettering to see if any of it came off.

Then he read:

Dear Mr. Beaton:

We are delighted to inform you that your novel, *The Beasts of Langley*, has been accepted for publication.

We will be contacting you in short order to discuss some minor revisions in the introductory sections. And, of course, your thoughts on marketing strategies are more than welcome....

His eyes swerved off the page. He found himself suddenly looking up at his father, who was looking back at him with a tense, suspended expression.

"You wrote a novel?" Patrick asked.

"Yes, son."

"That's what you've been working on? This whole time?"

And even as he asked the question, his own mind was answering it, his mind was actively *endorsing* the answer because until this very moment, nothing about Mr. Beaton had made much sense, and now everything seemed to. It was like a puzzle cube sliding into place.

A lifelong fantasist transformed into a *professional* fantasist—symmetry didn't get much more satisfying than that.

And wasn't it funny? Patrick had always resisted being curious about his father—he had always deemed it better not to know—and now he was in a state of almost permanent intrigue. He could feel the nerve endings prickling under his skin. He almost couldn't sit still. He wanted to run to the nearest Radio Shack, grab a tape recorder off the shelves, spend the next week or the next year or ten years setting down his father's oral history, every last event, every ancillary detail, every anecdote, wayward opinion.

But all he could muster was a modest query.

"What's the book about?" he asked.

"Murderous Cold War spirits."

"Murderous…"

"*Ghosts*, Pattie. See, there's this secret cabal of CIA conspirators planning to use their hoarded nuclear weaponry to establish a military world dictatorship. But they haven't reckoned for the ghosts of long-dead CIA *and* KGB agents. Collegial spirits of the dead, Pattie. Condemned to roam the nether world until the lawless Earth has found peace. The problem is, the only *human* they can communicate with is a voluptuous young medium named Marianne—and, of course, none of the idiot humans around her believe what she has to say except for a maverick young Navy lieutenant named—named Patrick. So anyway, at the end the conspirators are about to nuke the earth when the ghost spies rise up through the cracks of the floor and start knocking 'em off. One by one."

"Wow." Patrick's mouth began involuntarily chewing. "It sounds like a combination espionage and—horror story."

"*Spook* story, if you catch my drift. They tell me I've created practically my own genre." Mr. Beaton grinned. "They say it's bestseller-bound, Pattie."

And Patrick had to grin himself now. He was afraid, in fact, that it wouldn't end there, that he might start laughing, and he wouldn't be able to stop.

"That's why you were poking around CIA headquarters," he said.

"I had to, Pattie; they wouldn't respond to my Freedom of Information requests. Christ, they're thin-skinned bastards, aren't they?"

"And that whole nonsense about the personal defense system?"

"Well—yes, that was a bit of a ruse, Pattie, I have to say. I can't explain it, except—I just didn't want anyone to know I'd written a book. Until I could be sure it was publishable. You know, there's only so much stench of failure a man can carry around with him."

It was the first time Patrick had heard his father use the word *failure*. It made him sad; it was like hearing a little girl utter her first obscenity.

"So—so the whole time you were staying with me and—chasing Marianne—you were working on this book? That's what the laptop was for?"

"Yeah. Well, to be honest, Pattie, I'd practically finished the damn thing before I even got here. I was just stuck for an ending. I'm sure you can see, it needed some big apocalyptic finish, some great metaphysical retribution with a nice element of blood to it."

"Sure."

"And that's why I'm so grateful to you."

"Me?"

"Oh, Christ, yeah! If I hadn't stayed with you, I'd never have got the crowning inspiration. I might still be working on the fucking thing."

"I'm not following."

"Here," Mr. Beaton said, "I'll show you."

Once again, Mr. Beaton reached into his pockets—not his pants pockets this time but the inner reaches of his houndstooth jacket—and once again he pulled out a folded piece of paper and proffered it to Patrick, and Patrick, feeling almost dazed now, had the sense as he reached for it that he would be doing this for the rest of his life, custodian of his father's papers.

It was a single page with perhaps four lines of laser-printed, double-spaced text. Patrick flipped the page over, flipped it back again, glanced up at his father.

"It's the last sentence of the book," Mr. Beaton said. "Go ahead."

Patrick read:

> Their red eyes glowing like sirens in the black-ness of the Langley crypt, the squadron of Norway rats patiently chewed through the last strand of General Norsefeld's carotid artery.

Mr. Beaton's eyes were glowing too, a bit like sirens.

"The rats, Pattie! Called up by the ghosts of dead spies. The beasts of Langley!"

51

The last time.

That's what ran through Patrick's mind as he sat, collapsed as always, in Marianne's director's chair, his butt almost touching the ground. He was drinking his third or perhaps fourth glass of Maker's Mark, and Marianne was in *her* usual position, drinking a glass of white wine, perched on the edge of her glass coffee table with its faux-marble plinths, and she was wearing men's dungarees and a big roomy cable-knit sweater—almost a *Shetland* sweater, he thought ruefully—and it was their last time, their final salon. No more Madame du Châtelet and Voltaire. No more booze swilling, no more shit shooting. Everything had changed.

She's going to be my stepmother, thought Patrick.

And he was surprised that this had already lost its ability to surprise him. From the moment he'd woken up that morning, he'd been thinking of little else—and now, somehow, it had become just another rhetorical formation. *My stepmother. Marianne will be my stepmother.*

Then again it couldn't have been entirely rhetorical because 15 minutes earlier when Marianne opened the door, he'd been unable to say anything. And she, for her part, after giving him a particularly passionate hug, shrank into silence too, and they went through their usual rituals—the idle opening banter, the calibrated pouring of drinks, the positioning of bodies—but with a degree of self-consciousness that slowed their movements, as though they were recording everything for posterity.

No, it was awkward—it was definitely awkward—and it might have been hopeless if Marianne hadn't been so determined to rescue it, if she hadn't absolutely *needed* to talk. She had begun by cupping her glass in a strange way—from below the base, like a bowl—and sniffing a little around the rim. A lazy smile had sneaked across her face, and then she'd started talking in a rhythm that Patrick had never heard from her before—not a fast or slow rhythm, exactly, but a lyrical, continuous rhythm: You had the impression she was picking up a conversation she'd started somewhere else an hour ago.

"Well," she said, "we *will* need to investigate some of the better class of antidepressant drugs. 'Cause that's what the whole candy thing was about, you do realize that? It's just how he medicates himself—*inoculates* himself, really. He figures he can just—*sugar rush* himself through the whole thing, and I told him, 'No, honey, they got drugs now.' Drugs with very nice names, and they don't make your teeth fall out or give you insulin shock."

The last time, Patrick thought. The last time he would be listening to her musical chatter.

"And you know," she said, "we were wrong about him, you and me. We always talked about him like he was so dysfunctional, and the thing is—if you think about it—he's really *not*. 'Cause look at the facts: He moved here. He found a woman. He wrote a fucking novel, all right? Which everyone in Washington wants to do but never does. I mean, he accomplished his goals. He's kinda functional when you think about it; it's just he's lived alone too long."

She rattled on this way for about 15 minutes, telling Patrick things he had always known about his father, telling him a few things he would never have guessed. She discussed Mr. Beaton's scent, the clean unperfumed natural scent that seemed to her an emanation. She discussed his inexhaustible eye for beauty, the way he could choke up over a woman's pearl earrings. The way one of his eyelids quivered while he was asleep, like a pool of liquid settling in a cup.

"What I want to know," Patrick said, interrupting at last. And then he stopped. He closed his eyes. "I mean, it's all *reciprocal*, right?" he asked. "Da's not the only one driving this car, right?"

"Oh, fuck." Marianne's eyes seemed to be darkening and lightening at the same time. "No," she said. "No, it's my car too, Patrick. I just didn't—I mean, I *love* the guy." Her glass was resting in her right hand, and her left hand was making a kind of inverted peace sign—not a peace sign at all, Patrick recalled suddenly, but the cleft where she used to hold her cigarettes.

"Do you remember?" she asked him. "How I was always talking about setting your dad up with someone? And I'd always call you up and say, 'Hey, what about so-and-so?' And it wasn't just that Buddhist chick; I must have gone through about ten or 15 women in my mind—I even wrote out lists. I went through the names, and I just...I wound up rejecting every single one. At first it was, 'Oh, no, bad fit, the personalities don't match.' And after a while, it was, 'No. No, she's just not—she's not special enough.' Mr. B's got these very definite specs; he needs someone who can *appreciate* him."

She brought her glass to her lips, took a tiny sip. "So—what? It's just a hop and a skip to where you say, Well, fuck, *I* appreciate him—I mean, maybe *I'm* the one he needs. The funny thing is, I didn't get there." She stood up now, quite abruptly, so that Patrick instinctively fell even deeper into his director's chair, his legs kicking helplessly in the air. She stood and pointed to the long floral-printed chintz sofa in the opposite corner of the room, and as Patrick followed her finger, the image of his father rose up before them like a vapor.

"I woke up one morning," Marianne said, "and it must have been the second morning he was here. And I'm coming out of the bedroom, right, rubbing my eyes? And there he is. I mean, I've forgotten he was even there. He's lying on the couch, still asleep, and the covers are all thrown off, and he's doing—that thing with his toes? You know, curling 'em in, curling 'em out?"

"Uh-huh."

"I mean, let me tell you, those toes were going crazy," she said. "And I thought, 'Well, shit, Mr. B! Don't you ever settle down? Don't you ever just relax?' And—I don't know—it was like this whole big—*wave* of tenderness came over me, and I thought I was dying or melting or coming unglued or something. I just couldn't stand it. I couldn't stand to think of him ever sleeping on someone's sofa again."

She resumed her perch on the edge of the table.

"It's crazy," she said. "I mean, it's fuckin' *loony* tunes, Patrick. This morning I went in my boss's office, and I said, 'Well hey, I'm giving notice.' And she said, 'That's too bad; when you leaving?' And I said, 'Tomorrow.' And I didn't even wait around to, you know, get her approval or anything; I just turned around and flounced on outta there, and I thought, Marianne, you are one crazy chick. But I think it would've been worse if I'd stayed and tried to explain it all 'cause I mean, God, how *could* you?" She began reciting in a singsong voice: "'See, I spent a few nights with my best friend's father, and now we love each other, and he's written this book about—rats and KGB ghosts, and we're gonna go live in some beach bungalow for a few months, even though it's almost goddamn winter, and then we're gonna figure out what to do with the rest of our lives.' I mean, they would've just—called in the butterfly nets, you know?"

"It's not crazy," Patrick said. "Is it what you want?"

For the next few seconds, Marianne occupied herself adjusting the heel of her boot, and when she spoke again she sounded like she'd taken up a new subject.

"I wake up in the middle of the night now. Every night, like fuckin' clockwork. And, I mean, you'd think someone who just quit her job so she can go live in a bungalow with some guy she barely knows who's almost twice her age—I mean, you'd think I'd wake up *screaming*, right? The thing is, I'm—giggling, Patrick. For no particular reason. I mean, it's not like your dad's *tickling* me or anything; I'm just laughin' my ass off. And I think—well, this is good, isn't it? I mean, if every time I start thinkin' about the future, I start giggling, then that's kinda good."

This struck Patrick as her final word on the subject, but for the next 30 minutes Marianne kept adding more words—kept justifying herself, interpreting herself, throwing out propositions the way she had always done but with a new sense: the sense, maybe, that they might actually lead somewhere.

Patrick's eyes were closed now. The Maker's Mark was diffusing through him, and so was Marianne's voice.

"And anyway," she was saying, "I was sick of work, and it's pretty cheap living in Rehoboth in the winter. And your dad still has a lot of his savings—I mean, hell, I didn't even think he *had* savings—and the book advance is already kicking in. And then six months or so down the road, we should have a better idea about stuff. I mean, I kinda *do* want an honest-to-God wedding at some point. Otherwise I swear my mother's gonna hunt me down, come wavin' a deer rifle at me."

"Ow," Patrick said almost inaudibly.

"You know what, though?" Marianne's pitch rose suddenly. It made Patrick wary: She was getting ready to change the subject. "You need to stop worrying about your dad and me. You need to, you know, tend to your own shit."

"Yeah." He got a bolt of energy now. He rocked himself out of the chair—it was pretty easy, after all—went into the kitchen to pour himself another drink. "Can't I get someone *else* to tend to my shit?" he asked. "Aren't there any shit professionals?"

"Well…" Marianne pondered the question. "Listen, honey, if I were sticking around, I'd be happy to be your shit professional, but see, I *know* you, Patrick, and you gotta be your own shit professional. No one else can do it."

Patrick stifled a laugh. *Why didn't she say that a few months ago?* he thought. *Before I hired Seth.*

"Hey!" Marianne had risen too. She was standing in the doorway of the kitchen, snapping her fingers. "What about Mr. Shetland?" she asked.

Later, Patrick would think back fondly on his poise. He would remember how his head had lurched back only an inch or so before stopping and how his hand had stayed completely steady, poured out the remaining half inch of whiskey without so much as a hitch.

"Mr. Shetland?" he repeated.

"He's the only guy in the last two *years* I've heard you say anything nice about. I know you don't know his name or anything, but maybe you could—I don't know, go *hunting* for him somewhere. There's gotta be places he hangs out."

I've been to all those places. That's what Patrick wanted to say. He had journeyed to every place such a person could occupy. His efforts might someday form the text of an enlightening sociological treatise. Future generations of scholars would freely cite him in their footnotes: *Beaton, op. cit., p. 349.*

But he didn't want to talk about Scottie. They needed to discuss something else—anything else. His brain flailed, lunged for the first name that came in view.

"What about Rick?" he asked.

"Rick?" she repeated, frowning. "Oh, *Victor.* Did he tell you to call him Rick?"

"He must have," Patrick said. "I was only wondering 'cause— I mean, does he *know*? About the engagement and everything?"

"Oh, shit!" Marianne flapped her hand dismissively. "I don't have the time for that anymore. You know, this is gonna sound really strange."

"Yeah?"

"Well…" Marianne sidled past him, opened the refrigerator door, groped for the bottle of white wine, pulled it out, stared at the label, emptied the last few tablespoons of liquid into her glass. "It's just…" She put her glass to her lips, then lowered it again.

"What?"

"Well, call me paranoid and all, but I'm starting to think Victor's gay."

The dog was waiting for him when he got home that night, positioned about five feet inside the door, his head vibrating, a high-pitched mewl emanating from somewhere deep inside his body.

Is he ill? Patrick wondered.

No. No, he wasn't ill. It was his potty time.

Patrick almost wept, he was so taken by the pathos of being a dog—the pathos of having to wait for someone before you could go to the bathroom, having your most basic functions contingent on a human being's good will. Was that a life?

So as they walked up the street to the park, Patrick made sure to give extra rein on the leash, and when the dog relieved himself next to one of the park benches, Patrick had to fight back the urge to hug him around the belly, wrestle him across the whole expanse of grass—the way he'd once seen Alex do.

They walked companionably back to the house, the dog sniffing now and again at the wrought-iron fences or the tufts of alyssum still poking through the bricks of the sidewalk and then nimbly climbing the front steps. Once inside the house he broke into a slow trot, skidded slightly as he turned to go up the steps, then vanished upstairs into the guest bedroom. That was where he spent most of his nights: not in the guest bed but on a half-unraveled blue dhurrie rug that Patrick had bought three years ago at an estate sale.

It's really time to give the dog a name, Patrick thought. *It's only fair.*

The phone rang.

"Been thinking," Seth said.

"Yes?"

"You *shouldn't* call the dog Scottie."

"I wasn't going to," Patrick said. He was startled though. How had Seth known what he was thinking? Was he hacking into Patrick's mental circuitry?

Come to think of it, how did Seth even know he had a dog? And then Patrick remembered: The last time Seth called, they'd been talking, and the dog had interrupted their conversation. A single bark—a kind of warning bark—and Patrick was forced to confess everything.

"Don't call him Scottie," Seth was saying now. "Very irreverent. Or else just Freudian. Queasy."

"No," Patrick said, "I was going to call him—I don't know—Metrobus doesn't sing for me, but there's always Greyhound or *Trailways*." He was weaving a little on the kitchen floor; the Maker's Mark was still washing through him. It was better this way. This was the best way to talk with Seth.

"Or you could try Double-decker," Seth suggested.

"Or *Kramden*. Wasn't Ralph Kramden a bus driver?"

"What about Grant?" Seth asked.

"No, Grant's a shitty name."

"Patrick. I'm segueing. I'm asking about Grant. Did he call you back?"

Patrick stopped weaving now. "Um…no, in fact. He hasn't, in fact."

"Maybe you should leave another message."

"I could do that."

"Are you drunk?"

"Um…" He had been. A minute ago. "No," he said. He pressed his forehead against the freezer door, felt the chill creep down to his temples. "My father's marrying my best friend," he said.

"Oh." Seth was silent a few moments. "Is your best friend a woman?" he asked.

"Yes."

"Well, that's easier," he said. "That's much easier."

52

The week ended without a call from Grant. Each morning Patrick went to his office a half hour early, placed the call, listened with an ever-growing desolation to the sound of Grant's answering machine, hung up without leaving a message. He knew it was a silly ritual. He would be much better served, he knew, if he called at different times, and yet he felt mysteriously obligated to do it the same way every day. He remembered once suggesting to Seth that the best way to find Scottie might be to stay in one place and wait—and it seemed to him now he was actually testing the theory. He was staying in one place. Waiting.

Saturday morning—the day before Mr. Beaton and Marianne were scheduled to leave town—he awoke with barely a thought of Grant. Grant had been replaced by blueberry-buckwheat pancakes, and on an impulse Patrick decided to walk over to the Eastern Market diner for breakfast. He hadn't eaten there in about two years, but the idea energized him. He threw on a pair of sweatpants and a sweater and headed straight for the front door, began charging down the front steps. Halfway to the street, he stopped.

Sonya was coming out of the downstairs apartment.

She was wearing an olive-drab anorak with an elaborate hood that hung behind her neck like a backpack, and she was talking rapidly over her left shoulder. Talking to *Deanna*, in fact, who was following a few steps behind, shivering in a long gray woolen bathrobe that she'd wrapped around flannel pajamas.

Watching them, Patrick felt the fingers of dread climb up his breastbone. What were they doing together? They didn't even know each other—did they? How could they have met? What could possibly link them?

The thought that there might, in fact, *be* some link—some implicating subterranean connection—was too much to consider. He began casting about for an escape route.

They haven't seen me, he thought. *I can creep back into the house.*

"Oh, hi, Patrick!"

Sonya had already reached street level. Her face was flushed with the early December cold, and she was blowing big clouds of condensed breath. "How're you doing?" she asked.

"Fine," he said, the word clogging near his larynx.

"Well, great! I'll see you tomorrow morning, right?"

He nodded dumbly.

"Oh, and hey," she said, "why don't you start working on the Beethoven? You must be sick of that Paganini thing." She nodded once for closure, then leaned down the steps toward Deanna's apartment and extended one of her mittened hands. "Thanks again!" she said. And then she was off, striding down the street and turning the southwestern corner of the block with a flounce of good humor.

Gradually Patrick shifted his scrutiny from Sonya to the bottom of the stairs where Deanna was standing, rubbing her arms to keep warm.

"Hi," she said.

"Hi." He smiled wanly. "I didn't know you knew each other."

"Oh, we don't, really. Not very well."

"But she was thanking you?"

"Oh, right." Deanna nodded. "I guess she didn't tell you about that."

"No."

"Do you want some coffee?"

"Um...OK."

Always, he had felt this strange reluctance to enter Deanna's apartment—to stand on her home turf. He felt vulnerable even when he was in her garden.

"I'm sorry," she said, "all I've got is Taster's Choice. Is that all right?"

"Oh...fine."

She sat him at a round wooden Shaker table, its surface covered almost entirely by four large plastic table mats stenciled with roses and a Mason jar stuffed with yellow chrysanthemums. Patrick sat quietly in his plain ladder-back chair, watching Deanna bustle about the kitchen, boil the water, set out a tray of sugar and cream, pour butter cookies into a small ceramic bowl. She sniffled a little as she worked, and Patrick thought, *She's allergic to her own kitchen.*

"Here we are," Deanna said, setting the cup in front of him. "Do you need any sugar?"

"No, thanks."

She seated herself on the other side of the table but didn't quite pull the chair in. It reminded Patrick of how his mother would sit sometimes during meals: two feet from the table, angled away, forever poised to spring up.

"Sonya," she said absently. "How did I meet Sonya. Well, I guess it was a few weeks ago—I forget which day. I was coming down the street and—how did this work?—I saw you and Sonya talking—I think it was right outside your door."

Right outside my door, he thought. Of course. That Saturday afternoon. The failed attempt on Mr. Beaton's seed.

"*You* went inside," Deanna said, "and I didn't know Sonya, so I was just going to go inside myself, but, you know, she was coming down the steps, and she looked—a little distraught, I guess. So I just asked her if she was OK."

"Uh-huh."

"And she must have really been wanting to talk to someone because she started kind of spilling her guts. And before long she told me all about her husband's fertility problems, and we were discussing it a bit, and then without even thinking I said, 'Well, does your husband wear bikini underwear?'"

"Bikini…?"

"Because that can seriously lower men's sperm counts," Deanna said. "I read it in Ann Landers, believe it or not. Apparently, the briefs generate so much heat they kind of—*cook* the sperm. So I asked her about it, and Sonya said yes, her husband *did* wear bikini underwear, so I told her they might want to start experimenting with boxers and see what happened."

"And what happened?"

"Well, that's what she came to tell me. She said they've been trying the boxers for three weeks now, and the sperm counts have just—shot up, I guess. Whatever sperm counts do. She says they're on track to conceiving by the end of the year."

"Oh."

"She was so happy," Deanna said, tipping her head to one side.

Patrick felt his face. It was burning.

She doesn't know, he thought.

Deanna had no idea what she had accomplished. She had just

saved a woman's dream, rescued a very kind and patient violin teacher from a grueling round of screening interviews and essay contests—simply by passing on information from an Ann Landers column—and she didn't know.

Some people just naturally create good, he thought. *They spew it. Like carbon dioxide.*

"I'm really sorry you're going," he heard himself say.

"Oh, well, there's still a few days," she said vaguely.

No, he wanted to say. That wasn't the point. The point was he had run out of time. He had realized too late that she might have the necessary wisdom, that she and she alone, maybe, might have the necessary perspective on what had happened in his life or maybe the *foresight* to sift through his future. Whatever it was, he had failed to cultivate it. She was leaving in two weeks, and he would never be able to confide in her. He had permanently forfeited his chance.

The strange part was that after coming to this conclusion, Patrick essentially ignored it. He forgot that he had ever reached it. One minute he was sitting quietly in Deanna's upright wooden chair, circling his hands around a tepid cup of Taster's Choice, and the next minute he was talking. Without willing it, without offering any prologue, without even saying that he wished to speak to her, he began speaking—as though she had been waiting for him, as though they were the oldest friends in the world.

"See," he said, "I broke up with this guy last spring."

And to her everlasting credit, Deanna said simply, "Oh, Alex, yes."

Of course, Patrick thought, blinking away his surprise. Of course she would remember Alex. "So anyway—I kind of started dating this other guy, but it didn't work out."

"Oh, that perspiring man?"

"Per—no, no, that's *Seth*. See, Alex moved in with *Ted*, and *Seth* is the guy who *used* to live with Ted."

"OK."

"And, anyway, the thing is, I sort of—met this *other* guy a while ago. *Sort* of met. And he's not any of the people I just mentioned. And I think maybe, maybe *this* guy is the one. No, I'm sure of it. He is."

"That's great, Patrick."

"Well—no, it's not because I can't find him. And since I can't find him, I can't be sure he's the one. I mean, I *know* he is, but I'm not always sure of it. And then—I'm sorry. This is stupid."

"No, go on."

"Well, Alex and I are friends again, and there's so much—unfinished business, and I just don't trust the guy he's with now."

"Ted."

"Right. Ted. And I start thinking, Maybe I should give the whole Alex thing another shot—I mean, if Alex is *willing*, which I don't know that he is, which I don't know that *I* am."

"Why do you want to give it another shot?"

"Because I was such a failure the first time around." He said it very analytically, as though he were reading it off a prescription label. "I was—I don't know. I wasn't a *terrible* boyfriend; I just wasn't—I'm still learning, I guess. I think I would be better this time around."

"And you want to practice on Alex?"

"Um…" He looked up at her. "Wow, that sounds kind of callous."

"Oh, no, no." Deanna angled herself into the table. "It's just—I don't think it's like a sport or a job, do you? Where you just keep practicing at it, and your score goes up. I think you find someone, and you—you throw out the scorecard."

"Huh."

"That's my theory, anyway. Then again, What do I know? Look how long it took me to get married." She smiled at him, and then her eyes suddenly widened. "Oh!" she cried. "I forgot to tell you."

"What?"

"The rats have gone away."

"You're kidding."

"Not a sign of them anywhere."

"Wow." Patrick let out a gust of air. "You know, that's funny—I was thinking the same thing last night. I don't hear them the way I normally do." He leaned over the table, propped up his chin with his hand. "I can't believe they're really gone. Why would they go?"

"Oh, it's obvious, isn't it?"

"What?"

Deanna was smiling now—almost a teasing smile. "Your *dog*," she said. "He makes all the difference in the world. I mean, these rats aren't dumb; they've probably figured out by now, I don't have really have a cat, but they *know* you have a dog."

"The dog," Patrick said. "I never thought of that."

"Oh, he's better than the Pied Piper of Hamelin."

Later that day Patrick was sprawled out on his love seat, reading *The Palm at the End of the Mind*—he no longer asked himself if somewhere at this very moment Scottie was reading the same book—and the dog was curled up at Patrick's feet, the white necklace of fur continuous with the line of Patrick's toes, the nose hanging off the left front paw, the long-lashed lids curtaining the eyes. Looking at him, Patrick suddenly found himself so enchanted that he couldn't even read his book anymore—he let it fall into his lap. He stared at the dog and listened to the name that came falling from his own lips.

"Hamelin," Patrick said.

The dog opened his eyes, and for a moment he seemed to be actually considering the name—reviewing it the way he appeared to review all of Patrick's life choices. It was a taxing process, though: After a few seconds the dog's lids began to droop again, and in a few more seconds they were sealed shut. *So be it*, he seemed to be saying.

So be it, Patrick thought, feeling his own eyelids grow leaden. *Hamelin it is.*

53

He woke up two hours later. He might have slept even longer, but the dog, in his first official act as Hamelin, began barking at a squirrel outside the kitchen window. The sound was like a draw-bridge slamming down on Patrick's brain. He jumped up, spun his head around, squinted into the late afternoon shadows.

Oh, God.

Oh, God, he'd fallen asleep. He'd taken a nap.

Patrick rubbed his eyes, laced his hands across his face. Was the room really this dark? It couldn't be this dark, could it?

This is why a person should never take naps, he thought. *You never know if it's you or the room.*

He lay back down, stared up at the ceiling, felt the blood returning to his throat and head. *Jesus*, he thought. When was the last time he'd napped? He couldn't remember. Oh, no, wait—it was at Wolf Trap, wasn't it? At that damn Steve and Eydie concert. Lying on that muddy hill, six inches from Rick—he fell asleep—and an hour later he saw Scottie for only the second time in their mutual existence, saw him climb into a big red Plymouth Voyager, flash a red tattoo, and then disappear.

And that had been Patrick's first nap since—since the famous brunch party. Since the inaugural sighting of the Prince. Day 1 in Our Year of Scottie.

Patrick gave his head a shake—a fierce shake. Something was materializing in the recesses of his consciousness. Some tantalizing symmetry he couldn't quite get a handle on.

Napping.

Oh, God. Oh, of course.

Oh, it was so obvious! *Napping.* Napping led to Scottie. Almost inevitably.

And Patrick had just experienced a—a napping. He had just napped, and that meant—didn't it?—in five minutes or an hour or perhaps five hours—at some very near point in the distant future—the Scottish Prince would reemerge. Defying statistical probabilities, defying the joint dragnets of the Pink Posse and the D.C. police. Granting Patrick one last window of opportunity, one last chance to make his feelings known, one last chance to posit their common destiny. One last chance to fall to the ground and say "Stay!"

So it was a pregnant moment, Patrick felt that suddenly. A moment of imminent possibility. He felt it so intensely that when the phone rang, he almost thought it was ringing inside his head, vibrating against his temporal lobe. He lay there on the love seat, thinking maybe, just maybe, if he exerted his gray cells enough, he could answer without moving.

No. No, it wasn't working. The phone was still ringing.

He eased himself off the couch, gave his legs a couple of quick rubs, wobbled into the kitchen. Hamelin give one final bark before retreating into the living room, and Patrick lunged for the phone, grabbed it off its headset.

"Hello," he whispered.

"Patrick?"

"Yes?"

"This is Grant."

Grant. He groped, he groped. *Grant.*

"Grant Wallberger," the man said.

"Grant!" Patrick called out much too loudly. "Hi!"

"Hello."

"Wow," Patrick said. "It's Grant."

"You left a message on my machine," Grant said.

"Oh, right! That's right. I don't—did my message make any sense?"

"Well, no, it didn't."

"Oh, I'm sorry." Patrick pawed his face three times. "I was in kind of a hurry when—see, it's this friend of mine; he's had a break-in—"

"No, no, I understood *that* part. I just can't believe you have to ask me who was responsible. I mean, it was in all the papers."

"It was?"

"Oh, yes, about two weeks ago. This whole *rash* of burglaries. All masterminded by the same person."

"Oh, wow," Patrick said. "A *rash*. Wow. So who...?"

"Who what?"

"Who was the mastermind?"

And in the brief silence that followed, only one answer came to Patrick's mind.

Scottie.

That's what Grant was going to say: *It was Scottie, you stupid asshole!* And Patrick would have nothing to say in his defense. He would be forced to accept any reproach that came his way. He would be forced to say, *Yes, I fell in love with a felon. I unconsciously abetted his crime. I could have stopped him if I hadn't been so tired.*

"My cleaning woman," Grant said.

Patrick's eyes went dry suddenly. It was like someone was

blowing on them. "Your…"

"Her name is Johanna. Dutch woman. You must know her."

"No, I don't."

"Oh, no, you must have used her."

"I don't—actually, I don't use cleaning persons."

"That's too bad; she was really excellent. The Dusting Dutch Dervish, we used to call her. I have to tell you," Grant said, lowering his voice, "the house really hasn't been the same since she left. It's funny, though, she always used to go on and on about *Hispanics*, how you could never trust Hispanic cleaning people because they'd steal you blind. Which is ironic, don't you think?"

"Oh, yes," Patrick said.

"She was very clever. She spaced the burglaries out over months, and she always made sure she had an alibi whenever one of them happened. Usually she'd be cleaning someone else's apartment."

"Then how did she…?"

"She gave copies of the keys to her boyfriend. He's the one who handled the actual robbery part."

"Her boyfriend," Patrick said carefully. "Now did they—did they arrest him too?"

"Oh, yes."

"Was he…" He almost didn't want to ask now. "Was he Dutch too?"

Grant let out a horse laugh. "No, he was *Hispanic*. Don't you love it?"

Patrick's vision fell out of focus for a second. "Hispanic," he said. "So—so I'm guessing dark hair and swarthy complexion. Probably."

"Yes, he looked a little like Gilbert Roland. Have you ever seen Gilbert Roland?"

"No."

"You're too young for Gilbert Roland."

"Probably."

"Well, this fellow had beautiful, sleek black hair. A brilliant smile with one gold incisor. You know, if he hadn't taken my VCR *and* my electronic massage…"

"Pretty brazen," Patrick agreed. "A lot of brazenness there. Well—I'm really sorry to hear about your losses, but—I'm thinking, *obviously* these two can't be the ones who robbed my friend's house since—I mean, I assume they're in jail and everything."

"They are," Grant said. "May they rot."

"So—so *great*. I mean for you. Not for *them*, of course, but—good for you! Justice triumphs, and—good for you!"

"Yes…"

Five seconds went by, like half a day.

"So anyway," Patrick said, "I want to thank you so much for getting back to me."

"Not at all."

"It was very kind of you."

"Not at all. Please say hello to Alex."

Patrick was about to say "all right," but he stopped himself.

"Oh, that's right!" Grant said at last. "Never mind. Say hello to anyone you want."

In fact, the first person Patrick attempted to say hello to was Seth. He called him almost as soon as he was done with Grant. He *hummed* as he dialed—not a tune exactly, but an expressive murmur, a vocalized excitement. He was humming in lieu of screaming, because it seemed to him his whole body was ripening and swelling in preparation for a scream. Humming was the only way to keep himself quiet.

The phone rang four times before the answering machine kicked in, and as Patrick listened to the mournful opening tones of Seth's automated greeting, he found he couldn't bear to hear any more. He slammed down the phone, with a violence that made him step back for a moment, regard himself with a new interest.

Oh, he was just a little angry, that was all. He was angry because—because here he was with this *news*, bursting at the seams with *news*, and there was no one to tell it to except an answering machine.

Who else? he asked himself. *Who else can I tell? Besides Seth?*

And there was no one. That was the amazing part—not a single sentient being who would understand what he had to say.

It was a sad situation, an extremely depressing situation. Even if it was mostly his doing, even if it *was* the result of his reticence.

He had never sought allies. From the beginning he had made the search for Scottie an exclusive quest, an almost entirely private endeavor. So he should have been prepared, shouldn't he? He should have expected things to be like this—to be this constrained and ungratifying. But of course he hadn't. He hadn't anticipated it, and now he was so mired in funk that even the sound of his doorbell ringing couldn't rouse him at first. He heard it ring, and he thought, *I'm not going to answer. I don't care who it is.*

But his resolution suddenly, violently gave way to an even more powerful resolution—a hot, all-consuming desire to *speak*. He had to speak! It didn't matter who was at the door. His mind scanned the possibilities—UPS deliverer, Greenpeace shill, homeless woman, Jehovah's Witness. It didn't matter *who* it was; Patrick would tell them *exactly* what had happened. Before they could even open their mouths, he would be screaming the news at them.

He's innocent! He's innocent, I tell you!

He was almost dreading the moment because he knew he would have no control over it. He could only hope that whoever was on the other side of the door would just flinch a little—chalk it up to urban hysteria—get on with his business.

But the person standing on the doorstep was Seth.

And seeing him had the puzzling effect of completely silencing Patrick.

There were several possible reasons for this. It might have been simply a reaction to Seth's gay lumberjack outfit: the woolen pullover jacket, with huge black-and-red squares, the jungle-green U.S. Army pants, the black leather boots with eyelets that ran halfway to the knee.

Or it could have been simply the *way* Seth was wearing his clothes. The pullover, for instance, had been misbuttoned so that one side of it rose about two inches higher than the other, and the boots were a tangle of half-tied, double-helixed laces, and even Seth's *glasses* were a little askew. Patrick had never seen them like that—tilting down to the left and somehow taking the rest of the face with them, skewing the nose and the mouth, leaving the eyes naked and opaque.

"Hi," Seth said.

Stop staring, Patrick thought. *Don't stare.*

Instinctively he swept an arm toward the living-room couch, and Seth quietly followed—but then stopped about two feet inside the house. It was an awkward bit of positioning. His elbow was blocking the door, and Patrick had to tap him on the shoulder twice before he moved it.

"This is so funny," Patrick said. "I was just calling you."

"Uh-huh."

"Can I take your coat?"

"No, that's OK."

Seth involuntarily clutched at the pullover, pulled it tighter to his chest. He was going to stay right where he was.

So it was probably by way of compensation that Patrick began backing away. Something about Seth made him want to back all the way into the kitchen, continue through the back door and then out through the alley, making evenly spaced beeping noises like a garbage truck in reverse—but then he heard a sound directly behind him—a soft, dancing tread.

Hamelin.

It was Hamelin, and by the time Patrick registered who it was, the dog was already past him, sniffing the circumference around Seth's feet and then inspecting the feet themselves, scrutinizing the byzantine black lacing, the rows and rows of eyelets, then taking in the right trouser cuff, and so on up to the knee. And Seth, perhaps to keep Hamelin from venturing any further—or perhaps from the sheer pleasure of being touched—knelt down and ran his hand through the dog's matted brown hair.

"Oh," Seth said. "Oh."

"His name is Hamelin."

"Hamelin," Seth said.

"I think he likes you."

"Hello." Seth buried his nose in the dog's neck, inhaled deeply. "Hello, Hamelin. Hello."

Seth looked as if he could have stayed the rest of the day just like that: sniffing the dog, running his hand through the dog's coat, feeling the damp warmth of the fur and the jarring cold of the nose and then the resurgent warmth of the sandpapery tongue—but Hamelin was done for now. He walked away content, and once again Patrick found himself wondering if perhaps Hamelin was some kind of specially commissioned guardian, carefully vetting one more sector of Patrick's life, determining its suitability.

The dog padded over to the stairs, studied the first riser, then shot them a quick glance—a kind of prescient gleam, Patrick thought—before he made his way up the stairs.

"Hamelin," said Seth, watching him go.

Under normal circumstances Patrick would have taken the time to explain what an exceptional dog this was, what a clever and unusually *dignified* dog Hamelin was, how he never begged for food from the table and the only thing he did that was even remotely beseeching was to wander into the kitchen now and again but only, Patrick felt, to see how things were going, the way a headwaiter might tour the chef's quarters to get a better sense of the evening's menu.

There wasn't time to talk about Hamelin.

"I just got through with Grant," Patrick said. "It's great news. Scottie's *totally* in the clear. They arrested these two other people, the—the Dutch Dervish and Gilbert Roland, and he's not a felon, Seth! I can't believe I ever thought he was. I mean, I should have *known;* I should have had faith."

"I found him," Seth said.

54

And Patrick said, "Who?"

And now Seth's glasses seemed to tilt even further to the left, even as his eyes did their customary charge from their sockets. "Who!" He looked around the room uncomprehendingly. "*Who?*"

"You're not—are you talking about Scottie?"

"Who else?"

"No, you're kidding."

"Patrick." Seth leaned his head forward a few inches. "Would I kid? Would I *kid* you about something like this?"

A riotous thought came surging up in Patrick's brain.

The nap! It's the nap!

Oh, he would never again hate naps. He would embrace them forevermore. Where he had once loathed, he would revere. Where he had once resisted, he would accede.

He would fashion an entirely new religion around midday naps, convert the entire universe to permanent rest cure; he would consign the whole cosmos to eternal sleep because he knew, he *knew* that by letting down his guard—by allowing himself to nap—he had succeeded where nothing else had. He had brought Scottie out of the shadows, made him a creature of daylight.

Patrick lost all his poise. He began craning his head like a heron, looking to either side of Seth, sniffing the air.

"Where is he?" he cried. "Where is he?"

"Patrick. I didn't bring him *with* me."

"But—what? You lost him?"

"I didn't lose him. Sit down."

"Where?"

"I don't know. It's your house."

Patrick wheeled around. It *was* his house. There was his love seat. He could sit there. He could back up to the love seat, collapse his legs until the rest of him was sitting down on it.

Which he did. And Seth, for his part, simply perched himself on one arm of the mission rocker, leaving Patrick to wonder if the rocker's arm might not give way or maybe the whole chair would tip over—some disaster, some furniture-related disaster that Patrick would be powerless to stop. He didn't want to stop it.

"Tell me," he said. "Tell me everything."

"All right," Seth said. He extended his lower lip, blew out a forked stream of air. "OK. I went to the police station. This morning. 'Cause I thought about our discussion, yes? Justice, honor, truth. So I walked in there. Went to the front desk. Asked for the officer in charge. Said you know, maybe the sketch that was on TV wasn't so *good*. Now that I look at it. Not very close to life. Probably shouldn't use it."

"Uh-huh?"

"And they said, 'Well, great timing. We just arrested someone. We're putting together a lineup.'"

"Oh, my God!" Patrick felt his breath turn to ice.

"Well, just imagine," Seth said. "What went through my mind. I said, 'You arrested someone?' And they said yes, *citizen's* arrest. Undertaken by the vice president of the Pink Posse—"

"Oh, my God."

"Who *tackled* the suspect in Malcolm X Park this morning. Wrestled him into submission."

Patrick shut his eyes.

It was too much, that was all. It was completely and utterly and definitively horrible. The man he loved had been *tackled*, mauled and cudgeled and pummeled and—*pistol-whipped*, probably—*massacred* by a ferocious pink-shirted vigilante, set upon when he least expected it, for a crime he didn't commit, for a crime that didn't even *exist*. It was an outrage. It was *beyond* outrage, it was…

Patrick began sputtering with fury, but his mouth could form nothing coherent. *It's illegal!* That's what he wanted to say. *It's clearly illegal! Scottie is a prince; he has—he has diplomatic immunity.*

But the only word that came out was *thugs*.

"Thugs!" he cried. "These Posse men are fucking *thugs*."

"It was a woman," Seth said. "Actually."

"Oh."

"Powerful specimen. I felt her deltoid. In the waiting room."

"No!" Patrick put out one of his hands. "I don't want to hear about that. Tell me about the *lineup*."

"Oh! Fascinating. Really. They take you into this little kind of—cubicle. Sort of like the movies but dingier. A little scarier. You can't really believe it's a two-way mirror. You think they're sizing you up too."

"And did they bring in Scottie?"

"Well, they brought in *someone*. I mean, I was pretty sure who I was *supposed* to pick out. 'Cause he had this big violet bruise. Under his left eye. Where the woman clocked him, she told me."

"Uh-huh."

"So I thought, '*C'est l'homme. Oui? C'est le prince.*'"

"Uh-huh."

"So I stared at him. Very hard. Tried to airbrush the bruise away. Tried to see him in his normal—existential condition."

"Right."

"Went through the checklist. Height. Frame. Hair color."

"Right."

"Eye color. Jaw shape. Lopsided smi—well, of course, he wasn't smiling."

"Right."

"Spent, like, ten minutes just *looking*. Looking. And you know something?" Seth lowered his head, and the pupils of his eyes did the opposite—they began climbing.

"*It wasn't Scottie*," Seth said.

Patrick felt his own head lowering now. "You're—I mean, you're *sure*?" he asked. His heart was caroming against his rib cage. "You're absolutely *sure*?"

"Oh, please," Seth said. "Patrick, please. Remember all those times? The thousands of stores we've been to? The *millions* of men we've seen? And I always ask you, 'OK, what about *him*? Is *he* close?' And you say, 'Oh, no, Scottie's eyes were further apart. No, no, that guy's nose flares out too much. Scottie doesn't *flare* like that. And the jaw should thrust more. And *humorous*, Seth! I know I told you he was *humorous*.'"

Patrick's cheeks were flaming.

"So give me some credit," Seth said. "I've been listening. I *know* what Scottie looks like. I'd know him with my eyes closed. Could pick him out of a Reverend Moon wedding. This fella was not Scottie."

"But—the other men in the lineup?"

"None of them was Scottie. Police said, 'Take your time, sir.'"

And I said, 'Thank you, I will.' And I'm telling you. None of them was even *close*."

"So..." Patrick wanted to see all those faces now, all those pretenders' faces. He wanted to stare them in the eye. "So—did they send that poor suspect home?"

"Yeah, he's OK," Seth said. "Worry not."

Surely, though, thought Patrick. *Surely there are other things I can worry about.* Scottie was safe—it was true—but only for now, only for this minute. Who knew how many other vigilantes of various genders were lurking behind bushes, waiting to batter him into submission?

And even if Scottie's person could be protected—where *was* his person? Where was...

"Um..." Patrick cocked his head to one side. "Wait a minute. You said—you said you *saw* Scottie."

"I did."

"I'm not—help me out here."

"When I was leaving the police station."

"You were—"

Patrick's mouth closed suddenly, like a springe. He fixed his gaze on the square foot of space directly over Seth's head. The whole interview had taken a surreal turn, he decided. He could no longer believe that Seth was saying what he was saying.

"You were—"

"Coming down the steps," Seth said, overarticulating the words. "Here. I'll re-create. I'm coming down the steps." Without leaving the arm of the chair, he began jogging his torso, simulating a walking motion. "Down the steps comes Seth. 'Oh, shit! I still don't have the drawing. Patrick's going to kill me.' So I turn around." Seth executed a quarter turn of his torso. "Start walking back up. *Up* the steps I go." The torso began to bob again. "I *happen* to look to my left." His head swerved now toward the front door. "And *who* should I see? *Who* should I see? Walking down V Street." His head swiveled back around to face Patrick. The eyes narrowed to a tiny point.

"The Prince," Seth said quietly. "The goddamn Prince."

And for the first time since his arrival, Seth smiled. Not a triumphal smile, by any means. A smaller, more tentative thing— a worrying of the lips mostly, not even (if you really studied it) not even an actual smile.

"Quite extraordinary," Seth said in a dry monotone. "Evidence of God."

"You mean…" Patrick paused, carefully formulated his question. "The Prince was just—*walking by?*"

"Yes."

"And—I mean, you're absolutely, 100% *sure?*"

"As sure as death," Seth said, his voice mysteriously rising. "The hair. The eyes. The jaw, the facial ex—well, again, not a *humorous* expression. But not *un*humorous."

"Scottie?"

"Even had the sweater on," Seth said. And now the excitement of the moment seemed to be reaching him finally. He brought his hands together in a victory clinch. "*Shetland sweater,*" he intoned. "*Cranberry* color."

"Oh!"

Patrick pulled himself to the edge of the couch, then slowly fell back until his head was almost touching the wall. "Oh, God," he whispered.

He couldn't believe it. He didn't dare believe it.

"OK." He was speechless for a few seconds. He raised his hands in a gesture of supplication, struggling for the right response. "I mean, what did you—what did you *do?*"

"What did I do? I followed him. Of course."

"But he was in a cab."

"I know."

"So—how?"

"Oh, it's very corny. No, it's embarrassing. I saw *another* cab, yes? Coming down the street. I hailed it. I got in, said—"

"Follow that cab."

"Yeah. Well, actually I just said, "Follow." Which wasn't as helpful. But then I pointed to the other cab. And he figured it out."

"Uh-huh."

"So we followed the cab. And it—turned right on 16th..." Seth's eyes were looking inward now, retracing the journey. "Down 16th for a few blocks. Then—past the Australian Embassy. Oh, and then it went around! The circle. Scott Circle. We almost *lost* him there. And then—back up Rhode Island Avenue." He paused. "Very strange way to go. Don't know what the driver was thinking."

"Keep going," Patrick urged him.

"Across 14th Street. To Logan Circle. Another circle! Cab goes not quite—not quite halfway around. Turns right on P Street." He paused again. "You see what I mean? Why not take P Street the whole way? From 16th?"

"And then what?" Patrick could hardly control his voice anymore. It was tottering away from him.

"Well—the cab stopped."

"Yes?"

"And the Prince got out. Paid the driver."

"Yes?"

"Walked over to a house. On the south side of the street."

"Yes."

"Started fumbling with his keys. You know, like he's about to open the door. The door to his house." Unexpectedly, Seth paused. "His house," he said again, feeling the word's weight. "*House*. Anyway, he's about to open the door, yes? But then he turns around. Sees the cab."

"He saw you?"

"He actually caught my *eye*. Terrifying. I mean, I got spooked, I have to say. I—fundamentally *freaked*. Told the driver to keep going."

"You kept going!"

"Well, God, Patrick, I didn't know! I thought he might think I was *stalking* him! Call the police. And then—God knows. They put me in a lineup. That woman with the deltoid starts in on me."

"What about the *house*?" Patrick asked, almost sobbing. "Can you find the *house* again?"

A wrinkle of disgust bisected Seth's forehead. "Patrick, do you think I'm dense?" he asked. "Do you think I'm—some *novice* detective here? Some *Hardy* Boy?" He shook his head, made a loud clucking sound. "I wrote the address down," he said.

And without another word he reached into the pocket of his Army pants and pulled out a twice-folded sheet of green paper. Silently he passed it over, and Patrick, taking it, thought to himself, *Paper. Everyone gives me paper.*

His fingers worked with rare delicacy as he unfolded, carefully pulled each corner away. He made sure the paper was completely flat before he even looked at what was there—at the address that Seth had hastily scrawled in blotchy blue ink: 1214 P Street N.W.

"Red-brick facade," Seth said. "Three stories tall. I'm betting he's rich."

Scottie's house.

Patrick's hands closed around the paper. *The street where he lives.*

And even as he stared at the paper, he could feel the bitter pocket of air forming in his chest—the little balloon of irony. Here was Scottie's home. The place Patrick had spent 266 days trying to envision. The place he had journeyed to the farthest outposts to locate, and now—*now* they had found it—and it was *not* buried in the hindmost regions of Maryland and Virginia, it was not rubbing shoulders with an obscure retail nexus, it was *not* smuggled away in an exurban landscape. *It was here.* Buried in the city's midsection. Nine long months of searching, and Scottie had been here the whole time. A few miles away. Waiting for them to turn around, open their eyes.

Patrick didn't know whether to laugh or cry. He refolded the paper, then quickly opened it again—opened it in a kind of panic, as though the address might have changed while he wasn't looking.

But, no, it was still there. 1214 P Street N.W. Still there. And in a few more seconds he wouldn't even need the paper. The address would be inscribed in each of his brain cells, as integral to their functioning as DNA.

"It's only about 15 minutes away," Seth said.

Patrick looked up suddenly. Seth was no longer on the arm of the rocker; he was sitting *in* the chair, with his chin resting on his chest and his hands folded over his belly—like an old man on a porch swing.

"Fifteen minutes by *car*," Seth said. "Maybe less."

"You mean, I can go there now?"

"If you want."

"Go straight to his house?"

"Sure."

Patrick stood up. His legs, without permission, began bearing him toward the closet.

"Is it cold out?" he asked unthinkingly.

But Seth didn't answer. Patrick scanned the line of garments, rested his fingers on a camel-hair overcoat. He stared at it a moment, then pulled if off its hanger, slowly inserted one hand into an armhole, then the other hand. He pulled the coat around him, tugged twice on the gun flaps, felt the warm compression on his shoulders, his back, his underarms.

From behind him, Seth said, "Just one thing."

And Patrick was about to say, *What?* But he was a little thrown because the voice sounded nothing like Seth's—it was so much slower and thicker than Seth's. And as Patrick turned around he half expected to find a changeling waiting for him— some half human monstrosity cleaning Seth out of its teeth, belching up fumes of Seth.

But it wasn't a changeling, it was Seth. Still Seth, still reclining in the rocker, his glasses still askew—but his head thrown back now—and his eyes no longer opaque but actually—actually dissolving. *Extraordinary!* Patrick thought. Those curious blue eyes of Seth's were *melting down*—decomposing, dribbling onto his cheeks, running down the sides of his nose, bathing his entire face.

He was crying.

Patrick understood that now. Seth was crying. And he was saying something too, something barely audible. Patrick inclined his head, trying to make it out.

"Don't go," Seth was saying.

55

The next morning, Patrick was carrying down the last of 31 cardboard boxes from Marianne's apartment when he realized that the car waiting for him on the street below was an Oldsmobile Cutlass Cruiser.

What could explain it—paternal affection? What kind of complicated symbology had prompted Mr. Beaton to lease a rust-colored Oldsmobile for the journey to Delaware?

Whatever his motivation was, Mr. Beaton wasn't telling. All morning long, in fact, he'd been uncharacteristically silent, and now he was standing off to one side, staring down the street, and Marianne was holding onto the luggage rack, swaying back and forth in the wind, silently watching Patrick slide the last box into the station wagon's trunk.

And Patrick wasn't even there. He was somewhere far away.

"I thought you'd have more," he said, staring into the trunk. "More boxes."

Marianne waved her hand. "The rest's in storage. I mean, I don't think I'm gonna need my summer clothes anytime soon. What do you think?"

As confirmation, a cold blade of a wind blew through them, made the peak of Marianne's ski cap rotate like a weather vane.

She and Patrick shivered, rubbed themselves, and then gradually extended their arms around each other.

"You're not to worry about us," she said.

"No," he said.

"You just—be a shit professional, OK?"

"OK," he said.

And now Mr. Beaton was coming toward them, rubbing his gloved hands together, working his mouth around something. "Son," he said.

"Da."

And then they were hugging too, and his father's hand was wearing a smooth path along Patrick's spinal column.

It was Patrick who pulled away, slowly, and for about a minute the three of them simply stood there—in a kind of triptych formation with Marianne in the center, Patrick and Mr. Beaton angled toward the car, all of them shivering and kicking the ground. From the corner of one eye, Patrick saw Marianne's hand surreptitiously stealing into his father's.

"The rats are gone," Patrick said finally.

"You don't say!" his father cried.

"My dog did it. My dog Hamelin. He chased them all away."

"Well, then." Mr. Beaton's smile was beneficent as the sun. "It sounds like we're leaving you in good hands, Pattie. Good hands," he said. He nodded once, then released Marianne's hand and coiled and contracted his body until it was sitting in the driver's seat. He reached to close the door, then glanced back at Patrick, who was still standing on the curb.

"We'll send postcards," Mr. Beaton said.

"OK."

"You don't have to write back. We'll just keep sending 'em."

"OK," Patrick said.

Marianne pressed her lips against Patrick's cheek, then trotted around the car to the passenger door and disappeared inside. The engine gunned into life—as loud as a tractor. The Oldsmobile lurched forward a few feet, then stopped, and as if on command, a single disembodied arm flew out of each side of the car, made a curling, circling motion, then vanished back inside. The car grumbled down the street and around the corner.

I didn't know.

"I didn't know," Patrick had said. Standing by the closet, feeling the weight of the camel-hair overcoat on his shoulders. "I'm sorry. I didn't know."

And Seth's eyes fairly flamed. "Patrick. Did you think I would—spend all this *time*? All these—*months* just for—an intellectual exercise? I'm…" A final sob wrenched itself out of his body. "I just wanted to be with you."

By then Patrick's coat had come to feel entirely unnecessary. He peeled it off, carefully returned it to its hanger, closed the closet door. He shoved his hands into his pockets, studied the rug.

"There was a *plan*," he insisted. "We were going to…"

What was it? What was it we were going to do? He could barely remember.

"We were going to find Scottie," he started to say. "And it was going to suck, and I was going to want Alex back, and you were…"

Oh, there was something more. Something else that was supposed to happen, and he couldn't for the life of him remember. Alex would come back, and…

And Seth would go back to Ted.

Patrick remembered it now. Standing here, watching the

space that had just been occupied by his father's Cutlass Cruiser, he remembered, and it was amazing, in retrospect, how little thought he'd given to that last part of the equation, how little time he'd spent visualizing it: Ted running back, fully chastened by his latest adventure, consoling himself in Seth's arms.

That's how it was supposed to happen.

You said it yourself, Seth. You promised.

Six days after Marianne and Mr. Beaton left, Deanna moved out. Her fiancé had come down from Toms River especially for the occasion. He was a quiet, plump, bearded man who wore granny glasses and drove a Ford Explorer with a license plate that read: COGITO. He busied himself polishing the van's fenders while inside the basement apartment Patrick watched Deanna seal her last box of cooking implements.

"I don't know why I'm taking them," Deanna said. "I never use them."

"I'll miss you," Patrick said.

"I'll miss you too."

They couldn't quite bring themselves to embrace. Patrick sufficed himself with squeezing her gently on the forearm, and she made a soft clawing motion on the raglan sleeve of his sweater.

"Have a wonderful Christmas," she said. "And don't let Hamelin eat any of the poinsettias. They're very bad for him."

"All right."

"And give my best to your dad."

He didn't bother watching the van drive away. For the next half hour he stayed in Deanna's empty apartment, wandering through the rooms, running his hands along the walls (they needed new paint), smelling—he couldn't help smelling—the scent of cat dander still emanating from the kitchen floorboards.

He realized he was more comfortable here than in his own house. The house had too many associations, or rather, it had one particular association that seemed to crowd out all the others. Every morning now, preparing for work, he would find himself walking to the closet to get his coat—and then stopping dead in his tracks. Because this was where he'd been standing when Seth told him. This was where he'd heard the news. And suddenly the whole scene would play out again, as though it were happening for the first time.

He remembered how exasperated he'd become, watching Seth's body collapsed on the mission rocker. He'd become very cross. He'd given his shoulders an angry shrug, cast his eyes to the ceiling.

"I mean, God, Seth!" he said. "We were supposed to be looking for the Prince."

"I *was*," Seth said. "It was you."

And all of Patrick's anger had evaporated in a single pulse.

"Oh, Seth," he said. "I'm not. I mean—not a prince."

"Well—no one is. No, don't—I was going to tell you. When I first knew. You remember that dinner we had? With Ted and Alex? And I was so strange afterward. Couldn't even walk straight. Could barely speak because I *knew*. Some point in the evening. Early in the evening. I looked at Ted and everything—*hit* me. I thought, 'I don't want Ted anymore.' Imagine that. Ted doesn't interest me. Such a surprise! How did it happen? I couldn't figure it out. And then I looked at *you*. I looked at you. And it was, like, Wow! No shit."

Which was probably, Patrick thought, as good an expression as any for the revelation of love. *No shit! No shit, I love you!*

Ten days had passed now since Seth's confession, and Patrick was becoming increasingly successful at secluding himself from the world. He wasn't up to humanity. At work he closed his office door behind him as soon as he arrived—opened it only if someone knocked. He was barely cognizant of his surroundings. The compost heap in the adjoining office had now spawned whole colonies of insects—large black crunchy beetles—and the only thing Patrick could bring himself to notice about them was how they reflected the whole spectrum of light, the way spilled oil sometimes does.

Everyone had vanished now: his father, Marianne, Deanna. Even Sonya had disappeared for an extended procreative vacation. Patrick felt almost completely islanded. He didn't even watch television because he didn't think there was anything there he needed to know—that's why he was so unprepared for the blizzard.

Oh, he knew it was unusually cold for December, but it still shocked him that one moment he could be watching the evening sky—a bright tangerine sky as radiant as the Northern Lights—and the next moment that same sky could be filled with snow, *overwhelmed* by snow. Unimaginable quantities of snow exploding through the night and the following day and the following evening. A foot and a half—the weatherman said it was a new record.

The day it stopped snowing, Patrick took Hamelin for a walk. It was their first real walk in two days, and it took Patrick ten minutes just to force open the storm door. The cars outside were almost entirely buried except for the roofs, where the snow had left little mohawk stripes. The roads belonged now to the pedestrians, who walked in the ruts left by tow trucks and suburban vehicles. Down the street a pair of cross-country skiers glided across the powder. At the corner a delivery truck had been abandoned in the middle of a sloping drift. On the back a sign read: HOW'S MY DRIVING?

Patrick walked a good distance that day, with Hamelin laboring happily in his tracks. He walked up Pennsylvania Avenue, past the Tune Inn and the Hawk and Dove—already reopened. Past the Supreme Court building, where the statues of Poseidon and his subdeities wore frosted crowns. Past the Capitol, where the western steps had become a ramp for sleds and snowboards and toboggans. The snow had erased all stretches of grass, so the trees on the Mall seemed to merge now, to become the forest they had once been. The sun was just starting to emerge, and seagulls were making insane cries. Patrick saw one of them caught in a wind, blown along for a hundred yards.

"I mean, what can I say, Patrick?" Seth had sat up in the rocker. His hiccups had passed, and he was staring at his boots, at the byzantine skeins of lacing. "What can I say? You're cute and melancholy and a little screwy, and you have just the right amount of jadedness—not enough to be curdled—and we're really very much alike in ways that may not seem apparent at first, and I know you may think of me as this *creature*, this strange thing that's latched onto your life, but I improve with knowing, I really do, and I would be so nice to you, and you'd never have to worry about losing me—hell, I'm the tick, remember?—and even if you didn't love me, it would be OK, but I think you would, given half a chance, because you'd almost *have* to, you'd have no choice."

And Patrick didn't know what to say. He almost wept. A run-on sentence! Perhaps the longest unbroken concatenation of words that Seth had ever put together. What better proof of love was there?

And why—*why* had he never seen it? Amid all his failures, this was the one that stood out most prominently. How had he failed to see it?

And why had no one else see it?

It was quite remarkable in retrospect. Surely *someone*—someone with a better perspective than he—should have looked at the situation and understood exactly what was going on, should have seen it for what it was.

His father, for instance. His father was always forgetting Seth's name—and always cursing himself for forgetting, as though remembering the name were important. And hadn't Mr. Beaton declared Seth to be a great rat catcher—an occupation that in Mr. Beaton's cosmology ranked right up there with voluptuous medium to the spirit world.

And what about Deanna? What had been her first response when he told her he was dating someone?

Oh, that perspiring man.

And then Alex. Tacitly including Seth on all their prospective joint ventures. *Just the four of us*, he'd said. Two happy couples.

Oh, God, Patrick thought. *God, they all knew. And they didn't tell me.*

"So here's the deal," Seth had said. He was in command of himself now, or at least giving a good impression of it. He rose from the chair and began heading for the door, and Patrick instinctively peered into the closet for Seth's coat, and then remembered he was still wearing it.

"Two weeks, OK?" Seth was readjusting his glasses—finally!—making them straight, and he was looking at Patrick with an uninflected, almost businesslike expression. "I want you to have two weeks. To think about it. And if it doesn't make any sense—fine. You go off to your prince. Bon voyage. Aloha on a steel guitar."

"And what do *you* do?" Patrick had asked.

"I don't know."

And it was then that Seth's composure cracked briefly. He yanked off his glasses and pressed a finger against each of his eyes. It was another minute before he was ready to leave.

"Two weeks," he said, and he was gone.

And now it was 15 days since Seth had said that—two weeks and a day. And only now was Patrick able to leave his immediate neighborhood. The roads had finally begun clearing—not because anyone was clearing them but because the sun was blazing now, melting the snow into a gray granular paste.

It took Patrick two hours to shovel his car out. It took him another five minutes just to drive to the end of the street—he got mired briefly in a snow bank, and only a well-timed shove from one of his neighbors could extricate him. The Oldsmobile didn't perform very well in snow, he knew that, but today it would have to perform. Today he was going to Scottie's house. He was ready to see Scottie's house.

Under normal conditions, the trip really *would* have taken no more than 15 minutes. But with the roads in such a variable state, Patrick needed almost three times as long to get there. He drove in second gear, hunching his shoulders over the wheel, tapping his brake to warn away approaching drivers. It was hard going pretty much the whole way. The right turn off Massachusetts Avenue was particularly difficult—he had to plow through a series of moguls, each higher than the last—but then he caught sight of Logan Circle in the distance, and it gave him an infusion of will. He shifted into first gear and crawled down the road, his engine straining, the whole car vibrating as though it were about to implode.

Even moving as slowly as he was, the turn for P Street came on him sooner than he expected. He wrenched the wheel to the right, and the car lurched a few feet, like a sled, then came to a stop. Patrick inched forward, and seeing there was no space in the right lane, he carefully maneuvered the car to the left, then left again onto Rhode Island Avenue. He stopped on the north side of the road, flipped on his hazards, turned off the engine.

A hundred feet away, on the far side of a small triangular park, stood Scottie's house.

Number 1214. Patrick could see it from his driver's-side window, see it without even moving. It was the last in a row of identical red-brick edifices with English basements and double-hung windows and pediments—everything sheathed now in ice and snow. The roof of Number 1214 groaned under huge steppelike drifts, and a cataract of ice ran down the front, swelled out into an ice cavern where, three feet inside, a water meter sat cocooned. Over the front door a single three-foot-long icicle hung like a sword from the eaves.

It was a house under a spell.

He's inside right now, Patrick thought. *He's inside making cocoa or unsalted popcorn or building a fire or—pouring boiling water over the back stoop.*

And then his imagination froze up—as summarily as the world had. It refused to budge. It refused to imagine any more.

Patrick pounded the steering wheel. He buried his face in his mittens.

Oh, Seth. He pressed his eyes shut. *Seth, you ruined it. You absolutely ruined it.*

It was the only way to describe it. This was supposed to be Patrick's moment. The apotheosis, the final reckoning, the grand climactic confrontation with destiny—and Seth had destroyed it. Seth had gone and robbed him of nine months' delayed gratification, robbed him of resolution—robbed him of his *reward*.

Here it was, Day 281 in Our Year of Scottie, and here was Patrick ready to claim his prize—having no idea, of course, *if* it could be claimed or *how* to claim it, but that had never been part of the calculations anyway. The important thing had always been *finding* the Prince, and *now* the Prince was found. And everything had changed.

Now Patrick could think of nothing except Seth.

Even here in the car with Scottie perhaps a hundred feet away, perhaps 90 feet away—Seth was still closer.

Not that Seth had ever been far away, Patrick had to concede that. He had to concede that over the past few months, his thoughts had regularly and of their own accord run to Seth— and *lingered* there with a kind of surprised tenderness. It must have been, he thought, much the same feeling that Marianne experienced coming out of her bedroom that fateful morning and contemplating Mr. Beaton's recumbent, toe-twitching body: A kind of concentrated compassion that enveloped the watcher as much as the watched.

But that feeling for Seth only came over him when he was alone, Patrick realized. Whenever they were *together* the visual-auditory experience was too overwhelming for him. It seemed to produce a defensive reflex that kept tenderness at bay.

Seth's too much sometimes. How often he'd said that to himself! *He's exhausting. I can never get comfortable with him.*

And then, without permission, Patrick's mind went tumbling backward, out of the snow and ice, out of the winter, back through the fall—stopped abruptly on the near side of summer. And suddenly there was no more snow. Suddenly it was a beautiful September day, and he and Seth were sitting together in this very car—sitting rather *comfortably* together—in the Bulk Barn parking lot. Sitting for God knows how many hours, from early morning until well in the afternoon, scrutinizing the hordes of shoppers pouring in and out of the store. It was all coming back again. Patrick could see the pale brick warehouse with blue lettering and the cherry Saab on one side and the gray Mercedes on the other side and the shopping cart hangar and the bearded man who kicked their fender. He could feel the bands of sweat materializing on his back and under his thighs, and he could feel the air growing dense with heat and carbon dioxide.

And he could hear Seth's voice drumming in his ear. He could hear that better than anything, but he couldn't quite make out what Seth was saying—something about—something about *fantasies.*

Oh, of course, he was confessing his fantasy, his fantasy of domesticity—the dream man who would go shopping with him, two to a cart, and wait in line with him and complain about how long the line was and help him load the bags in a trunk and take the bags out again when they got home and use his keys to open the front door and greet the dog and sweep the back patio and clean the bathroom and iron the cloth napkins and discuss extremely banal things like their lightbulb shortage, things that would be of no interest to any reasonable human being except themselves.

And remembering all that, remembering the vision that Seth had conjured up inside that steamy car made Patrick feel almost unbearably warm now—almost *swaddled* in intimacy.

He couldn't understand it. It didn't make sense. Why should he feel this way now? So many months after it had happened? Was it simply because he'd been *happy*? For those few seconds?

Honestly, he couldn't say *what* he'd been. All he could say was that when he was sitting in that car, he had felt that nothing very terrible could happen to him. He had ceased, after a while, to even think about Scottie. He had ceased to wonder if the next wave of bulk shoppers would wash him onto their shore. He had been attentive to nothing but the present, to the living, breathing entity 30 inches away.

Of course, it was a fool's errand they were engaged in. It was *absurd*, the whole notion that Scottie would materialize before their eyes—but something about it had still resonated with Patrick.

The fantasy, he thought suddenly.

It was the fantasy that resonated. And for a very particular reason.

It's my fantasy too.

His eyes still closed, Patrick let his head fall back against the head rest.

It's my fantasy too.

Oh, God. Oh, God, why had it taken him so long to understand that?

Seth's fantasy rhymed with his—almost perfectly. In its contours, in its central vision, it was the very same fantasy he had erected around Scottie. It was the fantasy of Scottie coming home in the evening, having already stopped briefly at the corner store to pick up a carton of milk, and coming through the door and setting down the milk carton and walking over to Patrick, who was seated in a high-backed chair, and bending down and Patrick casually dropping his head back and their lips coming together—not *passionately*, Patrick reminded himself, but briefly, ritualistically, *routinely*. The same kiss they had exchanged that morning and the night before and every day prior to that and every day to come. The kiss of domestic covenants. The kiss of long and dear acquaintance.

That was the kiss Patrick Beaton had always dreamed of. His deepest, most compelling fantasy, and it had been defined by Scottie—and it had almost nothing to do with Scottie.

Patrick opened his eyes. The Bulk Barn parking lot was gone. It was winter again, winter everywhere, but the residual heat was still in his skin and his veins and his heart and his head, and he realized now that he would always be going back there, as long as he had a mind to take him, forever revisiting the car and the parking lot and the hot sun and the dense swamp of air— forever going back, without ever knowing why, knowing only that it made him feel good to do it.

Knowing only that it made *sense*. Which, he realized with a start, was the very criterion that Seth had proposed for making his decision: *If it makes sense.*

And it *does* make sense, Patrick thought. *Seth, it does make sense.*

It made sense then. It made sense now. It would make sense one second from now. And one minute from now. And maybe always.

56

"Hello?"

"Ted! Hi, this is—this is Patrick."

"Patrick."

"Listen, I'm sorry to bother you; I was—I *really* need to find Seth, and I was wondering if you guys have seen him recently."

"Seth?"

"I've been calling his apartment all day, and he doesn't answer, and I called his office, and they're still closed because of the snow, and I was just—wondering if you'd *seen* him at all."

"No," Ted said equably. "Not for about a week, actually, not since the snow. Oh, that reminds me—I'm supposed to apologize to you."

"Apologize?"

"Well—for the way I acted the other night. At the Fox & Hound."

"Oh, that's—"

"I mean, quite honestly, I didn't realize there was anything to apologize *for*, but Seth called me up a couple of weeks ago and asked me if I'd said or done something to upset you. And I told him we just had drinks, that's all. And he said you were a little bothered by something, and he said I wasn't to play with you.

He said you were different, and I wasn't to play any—any *games* with you, so…" Ted's glibness was abandoning him now. He was struggling a little. "So, anyway, I'm—I'm sorry if I made you feel weird. I didn't—that wasn't anything I meant to do." And then he groaned and called out to someone in the same room. "There!" he said. "I did it!"

And from somewhere in the near distance came Alex's voice. "Very nice," Alex said.

"And I get a reward, right?" Ted asked, his voice sliding away from the receiver.

"OK," Alex said.

Patrick grimaced, braced himself for the telltale slurping, the whole range of osculation—but the moment passed in silence, and when the phone conversation resumed, someone else was on the line.

"Patrick?"

"*Alex*. Hi! I'm sorry to bother—"

"That's OK; we were just making Christmas cookies."

"Oh, good, I—"

"Listen, I *did* talk to Seth."

"When?"

"Yesterday. He said you missed a deadline."

Patrick covered his eyes. *Two weeks. I'll give you two weeks.*

"And he told me, if you called, I was supposed to say—what? He's gone somewhere to—*cerebrate*, I think he said."

"Cerebrate?"

"Yeah, I thought at first it was *cel*-ebrate. But when I said it back to him, he said, 'No, no, *cer*-ebrate.'"

"Did he say he was leaving town?"

"Um…I don't know. I think I asked him that too, and he just said he was going out."

"Out."

"And I said, 'Well, good luck getting anywhere, it's'—oh, honey! The cookies aren't done yet. No, you're supposed to wait a couple of minutes. Oh, OK, *one*. That's it. I used a different kind of sprinkle. What do you..."

And for the next few minutes, Patrick was essentially on hold. He listened to Alex jabbering on about oven temperatures, the aging of Teflon, the differences between light and dark brown sugar, and he could hear Ted, his mouth half full, discussing the cookie's texture—and the feeling that came from all this sound—the feeling of being utterly and happily ignored—had a perversely warming effect on Patrick, like a eucalyptus rub on his chest. He found himself smiling in spite of himself. And it was in a spirit of inexhaustible good humor that he finally presumed to raise his voice.

"Alex!" he called. "Oh, Alex!"

"I'm sorry." Alex was giggling now, his breath rasping against the receiver. "He's impossible."

"Hey, I just..." Patrick took a gulp of air, plunged in. "I'm just *happy*, you know, that you're—happy."

"Oh." A last titter shook out of Alex, and then he fell silent. "Well, that's nice," he said.

"So that's all."

"No, great. That's great. The only thing..." Alex laughed softly. "The only thing left is for *you* to get happy."

"Right."

"And then I can be happy about *that*."

"Yeah, that'd be good," Patrick said. He stared at the ground. "I'm working on that part," he said.

"I know."

"I'll keep you posted."

"You do that, you do th—oh, *excuse* me, I think I said *one*. No, that looks like two. That looks like *two* cookies. Oh, all *right*, but really—they're better if you wait a couple of minutes. No, it's true! I read it somewhere...."

It was nice, Patrick thought, to have a mystery that was so eminently solvable. The Case of the Missing Seth, for instance. It really took only a few minutes to crack—only a little bit of *cerebrating*, as Seth would have it, and Patrick knew suddenly where "out" was, and it was such a perfect solution that he didn't stop to consider any other.

Hains Point. It had to be Hains Point.

Hains Point was Seth's favorite place in the world—Patrick had heard him say so any number of times. It was practically the only place they *hadn't* gone looking for Scottie. It was too sacred; it was spiritual ground. Hains Point was the place Seth went whenever he wanted to think about things. It was the place he went whenever he wanted *not* to think about things. It was where he went to watch the planes take off from National Airport and watch fathers fishing with their sons and worship at his very own temple.

Patrick had actually seen the temple—had even considered making it his own. It was an enormous stainless-steel sculpture of a buried giant—the only parts still visible above ground were a bearded face, an arm, a hand, the crook of a knee, a solitary foot. The piece was called "The Awakening," but it wasn't a happy awakening. The giant was either just emerging from or just about to be swallowed by the earth, and his mouth was torn open in a bellow.

"Always gives me goose bumps," Seth had said once. "Is it God? Maybe it's God. Boy, he's pissed."

Hains Point lay only about a mile from Patrick's house. The snow, of course, had transformed the city's geography—one mile was more like ten—but still it was easier to get there than Patrick would have expected. The Oldsmobile was moving more confidently now, and the roads leading into West Potomac Park were clear, and the lane that looped around to the point was packed down and easily navigable. Patrick drove slowly, peering over the walls of snow that rose up on either side of him, listening to the sound of his own churning engine bouncing back to him. He leaned forward until his face was almost against the windshield.

The snow had blanketed everything—the bubble of the indoor tennis court, the baseball field, the golf course, the willows and pines and oaks and Japanese maples—everything but the river itself, which was gray and dead, and a small yacht that was even now slipping out of the nearby marina, blinking a single dead light.

Patrick drove on for about a mile, following the line of East Potomac Park as it narrowed into Hains Point. He stopped his car in the right lane, turned off the engine, and as he opened the door an icy wind curled up inside his coat and raked his breastbone. He staggered a little, wrapped his coat more tightly around him.

It was cold! So cold and so quiet. The planes had just begun to return to National Airport, but they were still few and far between, and the only noise Patrick could make out was the sound of his boots leaving craters in the snow. He had the momentary sense of being a 19th-century explorer, miles from any Inuit settlement, seeking a lost party in the Northwest Passage. The snow, though, had buried all evidence of people. It had tried to bury the giant too, but the erupting god was too furious. His beard was frosted white, his fingers and toes were dripping snow—everything else lay writhing in the sun. His left hand made a kind of bowl, and a few feet from the bowl was Seth.

He was wearing a black overcoat and black leather gloves, and he was seated, his arms wrapped around his knees, his whole body rigid. He'd been watching Patrick from the moment the car arrived, peering guardedly over his knees, and now his neck was slowly retracting and his shoulders were rising, bracing themselves.

"Hi," Patrick said.

"Hello."

"I missed the deadline."

"I know."

Patrick looked at him for a moment, then made a slow circle, casting his eyes over the surrounding landscape, the dunes and whips of pure white meringue rising up over the flat gray water. *When it melts*, he thought, *this whole place will be underwater.* But there didn't seem to be any imminent danger of that. Everything was too cold to move. Patrick clapped his hands together, gave himself a couple of quick embraces.

"Aren't you freezing?" he asked.

"Never seen so much snow," Seth said. "In my whole life."

"How long have you been here?"

"Fifteen days."

"The whole time?"

"No, of course not," Seth said reasonably. "I'd be dead."

"So do you—come every day or something?"

"Yes." He nodded again. "I take a cab. Then I walk back to the Metro. Never stay for long. Hour at a time. However long I can stand." He rested his head on his thigh. "Sometimes I go and do holiday shopping. To get warm. But the music drives me away."

Grunting a little, Patrick heaved himself onto the patch of snow next to Seth. The cold went straight through him.

"Yow!" he cried.

"Tell me about it," Seth said.

Patrick pulled in his neck, buried his chin in his coat, rubbed the ends of his boots together. He stared at the space between him and Seth.

"I was wondering," he said, "if you would mind walking the dog in the mornings."

Seth raised his head a few inches. "Sorry?"

"See, I'm no good in the mornings. It's my biggest flaw. I can barely drag myself out of bed some days, and I've been—I've been known to be surly." Patrick poked at the snow with one of his gloved fingers, made a slow, lazy ellipse. "So I don't think I'd be an appropriate role model," he said. "For a young dog. Morningwise."

"Oh." Seth unclenched himself now, straightened his legs. His lips began to moisten and slide apart. "Well...I'm a morning person." He thought for a moment. "I could be."

"Well, that would work out well, then. 'Cause then I could walk the dog in the evenings."

"Uh-huh."

"And there's this really nice lady who'd walk him during the day. For a very reasonable price."

"Well—that sounds fine." Seth's nostrils were oscillating now, like someone picking up a scent. "Beaton," he said, his tongue lingering trancelike on each syllable.

"What about it?"

"Is that..." He stopped, scratched his head. "Is Beaton a Scottish name?"

"Yeah. Actually, it is."

"Ah!" Slowly, almost invisibly, Seth let himself tip backward, until he was lying flat on the ground, staring up at the sky. His black cloth coat, unbuttoned, fell open. "The Scottish Prince," he said.

Patrick reached over, picked Seth's head off the snow. It took only a few seconds of repositioning until his chest was supporting Seth's back and his legs were lying on either side of Seth's legs. He wrapped his arms around Seth's thin shoulders, which were shivering now through the coat.

"How easy are you about deadlines?" Patrick asked.

"So easy."

EPILOGUE

Almost every night, just as Seth was falling asleep, his arm would lash out and knock the alarm clock off the bedside table. It was a startling sound, startling enough to make Seth himself sit up with a half-suppressed shriek and gaze wildly about, and the only reason it didn't produce the same response in Patrick was that he was usually still awake. He generally needed more time to go to sleep. He had once regarded this as a disadvantage, but now, sometimes he deliberately kept himself conscious, sitting up in bed, breathing shallowly and blinking away the fatigue, just so he could see Seth's arm silently levitate, pause at the apogee of its arc, and then make that brisk, ruthless transverse slice, sweeping everything before it.

Seth was surprised every time it happened. He believed it was his body's way of informing him of the precise moment he was falling asleep. He claimed it was an atavistic survival instinct re-asserting itself.

"If it's a survival instinct," Patrick asked him, "what's it protecting you from?"

"Don't know," Seth said. "Something about being asleep. Very scary, yes? Being asleep and maybe someone else is awake. That's why I don't nap much."

So even in this—even in this most fundamental reluctance—they were alike. And only a few months ago Patrick had been wondering at how little they had in common. They couldn't even share clothes because Seth was several sizes smaller. In fact, when Seth had first dragged his suitcases up the stairs—February 2, an unusually warm, cloudless day—Patrick had stood there with his back against the bedroom wall, watching all this *clothing* come out, all these sweaters and boxer shorts and close-fitting undershirts and starched business shirts and slightly scuffed leather shoes—clothes he would never wear. And it felt as if he were meeting Seth for the first time or as if they would never meet.

And at the same time he couldn't deny the coursing, over-powering *love* that swept over him when he watched Seth placidly putting away his clothes in the scratched, wood-veneer dresser they had paid $20 for at Eastern Market. It was such a potent feeling that it paralyzed him. He thought, *Is this what love does? Freezes you on the other side of the room?*

He wondered that at night sometimes too, waiting for Seth's involuntary clock smiting. Because he could have stopped it from happening. He could have nudged Seth awake and said, "Honey, you're about to do that thing again." But something kept him from doing that. Something in him needed to see it happen, over and over again, because witnessing it was like an expression of love—the most private possible expression.

He got the same feeling, sometimes, watching Seth cook pasta or plant annuals (he was almost as skilled in the garden as Deanna) or wash whites or, really, do *anything* around the house. Seth was now so much a part of the place, it was hard to believe he had ever lived anywhere else. Within a day of moving in he had struck up an almost mystical rapport with Hamelin, so intense that whenever Seth was ready to take the dog for a walk, all he had to do was stand by the door and Hamelin would come running, no matter where he was.

Seth seemed to tap a more liberated feeling in Hamelin. Patrick would come home some nights and find them rolling around on the living room floor, Seth crying "Beast! Savage beast!" and the dog making explosive yelps of joy, and it all reminded Patrick of the first time he'd seen Alex, rolling across Dogshit Park with somebody else's dog, and seeing it now gave him an even more pungent sense of pleasure.

Of course, Hamelin would let himself go crazy with Seth in a way he wouldn't with Patrick, but then his relationship with Patrick was inherently more formal. Hamelin was the mentor. Now and again when Seth was absent and Patrick was sitting with Hamelin on the love seat and the dog's snout was resting on his thigh, Patrick would stroke behind his ears and lean forward and whisper to him, "So you approve, right? You think it was a good move?"

One night Seth crept up behind them at the very moment Patrick posed the question, and he responded in a perfect Hamelin voice. "Oh, *ruff, ruff,*" he said. "Oh, *ruff ruff ruff!*"

Mr. Beaton approved too, in his amused, indirect way. At least that's how Patrick interpreted the most recent letter:

Dear Pattie,

So nice to see you and Seth on our last go-through. I quite liked the Ethiopian restaurant, though I have to tell you, the phrase "dog food" came to mind more than once. Maybe we'll take Hamelin there the next time.

I'm off on my book tour in a couple of weeks. I thought of bringing a stuffed rat with me for photo ops. Speaking of which, Didn't I tell you Seth would be good at catching rats? Of course, I neglected to say, he's also good at catching PATS. HA HA!

Marianne continues to GLOW. You'd hardly know she's quick with child. Quick. What a strange word to describe something that isn't quick at all. Although it's quite nice...

Love, Da

Yes, Patrick Beaton had a new sibling on the way. It was strange to think that here he was, 33, and he had never fathered a child and likely never would (unless Sonya went the surrogate route again, and that was increasingly unlikely—according to the latest reports, she and her husband were reaching critical mass). And *still* he felt like a father in a way—a father-in-remove. Because without him, how could Marianne have met Mr. Beaton? Without his unwitting aid, how could *anything* have happened?

Things *had* happened, though. They'd happened, and they'd produced blessings. He could say that without a trace of irony. He could list his blessings on a piece of paper, which in fact he did one day:

1) An expanding family
2) A bearable job
3) A comfortable house
4) The world's most exceptional dog
5) Seth

He looked over that last entry and then underlined it—twice. Something about Seth seemed to require underscoring, and what Seth had accomplished required underscoring too. He had rescued Patrick Beaton, hadn't he? Reintroduced him to love, and love really *was* enough—for now and perhaps forever.

And yet. And yet. Lying awake at night, *late* into the night, hours after Seth had knocked off the alarm clock and only an hour, perhaps, before the *Washington Post* would come thumping against his front door, Patrick would find his thoughts moving inward, in a relentless peristalsis, toward Scottie.

Not in the way that they used to. He no longer tried to imagine what Scottie was doing or reading or who he was talking to or where he was eating dinner. His mind tended to dwell instead on those brief moments of intersection—in the library, in the parking lot—and he would find himself compulsively delineating the alternative scenarios, the things that might have happened if he'd been more awake, if he'd reacted more quickly.

Thinking about these possibilities never made him feel disloyal because the alternative scenarios were never particularly satisfying. They were just unrealized. Once a month or so, driving downtown, he would find the nose of his car suddenly veering up 13th Street, cutting into Logan Circle, and then taking that quick right onto P Street—returning, almost of its own will, to Scottie's house. And each time, he would drive past the house, then curve around onto Rhode Island Avenue, parking on the north side of the triangular park—and he would sit there, staring out the driver's-side window.

Of course he never went there seeking any particular outcome. In fact, almost any outcome would have been too much. He just liked the sense of being there.

I know I shouldn't, he thought. But he couldn't convincingly reproach himself, hard as he tried, because if he were honest about it, he would have to acknowledge that without Scottie there would have been no Seth. Oh, he doubtless would have *met* Seth—but there would have been no means, no *vehicle* for them to fall in love. It was Scottie who'd made it all possible.

And so the Scottish Prince had performed a service after all, Patrick thought, staring at the flat red-brick facade and the pediment and the water meter, no longer encased in ice, and the forsythia shrub and the wrought-iron fence. It could no longer be denied: The Prince had done well. Patrick's life was acquiring a form now, a pleasing shape. A shape, moreover, that mystically communicated itself to the world, driving off all the entropy that was once his life's defining principle.

What better illustration of this than his car—the much-maligned, much-besieged 1987 Oldsmobile Cutlass Ciera, which had gone more than six months now without a single assault? Its windows were still intact; its wheels were still spinning; its engine was gamely coughing and gurgling along. It might survive them all.

Sometime in the middle of spring, though—about a month into the Second Year of Scottie—the car began to blow heat whenever he turned on the air conditioning. This was less of a concern for him than for Seth, who sweat at the conceptual possibility of heat, and so it was mostly out of chivalry that Patrick resolved to take the car in for repairs. And it was probably fatalism that led him to decide on his usual garage, the one that had spent the better part of two years not repairing his engine strut.

Seth wouldn't let him do it, though. "Don't you dare take it there," Seth said. "I don't care how many Senators they have on their wall."

"Fine. Where am I supposed to go?"

"Try that *place*. That—Speedy Auto Service. It's three blocks away."

"Speedy Auto?"

"Yeah, they have cute ads. They even pick up your car for you. From your house."

The people at Speedy Auto were surprised, in fact, that Patrick had bothered to deliver his own car. They were politely amazed. They were also a good deal friendlier than the mechanics at his old garage, and after promising to call him back within two hours, they actually did.

"Hi, Mr. Beaton. This is Doug from Speedy Auto."

"Hi."

"Well, we've found your problem, sir. It's the wires leading into your alternator? They've been chewed to pieces."

"*Chewed*?"

"Yeah, I've seen this kind of damage before. It usually comes from vermin."

Patrick almost dropped the phone. His mind was whirring like a hive.

Vermin, he thought. *Vermin, vermin...*

The rats!

Oh, yes. Oh, it all made perfect sense. Patrick almost laughed at the dramatic symmetry of it. The Beaton rats—foiled by the resourceful Hamelin, flushed from their comfortable burrows—responding now with this final act, this climactic work of revenge. Cackling, no doubt, as they gnawed through the last wire and then scuttled down the street to their next unwitting host.

The beasts of Langley...

"Oh, and sir? There seems to be a problem with your engine strut."

"I know."

"We can take a shot at fixing it."

"Please do."

"And when would you like us to bring it by your home?"

"Bring it by?"

"Yes, sir, part of the Speedy Package. We bring the car back to you. No extra charge."

"Oh, that's—nice."

"We do it all so you won't have to."

"No, that's very nice, but I live three blocks away, so—I'll just come get it Saturday morning."

At 10 o'clock on Saturday morning, then, Patrick was putting on his jean jacket, getting ready to walk over to Speedy Auto Service, when he felt Seth's fingers tugging at the collar.

"You know, they *will* deliver it," Seth said. "If you want. No extra charge."

"I know," Patrick said, feeling strangely irked. "I need the walk."

"OK, OK." Seth smiled, ran his hands down the front of Patrick's jacket. "See you in a bit."

"OK."

And then they kissed, and it was like so many of their kisses—brief, almost mechanical—and at the same time an entirely new kiss, like so many of their kisses. Every kiss produced an entirely new tingle along Patrick's neck, climbed an entirely new distance up his scalp. The tingle was there to remind him: This was the fantasy. The fantasy he and Seth had created independently of each other. The diurnal domestic kiss, as unthinking as respiration.

He would never tire of kissing this way.

"Don't be long," Seth said. "I'm making molasses cookies."

Patrick didn't plan on being long, but then again, it was late

April, and the air was inching toward May. Pollen had gathered in the cracks between the bricks, and a neighbor's cherry tree had turned such a vivid pink, it looked almost synthetic, and a mourning dove had made a nest in somebody's breezeway. In Marion Park a man was standing behind a tripod camera, taking a photograph of a tulip tree.

Patrick was walking the way Hamelin sometimes walked: in feints and darts, his nose quivering, his eyes studying the ground. It wasn't a smooth way of getting places, but he reached the service station sooner than he expected. As he blinked up at the sign—SPEEDY AUTO SERVICE—he couldn't understand why it seemed to blink back at him. He stared at it longer than he needed to.

He walked into the front office, where a young woman with violet hair and violet fingernails sat behind the register. "Yes, sir," she said.

"I've come to pick up my car."

"Your name?"

"Patrick Beaton."

"Beaton. Beaton, Beaton, Beaton…*Beaton*…yes, sir, Mr. Beaton. Well, now, it looks like you're all paid up with the credit card, so we'll just find you a—Doug! Can you show Mr. Beaton his car?"

Patrick spun to his left. From the far end of the counter, a tall man with dirty-blond hair was staring back at him. A tall man with wavy dirty-blond hair and a powerful neck and chin and a lopsided smile.

Patrick's heart lurched to a stop.

"Yes, sir," the man said. "Right this way."

He pushed open a side door and motioned Patrick through, and when Patrick didn't move he walked through himself, and

Patrick, after a short interval, followed. They were standing in the garage now. A green Toyota Celica hovered about two feet over their heads.

Doug, he thought. How strangely it resounded in the ear. *Doug. Doug.*

"This way," said Doug.

He was wearing scuffed blue jeans and a short-sleeved uniform top, cobalt blue with a red insignia on its left arm. The very insignia that Patrick had been staring at five minutes before—on the sign—a red roadrunner, its legs in a cloud of revolution, its smile as chirpy as a Disney bird's. The logo for Speedy Auto Service.

Strange, Patrick thought. *Strange I should have thought it was a tattoo.* There wasn't much excuse, he knew—although he supposed there were extenuating circumstances. It had been dark, and the van was moving past him, and it was all at a distance, and he'd been so busy looking at the face, he hadn't really registered what was on the arm, not until a day later.

"We gave you a new engine strut," Doug was saying. "The thing's not rocking quite as bad as it used to."

"That's good," Patrick said.

"Just so you know, we *do* deliver your car to you if you want."

"Oh, I know, it's—I just live three blocks away."

Now Grant *Wallberger*, on the other hand, Grant Wallberger was the kind of a man who, even if he lived three blocks away, would want his car delivered to him. He was the kind of man who would happily pay for that privilege and would no more remember the man who had dropped off his car than he would remember the vendor he'd bought a pretzel from that morning.

"Cutlasses are the number one car for thieves," Doug was saying. "I don't know if you've had any problem that way."

How had it all begun? Something simple like—like maybe Grant hadn't had his checkbook on him. Was that it? Maybe Grant had gone to fetch his checkbook, and it had ended up taking him longer than expected, so the nice mechanic had begun to wander away from the vestibule. Completely ignoring the crowd of well-dressed men in the living room—he wasn't a guest, after all—he'd wandered down a hallway, to a small empty room, a library, poked his head in and chanced upon a nearly unconscious man, engaged in a brief and unmemorable exchange, and then made his way back to the front door—and just in time too because here was Grant Wallberger with the checkbook, and it was time to get going; he had other clients to see.

And, oh, yes, it was cold outside that Sunday in March—Day 1 in the First Year of Scottie—so Doug had worn a sweater over his uniform, a Shetland sweater.

"Just a heads-up," said Doug the mechanic.

Patrick shook his head. "I'm sorry?"

"You may find in a couple of months you'll need a new muffler and exhaust pipe. It's looking kind of corroded down there."

"Corroded. OK."

There were things Patrick would probably never know. The house, for instance: Was it really the house where Scottie lived—where Doug lived? Wasn't it just as likely a client's house? Wasn't it just as likely that after dropping off one car in Adams Morgan, the Prince had simply cabbed over to Logan Circle to pick up another? Which would make the house in Logan Circle the wrong house, the utterly entirely wrong house.

"And we went ahead and changed the oil," Doug was saying. "No charge."

"Uh-huh."

Of course it was the wrong house.

Of course it was the wrong house.

It wasn't the house Patrick had just come from. The house where even now the scent of ginger and cinnamon and molasses was filling the air, and a smallish, slightly built man was bending over a bowl of batter, beating it in large loopy strokes, occasionally letting his teeth slide through his lips in a largely unconscious gesture of joy, pausing briefly to greet the dog that had just wandered in—not to beg for food, mind you, just to monitor the situation—greeting the dog and saying, We'll play later, OK? Gotta finish these. Before Patrick gets home.

"Sir?" The voice of Doug the mechanic sounded as remote as church bells. "You're ready to go."

Patrick began pulling out his wallet, then he remembered he'd already paid. He looked up at the mechanic, who was leaning now on the hood of the car, one foot resting against the tire's spokes. The mechanic's jaw had eased forward, and his gray eyes were scattering rays of humor, and his smile rose a little higher on the right side than on the left.

"Is there anything else I can help you with?" he asked.

"No," Patrick said. "But thank you. Thank you very much."